THE NEW HOUSE

Tess Stimson is the author of fourteen novels, including top ten bestseller *The Adultery Club*, and two non-fiction books, which between them have been translated into dozens of languages.

A former journalist and reporter, Stimson was appointed Professor of Creative Writing at the University of South Florida in 2002 and moved to the US. She now lives and works in Vermont with her husband Erik, their three children, and (at the last count) two cats, three fish, one gerbil and a large number of bats in the attic.

By the same author:

Thrillers

General Fiction

TESS STIMSON

THE NEW HOUSE

avon.

Published by AVON
A division of HarperCollins*Publishers* Ltd
1 London Bridge Street
London SE1 9GF

www.harpercollins.co.uk

HarperCollins*Publishers*
1st Floor, Watermarque Building, Ringsend Road
Dublin 4, Ireland

A Paperback Original 2022

1

First published in Great Britain by HarperCollins*Publishers* 2022

A catalogue copy of this book is available from the British Library.

ISBN: 978-0-00-838608-5

This novel is entirely a work of fiction. The names,
characters and incidents portrayed in it are the work of the author's
imagination. Any resemblance to actual persons, living or dead,
events or localities is entirely coincidental.

Typeset in Meridien by Palimpsest Book Production Limited,
Falkirk, Stirlingshire
Printed and Bound in the UK using 100% Renewable Electricity at CPI Group (UK) Ltd

MIX
Paper | Supporting
responsible forestry
FSC™ C007454

This book is produced from independently certified FSC™ paper
to ensure responsible forest management.

For more information visit: www.harpercollins.co.uk/green

For my mother, Jane,
my father Michael,
my sweet sister Philippa
and beloved brother Charles.
Holding you all in my heart
until we're together again.

part one

chapter 01

millie

The silence of a house that's been broken into is unlike any other. It's as if you've flipped up its skirts and made it gasp, taking all the air with it.

Those first few stolen seconds of stillness are like a drug to me. I could spend a lifetime in this moment, at peace.

But it doesn't last long.

It's broken by the soft patter of feline paws running down the hallway. A grey cat slinks into the laundry room, ignoring me completely as she heads to her bowl. She isn't the least bit interested in me, or what I'm doing in her house.

Cats have refined survival of the species to an efficient minimalism. Even the most self-absorbed cat will nurture her own kittens. But by the time they're eight weeks old, the mother, having accomplished the important work of teaching them independence, is done with them. She'll still intervene if they're in trouble or get too rough in play, but she won't interact with them on a regular basis. She'll swat a youngster who disturbs her rest. And once they reach adolescence, at around twelve weeks, it's every cat for herself. The mother will hiss if they come near her food. She won't grieve when they disappear from the home. In fact, she'll be relieved.

We don't blame a cat for being a cat.

You knew what you were getting into, Tom says. *You're an intelligent woman. You knew what having children would mean.*

The cat twines herself in a figure-eight around my legs, seeking more food. I pick her up, stroking the back of her head, enjoying the sensual pleasure of her fur beneath my fingers as I wander into the kitchen.

I had high hopes for this property, but it looked a lot better on Rightmove than it does in person. The pictures were clearly taken with a wide-angle lens, and then Photoshopped. The kitchen has very little natural light, and even on a bright morning like this, it feels dingy.

The owners obviously renovated before putting the house on the market – the house smells of paint – but they've made the same mistake most people do when they remodel a kitchen: they've upgraded the cabinets and appliances, but kept the same inefficient, dated layout.

It's nicely done, with granite countertops and interesting stainless-steel backsplashes, but the way people live has changed a lot in the last few decades: a kitchen isn't just where you cook any more, but where you *live*. They should've taken down that wall to the dining room – who actually uses a dining room these days? – and created one large, open-plan space. It would've given them a lot of natural light, too, from the west-facing front of the house, and they could've put in some French doors at the back to get that indoor/outdoor feel.

I check out the cupboards. Emma Bridgewater crockery, yawn. Expensive Le Creuset saucepans but cheap knives, which tells me everything I need to know about the people who own this house.

Upstairs is equally disappointing. A cramped fifth bedroom that should've been used to expand the master bathroom, or, better yet, create a decent walk-in wardrobe. Original features

4

no one's had the courage to either eliminate completely, or assimilate into the new design.

None of the beds are made. The cupboard doors in the master bedroom are flung wide, as if they've left in a hurry. Her sweaters are neatly folded in colour-coded stacks, but his side of the wardrobe is a tangled mess, with ties dribbling down the shelves, and balled-up socks on the floor. In my experience, incompatibility in a wardrobe is a more reliable indicator of divorce than infidelity.

I open the cabinet in their ensuite bathroom, scrutinising the prescription labels.

She's had two bouts of cystitis recently. He's got bad haemorrhoids. She's missed a couple of her contraceptive pills this month. I wonder if her husband knows that.

Bored suddenly, I go back downstairs and scan the knick-knacks on the bookshelves in the sitting room, looking for a souvenir before I leave.

I never take anything valuable, or clearly sentimental. A fridge magnet. A bulldog clip. Nothing that will be missed.

There was a time I broke into houses on a weekly basis. Whenever life got too complicated, I'd slip away and disappear into the silence of a house that wasn't mine. I'd spend hours in other people's homes, perusing their wardrobes, reading their books. I find it profoundly soothing to exist in a world where I'm not supposed to be, for reasons I've never been able to explain.

It's been months since I allowed my darker self to call the shots, but I'm tense and exhausted. Some people drink or take drugs to relax. This is my addiction.

I know what I'm doing is wrong: I'm violating someone's private sanctuary. But I only visit houses that have been put up for sale, whose owners are inviting scrutiny. I'm careful never to leave a trace of my presence. I made a promise, and I never break my word.

First do no harm.

For a moment, I consider taking one of the photographs. Mr and Mrs Unmade Bed, with their two children, Boy and Girl. Here they are on their ski break in Zermatt. Oh, look! Boy and Girl have a new puppy, Dog! Look, Dog! Look!

They make family life seem so easy.

In the end I slip one of a pair of dice into my pocket, and go back through the kitchen, leaving via the same back door in the laundry room as I came in.

I even lock it behind me, which is more than the owners remembered to do.

Inside the mind of a psychopath | *Original Air Date 9 July*

The transcript below has been lightly edited for length and clarity.

I appreciate the introduction, Ken, but I'm guessing you all know who I am, or you wouldn't be here.

[Laughter]

I know you're all desperate to get to the juicy stuff, the Glass House Murders, and we will soon, I promise.

But this talk is supposed to be educational, so let's kick off with a statistic: one in a hundred normal people – and I'm putting *normal* in inverted commas here – is a psychopath.

I can see you all doing the maths, so let me save you the trouble. There's about a thousand of you in this room.

So that means roughly ten of you are psychopaths. But since the stat I just gave you rises to one in twenty-five when we're talking about business leaders and CEOs, we've probably got about forty psychos in here this evening. It could be carnage by the end of the night.

[Laughter]

But let's get serious for a minute. It's essential you approach this subject with something other than a pop-culture understanding of psychopathy.

Think of it as Psycho 101. I'll do my best to make it as painless as possible.

Thanks to Hollywood, when you hear the term *psychopath* you imagine a knife-wielding maniac with crazy eyes. Jack Nicholson in *The Shining*, Hannibal Lecter in *The Silence of the Lambs*, Norman Bates in *Psycho*. Well, I guess the clue's in the name with that last one.

[Laughter]

But what about this young lady who looks like Sandra Bullock sitting here in the front row? If you could just stand up – thank you. Lovely sweater, by the way. Looks like butter wouldn't melt, doesn't she? The archetypal girl-next-door. But trust me, *she's* the one you need to be scared of.

[Laughter]

Well, not literally. Thank you, Ms Bullock, you can sit down now. My point is, not all psychopaths are wild-eyed serial killers. It's a spectrum disorder, like autism. At one end, you've got Ted Bundy and Charles Manson and Jack the Ripper, Hollywood's bloodthirsty predators.

And at the other you've got the brain surgeons and TV presenters and tech moguls and corporate business leaders. The people everyone *needs* to be ruthless and focused and unemotional in a crisis.

People like me.

When I tell people I'm a psychopath, their response is usually a mix of horror and fascination. I mean, who *admits* to being 'deceptive, callous, manipulative, reckless, superficial, predatory', right?

[Laughter]

And I'm not going to lie to you: I'm all of those things.

You'd think it'd put people off me, but no. You might be nervous, but you're riveted and excited, too, aren't you?

And why wouldn't you be? I'm extremely charming when I want to be. I'm well-liked. I have lots of friends. Functionally, I'm a good person. I'm one of the 'safe' ones. I love to cook, and I've got a dark sense of humour. I often make people laugh. People come to me with their troubles.

So what makes me so different from most of you?

Well, I'm not going to bore you with lots of science about the amygdala and the orbital frontal cortex, but the bottom line is, psychopaths like me are biologically *incapable* of empathy.

A dozen scientific studies have confirmed it: we literally *can't* feel your pain. We don't experience fear or remorse. So we don't care about blending into society. We're not bothered by punishment or disapproval.

It's a miracle more of us aren't serial killers, to be honest.

We'll lie and cheat to get what we want, but we don't make moral choices; we make pragmatic ones. Usually we're not out to get you. We're like water: we'll always find the quickest and easiest route to where we want to be, and if you get in our way, you'll be washed away.

But we're as capable of love and nurturing as we are indifference and destruction. Most of us aren't a threat; remorse and empathy may not come naturally to us, but we can *learn* to care. It takes practice: it's like learning a different language, and it's exhausting. But we want to fit in, we want to be good people, and so we work at it.

Like I said, usually we're not out to get you.

Usually.

A small minority of psychopaths have a predisposition to calculated violence; violence that's cold-blooded and planned, and scary as hell.

I'm as terrified of people like that as you are. It's not like psychos give each other a hall pass.

I'm often asked how something as ordinary as moving house descended into such chaos and bloodshed, and the truth is, I honestly don't know. Hindsight is a wonderful thing, and, with retrospect, the signs were there. You'd think someone like me would have been able to spot them.

But at the time we had no reason to suspect anything.

We just wanted to sell our house.

chapter 02

millie

By the time I get back home, Tom is in the kitchen, organising breakfast, packed lunches, the day, our lives.

'How was your run?' he asks me.

'Good. Just what I needed.'

Tom and I have been married for nineteen years. He knows it's not the run that's rejuvenated me, and put a spring in my step.

I left a bouquet of pink roses on the doorstep of the house I borrowed to say thank you to the owners, with a cryptic note: *Pay it forward*. They'll be confused, but I hope the flowers will make them as happy as the house made me.

I hand Tom the dice I stole earlier as he puts two slices of wholewheat bread into the toaster. I don't permit white bread in the house, or sugar, crisps, fizzy drinks. No screens at the table, or in bed.

Tom pockets the dice without comment. Later, he'll add it to the other mementos of my extracurricular activities that he keeps in a drawer beneath his desk. I'm like a cat, bringing home a mouse as proof of my hunting skills.

Proof I still have my darker impulses in check.

The kids tumble down the stairs, already bickering and shoving at each other as they tussle for stools at the breakfast bar.

Medusa, our daughter, is thirteen, clear-eyed and knowing. She's inherited Tom's Black Irish hair and blue eyes, but in every other respect she takes after me. Sometimes this makes me sad; sometimes not. Naming her was my privilege, part of the deal Tom and I struck when we decided to have a child. I'd planned to call her Artemis, after the Greek goddess of the hunt, but that was before I endured a thirty-hour labour that ended in a forceps delivery and fourteen stitches.

Our son, Peter, named by Tom, is soft. Clay to her marble. He inherited my honeyed colouring, but people always say he takes after his dad. Amenable, sunny, accommodating. Ten years old, but he seems younger. He's cerebral and dreamy; he gets bullied at school, and frequently comes home without the new computer game or collectible for which he's saved for months.

I try not to play favourites, but if we were animals in the wild, Peter would be first to be picked off from the herd. He needs me in a way Meddie never has.

Peter sits down at the breakfast bar now and fills his bowl with plain yoghurt and granola. He reaches for the last banana in the fruit bowl to slice on top. His sister doesn't like bananas, but now that Peter's taken the last one, she wants it. She snatches his bowl away, and he sighs, but doesn't object.

'Give that back,' Tom says.

Our daughter regards him, flat-eyed, and spoons a mouthful of granola and yoghurt between her lips.

'Give the bowl back to your brother,' I say.

Medusa shrugs and sends it skittering across the counter towards him. 'I don't want it, anyway. The granola's got mouse droppings in it.'

Peter yelps and shoves the bowl back. 'Ewww!'

'Enough,' I say, in a tone of voice that silences the pair of them. 'I need to shower and change for work. You'd both better be ready to go when I come back downstairs. Your father doesn't have time to take you to school today, so I'm dropping you off.'

This is a rare event. Part of our deal when we decided to have a child was that Tom would assume the lion's share of hands-on parenting. We both knew that however good my intentions I'd quickly lose interest in the repetitive routines of childcare, perhaps with disastrous consequences.

I was quite clear when Tom asked me to marry him: I had no desire to replicate myself, no romantic longing to blend our genes. Frankly, given my childhood, I was a rotten proposition as a wife all round, but Tom was touchingly undeterred.

Perhaps it's because we grew up together. He was, quite literally, the boy-next-door. Our parents owned adjoining semis on Kennedy Road, a cul-de-sac in what an estate agent would no doubt call a 'leafy' part of West Sussex. My parents bought Number 17 when my mother was newly pregnant with me. Three months later, Tom's parents moved into Number 19.

My mother wasn't sick then. There are photographs of her and Tom's mother showing off their baby bumps together in the back garden. In some of them, my mother's even smiling.

We were born two weeks apart in June 1982, just as the Falklands War was coming to an end. We went to the same nursery school and we were inseparable. Even when we moved up to primary school, and Tom made friends with other boys, he stayed loyal to me.

I spent more time in his house than mine; his mother, Amy, showed me more love and care than my own indifferent, sometimes hysterical, mother ever did. Amy fed me when my parents neglected to, and gave me a lift home from school when my father was drunk and my mother had taken to her bed with 'nerves'.

Our bedrooms were separated by a thin partition wall, through which I'd hear Tom playing retro hits by Blondie and

The Cure well into the small hours. Sometimes I'd touch my palm to the wall and almost feel him breathing in the bed on the other side.

I wasn't like other teenage girls. I didn't care about the things they cared about: boys, clothes, approval. I couldn't afford to let myself care about anything. If I allowed myself to feel, the emotion uppermost would be *rage*.

Rage at my father, a violent narcissist who took pleasure in reducing my mother to a cowering wreck with his fist and his words. Rage at my mother, for letting herself be used as a punchbag and coming back for more again and again.

Rage at my own powerlessness.

In the absence of feeling, I'd do almost anything to force a jolt of emotion. I climbed higher up the chestnut tree to shake down conkers than any of the boys. I scaled a mobile phone mast for a dare. When I was thirteen, I sneaked out of the house in the middle of the night to climb the fence into a nearby railway yard, so that I could run the roofs of the trains parked in the sidings just for the hell of it; a fall into the gaps between carriages would have broken my neck. I hung onto the rear bumpers of passing cars on my skateboard to get a lift up the hill to our road. I was fearless, a daredevil, the leader of the pack. And Tom was my wingman.

Then – and now.

He never asked what I used to get up to when I disappeared, sometimes for days at a time, in the early years of our marriage.

We called these absences my 'prison breaks'. Afterwards, when I returned to him, the restlessness that fuelled me would be sated for a while. Without me ever having to discuss it with him, Tom understood.

Six years into our marriage, I was the one who put motherhood back on the table, because I wanted to please him.

And I was curious. A child was the ultimate challenge.

Tom's only condition was that my prison breaks must stop. As a mother, I couldn't disappear for days on end. If I was to teach discipline, I must practise it.

We agreed that when the need became too strong, when the stresses and frustrations of ordinary life drove me to act out, I would limit myself to day trips and ensure I was back by nightfall. And I would tell him afterwards. Not in so many words, but with my mementos. He knows he can trust me. And so I never stray too far outside the lines.

The key to our marriage has always been honesty. My loyalty to the truth is the bedrock of our relationship. If he ever asks what I do when I'm not with him, I will tell him.

He never has.

chapter 03

tom

My wife's very much an acquired taste. Even people who like Marmite rarely eat it out of the jar. She's very . . . *intense*. Very focused. She likes to think she lives in the shades of grey between *right* and *wrong*, but the truth is, her moral world is very black and white.

You're either with her or against her.

She's not the psychopath she thinks she is. She loves fiercely and furiously, but she doesn't wear her heart on her sleeve. She's had to fight for everything she's achieved: the child of an abusive drunk doesn't easily climb out of the pit. Her fists are still raised against a world that tended to hit first. She doesn't always follow the rules – or even the law – but she has her own personal code of honour, and she sticks to it. She *never* lies. And she's loyal to a fault. If she decides to fight your corner, she's all in – whether that's what you want or not.

To be honest, a little of Millie goes a long way. But she's a taste I've been hooked on for forty years. Back in the day, Victorians used to take arsenic regularly, using it as a tonic and an aphrodisiac. Who knows: maybe my addiction will kill me in the end.

I watch her now as she gets ready for bed, smoothing some kind of goo onto her flawless skin with deft upward strokes.

15

Millie Downton is the woman I should not have been able to get: a nine to my four. Her thick gold hair is twisted up into a loose knot, and she's wearing a plain white T-shirt and white cotton underwear. The soft glow from the bathroom light makes her look seventeen again. We're the same age, forty, but she looks a decade younger than me. She's in excellent shape, thanks to daily cardio and strength-training. She has an ortho-dontically perfect smile, a full mouth, and wide eyes that shift in shade between dark honey and black coffee, depending on her mood. If you were casting her in a movie, Rosamund Pike would be a good choice.

She catches my eye in the mirror as she snaps the lid of her lotion bottle closed. 'Did you have fun this afternoon?' she asks.

I took our son to visit the Holocaust Exhibition at the Imperial War Museum. It's not recommended for children under four-teen, but Peter said his class is doing a block on it later this term. 'Fun isn't the word I'd use,' I say.

'I'm sure Peter enjoyed it.'

I can't tell if she's making a crack about our son or not. Even after loving this woman for four decades, I still don't often know what's really going on inside her beautiful head.

My lovely wife would be quick to acknowledge she isn't easy to live with. She has rules for the children, rules for me: breakfast and dinner together, always. No shorts when we go out to dinner, even in Greece, even in August. Three peremp-tory strikes against each family member's friends, no questions asked.

Honesty, no matter what.

Yes, that dress makes you look fat.

No, I don't think you deserve to be on the school team.

The kids rebel on occasion. Sometimes I even join them. But Millie holds firm.

She's giving us structure. She's making us *safe*.

16

She's teaching us discipline. She's teaching us the power of family.

She has her issues, certainly. I'm the first to admit her habit of breaking into other people's houses is less than ideal. But she never takes anything they'll miss. No one ever knows she's been there. For some reason it soothes her soul – maybe because it reminds her not all families are as dysfunctional as the one in which she grew up. If it keeps her sane, what's the harm?

The truth is I don't care what she does, within reason: I'd never leave her. Not just because I love her, or because I love my children, although both those things are true.

I won't leave because I can't.

Millie is my obsession.

My dance with the dark.

I've loved her since we were infants in our prams. I never thought of her as a *girl* – she was just Millie, wild and fearless, tougher and braver than any of the boys. I took on all-comers to defend her right to run with us, frequently returning home with bruised knuckles and a bloody nose. I assumed we'd grow up and get married one day, because why wouldn't we? I loved her far more than she loved me, but there's always a lover and a lovee in any relationship. We complemented each other perfectly. Of *course* we'd get married.

The first time I proposed to her, the summer we turned eighteen, she laughed in my face.

In retrospect I can see I was suffering from some sort of romantic white knight syndrome. Millie made it clear she considered herself neither vulnerable nor in need of saving. As if to prove her point, I responded to my rejection with maturity and calm: I gave up my place at university and ran off to join the army.

I didn't see her again for three years, not till the summer my mother died and I was given compassionate leave to return home for the funeral.

17

On the long journey back from Basra, my head was filled with thoughts not of my dear, sweet mother, but of seeing Millie again. I knew she'd just graduated from Cambridge and returned home for the summer: her father was dead by then. As my taxi pulled up outside the house, I looked for her, but the curtains next door were drawn, the house silent and still.

That night, I was lying on my bed, my hands clasped behind my head, staring blankly up at the ceiling. A new tattoo with a Latin inscription poked out from beneath the left sleeve of my T-shirt. I thought it made me look cool.

A tap on the glass made me look up. Millie had climbed out of her window and used the guttering to traverse our houses from her room to mine, just as she had when we were kids. She swung one leg into the room and sat astride the windowsill, half-in, half-out, dangling an object from her fingertips.

'I have something for you,' she said.

'My mother's dead,' I said, without moving.

'I know.'

'Is that all you have to say?'

'What d'you mean?'

'You could at least say you're sorry.' I sat up and rubbed the palms of my hands back and forth against a buzz cut I still wasn't sure suited me. 'Jesus, Millie. I know feelings aren't your thing, but she *loved* you.'

'I know.' She twirled something between her fingers and held it out to me. 'Do you want my present or not?'

I'd had a front-row seat to Millie's messed-up childhood. I honestly couldn't tell you whether she'd have been a softer, easier person if her parents hadn't been such almighty screwups or if her spiky personality was written in her DNA, but even as a kid Millie threw up walls to keep people out, then dug a moat around them and filled it with Greek fire and barbed wire for good measure.

Of course I knew she cared about my mother. Just as I knew she'd never be able to admit it, least of all to herself.

'For fuck's sake, get in here before you fall,' I said.

She swung her legs over the windowsill and climbed into the room. 'I went to a lot of trouble to get this for you,' she said, holding it out to me.

I took the object. It was a solid silver keyring shaped like a scuba diver, complete with belt weights and two tiny silver oxygen tanks. 'Where d'you get this?' I asked curiously.

'Mr Taft.'

'Mr *Taft*? Like, our history teacher from school?'

'Yes.'

'Why would Taft give this to you?'

'He didn't *give* it to me, idiot. I took it.'

'You took it?'

She thumped down on the bed next to me. 'I know your mother's just died, but you need to stop repeating everything I say,' she said. 'I took it from his office. His *home* office,' she added. 'His stupid dog woke up. I'm surprised he slept through the barking. He must be going deaf.'

'Why would you do that?'

'He was so mean to you. And he loved that stupid keyring. He was always playing with it in class.' She shrugged. 'I thought having it might cheer you up.'

'You're crazy, you know that? What if you'd got caught?'

'I never get caught,' she said.

I put the keyring down, and kissed her.

It was our first kiss.

And it told us both everything we needed to know.

19

chapter 04

millie

I'm out on my morning run when I spot the *For Sale* sign going up outside the Glass House.

The property is a landmark in this part of south-west London, tucked away in the labyrinth of streets between Fulham and Putney. Most of the period housing stock in SW6 has a uniformity to it not found in other parts of London, because it was all built in a single thirty-five-year span when Fulham's prosperity turned from market gardening to housing after the District Line arrived in 1880. Rows and rows of identical Edwardian and Victorian terraced houses, punctuated now and again by post-war semis built on old bomb sites.

And then there's the Glass House.

The land sits on the inner right-angle of an L-shaped street, jammed between perpendicular rows of houses like a Trivial Pursuit wedge. A small workman's cottage used to stand on it, but after it was bombed to rubble in the Second World War, the land was considered too small to redevelop until people started paying three-quarters of a million pounds for a parking space.

The house looks like a glass lantern, with its milky translucent facade and black ironwork. It comprises two cubes, stacked at angles to each other, and has an almost glowing effervescence, thanks to the clear-and-frosted-glass exterior walls. According to the architect who designed it in the Sixties, he drew inspiration from an iconic Modernist glass house in Paris, a 1930s building known as La Maison de Verre.

The main living rooms are in the cube on the upper floor, which is capped by a rooftop garden, while three sprawling bedroom suites are all on the ground level. The inverted layout and walls of glass allow light to cascade into the living spaces, the effect enhanced by internal translucent sliding screens of the type found in traditional Japanese homes.

If the home had been built anywhere else, its asking price would run into eight figures. But the only access to the property is via a right of way less than six feet wide which slices from the street at an angle of forty-five degrees between the two adjacent properties. There's no parking, of course. There's no exterior space at all other than the rooftop and a narrow swimming pool – designed for exercise rather than recreation – that takes up the entire rear garden.

The house is smaller than ours in terms of square feet but the use of space is so effective the floorplan looks like a work of art. It's changed hands just once since it was built. According to land registry records, it's currently owned by Salome Ltd, a company with two directors, Felix and Stacey Porter. They bought it twelve years ago, just after Ms Porter got her gig on morning television.

I know all of this because I've stalked this house for years.

The first time I saw it was when I was out jogging with Peter in his pushchair, making efficient use of my maternity leave. We were living across the river then, in a two-bedroom flat in Wandsworth. At the time, it was all we could afford.

I stopped on the pavement so abruptly Peter almost got whiplash. It's the closest I've ever come to understanding the phrase *coup de foudre*.

A stroke of lightning: *this is my house*. It just didn't know it yet.

As soon as I got home, I told Tom I'd found the house we were going to grow old in. He knew better than to dismiss it as a fantasy, even though we could barely keep up the payments on the Wandsworth mortgage.

The following weekend, we stood on the pavement outside the home and agreed: the Glass House got a free pass.

Other couples keep lists of celebrities with whom they're allowed to sleep without recrimination should they ever have the opportunity.

We have a list of houses.

Five each. If any of them becomes available, and we're financially able to swing it, the other party has no choice but to agree.

I've had property crushes before, of course, but never like this. There was a stunning apartment in Narni, a hilltop town in Umbria, in central Italy, that captured my heart a few years ago. An extraordinary house on the Pacific West Coast with sweeping views of the ocean we saw on a trip to California the summer before last. But the Glass House is my one true love. There's something about the property's cool self-assurance, its uncompromising commitment to form over function. This is not a house that will ever apologise for being what it is.

It doesn't matter that I've never seen inside it. The Porters have a sophisticated security system I'd be a fool to attempt: I'm not a cat burglar. I know my limits. And the woman is notoriously private; unlike most small-screen celebrities, she's never allowed cameras inside her home for voyeuristic maga-zine spreads.

But I don't need to set foot inside. When you know, you *know*.

The estate agent gives the post holding the *For Sale* sign a good shake, to check it's solid. 'You interested?' he asks, as I stand transfixed on the pavement.

Tom and I can afford it now. I make good money, and the last ten years have been very kind to Tom's work in the high-tech security market.

'Yes,' I say. 'I'm interested.'

kyle and harper find their forever home!

1,309,564 views 👍 301K 👎 1.4K

Hi, my lovely Kyper peeps, welcome back! I hope you're all doing really well – oops, my hair's gone all static! I just brushed it before I turned the camera on, my bad, sorry about that, let me just tie it back. There we go.

Anyway, my loves, I'm so glad you're all here, because today's a really important day for us! This amazing house just came on the market and me and Kyle are going to see it now! We've got about an hour before our appointment, so I thought I'd take a minute to update you all, and then we can see the house together.

For those of you who've been following Kyle and me's house-buying journey, it's been a bit of a roller-coaster, hasn't it?

Just to catch you up if you haven't seen the show before – and we're so happy you've decided to join our Kyper Nation, my loves, it's so lovely to see you! – Kyle and me decided to put our house on the market this year. We love it here in Putney, and this is a such a sweet, sweet house, it's got so many lovely memories, but the boys really need their own rooms now, and we're just running out of space.

So anyway, we put our house on the market back in March and we were super lucky, we got an offer straight away, but then the problem was, we just couldn't find anything to buy. We were getting super stressed, but then we finally found a place in Brixton, the nice end, you know what I'm saying, my loves, don't you? But then two weeks ago the seller pulled out at the last minute and everything fell through.

Oh, God, it was awful, wasn't it? We were *so* disappointed.

But we kept looking and then yesterday this amazing house in Fulham came on the market, and I said to Kyle, this is it, this is the one. I just *knew*.

God, it's so scary, this whole house-buying thing, isn't it? You look round a place for, like, half-an-hour, and then you have to decide if you want to buy it. I mean, I don't know about you but I spend longer choosing a pair of shoes!

Between you and me, it *is* a teeny bit over our budget – well, a lot, really – but it's for our little family, so like I told Kyle, it'll all be worth it in the end. You can't put a price on love, can you?

And thanks to you, our Kyper Nation, we can just about manage it financially, we're so blessed, thank you, guys! Especially thanks to our sponsors at SugarPop. Seriously, peeps, I hope you're not paying full price when you shop online, because with SugarPop, you just download the app and they'll find the discounts for you! It's so awesome! Just click on the SugarPop link below this vlog and sign up, it's that simple.

Anyway, Kyle says I shouldn't get my hopes up about this house, there'll be loads of people interested and we can't afford it anyway, but we just *have* to get it, this is the one, I keep telling him. The thing is – I let my hair dry naturally again today, guys, I don't think I've straightened my hair for so long, what do you think? Tell me in the comments section below – anyway, the thing for me is, after everything that's happened, me and Kyle really need a fresh start, and I think this house could be it.

Honestly, my loves, I'm so glad you're here with me to share this moment. I know it's crazy, but the house feels like it's mine already!

chapter 05

tom

When Millie's in this kind of mood, she's almost impossible to resist.

'It's perfect timing,' she says, her eyes shining. 'The market's really strong right now, so we'll have no trouble selling ours. If we're quick off the mark, Tom, we could be settled into the Glass House before the new school year. The estate agent said he can get us inside first thing next week—'

'A strong market works both ways, Millie,' I caution. 'We'll be bidding against cash buyers. We may get over the odds for our place, but we'll be paying it, too.'

'We can afford it,' she says. 'It'll be a stretch, but I've done the maths. If we get our full asking price—'

'A big *if*,' I warn.

'Come on, Tom. If not now, then when?'

Millie's a risk-taker. She'll always spin the wheel, take the chance. She's not reckless: she assesses the odds rationally and makes an informed, considered choice. But while I'll always opt for the safer, higher ground, she's never afraid to step out onto the ice.

'You've only just finished renovating this place,' I say. 'The paint's barely dry!'

'Which is why it's the perfect time to sell.'

I sigh. 'Millie, I've got a shit-ton of stuff going on at work at the moment. It's my busiest time. And I'm not sure the kids need the upheaval right now, either. Peter's still finding his feet, and Meddie's already got to cope with changing schools in September.'

'The Glass House is closer to the Tube,' Millie wheedles. 'Meddie will be able to get herself to and from school without a long walk home in the dark during the winter. And you've been saying for ages we need more space,' she adds. 'You'll be able to have a proper office instead of having to use the basement. It's our *dream house*, Tom. You can't say no.'

I never could, not to her.

She senses me weakening, and laughs, throwing her arms around my waist. 'It's on the list, Tom,' she says. 'It's one of my five. You don't actually have a choice.'

She isn't joking. Her persuasive coaxing is no more than a fig leaf for my pride. There was never any question I'd agree. It's a shame: I like the area we're in now. We've got good neighbours – everyone turned out for the street party last summer. The kids have grown up here. It's going to be a wrench.

But Millie isn't asking for my permission. I should be grateful the twelfth-century stone tower she fell in love with in Italy a few years back never came onto the market.

'Can you imagine?' she says dreamily. '*Us* in the Glass House?'

Where we live, what car I drive, the number of zeros in my bank account – none of it's ever mattered to me, not really. But I understand why it matters to Millie.

Her father worked as a carpet fitter – when he was sober, anyway. Nothing wrong with that: good, honest work. And Millie's not a snob. But Terry Lennox knew he'd married up – Millie's mother, Charlotte, was a teacher whose family had

had money once upon a time – and he never forgave his wife for it. And he never forgave his daughter either: for being smarter than he was, for having ambitions beyond his horizons.

He blacked her eye when she won a scholarship to a private convent school at seven. He broke her arm when she was awarded a national science prize. He put her in hospital with a ruptured spleen when she came home with thirteen A* grades in her mock GCSEs. If he hadn't died before she got into Cambridge, he'd have probably killed her for doing so.

Terry Lennox worked for people who owned places like the Glass House. It doesn't take Sigmund Freud to work out why his daughter wants to buy it.

'We might not get it,' I warn. 'That house is a landmark. The owners are going to be fighting off buyers.'

'We'll get it,' she says confidently.

My wife is a mass of contradictions. She's cool and forensic; she's passionate and hot-tempered. She can be chillingly detached when she assesses our children's flaws, but she wouldn't think twice about killing to protect them. She has absolutely no self-doubt when it comes to her work, but she's so afraid of being hurt she's never learned to make friends. And she'd rather believe herself a sociopath incapable of human connection than admit *that* particular truth.

But when Millie sets her mind to something, there's no stopping her. Like I said: it's all or nothing with my wife. If she says we'll get the Glass House, I believe her.

Put it this way: I wouldn't want to be the person standing in her way.

chapter 06

millie

The estate agent twitches her high blonde ponytail forward over her left shoulder. It's her tell: she does it every time she's about to lie.

'The Conways are interested in several other properties,' Julia says. 'A bit more competitively priced, I'm afraid, Mrs Downton. But I'll let you know if they'd like to come back here for a second viewing.'

'That's fine,' I say. 'I've got several offers on the table already, so just email me before Friday if they want to put in a bid.'

'Friday?'

'I'm asking everyone to make their best offer by the end of the week,' I say. 'I'll review them and make a decision on Monday. I think it's fairer than the back-and-forth of a bidding war, don't you?'

She swallows. She's nervous and tentative just at the moment she should be assertive and bold. Most of her lipstick has gone now, a pale pink smear on the lip of the plastic water bottle she's been toting from room to room as I've shown her and her buyers around. Her white skin is stretched over birdlike bones; a blue vein pulses at her temple.

'The Conways have a lovely little pied-à-terre in Putney,' she says. 'I believe it's about to go under offer. I know they'd be able to complete very quickly if they decide to put in a bid after all.'

I watch the young couple as they confer beneath a silver birch tree in the small, walled garden to the rear of the house. Earlier, I pushed back the frameless glass accordion doors that run the width of the sitting room, opening up the entire space to the outdoors. Frankly, on a warm summer day like this, the house sells itself.

We're at the end of a row of classic Fulham terraced houses painted in delicate pastel shades of periwinkle and lemon and mint green, which means we only have neighbours on one side of us, so more light, less noise. You can get into the garden directly from the side street rather than having to go through the house, a boon when you have to deal with pushchairs and bicycles and all the rest of the paraphernalia that comes with children.

We had to renovate from top to bottom when we moved in eight years ago: we were among the last in our street to dig out the basement, but doing so increased our square footage – and property value – by thirty percent overnight. I had a floor-to-ceiling glass light well put in where the side return used to be, extending down into the basement and up through each of the three main floors of the house: the architect was sceptical, but it was more than worth the cost.

Smoked oak flooring. A Chesney fireplace, bespoke kitchen cabinets, Miele appliances and Carrara marble, a walkout rooftop terrace. Our asking price is simultaneously audacious and reasonable.

We're going to need every penny to buy the Glass House.

To be honest, I'm surprised a couple in their late twenties with two young children can afford a house anywhere near our price point, but apparently they're successful lifestyle vloggers with their own Instagram and YouTube channel, KyperLife, an irritating portmanteau of their names. The woman's been videoing herself as they've viewed the house, despite me asking her not to – I don't want our kids' bedrooms all over the internet.

They're holding hands now as they gaze at the house from the garden. It's clear they love it. They're already feeling a stirring of possessiveness as they imagine where they'll put their furniture.

When they come back inside, he's the one who reaches me first, squaring over-muscled shoulders and extending his hand with a simulacrum of spousal authority, but she's the one in charge. It's always the woman who picks the house.

'Kyle Conway,' he says. 'This is my wife, Harper.'

'Pleased to meet you,' she says.

He gestures around the sitting room. 'Julia says you reno-vated the whole house, top to bottom,' he says. 'You've done an amazing job.'

'The previous owner hadn't touched it in forty years,' I say. 'Some of the rooms didn't even have light fittings. It was easier to rip everything down to the studs and start again than try to fix it.'

I try not to wince as Harper scratches hot pink acrylic nails across the textured sisal wallpaper, a hungry look in her eyes. 'It must be hard to sell after all the work you've put in,' she says.

I'm impatient for them to leave. We need our house to go under contract as soon as possible to put us in the best nego-tiating position when we make an offer on the Glass House, and this couple are just tyre-kickers: they haven't sold their own place, and I can't afford to get stuck in an unreliable housing chain.

'I'm afraid I have another viewing in fifteen minutes,' I lie, heading towards the hallway.

'We want it,' Harper says instantly.

Her husband throws her a startled look. 'Harps—'

'Come on, Kyle. You *know* it's perfect. It's just what we've been looking for. It's our *forever home*.' She turns to me. 'We'll offer you full asking right now if you take it off the market.'

The agent's eyes gleam as she calculates her commission. Harper's offering nearly double the money we put into the house. Tom would kill me if he knew I was even hesitating.

I'm seriously tempted. We've had numerous viewings in the three days since we put it up for sale, but we're overpriced: no one has come back for a second look.

But I know what it's like when you find *the one*.

They say it takes just ten seconds when viewing a new house to see yourself living there. I recognise the property lust in Harper's eyes.

'It wouldn't really be fair to my other interested parties,' I demur.

'Whatever offers you've already had, we'll beat them,' she says.

'I really can't—'

'Fifty thousand over asking.'

Her husband grabs her arm. 'Harper!'

'Kyle, we've looked at, like, *forty-seven* houses,' she says impatiently. 'Do you want to trail round another forty-seven? And this one's so much nicer and more *homey* than that other glass one we just saw. I want *this* one.'

'We can't afford it!'

'We can if we get that new SugarPop deal,' she says. 'We'll get some great storylines out of moving here. You know we will.'

I can't decide if Harper Conway is exceptionally smart or a complete idiot. No one goes into a negotiation tipping their hand like this. Either she's caught up in bidding fever, or she's playing a clever game: an offer like this certainly cuts through the noise. Either way, it's a win for me.

'If you can provide a ten percent non-refundable deposit now rather than wait until we exchange,' I say, 'I'll give you forty-eight hours to prove your house is under contract and that you've got the financing to complete.'

Kyle looks shocked. 'Non-refundable? Harper, we can't—'

'It's a deal,' Harper says.

Inside the mind of a psychopath | *Original Air Date 9 July*

The transcript below has been lightly edited for length and clarity.

When I was eight, I fell through the ice while skating on a duck pond in Richmond. I was submerged in icy water for nearly fifteen minutes before being rescued by firefighters.

I was blue by the time they fished me out, and I wasn't breathing.

The paramedics rushed me to hospital, but, after forty minutes of CPR, my parents were told it was hopeless.

Doctors told them to say goodbye to me, and they were actually discussing transplant donation when I woke up.

Let me tell you, I played the guilt card for years afterwards: 'Clean my room? But you wanted to give away my *kidneys*!'

[Laughter]

The thing is, when my mother told me what'd happened, that I'd been clinically dead for over an hour, I *laughed.*

I wasn't afraid of death. I wasn't afraid of anything. The signs were there, if anyone had bothered to look.

Tell me, have any of you ever tried those immersive sink-or-swim language courses? Let's see a show of hands—

Almost half of you. Well, aren't we a roomful of overachievers?

[Laughter]

For those who haven't had the pleasure, you're basically dropped into a situation where you don't speak a word of the language you want to learn, usually with a host family.

No one explains anything to you, and if they do, you can't understand them.

It's not so much immersion as *sub*mersion. And these courses work because there's no way out. Even when you're tired, even when you're hungry and fed-up and frustrated, you can't break the fourth wall and appeal for help.

Your only option is to use the language you're learning to survive. Well, that's what it's like for a person like me to exist in a social world.

Thanks in no small part to Hollywood, the word *psychopath* is so loaded with meaning, it's hard to see past the stigma of the label to the human being beneath.

But I'm *biologically* wired not to feel shame or guilt. I was born without the ability to empathise, just as some people are born without limbs. It's not our fault.

To paraphrase the immortal Jessica Rabbit: I'm not a bad person: I'm simply drawn that way.

[Laughter]

If you have no inherent sense of right or wrong, being told something is 'bad' means nothing to you. Sociopathic kids need extra help with these kind of concepts, but most parents haven't got a clue where to begin.

Remember that statistic I gave you at the start of this talk? Psychopathy is as common as autism and bipolar disorder, but there are no support groups for the parents of budding sociopaths. Try typing 'I think my child is a psychopath' into a search engine and see how far you get.

You won't find online forums. No message boards filled with helpful advice.

Medical professionals are reluctant to diagnose a child as a psychopath, even if they've just strangled the family cat. They tiptoe around the elephant in the room with labels like *callous* and *unemotional traits*.

Because our 'condition' is considered untreatable. Tell a parent their kid is a sociopath, and it's like giving them a terminal diagnosis.

My own parents did a magnificent job of burying their heads in the sand. They ignored my awkward early attempts to manipulate those around me. They wilfully neglected to notice my lack of friends at nursery school.

I was left to sink or swim on my own. And to begin with, I sank. I lied all the time.

I broke things. I burned things.

I bruised people.

I stole from my classmates. I gave the little girl who sat next to me a wrist burn because she used the red crayon when I wanted it. Sociopathic kids don't 'grow out' of who they are. It's not just a 'phase'. But we live in a society where survival is dependent on fitting in. Better grades, better chances for college, better jobs, a better life: it's all better when you're part of a tribe.

So eventually we learn to swim. We figure out how to conceal our behaviour, and censor what we really think. At least the smart ones among us do. We hide in plain sight, though we never truly make friends. We endure relationships with people who don't really know us. We get jobs at places where we're tolerated, but never understood.

We learn the words, but we never feel the music.

We have no control over how we feel, but we know it bothers you. So we figure out how to blend in.

But full immersion in a foreign language is tough.

And it's *lonely*.

It might surprise you to know this, but sociopaths have an inbuilt longing to be loved and cared for, just like everyone else. It's a desire that often goes unfulfilled, because our natures make it so hard for us to get close to people, and that's where we tend to go off the rails.

The human brain wasn't designed to function without access to emotion – even in people like us. And the constant effort required to act like a 'normal' person and survive in your world is exhausting.

Overload the system, and eventually it short-circuits.

When I was three years old, Mrs Evans, one of the teachers at my nursery, brought in a papier-mâché model of her house that her teen-aged son had made her for Mother's Day. It'd taken him a month to build it in secret, and Mrs Evans couldn't stop smiling with pride as she showed it off to us.

That day was my day to have the class mascot on my table, a privilege that was shared out among the class on a strict rota system.

But then Mrs Evans gave Benjy to one of the other children, a mouth-breather with a permanent nasal drip.

'Sammy's doggie just died,' she told me, pulling a face I'd learned meant *sad*. 'You don't mind if I let him have Benjy today to cheer him up, do you?'

That afternoon, when Mrs Evans was supervising nap-time, I asked to go to the bathroom, which we were allowed to do on our own if we were potty-trained.

And then I went into her office, where she'd left her son's papier-mâché model sitting on her desk, pulled down my pants, and peed all over it.

chapter 07

stacey

The woman seems to know the house better than Stacey herself. She doesn't wait for the estate agent to show her from one room to the next: she's already moving ahead of them, clearly familiar with the property's inverted layout.

'I like the way you've redone the kitchen,' she says. 'Moving the island to run horizontally across the room makes for much better sight lines. And you get to take full advantage of the morning light.'

'That's what *I* thought,' Stacey says.

The other woman runs her palm over the smooth quartz countertop, custom-ordered an extravagant three inches thick. 'I always felt placing the island perpendicular to the western aspect was an odd choice,' the woman muses. 'I can only assume the architect didn't have a hand in the final decision.'

This is why Stacey insisted she be here herself when the estate agent showed prospective buyers around: she needs to be the one to choose exactly the right person for the Glass House. Someone who'll fall in love with the house, just as she did, and will do anything – *anything* – to get it.

'The architect died just before the house was finished,' Stacey says. 'The executors wanted to get it completed as quickly as possible in order to sell it, so they brought in a new building firm who cut corners to save money. When we bought the house we located the architect's original drawings and restored things in keeping with his design – not just in the kitchen, but elsewhere, too.'

'Did you remove that pony wall in the master bathroom? I can't believe the architect ever intended it to be there.'

Stacey laughs. 'We did, yes. You seem to know the house awfully well, Mrs—?'

'Millie Downton,' the woman says, extending her hand. 'And this is my husband, Tom.'

Stacey barely gives the man a second glance. 'Downton?' she repeats. 'Oh, as in—'

'Please don't,' Millie says. 'I nearly reverted to my maiden name when that programme came out.'

Stacey laughs again. She finds herself wanting to know more about Millie Downton: she's smart and funny, and clearly far more interested in the house than she is in Stacey, which makes a refreshing change.

She's a beautiful woman, too. Her bold red lipstick and immaculate blonde finger waves make Stacey think of Hollywood film stars from the Forties, an effect enhanced by a form-fitting grey dress and chic two-tone leather Spectator heels. Stacey has never met a woman who exudes such old-school glamour. Ordinarily, she'd be jealous, but Millie's beauty is oddly unthreatening. Stacey feels like an art student introduced to Van Gogh: there's no room for any emotion but awe.

She's pretty herself, in a girl-next-door kind of way. She looks her age, thirty-eight, but attractively so. Chocolate Duchess-of-Cambridge curls, good skin, athletic. Viewers love her. They can relate to her: her prettiness is aspirational and they tell themselves it's within their reach given the right styling and make-up and money. But Millie Downton's classic beauty is in a different league.

'Have you been here before, Mrs Downton?' Stacey asks. 'When the previous owners lived here?'

'In a way,' the woman says.

She turns from the window. Tiny diamonds catch the sunshine at her ears, and scatter prisms of light across the room.

'Mrs Porter, your asking price is higher than it's worth, objectively speaking, given its size and location, but we want this house, so we're willing to pay it,' Millie says. 'If you sell to us, it'll be a quick, straightforward sale. Or you could hold out for a better offer, and deal with an endless parade of groupies who come to see *you*, rather than the house.'

It's the first indication she's given that she knows who Stacey is.

Stacey likes her relative fame. Presenting a national mid-morning TV show four days a week means she gets reservations in restaurants that are booked up three months in advance, and sponsorship deals with brands like Marks & Spencer who pay her to wear their clothes.

But it also means she hasn't eaten a meal out with friends without being interrupted by someone wanting to take a selfie with her in ten years. In fact, she doesn't really *have* friends: at least, not civilians. The women she meets outside of work – at her HIIT class, on the board of the PTA – pretend her fame is irrelevant, but of course it colours every aspect of the relationship. They're either star-struck fans, or beneath their veneer of amity they're envious and resentful.

Stacey can't post anything on social media without running it past her PR: it doesn't take much to get cancelled these days. Every time she steps out of the house, she has to look camera-ready for the 'candid' pap shots that keep her in the public eye: it takes a lot of effort to make it appear as if she's made no effort at all.

Her celebrity also means her husband, Felix, lives in her shadow, a position even the most enlightened man would struggle to enjoy.

And Felix is not the most enlightened man.

'I'll have to talk to my husband,' Stacey prevaricates. 'We've only just put the house on the market.'

'Mrs Downton does have a number of other properties to look at,' the estate agent adds, keen to preserve the illusion he actually earns his commission.

Millie looks irritated. 'No, I don't,' she says. '*This* is the one I want. I recently discovered,' she tells Stacey, 'that sometimes you get what you want more easily if you just ask for it.'

Stacey has already decided she'll accept Millie's offer in part because the woman is right: she doesn't want hordes of the great unwashed trooping through her bedroom and poking around her bathroom cabinet. She can only imagine the headlines if information about some of its contents was leaked to the tabloids.

And Millie Downton is perfect for the Glass House.

'Your son went to Asher Brook Primary, didn't he?' Millie says as they walk back downstairs. 'My youngest, Peter, was in the same year as your boy. Archie, isn't it?'

'Gosh, you have a good memory. Archie was only at the school a term. We took him out because my husband wanted him to go to Fettes, where he went.'

'Eight's young to board.'

'Yes, I know, I feel awfully guilty, but—'

Millie laughs. 'Oh, I'm not criticising you,' she says. 'I'm *jealous*. I'd love to send my two off to boarding school, but Tom won't hear of it.'

'Don't believe a word of it,' Tom says.

'I'm really sorry, but I don't remember meeting you,' Stacey tells Millie. 'And I'm normally so good with faces—'

'We haven't met properly, though I saw you on that miserable mother-son fiasco at the Natural History Museum,' Millie says. 'I abandoned ship after half-an-hour, but I think you toughed it out.'

'If I'd left early, someone would've picked up the phone to the *Daily Mail*, and I'd have been pilloried as a bad mother.'

Millie smiles and holds out her hand. 'Call me when you've spoken to your husband. If you want to go ahead, I'll let my solicitor know and set things in motion my end.'

Stacey's sleeve rides up as she reaches across the kitchen island to shake Millie's hand. She sees Millie notice the ring of livid circular bruises on her forearm: the unmistakable grasp of violent fingers.

Quickly she twitches the sleeve back into place.

chapter 08

tom

Stacey Porter is very much taken by my wife.

As she should be: I put a lot of thought into making sure they'd hit it off.

I understand women in a way Millie never has. Stacey's a minor celebrity used to being the centre of attention in any gathering. The women she meets outside work will either fawn all over her, or resent her for being famous and wait for the right moment to slide a knife between her ribs.

The simplest way to make a woman like Stacey feel secure is to remove the element of competition. Counterintuitively that doesn't mean fading into the background.

People like beauty. In art, in nature, in architecture. In each other.

Ideas of beauty may change from one era or one culture to another – the curvy Fifties followed by the twiggy Sixties – but there are certain elements that remain the same. Symmetry. Proportion. Scientists have even come up with an actual measure of physical perfection: the golden ratio, which originates from the European Renaissance and is based upon the ancient Greeks' measure of perfect beauty. We find it when we divide a line into two parts so that the long part divided by the short part is also equal to the whole length divided by the long part. You don't need to know this, but the golden ratio is an irrational number that approximates to 1.6.

You don't have to be a mathematician to appreciate its importance, either. You recognise it instinctively a dozen times a day without even being aware of it. While you're looking at someone's face, and returning their smile, your subconscious is busy measuring: the length of the face, divided by the width.

All of which means Millie has a natural born advantage. Not using it would be like turning up with a knife to a gunfight.

My wife has no idea quite how beautiful she is. She makes the most of her genetic lot through exercise and hard work, but there's no vanity involved. When she looks in the mirror, she doesn't see the beguiling woman I see.

She sees her mother.

Millie rarely capitalises on her appearance. She seldom wears make-up and lives in jeans or work scrubs: I can't remember the last time I even saw her in a skirt. But I persuaded her to make an effort for Stacey Porter. And Stacey told herself a woman who looks like my wife doesn't need to feel jealous or resentful of her success. Millie's appearance lifts her out of the ranks of civilian non-celebrities and puts her on Stacey's level, giving her a passport to her world.

I went to all this trouble so she'd see Millie as a worthy successor to the Glass House: so she'd *want* her to live in it.

Because this is the third time the woman has put her house on the market in the last twelve months, only to withdraw it again before Millie had the chance to get her foot in the door. She's clearly reluctant to sell: I could see it in her face as she followed us around her house. Stroking marble countertops. Repositioning perfectly aligned blinds. She's still in love with this house. Who wouldn't be?

We all gravitate towards beautiful things.

Stacey needs to be coaxed, to be *wooed*, into giving up her home. She's only going to let it go if she finds someone she thinks deserves it. Her fingers have to be prised gently from the house keys one by one.

The viewing went better than I could have hoped. Stacey was clearly impressed by my wife: she barely even noticed me. I expect Millie to be bubbling with excitement on the drive back home, but instead she's unnaturally quiet.

'*Well*?' I say finally, as we turn off the Fulham Road. 'How d'you think it went?'

'Did you see the bruises on her arm?' Millie asks abruptly.

I'm taken aback. I'd anticipated elation, Christmas-morning exuberance: a stream of excited ideas and plans and a brisk to-do list. Maybe even a thank-you for helping make it happen. Afternoon sex.

'What bruises?'

'On Stacey's forearm. You *must* have noticed.'

'Not really,' I say, irritated.

Millie twists her left earring, her tell when she's anxious. 'It looked like someone had grabbed her wrists,' she says.

'Maybe someone pulled her out of the way of a bus,' I say flippantly.

'Did you notice how scared she looked when she mentioned having to talk to her husband?'

'She didn't look *scared*, Millie. She looked like selling a house is a decision a couple should make together. Not unreasonably,' I add pointedly.

I turn into our road. A Prius is pulling out of a parking space a few houses down from ours, and I quickly nab the spot. I bought the new Audi as a gift for Millie's fortieth birthday: she said it was a ridiculous extravagance, but to my mind there's no point earning money if you don't spend it. Business has been good recently, and as my mother used to say, there's no pockets in shrouds.

45

'The kids will be home from school soon,' Millie says distract-edly, as I unlock the front door. 'Can you organise dinner? I have to work.'

'Of course. The viewing went well, Millie,' I add, trying to get things back on track. 'We don't want to count our chickens, but I've a feeling we're going to get that house.'

My wife smiles, but it doesn't reach her eyes.

I follow her into the house. I have the oddest sensation I've just made a very bad mistake, and I've absolutely no idea why.

chapter 09

millie

When blood is fresh, still oozing from living tissue, it has the iron tang of a park railing just after it's rained. Clean, slightly salty, metallic.

But the longer it's out of the body, the muskier it becomes, acquiring the odour of everything it comes into contact with: sweat, decay, death. Sometimes I can still smell it beneath my fingernails, even after I've scrubbed my hands raw.

It's astonishing what blood does. There's no substitute for it: it can't be made or manufactured. Red blood cells disperse oxygen and nutrients to your lungs and tissues. White blood cells carry antibodies throughout the body to fight infection. Platelets help the blood clot when you're injured by gathering at the site and sticking to the lining of an injured blood vessel. Plasma transports blood cells throughout the body, along with nutrients, waste, hormones, and proteins that help maintain the body's fluid balance.

An adult female has approximately nine pints of blood in her body. If she loses more than three of them, she'll go into haemorrhagic shock, and die.

My fingers tingle as I spread my left hand against the pale expanse of exposed skin, widening the space between my thumb and forefinger to keep the flesh taut.

There's a purity to this moment, in the seconds before I cut. I savour the weight of the knife in my hand.

And then I slice. Without hesitation: through the epidermis, the top layer of her skin, through the thicker dermis, and on through the yellow wedge of subcutaneous fat she's spent years trying to diet away.

Her blood flows over my fingers, bright red, oxygenated, obscuring my field of vision. It doesn't matter: I could close my eyes, and still know where to cut. I have an almost supernatural intuition, as if my fingers can see, as if those red blood cells and platelets and plasma are communicating directly with my own blood, conveying messages along a sanguinary highway.

I only stop when I see white bone.

The heart is protected by the sternum, the organ's skeletal armour and the central bone to which ribs are attached. Cracking it with a saw requires pressure, power, and precision. Death is measured in millimetres.

But I'm good at what I do.

Once the sternum is bisected, I use a retractor to spread the two broken halves.

And then there it is before me.

Her beating heart.

The cavity is quickly filling with blood. She'll be dead in minutes, but I'm not going to wait that long. I'm going to stop her heart now. I inject a solution containing potassium ion directly into the aortic root. As her heart quiets, mine beats faster.

I haven't slept in twenty hours, but my mind is alpine clear as adrenaline courses through my system. I get the same rush when I ski a black mogul field in a blinding snowstorm, operating on pure instinct. One miscalculation, and the day is lost.

But I don't miscalculate.

The perfusionist gives me a brief nod across the table.

'We're good,' she says.

It's her job to run the cardiopulmonary bypass pump while I operate. My patient has an aortic aneurysm: a bulge in the main blood vessel that carries blood from the heart to the rest of the body. Arteries usually have strong, thick walls. But sometimes the force of blood constantly pushing against an area with weakness can make them swell. The result is a balloon-like bulge: an aneurysm. When it bursts, it causes huge internal bleeding and is usually fatal.

The woman on the table is unlucky: she's young and a non-smoker, and nearly two-thirds of aneurysms happen to men. But she's six months pregnant, which is probably what caused it to rupture. Until it happened, she wouldn't have known it was even there.

The woman on the table is lucky: she has me.

I work quickly and efficiently to save her life. My surgical team know me well, and anticipate my needs effectively and without drama. Once the heart has been repaired, I put the sternum back together, using plates and screws to hold the breastbone and ribs in place as they heal.

Finally I close the incision with three layers: no suture material is visible on or above the skin. I use vicryl sutures for the first two layers and monocryl sutures for below the outside layer of the skin. Both are absorbed by the body within two or three months. My aim is to minimise the trauma to the chest to allow my patient to recuperate faster. I have the lowest mortality rate of any doctor in the hospital, and one of the lowest of any heart surgeon in the country. I intend to keep it that way.

My surgical registrar catches me as I change my scrubs.

'Ms Lennox, do you have a moment to talk to the husband?' she says. 'He's very anxious.'

49

Someone will have kept my patient's family apprised of her progress, but relatives always want to speak to the surgeon. We're the closest they get to talking to God.

I follow the registrar to the family waiting room. The husband is at least a decade older than his wife, and a good three stone overweight. Nicotine stains his fingers. He should have been the one on my operating table.

He grabs at my arm. 'Dr Lennox, please, how is she?'

'It's *Ms* Lennox,' my registrar corrects.

In the UK, surgeons are never called *doctor*, a convention that harks back to the days when surgeons were butchers without medical degrees and were not considered worthy of the prefix. Americans get very confused.

'The surgery was very successful,' I say, gently extricating myself from his grasp. 'We were able to—'

'Is she all right? What about the baby?'

'Your wife and baby are both doing well,' I say.

'She couldn't be in better hands, Mr Sharp,' the registrar adds.

He's right. There's a reason I became the country's youngest Professor of Cardiac Surgery three years ago at just thirty-seven, leapfrogging surgeons with decades more experience. Since I joined the Princess Eugenie Hospital as a consultant I've performed more than two hundred Norwood operations and nearly three hundred arterial switch procedures. My outcomes are among the best in the world.

No one would describe me as a touchy-feely person: I'm aware my bedside manner leaves something to be desired. But if someone you love needs a miracle, I'm the one you want carving up their chest.

I try hard not to see my patients as people: it gets in the way of my clinical judgement. And I avoid their relatives at all costs for the same reason. But there's something so desperate in this man's expression, I can't just walk away.

'Mr Sharp, I'm not going to let your wife die,' I say gently. 'What happened to her was a freak accident, like a burst pipe. And I've just fixed it. She's not sick or fragile. She's a very healthy woman. They're both going to be absolutely fine.'

He starts to sob.

I absolutely don't do tears. I leave before he throws himself bodily at my feet in gratitude: it wouldn't be the first time.

I'm walking down the ramp into the underground car park when my phone bleeps with an incoming text.

We got the Glass House.

chapter 10

millie

I toss my phone onto the passenger seat within easy reach and put on my sunglasses. Sunlight streams through the panoramic sunroof as I emerge from the car park. In its way, this vehicle is a work of art just as much as the Glass House. Every aspect of the cockpit is a masterclass in efficient simplicity.

An extravagance, yes: but I'm a connoisseur of beautiful things.

The traffic on the Brompton Road is heavy, but moving quickly. On impulse, I stop at the Flower Yard to pick up a bouquet of summer blooms: I'm in the mood to celebrate. Not only did we get the house, but Stacey Porter has just agreed to come to the upcoming hospital gala to raise funds for a new hybrid OR in the Emergency Department.

Even better: she thinks it was *her* idea.

It wasn't difficult: it just took an off-the-cuff remark about sick babies and a comment on the power of celebrity when Stacey called me personally to ask me to forward my solicitor's details.

I tap my fingers on the steering wheel in time to Glenn Miller. The fundraiser will be the perfect occasion to get to know her better: a professional event, but one that's emotional, too. It's hard to keep your guard up when you're talking about desperately sick children. And I need Stacey to trust me if I'm to be able to help her.

Those livid bruises on her forearms: I can guess whose violent hands put them there, but she has to *tell* me—

I jump as something slaps against my windscreen.

An empty Styrofoam cup bounces from my car into the road. Someone in the car ahead of me tosses a balled-up fast-food bag from the window. Another plastic cup follows.

As we slow for a red traffic light, I pull into the inside lane and draw level with the vehicle, a gas-guzzling Chelsea tractor. The littering is so blatant I expect to see a harassed mother or French nanny wrestling with a bratty child.

But the environmental vandal is a lone middle-aged woman: glossy, expensively dressed, white. She glances briefly across the car at me, and then shamelessly lobs an empty Perrier bottle out of her window.

A *glass* Perrier bottle.

It misses a young cyclist by inches, shattering on the road next to him. The boy swerves, too shocked to do more than shout in alarm as he passes the woman's car. Her response is to give him the middle finger.

Usually I keep my darker angel on a very short tether. We have an accommodation: she holds herself in check and agrees not to set my world on fire, and occasionally, just occasionally, I allow her to have her head.

I never *lose* my temper. But sometimes I choose to unleash it.

As soon as the traffic lights change, I drop back into the lane behind the Mercedes 4x4. The woman drives with all the consideration I'd expect: cutting in front of other cars, failing to signal, swerving between lanes – I see her texting – and driving straight through a pedestrian crossing without stopping. I lose her briefly near Fulham Broadway when she jumps a red light, but she stops at a patisserie and I soon pick her up again.

The woman finally turns off the Fulham Palace Road into the warren of alphabetically named streets that run down to the river. She stops next to a parking space outside a red-bricked terraced house with an immaculate black-and-white tiled path to the front door, and a glorious riot of phlox and lavender and overblown roses lining the low wall separating it from the street. The parking spot is too small for her outsized SUV, but she elbows her way into it anyway, and parks with her offside back wheel almost fully on the pavement. Anyone with a pushchair will have to go into the road to get past it.

I wait till the woman's gone inside, and then double-park twenty feet away beside an empty motorcycle bay, and walk down the street to her car.

I don't have a plan. I don't need one: the devil looks after his own.

The woman's left her sunroof open.

In the front garden of a nearby property three wheelie bins are neatly lined up behind the wall: rubbish, recycling and compost. They're all full; they must be due for collection in the next day or two.

I take a full bag from the rubbish bin, return to the woman's car and shake the entire contents through the sunroof.

Stinking cat litter. Oozing plastic meat packaging, half-consumed ready meals and – oh, joy – *used tampons*. I go back to the compost bin and add a scoop of coffee grounds and eggshells and rotting tomatoes to the mess.

When people think of angels, they usually picture cute cherubs with wings floating on clouds. Beneficent guardians taking the wheel to make them swerve just as a tree was about to fall and crush them. Kindly messengers leaving white feathers around the house to let them know their loved ones are watching over them.

But that's not all they do.

Angels are capable of pitiless destruction, and can destroy a city with a mere gesture of the hand. Just ask the citizens of Sodom and Gomorrah, whose cities were reduced to nothing but charred ash by two angels raining down sulphur and fire. Every firstborn Egyptian male was killed by the Angel of Death when the Pharaoh refused to let the Israelite slaves go. Whenever God needs to do something really awful, She sends an angel.

The litterbug got off more lightly than she'll ever know.

kyle and harper get ready to party!

Hi, Kyper Nation! Welcome back! I hope you're all enjoying this amazing weather! I've been in the garden working on my tan, I think it's coming along OK? I missed a bit when I put on my sunscreen, look, you can totally see on my shoulder where I couldn't reach, it's so annoying!

So, anyway, my loves, you have to help me, because I've changed my mind a million times about what I should wear for the party tonight. I love getting glammed-up, don't you? But it's so *stressful*. It's so much easier for men, isn't it? They just wear the same old boring black tie and they all look like James Bond.

Anyway, since I can't decide, I thought I'd let all of *you* choose for me!

I've narrowed it down to these two. There's this red dress, it's by Ver – oh, God, I'm going to say this wrong, aren't I? I've never been any good at French – Versatch. Is that right, Kyle?

Versatchee. I knew you'd know, babes.

So I got it online from this fab new designer outlet store, Poshnet. They're one of our new sponsors and I can't believe how lucky we are to be working with them, because they're just amazing! For those of you who don't know, Poshnet is a discount site selling genuine designer labels at, like, a *tenth* of retail. Some of their clothes are samples from shows so if you're super-skinny you'll get your pick of the current season, but for the rest of us normal girls who actually have boobs and a bum – *you*

56

know what I'm saying, ladies! – they're basically from last season or pre-owned but you totally wouldn't know.

Anyway, you have to check them out, Poshnet.com, they're just awesome. I'll pop a link in the description bar below.

So there's the red dress. And then this one, I know black's a cliché, but it's totally classic and sort of Audrey Hepburn and I think it makes me look sophisticated, what d'you think, guys?

Let me know which one you prefer, my lovelies. There should be a button for you below so you can vote, or tell me what you think in the comments section below.

By the way, what do you think of this hairstyle for tonight? Oops, let me turn the camera so you can see the magazine better. I thought I'd try out something new for the party, kind of like a messy up-do. You know, formal, but in, like, a *young* way.

OK, now Kyle's out of the room, I can tell you a bit more about this party tonight. Actually, between you and me, it's not really a party, it's a charity gala, you know, one of those posh dinners where people auction a week on their yacht or a private recording session or whatever to raise money. Kyle will kill me when he finds out, he hates this kind of thing, but I kind of feel we're so blessed, we need to give back more, you know? I often ask myself, what would Meghan or Amal do?

And the other reason we're going is because the woman we're buying the house from, she's going to be there.

I know what you're thinking, peeps, and hear me out, I'm not some kind of crazy stalker! But it's really, *really* hard to get into a good school where we're moving. And with these things, it's always about who you know, isn't it?

I don't want to sound shallow, but people judge you by your friends, don't they?

And you don't have to *like* someone to be friends with them.

I'll be honest, I thought this woman was a bit of a bitch when

I met her. But then our estate agent told me she's a surgeon, which makes sense. They're always a bit spectrum-y, aren't they? If we're allowed to say that. No offence to all the spectrum people. But you know what I mean.

Oh, God, I know it sounds *totally* stalker-y, but we really need to make the right sort of friends if we're going to fit in properly, so *please* don't judge me!

Anyway, it's just a party! What's the worst that can happen?

chapter 11

millie

Peter sits cross-legged on the floor, watching me put on my make-up. He isn't annoying me exactly, but the boy's ten. He should be playing Fortnite on his phone, not hanging around watching his mother apply her lipstick.

His sister appears in the doorway. 'Mummy's boy,' she says. 'You're so freaking lame. What are you, *gay*?'

'I'm not gay!'

'Don't be a bitch,' I tell my daughter.

My son is already running from the room. In the wild, certain shark embryos cannibalise their littermates in the womb, with the largest embryo eating its siblings. It's Darwinian out there.

'Dad told me to tell you Hatley's here,' Meddie says.

'*Mrs* Hatley,' I correct.

'Why do we need a babysitter, anyway? I'm thirteen. I don't need someone to look after me.'

'Peter does.'

We both know why.

Meddie lounges against the doorjamb, watching me with Tom's eyes. 'You look very beautiful,' she says.

I spritz Chanel No. 5 on the inside of my wrists. 'Thank you,

Meddie. Please don't give Mrs Hatley any trouble,' I add, standing up and putting my phone in my jewelled clutch.

Stacey Porter must be watching out for us: Tom and I have barely checked our coats before she finds us.

'I love your dress!' she exclaims, holding me at arm's length as she surveys me from head to toe. 'Is it vintage? And your hair! Very Veronica Lake.'

Tom's idea: he knows how much I hate getting dressed up for these things. *Let's go vintage*, he suggested, when he presented me with this dress, a gift to celebrate our house going under contract. *It's glam, but not obvious, and you won't have to show too much skin.*

'Have you found your table?' I ask Stacey, keen to change the subject.

'We're right at the front of the ballroom,' she says. 'You must have twisted a few arms to arrange that at such short notice.'

I smile. 'I don't know what you mean.'

'I think you do. Don't worry, I'll make sure my husband spends far more than he should in the auction.'

Tom is good at tracking people online, even those who're careful to minimise their digital footprint, but he didn't manage to dig up much about Mr Stacey Porter. The man doesn't have any social media presence at all, and apart from a few unavoidable listings – birth and marriage records, land registry details – Tom found next to nothing.

'You remember my husband, Tom,' I say, as he comes up behind me.

'Of course. Good to see you again,' she says. She glances around the hotel lobby, which is rapidly filling with barely-there dresses and too-tight dinner jackets. 'Felix is somewhere around. I'll introduce you in a minute.'

'Mrs Downton!'

A woman in a scarlet dress with an elaborate up-do is bearing down on us in improbable heels, an impressively muscular man trailing in her wake. It takes me a moment to place them.

'Mrs Conway,' I say, as Stacey takes advantage of the distraction to slip away.

'Call me Harper, please. Is this your lovely hubby?'

'Tom Downton,' he says, extending his hand.

'We're *so* excited to be buying your house,' Harper gushes. 'We're doing a special Countdown to Move-In Day on our vlog. We've got a competition to choose the new paint colour in the lounge – not that there's anything wrong with the one you've got,' she adds quickly. 'But our Kyper Nation fans like to feel *involved*, you know?'

'Absolutely,' Tom says.

'And when you're on TV, you need some colour on set to *pop*. Brighten things up a bit. Though our fans love your office, Mrs Downton,' she adds. 'It's got loads of likes, almost as many as the terrace, hasn't it, Kyle?'

Tom takes a couple of glasses of Prosecco from a passing waiter and hands one to the woman. Given her flushed cheeks and overbright eyes, I suspect it's not her first. 'What's your connection to the hospital, Harper?' he asks.

'The hospital?'

'Well, since you're here to support its fundraising efforts I assumed you must have a connection,' Tom says. 'Nothing unhappy, I hope?'

Oh, my husband can be wicked sometimes.

Harper looks uncomfortable. 'Just supporting the community,' she says. 'I mean, since we're going to be part of it and everything.'

'I do hope you'll bid for something in the auction,' I say sweetly. 'We've been so lucky with our donors. Last year,

61

someone paid ten thousand pounds for a reserved parking space outside Asher Brook Primary.'

'I'm surprised it didn't go for more,' Tom says. 'A parking spot near that school is rarer than hen's teeth.'

'Oh, your son goes to Asher Brook?' Harper says, with a creditable attempt at surprise. 'We're hoping to get *our* boys in there.'

'Then you must let me introduce you to Mark Bristow,' Tom says kindly. 'He's in charge of admissions there. Good friend of mine.'

I can almost hear Harper's knicker elastic snap.

Her husband, Kyle, hasn't yet said a word. He looks as awkward in his black tie as Tom looks at ease in his.

A colleague of mine intercepts us as we merge into the throng heading towards the ballroom. An informal consult on a complex case: I lose track of Tom and the Conways, and don't pick them up again until we are all about to sit down.

Stacey's table is next to ours, of course. Our gilt chairs are back to back, and as I sit down, she taps me on the shoulder.

'That's Felix,' she says, indicating the man two seats away from her.

Not what I expected. Much older, for a start: at least twenty years older than Stacey. Better looking than the few photographs Tom managed to find online: sharper jaw, sharper eyes. Clean-shaven, thick brown hair. His expression is flinty.

He nods curtly at me when he sees his wife pointing, and carries on talking to his neighbour, a middle-aged woman I vaguely recognise from a gardening show that was cancelled a few years ago. She looks as if she's been kidnapped by a murderer and dressed in his mother's clothes.

Harper waves enthusiastically from her table on the far side of ours. Clearly her presence at the gala is not a coincidence. She's done her research: she's found out where I work, the causes I support, the school my son attends. I assume it's for much the same reasons I've gone to so much effort to make a friend of Stacey: until we exchange contracts, none of us have a done deal.

At least I hope that's the reason.

SETtalks | psychologies series

Inside the mind of a psychopath | *Original Air Date 9 July*

The transcript below has been lightly edited for length and clarity.

Who remembers the name Susan Atkins?

Well, I don't blame you for not recognising it: it's a common enough name. What about Patricia Krenwinkel?

Ah. We're getting closer now. Show of hands . . . a few of you. Charles Manson?

Oh, you've all heard of him.

Of course you have. We all know who *he* is. Charles Manson is the man who broke into Hollywood director Roman Polanski's house with his so-called 'Family' and stabbed five people to death, including Polanski's wife, Sharon Tate, who was nearly nine months pregnant with their baby.

Except he didn't.

Charles Manson wasn't even *there* that night.

Susan Atkins, Patricia Krenwinkel and a former airline baggage handler called Tex Watson were the ones who actually invaded the Polanski house on Cielo Drive on August 9, 1969.

According to Manson's biographer, Jeff Guinn, even as a child Manson liked to recruit gullible classmates, mostly girls, to attack other students he didn't like.

Afterwards, he'd swear to teachers his followers were just doing what they wanted – he couldn't be held responsible for their actions. And because no one thought a six-year-old was capable of such Machiavellian manipulation, he got away with it.

Manson was clearly a psychopath, of course.

He showed all the classic signs: a devious, manipulative personality from a very young age, total lack of empathy or remorse, callous arrogance and indifference to the suffering of others, thrill-seeking recklessness, superficial charm.

Just like me, in fact.

But what about his disciples?

Susan Atkins and Patricia Krenwinkel were just twenty-one when they cold-bloodedly stabbed a heavily pregnant woman to death as she pleaded with them to let her live long enough to give birth to her baby. Were *they* psychopaths, too? If these young women had never met Manson, would they have still have become killers?

Or would they have drifted along in obscurity: settled down, married, raised children, become apple-cheeked grandmas?

It's an interesting question, isn't it?

Unlike Manson, neither of them had shown any sociopathic tendencies before the killings. In fact, Krenwinkel had considered becoming a nun before deciding instead to attend a Jesuit college, only to drop out after one term.

Admittedly, they both came from unhappy homes, which made them vulnerable. But until they met Charles Manson, they were just sad, lonely young girls. It's enough to send a chill down your spine, isn't it?

What if Manson hadn't played guitar at the house where Atkins was living with friends?

What if Krenwinkel hadn't bumped into him at the beach and been told, for the first time in her life, that she was beautiful?

Charles Manson was a natural born killer: his life was going to erupt in violence sooner or later. But if they hadn't met him, those young women might have gone all their lives without harming anyone.

I'm not making excuses for them, of course.

They *chose* to follow Manson, to join his doomsday cult, to kill without pity, without remorse, and take pleasure in it.

But to coin a phrase, some people are born psychopaths, and some have psychopathy thrust upon them.

The first time everyone in our property chain met was at the charity gala for the Princess Eugenie Hospital.

Everyone knows about that night now, of course. The newspapers did it to death after everything came out. There was even a reconstruction-for-TV of the whole evening, including the auction, although they made it a lot more dramatic than it seemed at the time. None of us knew it then, of course, but a terrible chain of events was set in motion that night.

Our meeting was no less fateful than the day a teenager called Susan Atkins sat down to listen to a young man with hypnotic eyes play his guitar.

And it would end the same way.

In murder.

chapter 12

millie

Tom is sitting on the opposite side of our table from me, back to back with Harper, with whom he's been conducting an animated conversation all through dinner. I watch them, wondering what they can be talking about.

I worry about Tom sometimes. He has a weakness for dangerous women. And something tells me that despite outward appearances, Harper Conway could be very dangerous indeed.

As the wait staff clear away our plates after the main course – overcooked salmon, but the hollandaise sauce was decent enough – one of the men at Stacey's table, a middle-aged sports presenter running to fat, starts to complain loudly about the quality of the wine to a poor waitress young enough to still have braces on her teeth.

'He wouldn't know a good claret if he had a transfusion with it,' Stacey murmurs in my ear as she gets up from the table. 'Excuse me, I'll be back in a minute.'

The hospital's chief executive, a whip-smart Wharton grad called Michèle Harrington, approaches a podium set up on the small dais usually used by the band. While the dinner has been underway, a silent auction has taken place: guests have had the opportunity to sign up to bid on a number of items laid out on linen-covered trestles at the back of the ballroom, including a pink sapphire Dinny Hall ring and a week in Nevis I found rather tempting.

Michèle begins to announce the winners in advance of the live auction just as Stacey slides back into her seat. The bids far outstrip the worth of the items; this is a charity fundraiser, after all. And nothing opens wallets like having your name and ability to pay written on a bid sheet visible to your peers.

The aggressive walrus at Stacey's table visibly jumps in shock when his name is announced as the winner of a case of vintage 2009 Margaux.

'Incredibly generous bid,' Michèle says, beaming at him as she leads a round of applause. 'Ten thousand pounds, ladies and gentlemen!'

He pales beneath his fake tan.

'I didn't – I don't remember bidding on that,' he sputters to the table at large.

'It's for such a good cause,' Stacey says, winking at me.

At the next table, Tom roars with laughter at something Harper has said.

'By the way, Millie,' Stacey says, 'I have a few pieces of furniture we can't take with us to our new apartment, and I wondered if you'd be interested in having me leave them behind? That teal Julian Chichester cabinet in the sitting room, and the Agostino mirror. They're simply too big.'

'Are you sure? They're so beautiful,' I say.

'You'd be doing me a favour taking them off my hands. In fact,' she adds, 'why don't you come and take another look at them and then decide? Maybe Saturday morning? Felix makes a mean mimosa.'

'I could do Sunday,' I say. 'I have surgical rehearsal this Saturday.'

'Sunday works.'

Felix leans behind the man seated between him and his wife. 'Stop it, Stacey,' he says.

His tone is cold. I don't know if he objects to the brunch invitation in general, or me in particular.

Michèle launches the live auction, perfectly timed for this point in the evening when the guests are nicely lubricated. The bidding is lively and even raucous at times as donors compete to flex their philanthropic muscles.

I act as a stalking horse on a number of big-ticket items, drawing out the high rollers and gracefully conceding defeat when I'm outbid. I've already made a private donation: when Tom gave me my Audi, I made a matching gift to the hybrid OR, though I didn't tell him that. We can't quite afford it, but I wouldn't have been able to drive the car with a good conscience otherwise.

At the adjacent table, Harper squeals when she wins a photo-shoot with society photographer Hugo Burnand. 'Kyle, he took the wedding pictures of Prince William and Kate Middleton!' she cries. 'And now he'll be taking pictures of *us*!'

A couple of well-known television personalities approach Michèle at the podium to make pre-arranged 'spontaneous' offers to share their talents or open their homes, the sequence carefully choreographed to make other guests feel like they're in at something rather special and unexpected.

One excitable woman bids five figures to be a guest weather-girl on morning television. Another buys her daughter's name for a character in a bestselling thriller writer's new novel. A champion show jumper stands up at the back of the ballroom, and offers riding lessons on the horse she rode in the Olympics.

'I'll pay double if you take the place of the horse!' a man calls.

Laughter.

Harper leaps to her feet, swaying slightly. It's clear from

the feverish light in her eyes that she's very drunk. 'Who'll bid a thousand pounds for private training sessions with Kyle?' she cries.

There's a slightly sticky lull.

'You can be on our vlog, too!' Harper adds.

Most of her audience is too old to know what a vlog is. People cough, and shuffle their feet. A few chairs scrape as they're pushed back. I don't want the auction to end on this note.

'Shit,' I mutter, and raise my hand.

Michèle points my way. 'A thousand pounds from Mrs Downton! Wonderful! Do I hear fifteen hundred?'

'In for a penny,' Stacey murmurs, lifting her arm.

'Fifteen hundred!' Michèle says delightedly.

I glance across at Stacey's husband. A muscle works at his jaw, and his body is rigid in his seat.

'Two thousand,' I call.

Tom throws me a look: amused, rather than irritated.

Now that we've set the ball rolling, other guests join in. Kyle's training session eventually goes for just under five thousand pounds: the winner is a very pretty male soap star with glass cheekbones and boy-band hair.

As the auction comes to an end, Stacey is sucked into industry shoptalk with the rest of her table and I leave to go to the bathroom. On my way back to the ballroom, I notice the same obnoxious sports presenter who accosted the young waitress earlier jammed in a corner with the coat-check girl. His hand is on her bottom, and he's whispering something in her ear. Her back is arched like a Russian gymnast in her attempt to avoid him.

'Is there a problem here?' I ask loudly.

The sports presenter releases her, and she leaps back as if scalded. 'Did you not get the MeToo memo?' I demand, in a tone that makes sure everyone within five metres of us can hear. 'I'm sure your *wife* would be happy to fill you in.'

Several phones are being raised in our direction. The slime-ball flushes puce, and can't slither away quickly enough.

'Next time, kick him in the balls,' I tell the girl. 'You don't have to take that shit from anyone, however famous they are.'

Felix Porter is waiting near the auction tables when I finally return to the ballroom. As I approach, he steps into my path, blocking the way.

'Stay away from Stacey,' he says.

The moment is oddly intimate. Just inches separate us: I can feel the heat radiating from him.

'Are you policing your wife's friends?' I ask lightly.

He grabs my forearm. 'I'm warning you,' he says. 'Stay away from her. I'm not going to tell you again. You don't know who you're dealing with.'

I snap my arm free.

Neither does he.

chapter 13

stacey

Stacey stares out of the window of the black cab. While they've been at the charity fundraiser, a sudden thunderstorm has broken the summer heat. The London streets are slick and the cab's tyres whoosh through the glistening puddles.

Her heartbeat quickens as the taxi turns into their road. She knows what'll happen when they get home.

She still has the bruises from last time.

'Nothing like a good storm to clear the air,' the cabbie says over his shoulder. 'And we need the rain, the summer we been having—'

Felix leans forward, and slams the partition shut.

When the cab pulls up outside the Glass House, her husband gets out and stalks into the house, leaving her to pay.

'Everything all right?' the cabbie asks her.

'Of course,' she says. 'He's just tired. Long day.'

The driver makes a tepid attempt to proffer her change, and gives an old-fashioned doff to his forehead when she indicates for him to keep it. 'Thanks very much, miss.' He pauses. 'I hope you don't mind me saying, but I love your show. Me and the wife, we watch you every day.'

'Thank you—'

'That Brendan. He seems like a decent bloke?'

72

Stacey's co-host on *Morning Express* is a misogynistic, homophobic, smug bigot. She's supposed to be the lead anchor, but the show's – male – executive producer lets Brendan get away with murder.

'Lovely man,' she says. 'A real sweetie. One of the good guys, you know?'

'That's nice to hear,' the cabbie says, satisfied. 'You never want to find out Tom Hanks is a wife-beater, do you? Take care, love. Mind how you go.'

Stacey's stomach fizzes as she walks into the darkened house. Felix hasn't left any lights on for her, and she gropes around in the dark for the switch.

A shape looms out of the darkness. Felix shoves her against the wall, his forearm pressed against her throat, choking her. She gasps and scratches at his arm, trying to loosen his grip. His breath is hot and wine-sweet against the side of her neck.

She can't breathe.

The room starts to spin. Black spots dance before her eyes, and she's about to pass out when he suddenly releases her.

Stacey sags forward, her hands on her knees, and inhales deep, ragged pulls of air.

Felix stands there, watching her, his arms hanging loosely by his sides. He's breathing heavily, as if he's just run a race. She waits to see what he'll do next.

Sometimes he walks away.

Sometimes he sobs, and begs her to forgive him.

Sometimes he hurts her more.

Tonight, he lunges at her and grabs her wrist, yanking her towards the bedroom. She kicks off her heels as she stumbles behind him so she can keep up without falling.

Felix flings her onto the bed and she scrambles across the mattress, trying to get out of his reach, but he's too quick for her. He seizes her leg, and hauls her towards him on her

73

stomach, jamming his knee against the small of her back and forcing her face into the bedcovers.

For a brief moment, he relaxes his grip, and she gasps a lungful of air.

'It doesn't have to be like this,' he says. 'You can make all this stop, Stacey.'

She turns her head aside, refusing to look at him.

He shoves his leg between her thighs, forcing them apart. Her expensive dress rides up and bunches around her waist. He holds her arms above her head against the mattress and puts his mouth against her ear.

'Tell me this is what you want,' he whispers.

'I want it,' she pants.

He hits her. Not her face: he knows better than that. He punches her stomach, where the marks can't be seen. He's always careful to make sure her bruises can be hidden with a long-sleeved blouse or a high-necked sweater. He's never broken a bone or left her needing stitches. She's never had a black eye she's had to explain away, laughing as she insists that yes, she really *did* walk into a door.

Felix is a good man. He's never cheated on her. He doesn't smoke, or drink to excess, or burn through her money. He doesn't belittle her in public, or embarrass her. He'd do anything to make her happy: he's proved that a thousand times. He's been a wonderful father to Archie. All her friends envy her. They have a beautiful home, a glamorous lifestyle, a wonderful life.

She's lucky to have him.

They're lucky to have each other.

Every relationship has its ups and downs. This aspect of their marriage, this shameful, violent, unhappy side, is a small price to pay for an otherwise perfect partnership.

Their counsellor – they don't go any more, it just seemed to make things worse – their counsellor said their relationship is *codependent*. What that means, he told them, is that one partner, the codependent one, feels worthless unless they're needed by – and making extreme sacrifices for – the other partner, the enabler, who's only too glad to receive their sacrifices. *It takes two to tango*, he said.

Stacey doesn't understand why that's a problem. Surely if two people have a relationship that makes them both happy, that's a *good* thing?

Except she's not happy: not any more.

Ever since Archie went off to boarding school, things between them have escalated. Their son's absence has allowed them to fight without boundaries. They don't have to wait till he's asleep and keep their voices down as they tear into each other behind closed doors. It's almost as if they've come to relish the chance to plumb the depths of their sickness together.

Her head slams violently against the headboard.

It's not rape if she's complicit.

Afterwards, Felix cries. He cradles her against him and murmurs how sorry he is and covers her bruises with tender kisses. *This has to stop*, he says, *we have to stop this, I can't keep doing this to you. We need help.*

Even she can see they can't go on like this.

Something has to give.

chapter 14

tom

Harper Conway reminds me of my wife. At first glance, they've got nothing in common: Millie with her classic, pale, unvarnished beauty, and then Harper, all thick make-up and Scouse brows and fake orange tan, and that poker-straight Kardashian black hair almost to her bottom. One a brilliant doctor, the other a vlogger who makes a living out of videoing herself . . . *living*.

But scratch the surface, and things change. Harper's not the airhead she appears: underneath that dim-bulb media persona she's smart and clued-in. Maybe not as ferociously clever as Millie is – we can't all be world-class heart surgeons. But she's streetwise and savvy: she knows how many beans make five. You don't get one-point-nine million Instagram followers and sponsorship deals worth tens of thousands by actually *being* an airhead, even if that's the part you're playing. It's just a pity she has to dumb herself down to be successful. I get it: it's all about image these days. Anyone tuning in to a reality show knows *reality* is the last thing they're going to get. And you're never going to go broke underestimating the intelligence of your audience. Still. It's a shame. In another life she could've given Emily Maitlis a run for her money.

She's funny, too. Doesn't take herself too seriously. What

she's doing with that dimwit of a husband is beyond me. I don't think he said ten words to anyone all night at the gala last week. But Harper's got a spark to her – a whiff of mischief.

OK, I admit it: I wouldn't kick her out of bed.

Don't get me wrong – I'd *never* cheat on Millie. She's the love of my life. And I have a keen urge to hang onto my balls. But just because you're on a diet it doesn't mean you can't look at the menu.

I enjoyed myself at that gala a lot more than I expected. Harper was bloody entertaining company, actually, even if she was a bit wasted by the end. To be honest, I feel a bit guilty about that: I was the one topping up her glass most of the night, so it's my fault. She'd clearly pre-gamed before she got to the event out of nerves. And I shouldn't have teased her about her connection to the hospital just to amuse Millie. Obviously the girl was there for a bit of social climbing, but so what? Isn't that what we all do? Calling it *networking* doesn't make the rest of us a cut above.

Oddly, I get the feeling Harper's in on the joke. Like she knows exactly what everyone thinks of her and doesn't give a damn as long as she's getting what she wants.

As I said: she reminds me of my wife.

'Of course it's OK,' I tell her, getting a packet of Hobnobs out of the cupboard where I keep my secret stash – Millie's not big on *empty calories* – and putting some on a plate. 'I told you: drop by any time. Tea? Or would you prefer coffee?'

'Coffee, please.'

'Still sobering up?'

Harper laughs ruefully. 'I'm not gonna lie, it took a couple of days.'

'Wait till you hit forty.'

'You were really kind to me the other night,' she says, suddenly serious. 'I'm sorry if I embarrassed you.'

'Not at all. You didn't. I had a great time. And at least you didn't puke on my shoes.'

She produces a glossy bag with string handles and pale blue tissue paper peeping out of the top. 'I just got you a little something to say thank you for looking after me,' she says, pushing it across the counter. 'It's not much—'

'You didn't need to do that!'

'I wanted to.'

I move the plate of Hobnobs aside and take out the wad of tissue paper. Nestled in the bag is what is clearly a very expensive linen shirt.

'I saw this, and I thought, it's the exact same shade of blue as Tom's eyes,' Harper smiles. 'I had to get it.'

Millie doesn't do personal gifts, not like this. She never forgets a birthday – she's far too efficient – and she knows what I like, but her presents are practical, something she knows I want or need. An all-singing, all-dancing power tool. Tennis lessons. Tickets to see ZZ Top. But romance isn't her thing. We've never celebrated our anniversary or Valentine's Day, though she lets the kids make a fuss of her on Mother's Day. But that's more for them than her.

Not that Harper's gesture is romantic, of course.

'That's incredibly kind,' I say, touched. 'But I can't accept this.'

'Well, it's too late to take it back,' she says.

'I'm sure your husband—'

'I want *you* to wear it.'

'OK. I don't know what Millie's going to say,' I laugh, putting it back in the bag. I'm only half-joking. 'But thank you. It's lovely.'

I know what's going on here. I'm not an idiot, and I don't think I'm flattering myself by picking up on a little subtext. If I wanted to try my luck, I don't think I'd be slapped down.

Except she's nearly fifteen years younger than me, and I'm

hardly a sex symbol: more Gérard Depardieu than Timothée Chalamet. Even if I didn't love my wife, I'm not *that* much of an old fool. Whatever daddy issues Harper has going on, a fling with me isn't going to solve her problems.

'You were really nice to me at the gala,' she says earnestly. 'You didn't have to be. Everyone else looked down their noses, but you treated me like I was just as good as them. No, they did,' she adds, as I start to protest. 'It's OK, it doesn't bother me. I'm not doing this for me. I'm doing it for my boys. I want them to have a better start than I did, you know?'

'I do know,' I say.

'Kyle thinks we shouldn't *get above ourselves*,' Harper says, pulling a face as she draws quotes in the air around the words. 'He thinks if something was good enough for us, it should be good enough for our kids.'

'You don't?'

'I've been hustling my whole life and what I do, it's not a great career but it's not nothing,' she says. 'I want more for the boys. Good schools. *Connections*. Maybe they won't turn out to be very clever, but if they are, I want them to feel like they can be anything they choose. Lawyers and doctors and that.'

'Is that what you wanted? To be a doctor?'

She picks up her mug of coffee, and wraps both her hands around it. 'I grew up in a car,' she says, after a long moment. 'Well, a few cars, really. Sometimes a van, depending on what Mum's latest boyfriend was driving. Now and then we'd wind up in a shelter or a B&B, and I'd go to school for a few weeks. Once, I even made it through an entire term.' She puts the mug back down on the counter without drinking from it. 'I didn't have friends, because we were never in one place long enough. Mum killed herself when I was fifteen, and my dad was an addict who OD'd before I was even born. I'm not telling you because I want you to feel sorry for me,' she adds quickly.

'But maybe if things had been different, I could've got some exams. *I* could've been different.'

I guess that explains the daddy issues. She and Millie have more in common than I imagined: parental addiction, neglect, suicide – Millie's mother took the better part of two decades to starve herself to death after her dad died, but her story ended in the same place as Harper's mother's.

I know what it takes to make it through the kind of childhood she had, because I know what Millie had to do to make it through hers.

Harper's learned how to make hard choices. She's aware the world's a cold, unforgiving place, and that life is nasty, brutish and short. The weakest in the herd are picked off: only the fittest survive.

Kill or be killed.

'Look around you,' I say gently. 'In a few weeks, this house will be yours. *You* did this. You've come a long way from the back seat of a car.'

Her eyes are bright. 'Thank you for saying that.'

I hope Millie can find it in her heart to be kind to this girl. Compassion's not her strongest suit: it's hard to show kindness when you've never experienced it yourself. And for some reason my wife is fixated on the woman on the other side of our housing chain: Stacey Porter.

I don't know what it is about her that presses Millie's buttons, but every time my wife mentions her name, I get nervous.

chapter 15

millie

I hear voices coming from the kitchen as soon as I walk into the house.

Annoyed, I hang my keys neatly on the hook, and put my sunglasses back in their case on the hall console.

Tom knows I've been on my feet in theatre for close to thirty hours. I've rehearsed for today's procedure – the separation of eighteen-month-old conjoined twins – for close to four months: the surgery has been on my calendar for weeks now. I don't normally operate on paediatric patients, but the team handling the separation were unable to find a paediatric cardiac surgeon sufficiently skilled to take on the case. Successful separation of twins with a thoraco-omphalopagus connection is extremely rare for obvious reasons: you can't divide a heart in two the way you can a liver. The girls shared a connection at the atrium, the upper chamber of the heart, close to several vital veins. The chance both babies would die during surgery was almost one hundred percent: no rational surgeon wants to take on those odds.

Which is why the team came to me.

I used cardiac CT and MRI scans from both before and after the twins were born to create a 3D printed model of their heart, which allowed me to examine the shared structures and meticulously plan how to separate them. I spent weeks experimenting with different options until I found the 0.001 percent chance that'd give both girls a shot.

I rarely get nervous about my cases, but for some reason this one got to me. It's why I needed the therapy of drifting through a stranger's house after successfully keeping my addiction in check for so long.

But my efforts paid off. The girls didn't die on *my* table.

We're only a few hours out, but Hope and Faith are in separate ICU cots.

As a surgeon, I'm used to long hours and lack of sleep, but the fierce concentration required for today's surgery has left me drained. I've been running on adrenaline and caffeine for two days. The last thing I need now is to have to deal with Meddie and her teenage friends.

I made the assumption it's my daughter and her posse in the kitchen because of the high-pitched laughter drifting down the hall . . . but it's Harper Conway I find sitting at my marble island.

'Harper came round to take a few measurements,' Tom says, the tips of his ears pinking slightly. 'She wants to order curtains so they're ready when they move in.'

We have custom-made whitewashed plantation blinds in every room, and UV filters on the panoramic doors to the terrace. I can't abide the fuss of curtains. They remind me of my mother.

'I hope you don't mind me just dropping in, Millie,' Harper says. 'Only Tom did say the other night that if I wanted to stop by—'

'It's fine,' I say.

'And I was just passing, and I thought, it won't take five minutes.'

To judge from the cold coffee mugs and empty packet of Hobnobs on the kitchen island, she's been here a lot longer than five minutes.

'Did you get what you wanted?' I ask.

'Your hubby's been ever so kind,' Harper says. 'I'm sorry to be such a bother.'

'No bother at all,' Tom says, equably.

There's a gift bag perched on one of the island stools next to him, with wisps of pale blue tissue paper poking out of the top. Harper sees me notice it.

'Kyle and me get a lot of freebies because of our vlog,' she says, a little too quickly. 'It's just a shirt. Kyle will never wear it, he hates anything formal. He's more a T-shirt kind of man.'

Tom opens the bag to show me. 'Wasn't that kind?' he says.

'Very.'

She doesn't linger now I'm here, and Tom walks her to the front door. Their goodbyes take longer than strictly necessary: I've ground my coffee beans and pressed a carafe of Colombian bold roast by the time my husband returns.

'Lipstick,' I say.

He glances at his reflection in the kettle, and hastily wipes the sticky red imprint from his cheek. There's more lipstick on his mouth, but I don't tell him that.

I rinse my mug in the sink and put it in the dishwasher. Tom snakes one arm around my shoulders, his other hand sliding between my legs. His erection presses into the small of my back. 'You're not jealous, are you?' he murmurs.

'Of course not.'

I look up and see our reflection in the window, Tom's arm looped loosely across my neck. And I'm suddenly, unexpectedly, assailed by a memory of my mother at the kitchen sink, my father behind her just as Tom is now.

But my father's embrace isn't affectionate.

I don't know how old I was: in my memory, my eyes are level with the top of the kitchen island, so perhaps four or five. Five, I must have been five: my mother was pregnant with my sister, Gracie.

My father's hands are around my mother's throat.

He's forcing her head down into the sink, which is full of greasy water. She's coughing and gasping, fighting for air. Her arms flail impotently, unable to reach him. She's drowning.

I despised my mother, even at the age of five. I despised her for her weakness: not her physical inability to stand up to him – she was only five foot two and a hundred pounds lighter than he, and pregnancy made her even more vulnerable – but for willingly ceding him her power in return for the ring on her finger. She was a beautiful woman, a *smart* woman. As young as I was, I could see she had other weapons in her arsenal. She could have made him love her. She could have made him love *me*.

I wasn't weak like my mother.

So I picked up the paring knife she'd been using to prepare dinner, and plunged it into the back of my father's bare leg.

I couldn't have known where to cut to cause maximum damage, of course. I was *five*. And yet instinctively I avoided the big muscles of the thigh or calf: he'd brush off the slender paring knife like he was swatting a mosquito. Instead, I went for the vulnerable point between the joints of his knee. I sliced straight through the posterior cruciate ligament and severed the popliteal artery, though of course it'd be years before I learned what they were called. Had my mother not called an ambulance, my father would have bled out on the kitchen floor.

She never thanked me. On the contrary: she blamed me for making his vicious temper worse because of his chronic knee pain.

Perhaps she was right. Violence is never the answer, of course.

Until it's the only option.

chapter 16

millie

Stacey's yellow Mini convertible pulls up opposite the gates of the Hurlingham Club. The top is down, and she waves at me over the sun visor.

'Oh, God, I'm *so* sorry I'm late,' she calls, as I cross the road to meet her. 'I got caught up at work. Have you been waiting long?'

'Two minutes,' I say.

She flings open the passenger door. 'Get in. I'll drive us to the clubhouse.'

The porter comes out of the lodge and raises the security barrier as Stacey pulls into the driveway.

'Hi, Fredo,' Stacey says. 'You look like you've caught the sun.'

'Welcome back, Mrs Porter. Nice day to be on the courts.'

'It's yoga this morning,' Stacey says. 'But we might stay and have some lunch afterwards, as it's such a lovely day. This is Millie Downton, a friend of mine.'

'Nice to meet you, Ms Downton. I'll phone ahead for you, Mrs Porter, and reserve a table.'

I've never had a female friend before. I didn't want one: Tom was always enough for me. I've never really understood the mysterious and strange nature of female friendship: the emotional intimacy and need to share the innermost details of each other's lives which from the outside seem to make the relationships as fraught as they are gratifying. It's a common trope that men are more competitive than women, but in my experience women are simply competitive in a way that's less obvious – they're competitive about *connection*.

The girls I knew at college, the women I worked with at the hospital: what appeared to matter to them most was the degree to which they were privy to each other's secrets. And I was always too ashamed to share mine.

Stacey noses her car around a group of women in tennis whites walking three abreast and follows the gentle sweep of the drive towards the Georgian clubhouse. Sitting beside the Thames in Fulham in forty-two rural acres surrounded by the stressful clamour of central London, the Hurlingham Club is an anachronistic survivor of a different age. It lost its polo grounds after the Second World War when the London County Council nabbed them by compulsory purchase for council housing, but it's somehow managed to hold off all-comers since then. The goalposts of the so-called class war may have shifted, but the Hurlingham is still an unapologetic oasis of privilege.

'How long have you been a member here?' I ask as she parks behind the clubhouse.

'All my life. My parents were members, though we didn't come here much after they moved back to Norfolk when I was about seven.'

Tom and I have been on the waiting list for nineteen years, ever since we first moved to London when I was a medical student at Guy's Hospital. Actually, we're still *waiting* to get onto the waiting list proper, which is currently closed: the only way to become a member is to be born to someone who has membership, and then wait for them to die. Full membership is the holy grail.

'Do your parents still live in Norfolk?' I ask.

She scoops her yoga mat from the back seat. 'They died twenty-three years ago,' she says. 'Killed in a car crash on their way home from a New Year's Eve Millennium party. They'd both been drinking, of course. I was in the car, but somehow I walked away with barely a scratch.'

'How old were you?'

'Fifteen.'

'How awful. That must've hit you hard.'

'It hit my brother harder. Adam always felt guilty for not being with us, as if he could have done something. He was six years older than me, so after their deaths he became my legal guardian.'

'You must be close.'

'He overdosed on heroin when I was nineteen.'

Her tone is matter-of-fact, without a trace of self-pity. But in this context, Felix makes more sense. You don't have to be an armchair psychologist to recognise that a child orphaned young will seek out a father figure, especially when she loses her substitute parent just a few years after the initial bereavement.

I know what it's like to lose a sibling.

Gracie, my sweet Gracie—

No. I refuse to go there.

I'm already aware of Stacey's personal history, of course. She's talked about it just enough in the press to have a relatably tragic backstory without seeming to exploit it. But I know it's important for our new friendship that she tells me herself.

And that friendship suddenly matters to me.

I care about Stacey. This isn't about the Glass House any more. It hasn't been since the moment I saw the bruises on her wrist.

This is the second time she's invited me to join her for yoga at the Hurlingham. The classes here are less physically demanding and more woo-woo 'spiritual' than my normal vinyasa power yoga practice, with rather too much third-eye navel-gazing for my taste, but I'm not here to strengthen my core.

'Nice leggings,' I comment with a smile as I follow her into the studio.

'Hope you don't mind,' she says, slightly embarrassed. 'I'm a bit tired of being a Lululemon clone.'

The first time we met up for yoga a couple of weeks ago, she admired my athletic wear. I sent her a link to the niche US site in California where I bought them. She must have gone straight home and ordered a pair: I'm flattered more than I care to admit.

After our class, we change and stroll over to the clubhouse brasserie for lunch. The average age of the other diners on a mid-week morning is approximately seventy-three; pearls, blazers and brick-red jeans are the order of the day.

'Are your parents still alive?' Stacey says, as we sit down.

Clearly our earlier conversation is still preying on her mind. I don't usually talk about my parents, even with Tom. I try not to think about them. But I understand the rules of engagement: Stacey has shared something of her family history, which requires me now to share something of mine.

'My mother died a couple of years ago,' I say. 'My father killed himself when I was in my final year of college.'

Not strictly true, of course.

But close enough.

'How dreadful,' Stacey says.

'Not really,' I say. 'He beat her. He beat us all. He was a vicious, inadequate man. He spent thousands of pounds on expensive hobbies while Mum went without dinner to pay the electricity bill.' Ice cubes clink in my glass as I take a sip of water. 'I used to fantasise about killing him with my bare hands. It was a relief when he did the job himself.'

Stacey tugs at the sleeve of her summer dress. The fabric covers her shoulder now, but I saw the bruises when she was in her yoga clothes.

'Did your mother ever think of leaving him?' she asks, without meeting my eye.

'She should have done,' I say. 'She didn't have the courage. She was too afraid of being alone. She couldn't support herself: she hadn't taught since they'd got married, and she was too scared to retrain. She thought it'd be better for me to have a father, but no father is better than a violent one.'

Stacey stares down at the table.

'He promised he'd change,' I say. 'Every time he knocked out a tooth, or blacked her eye, or broke a bone, he'd swear it was the last time he'd ever hurt her. And it was. Until the next time.' My voice takes on a bitter edge. 'She couldn't even leave him for us.'

'Maybe she was afraid he'd come after her,' Stacey says.

'She could have—'

'Maybe she knew he wasn't the kind of man to give a damn about things like restraining orders,' Stacey adds rapidly. 'Maybe she realised he'd never let her go. He'd kill her first, even if it meant he'd spend the rest of his life in jail.'

The knuckles of her clenched fists are white.

The waitress stops beside our table, notepad in hand. 'Have you decided what you want, or do you need a bit longer?'

'Give us five minutes,' I say tersely.

The girl nods and backs away.

'There are always options,' I tell Stacey, once the waitress has gone.

'Only on paper.' She looks up, and her eyes are filled with

despair. 'In the real world, might is right. You know that as well as I do.'

My phone rings in my bag. I want to ignore it, but the ringtone tells me it's Tom, and he wouldn't interrupt unless it was important.

'It's Peter,' he says, as soon as I pick up. 'There's been an accident. The ambulance is on its way, but you need to get home right now.'

chapter 17

millie

You don't realise how much you love your child until you might lose them.

There's been an accident.

I arrive home just in time to watch the paramedics load the stretcher into the back of the ambulance, knowing better than to get in their way. My baby looks so small and vulnerable suddenly, dwarfed by the vehicle.

Tom is already clambering inside it. 'I'll meet you there,' he says.

'It's going to be OK,' I say, the reassurance more for myself than for him. 'They have to do this with head and neck injuries, just in case. It's just a precaution.'

'I should never have left them alone,' Tom says.

The summer holidays have just started. Our children are thirteen and ten. Tom works from home most of the time: the majority of his client meetings take place on Zoom these days. The kids are old enough to look after themselves for a couple of hours on the odd occasion he has to go into central London for lunch.

He should never have left them alone.

Tom and I knew we were taking a risk when we had children: psychopathy is an inherited trait. The genes that make us unfeeling or narcissistic are often selected in evolution because they have benefits, especially if you are in a profession where a cool head is paramount. Evolution doesn't care about how altruistic you are, or how much good you do. Only that you *win*.

Genetics is just part of the story, of course. Psychopathy is frequently linked to familial violence and abuse. A child who grows up with a violent father and a neglectful, self-absorbed mother will discover they can only get attention and resources by becoming manipulative. They'll learn that negative behaviour is encouraged, and even rewarded. Their psychopathic-behaviour muscles will get stronger, until this pattern of being becomes hardwired into their personality.

I'm living proof.

When we decided to have a baby, we knew we couldn't do anything about the DNA it would inherit, but we could make certain it wasn't amplified by violence or neglect. Tom and I spent a year hammering out the parameters of our parenting before we tried for a child. He agreed to take on the scut work: ferrying the kids to school, chivvying them with their homework. I know my limitations. But I wanted to be the best mother I could possibly be. I might not be a natural parent, but I was determined to be a *good* one.

Psychopathy can't be 'cured' any more than you can change the colour of your child's skin. But it can be *channelled*. Given the right parenting, it can be modified with a reward system that taps into a child's self-interest.

A little girl can grow up to be a life-saving heart surgeon instead of a serial killer.

Because of my dysfunctional home life, I was forced to develop a certain callousness and lack of emotionality to survive. But my children have grown up in a good, loving home. They've been nurtured and listened to and given healthy rules and safe boundaries. I've done everything I can to make sure they grow up into kind, loving, normal human beings.

And yet one of them is more dangerous than I've ever been.

Some genetic variants get weaker with each generation as evolution picks and chooses those traits best suited to ensure survival. Frequently, a negative mutation burns itself out: those who have it are either infertile, or die before they can reproduce and pass it on. Other mutations become stronger. A part of me is almost in awe: I feel like a talented amateur musician who's given birth to Mozart.

Meddie and Peter have the same biological parents and have been raised in the same home, but one is happy to spend the day curled up in a window seat reading a book.

The other has just pushed their sibling from a second-floor window.

I've watched for the early warning signs since the moment my children drew breath. The first red flags appeared in nursery school, when we were called in for conferences with the teacher three times as often as other parents.

Your child doesn't seem to care about getting into trouble.

We need to work on our socialisation skills.

There's been an incident of spitting . . .

. . . of kicking.

. . . of biting.

Tom used to remind me kids aren't good *or* bad. Psychopathy is a continuum and some elements will be found to some degree in most children.

He was right, of course. Kids can be unkind, even cruel. They form gangs, bully each other, squash caterpillars; they lie and cheat and steal. Girls just as much as boys. Most kids' childhoods are less *Little Women* and more *Lord of the Flies*.

But I knew. Meddie was nine and Peter six when I discovered exactly what I'd given birth to.

My daughter was in an exceptionally good mood that morning. She'd got herself up and ready for school before I was even awake, and then ate the breakfast I prepared for her without her usual raft of complaints. When Peter sat on the papier-mâché artwork she'd spent the previous evening working on for class, she didn't say a word.

I discovered why when I came home that night.

'The class *rabbit*, Tom?' I said, when the kids had gone to bed. 'I told Meddie she couldn't sign up to the roster to look after him because you had allergies.'

'She's not stupid. She knows that's bullshit.'

'Remember what happened with the tortoise? You don't think bringing home a baby rabbit is asking for trouble?'

'The tortoise was an accident.'

'You don't put a tortoise in the microwave by *accident*.'

'You do if you're five years old and think it's hibernating because it's cold,' Tom said irritably. 'Stop looking for something that isn't there, Millie. Our kids are perfectly normal. They're just *kids*.'

He stuck to his see-no-evil stance even when the rabbit 'escaped' from its hutch that night and climbed into the dishwasher and ran the steam-and-sanitise cycle all by itself.

He maintained it the following year when the little boy next door nearly lost his finger in a garden gate that mysteriously jammed shut, insisting it was just another unfortunate accident.

But even Tom can't hide from the truth now.

The only reason we're not planning a funeral is because the magnolia tree beneath the hall window broke what would have been a fatal fall.

We won't always get this lucky.

It's just a question of time.

chapter 18

tom

I hold my daughter's hand under the blanket as the ambulance races to the hospital, sirens blaring. I can't forget Peter's face as the paramedics loaded his sister onto the stretcher. Practically *salivating*.

Meddie is very much my wife's child, made in her image: cool, unemotional, self-contained. But Peter was supposed to be *mine*. I gave him a straightforward name, an ordinary boy's name for the ordinary boy I'd longed for: tousled and tow-haired, all scraped knees and conkers and smelly socks, a sunny-natured ally in a hitherto all-female household.

He was an easy baby: he slept well and rarely cried. He grew into an affable, good-natured child. That open, sunny smile, the dishevelled mop of hair like macaroni curls, the freckles and the wide-eyed, innocent gaze: the little boy I'd always dreamed of having.

On the *out*side.

I'll never admit it to a living soul, but there's something about our son that gives me the creeps. Even when he was a baby, I didn't warm to him the way I did to Meddie. He has my wife's eyes: the same shape, the same rich amber flecked with green, but they lack their mother's . . . I don't know, I'm not good with words – *aliveness*, maybe? Millie's eyes change with her mood, from warm honey to cold coffee, her emotions scudding across the surface like clouds in the sky. Peter's eyes are flawed stones, absorbing the light instead of sparkling it back at you. There's a deadness to them, a flatness, like the eyes of a shark.

What kind of father thinks like that about his own kid? I feel guilty about it every day. I've done my best to get past it. Bent over backwards, in fact: I've always been the first to defend him – that business with the school rabbit, for example. I told Millie she was being paranoid. Peter was *six*.

But I saw him at the Holocaust Museum the other week as he pressed his face to the glass, transfixed by the exhibition of clothes and letters and shoes from the Auschwitz death camp. I felt sick just watching him. There was a dark, crackling energy to him, as if he was *feeding* off the misery and suffering the artefacts represented.

Adults always love Peter, but other kids know better. They can sense there's something not quite right about him. He rarely brings a schoolfriend home, and when he does, they don't come back.

Maybe my wife was right after all.

Before we had kids, I never bought into Millie's genetic curse nonsense. Her parents fucked her up, sure, but underneath all that emotional repression she's a good person. With her background, she could easily have become an addict, or a drunk, or just married a man like her father and repeated her mother's mistakes. But despite everything that happened to her, she chooses every day to go out and *save lives*.

The first time we discussed having a baby I told her: we weren't like her parents. We'd give our children a stable, loving home. There was no reason our kids shouldn't turn out perfectly fine. And our daughter was the proof of the pudding: fearless, loving, loyal to a fault, a stickler for fair play. I'd lay down my life for her in a heartbeat.

No, if we'd stopped after Meddie, I wouldn't have given Millie's dire prognostications about bad seeds and psychopaths another thought.

I squeeze my daughter's hand beneath the blanket, my whole being concentrated on a single wordless prayer: *please let her be all right please let her be all right please let her be all right.*

The worst of it is, this is all my fault.

Harper called me in a panic this morning, insisted we had to meet, wouldn't tell me what it was about. If it'd been as innocent as I told myself it was, I'd have invited her over to the house instead of arranging to meet her at a restaurant in Chelsea. But the truth is, I didn't want the kids to see us together.

Didn't want my wife to know.

Millie's enough for me. She's *always* been enough for me – I literally can't remember a time in my life without her. And I know her veneer of cool self-sufficiency is just that: a veneer. She's vulnerable and insecure and fragile, just like the rest of us.

But now and again, it's nice to be *needed*. Millie loves me, I've never doubted that, but she's never *looked up* to me. She's the one with the big job: I make more money than she does, but I'm fiddling with computer codes and she's *holding people's beating hearts in her hands.*

I'm not some unreconstructed Neanderthal who thinks women should be barefoot and pregnant in the kitchen. But I am still a *man*. It feels good when a pretty woman hangs on your every word.

Especially a pretty woman in tears.

Why Kyle Conway is having an affair is beyond me. Harper's a lovely girl: she works hard, she's a good mother, and her heart's in the right place. Why would her idiotic husband risk it all for a quickie with the woman next door?

The poor girl's heartbroken, and obviously I'm flattered she turned to me for advice. But while I was congratulating myself on navigating the dangerous waters of her daddy issues with skill and care, I took my eye off the ball at home. And now my daughter's in an ambulance, and my son is a—

—no. Even Peter wouldn't go that far. He loves his sister. It was an *accident*.

He didn't mean to hurt her.

chapter 19

millie

'Jesus Christ, Tom,' I say. 'What's it going to take for you to see it?'

Tom casts a glance at the medics conferring by the desk along the hall. 'Keep your voice down,' he says. 'We'll have bloody social services on us.'

'That might not be a bad thing.'

'You don't mean that.'

'This wasn't an *accident*, Tom.'

'We can't be sure of that.'

'Yes, we can,' I snap.

Tom takes my elbow and steers me down the corridor. 'OK. Let's say it *wasn't* an accident, Millie,' he says, keeping his voice low. 'You think having the kids taken into care would help? This is my fault. I should never have left them alone.'

'If that magnolia tree hadn't been there, we'd be standing outside the mortuary right now, not a hospital room.'

'You don't have to remind me.'

'Well, it seems like I do,' I say.

Tom rubs his hand over his face. His skin is grey. I don't blame him for not wanting to face it. No parent wants to acknowledge they've created a monster.

He's always got off on my dark side. There's a sexual element to our dance with my shadow self, an erotic danger. But it's a whole different ball game now he's seeing those same traits manifest in our child. Our *baby*. The same helpless little being with the gummy smile whose nappies he changed and whose back he rubbed to bring up wind.

'It doesn't make any sense,' he says helplessly. 'If he pushed her, there must be a *reason*. You don't do something like this just for the hell of it!'

Surely he's lived with me long enough to know that's not true.

The double doors behind us swoosh open, and the triage nurse emerges from the Emergency Department.

'Would one of you like to come back with me while we set her shoulder?' she asks. 'I'm afraid it's rather painful, even with medication.'

'I will,' Tom says instantly.

It should be me: I'm the doctor, and far better equipped than Tom to cope with the trauma of watching our child suffer.

But we have another child sitting at the end of the hall.

A ten-year-old boy who just pushed his sister out of a second-floor window.

Tom can't even bear to look at him. He follows the nurse through the double doors, and I walk back down the corridor towards our son.

I want to run from this, too, but we're Peter's only hope, Tom and me. The difference between a CEO and a serial killer can sometimes hinge on the single question of the family into which they're born. How we respond to this crisis could be the turning point in our son's life.

Peter is sitting peaceably on a hard blue plastic chair in the waiting area, gently swinging his legs. He smiles as I approach. The summer sun has brought out a smattering of freckles across his nose: he looks wholesome and oddly old-fashioned, like he's stepped from the pages of an Enid Blyton novel.

'Is she dead?' he asks, matter-of-factly.

'No,' I say, sitting down next to him. 'She has a number of rib fractures, lung contusions, and she's severely dislocated her shoulder. Your dad's with her now while they set it. She's in a lot of pain, but she's not dead. And she's going to be fine.'

My son nods, as if making a mental note for future reference.

I don't waste time asking *why*. For people like my son, there's only ever one answer to that question: *because I wanted to*.

I wanted to see what would happen.

I wanted to know if I could.

I wanted to *hurt*.

The signs have been there since Peter was a toddler, but stupidly I convinced myself Tom was right and I was wrong: that accidents *do* happen and rabbits can crawl into dishwashers and toddlers' fingers sometimes get stuck in garden gates. I told myself that even if I *was* right about him, Peter would eventually learn what was allowed and what was not, and curb his natural impulses out of self-preservation, if nothing else.

But then he pushed his sister out of a second-floor window.

He's *ten*. He knew Meddie could've been killed. He must have known, too, he couldn't explain this one away: the trouble he'd be in.

And he did it anyway.

I remember what it was like when I was his age: when I walked along a roof ridge line or played chicken with an inter-city train just to be able to *feel*. You'll do anything to end the torment and break through the numbness. It's why my heart aches for him, despite what he's just done. When I look into his eyes, what I see is triumph – and despair. Our daughter's physical injuries will heal. Peter's psychic wounds are incurable.

I can't bear to think how lonely my son must be. In violent psychopaths, there's a strong relationship between the intensity of loneliness they experience, and the degree of violence and

102

recklessness in their actions. Peter has few friends, despite his outward charm and affability. He spends far too much time in his own head, which is why he gets bullied at school.

I remember watching the CCTV of the two shooters at Columbine High School strolling the corridors with no semblance of fear or remorse for the appalling atrocities they were committing. And in addition to my shock and repulsion, I experienced one other very acute sensation: recognition.

I understood those boys. Worse, I could identify with them.

Not with what they *did* – dear God, *no*, not with that, *never* that. The pain and suffering they inflicted on the children they murdered, on those who loved them – unimaginable. But I think I understand why those two boys did what they did. Their loneliness and alienation must have been truly agonising for them to do something so inhuman.

Peter already thinks the world is against him. If I can't turn things around for him now, eventually he'll reach the point of no return. He'll cut through the last thin connection to the normal world.

Shoot up a school. Abduct and smother a child.

And there'll be nothing I can do to stop him.

Inside the mind of a psychopath | *Original Air Date 9 July*

The transcript below has been lightly edited for length and clarity.

For most people, the ninety-nine out of a hundred who aren't psychopaths, murder is unquestionably wrong.

You don't even have to think about it.

It's the ultimate crime, right? Taking a life.

We could get into the weeds debating whether child abuse or betraying your country are actually worse than murder, but generally speaking I think most people can agree stabbing an old lady to death for her handbag is one of the most heinous crimes there is.

Psychopaths are biologically incapable of understanding *why* that's wrong – it's like asking someone who was born blind to grasp the concept of *green*. But even we can see that, according to your rules, going round slaughtering people isn't going to win you any popularity contests.

But there are some exceptions to this rule, aren't there?

Sometimes it's OK to kill people.

Let's take the military, for example. Soldiers are actually *paid* to kill each other.

Yes, I know that's not the same. Legally the killing of an enemy in the heat of war is allowed. It's fine to kill people if it's for the right reasons. If you're defending your country, you can actually get a medal for it.

And what about the death penalty? In Britain, it was abolished in 1965, though treason remained punishable by death until 1998. But across the Pond, Texans are happy to stick the needle in the arm of anyone who looks at them funny. They call it justice.

My point is: sometimes killing people is a heinous crime, and sometimes it's the right thing to do.

And the line between the two is much more blurred than you might think.

Murder one or manslaughter?

Second-degree murder or self-defence?

The Americans have a legal defence they call the 'castle doctrine' which is actually based on English common law: your home is your castle and you have the right to defend it. You don't even have to prove you're in danger at the time: if your drunk neighbour breaks into your garage one night to take back some tools he lent you, you've every right to shoot him in the back.

Seriously, is it any wonder people like me get so confused?

We don't have an instinct for right and wrong, remember. We have to learn your rules, and the goalposts are constantly shifting.

So you tell me: when is it OK to take a single life to save many?

If the 'single life' in question is a teenage boy wielding an AR-15 assault rifle in a primary school, taking him out is a no-brainer.

But what if he hadn't yet picked up the gun?

What if he hadn't even *bought* it?

Suppose you've known him since he was a kid. A neighbour's boy, maybe, or your nephew.

Say you'd found him trying to drown a kitten when he was seven years old. A year later, he attempts to strangle his little brother.

His mother doesn't want to hear it: says you're making something out of nothing. It's just roughhousing, she says. *Boys being boys.*

So you keep a quiet eye on him. And one day you find a notebook he's filled with images and descriptions of the horrific things he'd like to do to people.

A kill book.

He hasn't actually done anything criminal. Not yet.

No one can see who he really is, except you. But you recognise the darkness in him. You know, you *know*, this boy will kill sooner or later.

Ask yourself: if you'd been in my shoes, what would *you* have done?

chapter 20

millie

There's a strange atmosphere in the house in the days after Meddie's accident: an unnatural stillness. I can't shake the sensation that despite everything that's happened already, we're in the calm before the real storm.

I say as much to Tom as we're getting ready for bed one evening a week or so later. The August night is sultry and humid, and the breeze from the open window too tepid to be refreshing.

'You're reading too much into what happened,' he tells me. 'How many times do we have to go over this? It's summer, the kids are hot and bored, and I should never have left them to their own devices all afternoon.' He strips off his T-shirt, and tosses it on the chair in the corner of our room. 'Maybe Peter just got fed up being goaded by his sister, and gave her a shove to shut her up. You know what Meddie can be like when she presses his buttons.'

'He could've *killed* her!'

'He's only ten, for God's sake! He lost his temper. He didn't mean to hurt her. Of course he shouldn't have done it, but it doesn't make him a bloody psycho.'

He knows that's a loaded word for me, not just a turn of phrase.

Tom flips the covers back so far they fall off the end of the bed. The duvet is too warm for a night like tonight – I can't wait for the Glass House and its air-conditioning – but the careless messiness of the gesture irritates me. I like getting into a properly made bed.

Tom wants to have his cake and eat it: he refuses to admit Meddie's fall was anything but an accident, and yet he won't let our son within ten feet of our daughter as she recuperates in her bedroom.

So it's down to me. I've spoken to Peter, and made it very clear I'll be watching him like a hawk from now on. I talked to him in the only language he understands: *I will hurt you*, I told him. *If you ever do anything to harm your sister again, I will hurt you.*

He believed me.

The problem is, I don't believe it myself.

I'm a tigress when it comes to my children, just like any other mother: which of us wouldn't do anything to protect our young? If someone threatens our child, we'll crush their eyeballs with our thumbs and rip out their heart with our teeth if necessary.

But Peter is my child as much as Meddie. I could never hurt him, not even to save my daughter.

So I talk to Meddie, too. My abiding fear is that Peter will try to hurt her again, sooner or later: he won't be able to help himself. And Meddie knows this as well as I do, which means I'm afraid for my son, too. She's smarter than Peter, older and stronger. Unlike him, she has guile and the ability to control her temper. Peter doesn't scare her.

In our house, Tom is the only one who's afraid.

And then I do what anyone struggling to keep the peace between warring factions does to unite them: I find them a common enemy.

I ground them both, take away their screens, and force them to spend the long summer days sorting through clothes and toys and books in their bedrooms in preparation for our move next month. They're both so furious with me, they forget to be angry with each other.

But I know the detente won't last.

I untangle the bedding on the floor now and get into bed, floating the sheet across us both and settling back against the pillows. I pick up my book, but I'm too tense to read. I don't know what more I can do to keep my family safe. My father was right: I should never have been allowed to have children. Tom is a good man: I'd always hoped his genes would win out over mine, but clearly that's not the case with our son. Poor Tom.

Peter has known nothing but love. Neither of us have ever raised a hand to him, not even to slap his fingers away from a hot stove. I have to hope it's not too late for him. I managed to channel the liabilities of my personality into an arena where they became *assets*: my inability to connect emotionally with my patients and feel their fear is what enables me to stay cool under pressure and save their lives. I have to believe I can help Peter do the same.

Maybe moving to a new house will give us all a new start. I know I'm pinning too much on the idea, but what else do I have?

Tom switches off his bedside light and turns towards me. His bare torso is gilded amber by the streetlight outside. He's been working out, I realise suddenly: he has the sharply defined abs of an Olympic swimmer.

'Millie, you've got to let this thing with Peter go,' he says, taking the unread book from my hand. 'He's got some problems, we know that, but he hasn't inherited some sort of "bad seed" from you. What happened with your father wasn't your fault. You're not a bad person. If you wanted to, you'd be perfectly placed to kill dozens of people without anyone ever knowing, but you go into that hospital and save lives every day.'

'I break into people's houses, Tom.'

'And steal *paperclips*!'

He thinks he knows me. Poor Tom. He doesn't realise honesty can be as big a smokescreen as deceit.

I take my book from him again.

He has no idea what I had to do to survive.

kyle and harper share their truth

1,841,002 views 👍 432K 👎 2.6K

Hi, my lovely Kyper Nation, I'm *so* grateful to you for showing up today, because it's been a really, really traumatic week and this is going to be a super emotional episode. I'm, like, baring my soul to you today, and this is so, *so* incredibly painful, but I feel like I need to share my truth with you, because I need to be my authentic self with you even when it hurts.

You know me and Kyle think of you all as our family. Some of you have been following our story since the beginning and it's been a roller-coaster ride, hasn't it? Honestly, we couldn't have made it without you.

We've been super lucky with this vlog and all our lovely sponsors like SugarPop and Poshnet – and don't forget to check out the links to their websites below before you go, peeps, because they're totally awesome and they've got some amazing deals right now.

But me and Kyle have had our rough patches, too, like everyone, and sometimes you have to nearly lose something to realise how precious it is, like in that song, you don't know what you've got till it's gone, it's just so *true*.

Sometimes it feels like a relationship is over but really it's a moment for growth and understanding and to lean into your partner, you know?

The thing is, what you all need to know is, this week Kyle came to me and confessed, oh, this is, like, really hard for me to say—

[Sobbing]

So, Kyle told me, he admitted he'd been intimate with someone else.

I was in absolute bits, I'm not going to lie. I just never thought this could happen to *us*. I couldn't understand how my Kyle could do this to me.

So I said to Kyle, you have to leave now, I can't trust you, and he was devastated too, because he didn't want to lose me, and he said he didn't *want* to cheat, but he couldn't help it because it turns out he's basically suffering from an addiction. He said sex is his addictive behaviour, that's where he goes to hide his feelings, to run away from reality, it's like it's his *drug*.

And once I started to understand it wasn't his fault, I realised I had to help him, because that's what Meghan would do, isn't it?

So I told him, look, I'm *here* for you. I'm willing to work on this. I want this family to work. Our sponsors said they were behind us one-hundred-and-ten percent. The amazing people at Poshnet even arranged for Kyle to have therapy for his sex addiction and that's why you haven't seen him so much in the last few vlogs, he's been working on himself.

Seriously, peeps, I love Kyle so, *so* much. It's been super hard recently, because it's not easy to get the trust back, is it? But we've both been putting in the work to repair our marriage, and I just wanted to share where we are on our journey with you, because I know lots of you have been in my shoes and I'm just humbled by all the messages of support you've been sending.

So I thought, why not use our trauma to help people? I mean, if you guys can learn from our experience, it'll have been worth it, you know?

Kyle and me are going to be doing a special live show with Kyle's therapist, Jana, and I know it's going to be really deep and authentic and a really private moment, so I hope you'll all be able to join us. I'll pop a link in the description bar below.

I still believe so, so much in marriage, love, and rebuilding. And one of the biggest lessons I've learned in life is you've sometimes got to go back and deal with really uncomfortable situations and be able to process them so you can heal.

Because otherwise the past catches up with you, doesn't it?

chapter 21

millie

Tom's changed the password on his phone.

It's been set to Meddie's birthday for as long as I can remember: 010409. I tap the six digits into the screen again, one ear cocked to the sound of Tom in the shower, but the phone stays resolutely locked.

There's only one reason a man suddenly changes his password.

He hasn't been himself for weeks now. It's not just the time he's spending working out or the new clothes in his wardrobe – he seems to have lost his *spark*. Tom's always been the upbeat, positive one: he believes in the fundamental *goodness* in human nature, while I lean towards a Hobbesian vision of life as nasty, brutish and short. But recently he's been moping around the house, a heavy black cloud almost visibly hovering over him. He's short with me, grumpy with the kids. And things have definitely tailed off in the bedroom: it's been *weeks*.

There's something going on with him and Harper Conway, I'm sure of it. Maybe not an affair, not yet. But *some*thing.

I hear the sound of the shower cease, and quickly put Tom's phone back on the bedside table. I don't feel great about spying on my husband, but I tell myself the ends justify the means.

I've never doubted him before. He's been my biggest cheerleader and staunchest supporter since we were kids in the playground. He knows my darkness and he still loves me. I can't imagine many men who'd be able to live with me. He knows how much I love him, but I'm aware I'm not very good at showing it. I don't know *how*.

But he's not a saint. He wouldn't be human if he didn't sometimes long for a simpler life. A simpler woman.

The mistake he's making is thinking Harper is his gateway to either.

'You need to wake the kids up,' Tom says, towelling his hair dry as he comes back into the bedroom. 'The surveyor's coming today. I thought you said we had to get the house ready for him?'

'Shit,' I exclaim.

I'd completely forgotten. Our house is more than a hundred years old: its foundations have shifted and none of the floors are level, so some doors stick and certain windows have to be opened with care. When we renovated the property and dug out the basement, we underpinned the house structurally, but even I can't turn back time. If you put a marble on the floor at one end of the kitchen, it'll roll slowly but inevitably to the other side.

Selling a house to a prospective buyer is the easy bit. A property is sold in the first ten minutes based on the emotions it elicits. You're selling a lifestyle, not a pile of bricks and mortar: a dreamworld of crisp white linen duvet covers, vases of fresh lilies in every room, Pol Roger champagne in the fridge and a single bowl filled with gleaming fruit on the kitchen island. In this fantasy world, there are no phone chargers snaking across sticky countertops, or jumble of shoes tossed inside the back door.

But a surveyor isn't interested in the characterful idiosyncrasies of an older property. He's looking for reasons to knock thousands off our asking price – thousands we simply can't afford to lose given how much we're paying for the Glass House.

We whirl into action: I take the ground floor and basement, and Tom looks after the rest of the house. Humidity and the heat of summer have caused the floorboards in the kitchen near the sink to buckle, so I throw an expensive grey and white rug from the dining room over the offending area. Upstairs, Tom puts all the batteries back in the smoke and carbon monoxide detectors, which chirp in the middle of the night at random intervals for no reason we've ever been able to find, and turns on the lights in our bedroom from the bedside dimmers to hide the fact that when you use the main wall switch, they flicker.

'Did you put the suitcases in front of the dodgy air handler in the basement?' Tom asks, when we meet back downstairs with the kids.

'Yes. Has anyone seen my phone?'

'Christ, Mum,' Meddie says. '*Again*?'

We spend a fruitless five minutes looking for it before Tom thinks to call my number and I track it to the top of the cistern in the downstairs bathroom.

Time is short and we hustle the kids out to the car. Meddie's arm is still in a sling, and Peter solicitously helps her with her seatbelt and checks she's comfortable against the extra cushions I put in the car. Tom throws an approving glance at him, and then looks meaningfully at me: *see, I told you it was nothing to worry about.*

This is our first excursion since Meddie's accident, and Tom has decided on brunch at the Pizza Express on the King's Road, because this is what normal families do, and *we are a normal family*. It takes us a while to find a parking space nearby: in the end, Tom ruthlessly nips in and steals one from a car patiently waiting with its indicators on.

'Nice one, Dad,' Meddie says.

The other vehicle beeps angrily at us, and then drives on.

I'm just sorting out the parking meter when Tom comes up behind me and nudges my arm.

'Isn't that—?'

Across the road, Harper Conway is in animated discussion with a man half-hidden in the doorway of an office block. As we watch, she leans towards him and wreathes her arms around his neck.

The man with her isn't her husband.

It's Stacey's.

chapter 22

stacey

Felix knows better than to hit her where it shows. He's skilled at causing her pain without leaving marks. He punches her in the kidneys, or kicks her between her legs.

She's miscarried twice since they had Archie.

But she'd forgotten she was presenting a special swimwear programme today, part of the *Morning Express* 'Real Women' series. She agreed to model a one-piece swimsuit – she draws the line at a bikini on national television – so at least the marks on her stomach will be hidden. But she can't do anything about the livid bruises on her arms and legs.

'What on earth happened to *you*?' her wardrobe stylist, Kym, exclaims when Stacey disrobes in her dressing room.

Stacey summons a rueful smile. 'I tried out one of those electric bikes.'

'Oh, my God! What happened?'

'They go faster than you think. Don't tell anyone – I feel silly enough as it is.'

'Those things are a menace,' Kym says, picking up her make-up brush. 'My friend was working on *America's Got Talent* when Simon Cowell came off one of those and broke his back. He couldn't hardly walk for months.'

Stacey's co-anchor, Brendan, is smug in his trendy board

shorts and bare chest when she walks into the studio. He's not part of the 'Real Women' segment, but he revels in his reputation as the housewives' wet dream, and isn't going to pass up an opportunity to show off his six-pack.

'Nice outfit,' he says, as she settles herself on the sofa and waits for the sound guy to mike her up. 'Covers up the old mum-tum a treat.'

He knows how sensitive she is about her weight. Stacey's battle with the bulge is familiar to viewers: they did a whole series around her 'weight-loss journey' a couple of years ago. Her personal ratings went through the roof. Thanks to her nutritionist and personal trainer, at thirty-eight she's in better shape now than she's ever been, but she'll never have flat abs or a thigh-gap, because she's not a pre-pubescent girl.

'You're gonna need to put on a shirt, Brendan,' the sound man tells him. 'I have to clip your mike to something.'

The floor manager is already counting down to record the trailer for the upcoming show. As soon as the light above the camera facing her blinks red, Stacey produces the warm, welcoming smile that's endeared her to the nation.

'Coming up in today's show: the heartbreaking story of the "milk carton kids" who disappeared thirty years ago and never came home,' she says.

'And we meet the war hero defying the odds to parachute off Mount Everest,' Brendan says.

'Plus the latest in our series on Real Women: are any of us really "beach-body ready" and should we even be trying?' Stacey asks. 'All that and more in today's *Morning Express Show*, coming up right after the news in your area.'

She's too much the consummate professional to let her distraction show while they're on-air, but a low-level anxiety gnaws at her all morning. She's planned her escape from Felix down to the last detail, but so much depends on whether Millie

Downton will help her. She's grateful for the swimsuit segment: once the parade of women in bikinis comes on set, Brendan's leering misogyny ensures the programme descends into organised chaos, which masks her inattentiveness.

After the show, she joins the production team in the editor's office for the usual post-mortem. To her disgust and Brendan's smug delight, three-quarters of the morning's viewer calls and emails are to ask for more shots of his waxed abs. One of the feature producers suggests sending him out to various scenic locations to recreate famous 'knicker-wetting' moments: scything in a field like *Poldark*'s Aidan Turner, or emerging from a lake like Colin Firth in *Pride and Prejudice*.

Stacey excuses herself from the meeting and leaves, texting her agent as she takes the lift down to reception where her car is waiting. She's anchored the *Morning Express Show* for more than a decade. It's time the network gave her a show of her own, something that'll give her a chance to show off her serious journalistic chops. She knows her own worth: she's won the People's Choice Award for Best Presenter eight years running.

She's grateful Felix is at work when her driver drops her off at home. She needs time to sort through all their joint paperwork, and make sure she has everything she needs before she pulls the trigger on her plan.

And then her phone beeps with an incoming message from her husband just as she opens the front door:

I'm waiting for you upstairs.

chapter 23

millie

I'm running along the Embankment when Stacey phones me. Exercise helps me come down from my surgical high: I've just finished a fourteen-hour coronary artery bypass graft on a fifty-six-year-old woman. The CAPG itself was successful, but my patient suffered a number of complications on the table which tripled my time in theatre. She'll survive the surgery, but I doubt she'll live to draw her pension: she's four stone overweight, and the obese don't generally make old bones. There's nothing like slicing down through several inches of yellow adipose tissue to make you want to hit the pavement and work up a sweat.

'I shouldn't be ringing you,' Stacey says. 'But I didn't know who else to call.'

I slow my pace and jog away from the river towards a bench near a child's play area. Two boys of maybe six and eight are swinging from the jungle gym. A couple of glossy-haired girls far too young to be their mothers sit on another bench, gossiping over their lattes. Snatches of French drift towards me on the summer breeze.

As I stretch out my calves against the bench I see the older boy shove the younger one from the jungle gym. The kid falls six feet onto the rubberised matting, landing heavily on his left shoulder and letting out a yelp of pain. The French nannies don't even look up.

'You're not at work, are you?' Stacey asks me.

'Out for a run,' I say, still slightly breathless. 'What's up?'

'If my lawyer finds out I'm talking to you—'

'Wait,' I say, instantly alert. 'This sounds like a conversation we shouldn't have on the phone. Are you at home?'

'Yes.'

'I'll be there in fifteen.'

The older boy is sitting on a swing now, playing with an ice-blue robotic dragon that seems to be breathing smoke. The smaller kid is on the ground beneath the jungle gym with his arms wrapped around his knees, sobbing.

I jog back towards the river. As I pass the obnoxious bully, I snatch the dragon out of his hands and toss it into the Thames, winking at the little kid without even breaking my stride.

I'm surprised when Felix answers the front door.

'I told her not to call you,' he says sourly, but stands aside to permit me entry.

Despite all the glass, it's cool inside the house. The whisper-quiet central air-conditioning keeps it a temperate twenty degrees.

I follow Felix upstairs to the kitchen where Stacey is sitting at the island, still dressed for the television studio in a pink capped-sleeve dress. The heavy camera make-up ages her, and fails to conceal the dark shadows beneath her eyes.

Or the bruises on her arms.

Felix leans against the fridge, his arms folded. He looks as defeated and exhausted as his wife.

'Who wants to tell me what's going on?' I say.

Stacey glances at her husband, and then quickly looks away.

'My company's about to go bust,' Felix says baldly.

122

He works for a private investment firm called Copper Beech Financial: I've seen it mentioned in the financial pages more than once.

'Does that mean you'll be out of a job?' I ask.

'I'm a director,' he says. 'If the company goes down, I go down with it.'

'I'm sorry to hear that,' I say. 'But I'm not sure why you're telling me.'

Felix pushes away from the fridge and moves towards his wife, one hand resting casually on the back of her stool. It's the first time I've seen them interact as if they're a couple. 'We can't sell you the house,' he says.

My stomach plunges. If the sale falls through now, we won't suffer financially, beyond the money we've laid out for the survey, but emotionally it's a different story. In my head, I've already moved into the Glass House. Even the kids have finally been getting excited about their new bedrooms. The movers are booked. I've arranged to have our electricity and gas supply terminated. I've ordered a new sofa that's far too large for our current house, but'll go perfectly here.

I need this move. *Peter* needs this move.

'We wouldn't do this to you if we had a choice, Millie,' Stacey says. 'Hopefully it'll just mean a bit of a delay while Felix sorts everything out—'

'How long of a delay?'

'I don't want to get your hopes up,' Stacey says.

'If Felix has lost his job, surely selling the house would be—'

'I'm a *director*,' Felix says again. 'My assets are up for grabs.'

'It's the company that's going bust, not you,' I snap. 'Your home should be legally protected from creditors.'

'Not necessarily,' Felix says.

'What does that mean?'

Stacey looks nervously at him, and then back at me. 'It

123

means they can come after your personal assets if they can prove wrongful trading,' she says. 'I'm sure it'll all be fine in the end, because obviously Felix hasn't done anything wrong,' she adds hastily. '*Obviously*. But his lawyer says it's a lot harder to make someone homeless than it is to seize a pile of cash sitting in a bank account. He says we shouldn't sell the house till this is all sorted out.'

'You could transfer it into Stacey's sole name,' I tell Felix. 'Your creditors couldn't come after the money then.'

'It'd still be a marital asset,' Stacey says.

Felix gives me a cold stare. I imagine slicing neatly around his eyeballs with my scalpel and pocketing them, like marbles.

As if conjured by my ill-wishing, a sudden gush of blood bursts from Felix's nose. He tilts his head back and gropes around for something to staunch it as he pinches the bridge of his nose. A light spray of blood spatters the counter and my running shoes.

'It's the stress,' Stacey says, her tone oddly flat. 'He often gets nosebleeds.'

There's a tea-towel on the kitchen counter in front of me and I hand it to him.

'Lean forward and breathe through your mouth,' I say. 'It'll drain blood into your nose instead of down the back of your throat.' I open the freezer compartment of their shiny American refrigerator and rummage for a bag of peas. 'Take this. It'll help stop the bleeding.'

'Fuck this,' Felix says, waving me away. *Duck dis*. 'I'll be in my study.'

We listen to his footsteps recede downstairs.

Stacey suddenly reaches across the kitchen island and seizes my forearm so tightly her nails dig into my skin.

'Don't believe him,' she says urgently. 'Please, Millie. This has nothing to do with him losing his job. He won't let me leave. You have to help me.'

chapter 24

tom

I can't say I'm sorry about losing the Glass House.

Millie's upset, of course, but the prospect of that huge mortgage was already giving me sleepless nights, and it's a lot of upheaval to put the kids through just to move a dozen streets away from where we are now. The last thing Peter needs is any more disruption.

And now that her *dream house* is off the table, maybe Millie will stop obsessing about Stacey Porter—

Some hope.

I'm not sure what it is about her friendship with Stacey that sets off alarm bells. The woman seems nice enough, though it's hard to know how much of that is a carry-forward from her cuddly, approachable screen persona. But her friendship with Millie has gone from nought to sixty in thirty seconds: it's the intensity of it that makes me uneasy. Something about their relationship just feels overheated, the emotional equivalent of a housing bubble. My wife can be very focused when she gets her teeth into something. Very determined.

Given her personal history, it's not surprising Millie has a hair trigger for domestic violence. She's got zero tolerance for any kind of physical abuse: quite rightly, of course. I've rarely seen her lose her temper, but when she's confronted by any kind of violence or bullying – of defenceless animals, children, other women – it's like red mist descends and some external force takes over. Her *dark angel*, she calls it. I honestly think when it happens she's capable of pretty much anything. And I can feel her champing at the bit to go into battle on Stacey's behalf.

Maybe I was wrong to put an end to her prison breaks. Perhaps she needs more than her wistful visits to other people's houses.

Maybe we both do.

I'm not going to lie: I miss the thrill I used to get when she'd come home from one of her extracurricular adventures. We never discussed the specifics of what she did when she was away – we didn't need to. She'd return with a certain look in her eye: a lightness, like a brand new leaf under the sun. As if whatever fever had consumed her had abated, at least for now. She'd be gentler in bed, and more kind out of it. I miss that Millie.

My phone vibrates on the table, jerking me from my reverie. I glance at the screen, and then flip the phone facedown and cover it with the café menu.

Harper must have called me a dozen times in the past few days. It's my own stupid fault: I don't know what I was thinking, letting myself get sucked into – well, I'm not exactly sure what it was. Let's call it a middle-aged man's foolish ego trip and leave it at that.

Nothing untoward happened: just a few shopping trips to *freshen up* my wardrobe, and a bit of encouragement to go back to the gym. And yes, maybe a kiss or two that weren't quite as platonic as I told myself at the time. I'm not naive: I know where things might have headed if it'd gone on much longer. It doesn't matter how you slice it: the fact I changed the password on my phone and started deleting Harper's texts tells its own story.

I can't believe I was such a bloody idiot. In my defence, I felt sorry for the girl, carrying the weight of keeping the whole KyperLife show on the road while her husband was busy dipping his wick next door, but obviously that's no excuse. I'm soaked in shame. If I hadn't spotted Harper draped all over Felix Porter in the street last week, who knows how things would've ended.

'It's not what you think,' Harper said, when she phoned me the next day. She'd seen me going into Pizza Express with Millie and the kids: she'd known she'd been rumbled.

'You don't owe me an explanation,' I said.

'But I *want* to explain—'

'Honestly, Harper, it's fine. My pride may be a little dented,' I added honestly, 'but there's no harm done. What you get up to with Felix Porter is entirely your own affair, although I'm not sure I'd want to tangle with his wife if I were you. She's a bit of a national treasure. I don't think it'd do you or your brand any good if it all came out.'

'But it *isn't*,' she insisted. 'An affair, I mean—'

'Look,' I said, 'I genuinely hope you and Kyle manage to work things out. You've got those two lovely boys to think of. And now I'm afraid I really do have to go.'

So I was relieved on multiple fronts when the Porters pulled out of the sale. It meant our sale to the Conways was off, too, because the Glass House was the only reason we were moving in the first place. There should be no reason to come into contact with Harper again. We can safely turn the page. Disaster averted. All's well that ends well.

Except Harper just won't let it go.

My phone buzzes again beneath the menu. Obviously it's unfortunate the Conways had already exchanged contracts with their own buyer before we told them the sale was off, but there's not much I can do about it now. I've told Harper they'll find somewhere else she likes just as much, but she still *keeps calling*.

Stupid of me. Stupid stupid *stupid*.

I'm jolted out of my self-flagellation when Felix Porter approaches my table.

'Sorry I'm late,' he says tersely.

He pulls out a chair and sits down, his long legs tangling beneath the wrought iron table as he shifts restlessly, trying to get comfortable in the tight space between the table and the concrete planter separating the café from the street.

'I appreciate you coming,' I say. 'I know how—'

'What's this about?'

Not wasting any words, then.

It's hard to know what to make of Felix Porter. He's a good-looking man: probably pushing sixty, but trim and physically fit. When he walked into the café there was an imperceptible flutter among the women, a smoothing of hair and recrossing of limbs. He's a bit of a cold fish if you ask me – he eyes the glass of white wine I ordered while waiting for him with evident disapproval – but there's no denying he has a certain alpha magnetism about him, despite the permanent scowl.

'What happened?' I ask, gesturing to his face. 'Don't tell me: I should see the other guy?'

He touches the fresh bruise purpling his eye socket. 'Kitchen cabinet,' he says shortly.

There are livid red scratches on his wrists, too.

It's no wonder the situation with the Porters pushes all Millie's buttons. But I have a hunch their relationship is a lot more complicated – and a lot darker – than my wife thinks.

'Would you like something to drink?' I ask Felix, glancing around to catch the eye of a waitress. 'Coffee or—'

128

'Can we just get on with this?'

'You got it. How are things at work?'

His expression tightens. 'I'm trying to save the pensions of tens of thousands of people so they don't end up on the streets in their old age,' he says. 'But thank you for asking.'

I haven't read anything in the financial pages about Copper Beech yet, but when I made discreet enquiries with a journalist friend who works at the *Financial Times* after the Porters pulled out of the house sale, he confirmed the company's definitely in trouble. Oddly enough, Felix Porter seems to come out of it surprisingly well. The firm's board of directors has been sailing close to the wind for a while now, but Felix has apparently been holding their feet to the fire, trying to get them to clean up their act before the FSA is forced to intervene. I know Millie thinks he's the devil incarnate, but he may be in the clear on this one.

'You can probably guess why I wanted to see you,' I tell Felix. 'I know you've got a lot on your plate, and I'm not trying to add to the pressure. But if there's any way we can get the sale back on track—'

'You're wasting your time.'

'Hold on a minute and hear me out,' I say, holding up my hand. 'I'm not going to pretend to know your business, but I've done a bit of research and if all that's really holding you up is concern over your vulnerability to asset seizure, I think we can find a way round it. And,' I add, sitting back as I deliver the pièce de résistance, 'we're prepared to up our offer by a hundred-K.'

It's going to hurt us financially, there's no two ways about it. But I reckon we can swing it if I take a couple of IT jobs working for a space cadet whose calls I haven't been returning.

I love my wife. I don't care one way or the other about the Glass House, and I don't particularly want to encourage Millie's friendship with Stacey Porter. But if it's in my power to give her what she wants, I'll do whatever I can to make it happen.

'I told you,' Felix says. 'You're wasting your time.'

'Come on, mate. It's a good deal. Another hundred thousand—'

He pushes back his chair. 'You're talking to the wrong person.'

'What's the problem?' I demand, irritated now. 'Why are you so wedded to that house? Your wife wants to sell, my wife wants to buy. You know what they say: happy wife, happy life. I'm sure we can—'

He cuts me off. Again.

'I told your wife,' he snaps. 'I've warned her to stay away from Stacey more than once. If you really want to look out for her, tell her to listen to me.'

'What's that supposed to mean?'

Felix gets to his feet. '*I'm* not the one who pulled out of the sale,' he says.

chapter 25

millie

Tom thinks it's a good thing the Porters have pulled out. *Peter needs stability*, he says. *Maybe now isn't the time to uproot him. And besides, we were biting off more than we could chew with that mortgage, weren't we?*

Next time, he says. *There are other houses.*

I tell him it's not about the house, not any more.

'You know what that man is doing to her, Tom!' I say. 'How can I just walk away?'

'You're only hearing one side of the story,' he says. 'You barely even *know* this woman. You've been friends for what? Six weeks? Eight at most. We don't know what their relationship is really like behind closed doors. These things are complicated—'

'I've seen the bruises! There's nothing *complicated* about it!'

'And I've seen his!'

'Come on!'

'Millie, you've got absolutely no proof Felix is abusing her.'

'She *told* me. Well, as good as.'

He sighs. 'Millie, I know how raw this subject is for you, but I don't think it's that straightforward. I think there's more going on than we—'

'Are you saying she's lying?'

'I know, I know,' he says, holding up his hands. 'Believe the woman.'

It's clear he doesn't like Stacey. I don't know what he's suddenly got against her: they seemed to get on fine when we all met at the gala. Perhaps he's jealous. Until now, I've never wanted anyone but him.

'She *needs* me,' I say.

Tom retreats. He knows better than to challenge me on this.

There was a Spar shop at the end of the road where Tom and I grew up. It was run by a short, immensely fat Polish woman called Marilla who'd lived above it since before we were born. She seemed ancient to us when we were nine years old, but she was probably no more than sixty at the time. She had a thick foreign accent and more than a hint of a moustache, and always wore a long-sleeved black dress, even in the height of summer.

One day, when she was clearing up a spill in one of the aisles, she rolled up her sleeves to squeeze out a sponge and exposed a blurry blue six-digit number tattooed on the outside of her forearm.

I knew about concentration camps. We'd done a whole block about Auschwitz in our Social Studies class only the previous term.

'Marilla lost her whole family in the camps,' my mother said when I asked her about the tattoo. 'Her parents were sent to the gas chamber, and her sisters died from starvation in labour camps. She told me once she always keeps a bread roll in her pocket, even now.'

'But she isn't Jewish,' I said. 'She wears a *cross*.'

'The Nazis didn't just murder Jews,' Mum explained. 'Marilla was a twin, and there was a doctor in that camp who did wicked experiments on twins. It's why Marilla couldn't ever have children.'

I burned with curiosity to know *what experiments*, but I was smart enough not to ask.

My mother's tone when she spoke about Marilla was filled with pity. But where she saw only a victim, I saw a survivor: someone who'd found the will to keep going, to *stay alive*, no matter how viciously she was brutalised.

A woman as unlike my mother as it was possible to be.

Marilla fascinated me. She'd been the same age as me when she was sent to Auschwitz. How could she have survived in such a place? So many people older and smarter and stronger than she had died. What made her different?

I started to find excuses to go to the Spar shop, volunteering to fetch my father's cigarettes and beer. Some days when I couldn't face going straight home from school Marilla let me hang out in the storeroom or help her stack shelves.

'Why are you nice to me?' I asked one afternoon.

She put down the heavy boxes of soap powder she'd been stacking. 'You think I survived the camps because I was stronger than the rest, *kochanie*?' she asked: I knew that was Polish for *sweetheart*. 'You think I was smarter or luckier than the others? No, Millie, the *worst* of us survived: the selfish, the violent, the brutal, the cruel. The best all died.' She rubbed at her tattoo as if the numbers burned, her expression suddenly bitter. 'I became like *them*. I let them kill my humanity. I need to atone.'

I didn't understand what she meant: I was only nine.

One afternoon in late December I was sitting at the dining table doing my homework when my father came home. He'd been at the pub all day: he reeked of beer, and his trousers had a suspicious stain at the crotch.

'Why's she still up?' he demanded, jerking his thumb at me.

'It's only five-thirty, John,' Mum said.

My mother was a beautiful woman. A *clever* woman. She had tools she could have used to manage my father, since she

133

clearly didn't have the guts to leave him. Occasionally, after one of their fights, she'd flee with me and my sister to one of those battered women shelters, with their walls in neutral colours and their rubber mattresses and their giant jars of peanut butter. But after a night or two, she'd call him, and there'd be tears and promises of change, and then she'd go back and drag us with her. I hated her for her weakness. Sometimes it felt like she *wanted* him to hurt her.

I fled upstairs as the fighting started. I'd learned a lot since I'd stabbed my father in the back of the knee with a paring knife. I knew better now than to come between them. My mother wallowed in her victimhood. Sooner or later, she'd drown in it, and I wasn't going to get caught in the undertow.

The shouting intensified. But as bad as the yelling was, the silence that came next was always worse, because that meant he was hitting her. I watched helplessly through the bannisters as he dragged her along the hallway towards the kitchen by her hair. I didn't hide in my bedroom beneath the covers with my four-year-old sister Gracie because I needed to *see*: to remind myself what happened when you ceded your power to a man.

Mum thrashed back and forth trying to get out of his grip, flopping around like a landed fish, her hands clawing above her head. I wondered if he'd kill her this time. I wondered if I was strong enough yet to kill him if he did.

And then suddenly the kitchen door burst open below and Tom launched himself bodily on top of my father: Tom, nine years old and skinny as fuck, screaming and shouting, his small fists beating my father's back.

Dad brushed him off as if he were no more than a mosquito, but he had to let go of my mother's hair to do so. She scrambled frantically away on her hands and knees like a feral cat. And then Dad picked Tom up like he was a bag of flour and

134

threw him against the kitchen wall. Tom smashed into it so hard his head punched a hole in the Sheetrock.

I tore down the stairs, screaming at my father to stop.

My mother grabbed my arm as I reached the bottom. 'He'll kill you!'

Dad was lurching around trying to find my mother, a blundering bear of a man. A large cut on his forehead bled heavily into his eyes, obscuring his vision.

I broke free from my mother and ducked beneath his flailing arms. In the kitchen, Tom sat up, disorientated but alive.

'Run!' my mother cried.

Mum didn't defy my father very often. They fought like this all the time: what had happened tonight wasn't out of the ordinary. Sometimes she'd even hit him back, because in my parents' world, violence masqueraded as passion and a beating meant you *cared*. So when she yelled, '*Run!*' I seized Tom's hand and we ran.

We didn't run to Tom's house next door, or to the neighbours, whose lights were going off as we passed them because nobody wanted to get involved. We ran to the one place I knew would give us sanctuary: the Spar shop on the corner.

I sped barefoot over broken glass and rough tarmac in my jeans and T-shirt, heedless of the biting December wind as I hauled Tom behind me. My mother was screaming like a banshee, but I didn't scream. I didn't cry.

I just ran, because I knew that was how I was going to live.

chapter 26

millie

Stacey Porter: (No Subject)

I stare at the email on my phone. I don't click on it, because I already know what it contains. Once I open it there'll be no going back.

I haven't told Tom what Stacey has asked me to do. He'll tell me she's using me: that I'm the one who'll be taking all the risk. *Even if you're right,* he says, *even if Felix is abusing her, what happens when she goes back to him? Because you know she'll go back, Millie. Women like her always do.*

After the terrible night when Tom rescued me from my father and we fled the house, after everything that happened afterwards, I thought that now, *surely,* my mother would find the courage to leave him. But in the end the gravitational pull back to him was just too intense. I wasn't strong enough to drag her free.

She went back because she was addicted to him: to the cycle of abuse and remorse. When he beat her, he was in control, but when he was sorry and filled with apology and regret, *she* was the one in charge. She thought she could save him. She thought she could *rescue* him. The abuse actually made her feel special and wanted: she was convinced if she could just prove to him how much she loved him, she'd be able to fix him.

Gracie was your mother's responsibility, Tom says. *She's the one who should've saved her. She's the one who put her in jeopardy in the first place.*

But I was her big sister: it was my job to look out for her.

I left her behind.

She was just four years old.

Stacey Porter: (No Subject).

My thumb hovers over the subject line. I understand now what Marilla meant when she said, *I need to atone.*

My secretary buzzes in my next patient, and I put my phone away, the email unread.

I pull up the patient's chart on my computer. She's a fifty-two-year-old woman who came to me five months ago complaining of dizziness and shortness of breath, neither of which were surprising given she was at least forty pounds overweight. Unlike many of my colleagues, I don't see obesity as a moral failing. But as a heart surgeon I know there's no such thing as *fat but fit* either. Healthy obesity is a myth propagated by a laudable body positivity culture that's unfortunately missing the point: fitness is the body's ability – and specifically the ability of lean tissue, or muscle – to take in and use oxygen. Which means it's really all about your heart and lungs. You may get away with those extra rolls around your waist at thirty, but by fifty, your heart is exhausted from all the extra work it has to do.

The first time this patient came to me, I told her to come back when she'd lost three stone. She cried, and complained to the hospital she'd been 'fat-shamed'. And then she went home and lost the weight.

I tell my patient that I'm proud of her, and ask my secretary to schedule her surgery. She's my last appointment of the day: for once I'm only running a few minutes late. I'll be home in time to have dinner with Tom and the children.

'Liz,' I say, putting my head around the door to my waiting room, 'what date was that board meeting with the trustees again?'

'The eleventh,' she says. 'And there's someone here to see you, Ms Lennox. She doesn't have an appointment. I told her you were busy, but she insisted she'd wait—'

'It won't take long,' Harper says, rising to her feet.

I'm not even slightly surprised to see the woman at my hospital. She clearly has issues with boundaries, as she proved when she gatecrashed my gala.

'Thanks, Liz,' I tell my secretary. 'You can go home now. I've got this.'

Harper follows me into my office. I shut the door, and take my seat behind my desk. She has no choice but to sit opposite me in one of my patients' chairs: deliberately lower, so the occupant has no choice but to look up to me. It has nothing to do with ego: it's an effective psychological trick, because a patient who respects their surgeon is more likely to do as they say pre- and post-op and thus achieve a better surgical outcome.

I've been waiting for this shoe to drop since we told the Conways the sale was off. She'll have gone to Tom first, and he'll have given her tea and sympathy and *there'll be other houses*. It was only a matter of time before she came to me.

'I assume this is about the house,' I say.

'Our *forever home*,' Harper says, pressing both hands to her heart. 'Kyle and me feel like the bottom's *literally* fallen out of our world—'

'You can drop the act, Harper. There aren't any cameras here.'

She hesitates a moment, and then suddenly her face transforms from vapid to shrewd like someone's shaken an Etch A Sketch.

'Look, we've got a contract with our sponsors,' she says briskly. 'This move has got to happen ASAP or we're going to go broke, and I know you're not going to sell to us unless you get the Glass House.'

'And you've figured out a way to make that happen.'

'Yes,' she says. 'I have.'

Inside the mind of a psychopath | *Original Air Date 9 July*

The transcript below has been lightly edited for length and clarity.

Let's get back to the Glass House Murders, because I know that's why you're really here.

Well, I take issue with whether any of them were actually *murders*, but we'll come back to that.

You want the gory details, don't you? You want to climb inside my mind and know what it's like to break the ultimate taboo: to kill another human being.

I'm not going to judge you for that.

It's fascinating to engage with our deviant capabilities and watch what human beings are willing to do when morality's taken out of the equation, isn't it?

And trust me, we're *all* capable of killing someone.

You know that as well as I do. It's why you're addicted to true crime television and murder mysteries: you're fascinated by your own dark side. Watching *The Ted Bundy Tapes* is like driving past a car crash: hard to look at, but even harder to look away.

Come on, admit it. You get a secret thrill when you're driving down the motorway and you see flashing lights and ambulances on the other side of the crash barrier. You hate yourself for it, but it doesn't stop you slowing to a crawl so you can get a good look, just in case there's a bloody corpse sprawled across all that twisted metal.

Bizarre, isn't it? I don't suppose many of you actually get off on crime scene photos, but you still crane your neck looking for gore. Because it's *cathartic*.

There but for the grace of God.

And you're here for the same reason.

I look like one of you, don't I? Even now you're asking yourselves how someone like me could have done something like *that*.

Being here, listening to me, is like interacting with your darkest thoughts, the ones you usually do your best to ignore. Because society tells you they're taboo, which only makes them more exciting.

You know the ones I'm talking about.

But that nagging little voice at the back of your head, your *conscience*, makes you shy away from the very idea almost as soon as it takes shape.

Honestly, I don't know how you neuro-typicals manage. It must be like having tinnitus or one of those ear-worm songs you can't get out of your head.

But when you watch a slasher movie, or read a novel about a serial killer, you finally get to indulge the greedy, voyeuristic parts of your soul you like to pretend aren't there.

And you know what? It's *good* for you.

Seriously. A nice juicy murder-by-proxy gives you a hearty adrenaline rush from the comfort of your own home. It's the same buzz you get when you ride a roller-coaster.

It's evolution looking out for you. Back on the plains of the Serengeti, you needed to kick things into high gear the moment you sensed a threat. So your body would release adrenaline, which increased your heart rate and respiration and sent oxygen and energy to your muscles to ready you for fight or flight.

These days we don't often have to worry about sabre-toothed tigers or sharks or poisonous vipers – well, not unless we go into politics.

[Laughter]

The stresses *we* face are whether we can make the rent this month, or if we're going to hang onto our job.

But our bodies haven't evolved to keep up and so they still go into adrenal overdrive if we perceive a threat, real or not. Your survival instinct isn't able to do what it was designed to. Which means now

141

and again we need to give our bodies a reboot and really *feel* the fear.

That's why you enjoy stories about serial killers. It's not because you're sick people. You're wired to feel this way. It's natural to experience a vicarious close call and, well, *survive*.

Why am I telling you all this?

Because I want you to know it's OK that you're getting off just a little bit by being in this room with me. It's even OK for you to *like* me. I won't tell.

[Laughter]

I told you, I'm one of the *good* ones. If I do something bad you can be sure it's for a very good reason.

Sometimes you have to cut out a cancer to save the patient.

Don't think about the lives I took.

Think about the ones I *saved*.

chapter 27

millie

I always sleep well: one of the benefits of being a doctor and years of working on-call. But Tom and the children know not to wake me before my alarm goes off when I'm operating the next day: the house had better be burning to the ground if you're going to disturb me.

So when Tom shakes me awake in the grey light of dawn, I know it's serious.

'You need to get up,' he says.

'Are the kids OK?'

'They're not hurt, if that's what you mean.'

'What time is it?' I ask.

'Five-thirty.'

I get out of bed and grab an old pair of clean scrubs from the stack in my wardrobe, my go-to attire when time is short. 'What's going on?'

'Jesus. You didn't hear the hammering at the front door?'

'Obviously not.'

Tom sighs. 'Just hurry up and get dressed.'

I pull on my scrubs and follow him downstairs. The front door is open: standing in the street outside is our elderly neighbour from across the road, Mr Maxwell. Marshall. Something like that.

He has his arm around our son.

'Why are you out of bed?' I ask Peter. 'Why are you *dressed*?'

'Mr Mitchell was disturbed by a noise in his kitchen this morning,' Tom says, his tone preternaturally calm. Only I can see the muscle working at the corner of his jaw that signifies how angry he is. 'When he came downstairs, he found Peter going through his fridge.'

Peter ducks his head, looking suitably contrite. It's an act, of course, but a convincing one.

'You broke into Mr Marshall's house?' I demand.

'It's Mr *Mitchell*,' the man says, apologetically.

'I woke up early and I couldn't find Pumpkin,' Peter says innocently. 'I was worried about her, so I went outside to look for her. And I saw her go into Mr Mitchell's house so I went to rescue her. The kitchen window was open,' he adds. 'I didn't *break* in.'

He's so full of shit.

The only time he bothers with Meddie's cat is when he wants to torment her. I know exactly why he broke into the man's house: like mother, like son.

But Peter is *ten*.

'You thought the cat was in the fridge?' I ask sardonically.

'I was looking to see if there was any cream,' Peter says. 'I thought Pumpkin might come out from wherever she was hiding if I put some out for her.'

'I'm sure the boy didn't mean any harm,' Mr Mitchell says, releasing Peter.

Tom clamps his arm around our son's shoulder and pulls him close. 'I can't apologise enough for Peter's behaviour,' he says. 'We're so grateful to you for bringing him back safely, Mr Mitchell, and for not taking this any further. I promise you, we'll be having a serious talk with our son once we've all got some sleep. You'd better apologise to Mr Mitchell, Peter,' he adds. 'You must have given him the fright of his life. And we'll be thinking of ways our boy can make this up to you, Mr Mitchell. I'm sure he'd be happy to do your weeding for the rest of the summer, for a start.'

'I don't think there's any need for—'

'Tom's right,' I say. 'Peter has to learn actions have consequences.'

'I'm just glad the boy's all right,' Mr Mitchell says. 'I wouldn't want any child of mine wandering the streets in the middle of the night.'

'I'm really sorry, Mr Mitchell,' Peter says, eyes wide. 'I didn't mean to scare you.'

Oh, but he *did*.

'All's well that ends well,' our neighbour says cheerfully. 'I shouldn't have left that window open in the first place. Invitation to burglars. Lesson learned. I'm lucky it was you and not an axe-murderer, eh, Peter?'

Tom apologises to the man again, and closes the door.

'Get to bed,' he tells Peter through gritted teeth.

Peter bounces up the stairs, a shit-eating grin on his face. He's still on an adrenaline high, too buzzed to give a damn about the trouble he's in.

Despite what I've just said, I know it doesn't matter how we punish Peter: he'll never learn *actions have consequences*. When most children do something that makes their parents sad or angry, they observe that reaction and feel bad about it: it's how they learn to feel guilt. But Peter has zero regard for the feelings of others and is therefore unable to internalise social emotions like shame.

The only thing he'll learn from this is that he can get away with it.

Tom goes into the kitchen and puts a coffee pod into the machine. 'Unbelievable,' he says tightly.

'How d'you want to handle it?' I ask.

'Ground him. Take away his phone. Handcuff him to the bed.' He lifts his hands. 'Jesus, I don't know.'

'Grounding him's the worst thing we can do,' I say.

'Then what do you suggest?'

'I don't have all the answers, Tom.'

'We're lucky it was Mitchell's place he broke into,' Tom says. 'He's a decent man. If it'd been anyone else's home we'd be in trouble. It's a good thing we lost out on that Glass House, Millie. I told you, Peter needs stability. The last thing we should do is uproot him now.'

I throw Tom's coffee pod in the recycling bin and insert a new one for myself.

'It doesn't matter if we stay here or move to Timbuktu,' I say. 'Peter isn't going to change. He can't help it. It's just the way he's wired.'

'Bullshit! It's nothing to do with the way he's *wired*, Millie! Stop making excuses for him. The only reason our son is breaking into people's houses is because he thinks he can get away with it!'

'It's not his fault if he's inherited—'

'Christ, Millie!' Tom explodes. 'Enough with the psycho shit! You had a shitty childhood and shitty parents, that's all! So, you have baggage. What's Peter's excuse?'

He doesn't wait for an answer. I watch him as he storms out of the kitchen, slopping coffee from his mug onto the pale wood floor as he goes. Automatically I pick up a sponge and mop the spills before they stain.

Tom may refuse to face it, but I can't hide from the truth any longer. Whatever small seed of darkness there is in me has rioted uncontrollably in my son like Japanese knotweed.

I'm torn between protecting him and protecting the world *from* him.

And I'm coming to the dreadful realisation I can't do both.

146

chapter 28

millie

There's only one place I feel safe. In control. One place where I know who I am: where *being* who I am is a good thing, not a bad one.

The patient on my table is in his mid-sixties, a Catholic priest who was more afraid of dying when we met for his consult than one would expect, given his calling. An arterial switch operation is complex, but it's a surgery I've done many times. I don't expect any complications.

I start to cut. The familiar procedure is as soothing as a meditation: first expose the aorta and pulmonary arteries, and perform multiple cardiovascular cannulations in order to initiate a cardiopulmonary bypass. Transect the arteries and resect them together with a small patch of aorta. Implant the coronary arteries to the neo-aorta, formerly the main pulmonary artery, and switch the transected great vessels. Then shift the proximal transected pulmonary trunk posterior to the branch pulmonary arteries, and patch the proximal transected aorta at the site of coronary artery explantation. Finally, repair the atrial septal defect via a right atrial incision.

I work swiftly, and we finish ahead of schedule. Changing into a clean pair of scrubs, I head back up to the ICU to check on my patient.

'Let me know if his condition changes,' I tell my registrar.

For the rest of the day, I cut and sew, break ribs, stop and restart hearts, my powers undiminished. Whatever my failings as a mother, I am still God in my operating room.

It's almost nightfall by the time I leave the hospital. Tomorrow will be another long day, starting with a heart transplant on a young athlete with heart failure brought on by dilated cardio-myopathy. A viral infection, probably, though the cause is uncertain. I can do nothing about the monster at home, but here I save lives. *Here*, I am a good person.

A shadow looms out of the darkness as I cross the car park.

'Jesus Christ, Harper,' I exclaim.

'You didn't answer my texts,' she says.

I unlock my car and toss my bag onto the passenger seat. 'You can't keep coming to my place of work like this,' I say.

'It's been almost a week,' she says. 'You told me you'd handle it.'

I roll my shoulders, too tired after a long day on my feet in theatre to play nice in the sandpit. 'Back off, Harper.'

'Do you have any idea how much I've got riding on this?' she cries, grabbing the car door as I get in. 'I pitched the entire new season of our show around this move, Millie! My sponsors will pull the plug if we don't get things back on track. I won't just be homeless, I'll be out of a job!'

I don't like the assertive way she calls me *Millie*, as if we're friends.

'I'll deal with it,' I snap. 'I'll let you know when it's done. Please don't come here again.'

'Let's hope I don't have to,' Harper says.

I watch her in my rearview mirror as I pull away. I neither trust nor like her, though anyone who can build a brand the way she's done deserves respect. And the information she gave me about Felix may still prove useful. But I already regret

148

getting into bed with her on this. The disconnect between her vlog persona and the woman waiting for me in the dark in the car park is disturbing. Her Instagram life is no more unreal than that of any other influencer who shows you only the bright, shiny bits of their Photoshopped life: frankly, if you're foolish enough to believe it's real, you deserve to be duped.

But Harper's emotions are too close to the surface. She's brittle and impulsive and unpredictable, and that makes her dangerous.

I pull up Stacey's unanswered email from my inbox. OK, I type, before I can change my mind. I'll do it.

kyperlife

harper admits she's not OK

Wow, Kyper Nation! We just passed a really awesome milestone! Two million views! It means so *so* much to me, because it's been such a difficult time recently, and knowing you're all there supporting me and sharing my journey – seriously, guys, you just mean the world to me, you're like my family, you know?

This whole situation with me and Kyle has been devastating and I'm super grateful for all your messages and support and all the love. Because sometimes it's really *hard*, you know? There are all these negative voices out there and there are times I just want to run away and hide because I'm only *human*. We're not meant to be breaking each other down, we're meant to be building each other up, that's what KyperLife is about. And I know you guys will use your voices to support each other because your voices are the voices of *truth* and *hope*.

I'm so proud of my Kyper Nation, you're standing up and demanding to be heard and demanding to own the conversation, and you can make a *difference!*

Because when one person speaks their truth, it opens the door for all of us to do the same, and if we listen with an open heart and mind the pain becomes lighter for all of us.

What I've learned from this is, you can't let the haters win. You have to speak out, even if you're nervous about saying the wrong thing, because really the only wrong thing to say is to say nothing, you know? It's not enough to just *survive* something, right? Like, that's not the point of life.

I know what it's like to have someone let you down and trample on your dreams. People make promises and they say they'll do something and then they let you down. They think they can walk away but you have to hold them to account. You can't let them get away with treating you like you don't *matter!*

At a certain point you have to stand up for yourself because no one else can do that for you. You have to take back *control.*

And if that comes with risk, well, there's a lot that's been lost already.

chapter 29

millie

The window is unlocked just as Stacey said it would be.

I glance up at the properties overlooking the pool to the rear of the Glass House. Once I'm certain I'm not being watched, I slide my credit card beneath the window catch and open it an inch.

Tensing, I wait for the scream of the alarm. Stacey said she wouldn't set it, but there's always the possibility Felix did it himself.

The light on the sensor stays green.

I push the window fully open, and climb inside. The inverted layout of the Glass House means the bedrooms are all downstairs; judging from the dirty boxers puddled on the floor and the rats' nest of cables trailing across the desk, I'm in their son's room. I step over a sweaty trainer with its heel ground down, and go out into the hall. Felix's study is at the far end of the corridor. According to Stacey, he keeps it locked twenty-four/seven.

Privacy is one thing: every healthy marriage has its secrets. I've never bought into the notion that husbands and wives should be open books to one another. Who wants to read a novel when you know every twist before it happens and how the story will end? But Stacey says Felix guards his study as if he has a body hidden in there. He locks it even when he goes to the loo.

'It's not Fort Knox,' she said, when she begged me to help her. 'I don't think it'd be difficult to break into his office. But he's been working from home for the last few weeks and there's no way I can get into his study while he's here. If I can come up with a reason to get him out of the house, *you* could be in and out without him ever knowing.'

She had no idea she was tapping into my particular skill set, of course. It was just serendipity.

'What do you need me to find?' I asked.

'The deeds to the house,' Stacey said. 'The bank sent them to us when we paid off the mortgage four years ago, but I don't know what Felix has done with them. I can't sell the house without them.'

'The Land Registry must have a digital copy,' I said.

'We can apply for one but the backlog has been ridiculous ever since Covid. It could take *months*. I need the deeds, Millie,' Stacey said urgently, her hand tightening on mine as she reached across the kitchen island. 'I'll never be able to get away from him if I can't sell the house.'

It takes me less than a minute to break into Felix's office. His study is far messier than I remember from my initial tour of the house. Several lever arch files lie open on the slab of glass that serves as his desk. Others have been hastily and unevenly shoved back into place on the shelves behind it. The wastepaper bin is overflowing, crumpled paper spilling onto the floor. Beside it, a shredder is so full it's jammed. The room looks as if it's been ransacked by MI5. How can a man this controlling in his personal life be so *disorganised*?

I skim the business files on his desk, and then turn my attention to the filing cabinet in the corner. It's unlocked: the top drawer contains an empty bottle of Scotch that rolls towards me with a clang when I open it. The rest is filled with folders from Copper Beech. I rifle through them, but there's nothing personal there.

I'm not worried about getting caught – Stacey's taken Felix and their son to a lunch with friends in Cheltenham, so I have plenty of time – but I don't want to be here any longer than I have to. This is business, not pleasure.

I pick up a painted rock emblazoned with the word *daDdy* in red paint, and toss it idly from hand to hand. If I wanted to hide important documents, where would I put them?

Felix doesn't have a safe. There are no drawers attached to his minimalist glass desk. No other cupboards or cabinets in the room. Where does he keep his pencils and paperclips, for God's sake?

I suddenly spot a navy folder slotted in horizontally along the top of some of the files on a high bookshelf above his desk. Putting the rock down, I reach for it and flip it open. The letterhead on the first page is gilt-embossed: *Lyon Raymond & Lyon*. Harper was right: it's a letter confirming the law firm's retainer to represent Felix in his divorce.

The divorce Stacey knows nothing about.

Harper ran into Felix coming out of the lawyers' office the day Tom and I saw them hugging on the street. If we threaten to tell Stacey about the divorce, she reasoned, Felix might agree to sell the Glass House to me in return for our silence. But first we need proof.

I doubt Felix will be that easily intimidated. But since I'm here anyway, it can't hurt to take copies of the paperwork and give it a shot, just to get Harper off my back.

I'm a little surprised he wants a divorce, to be honest. Abusive, controlling men like him don't usually let their wives out of their clutches. But according to Harper, Stacey has family money. A lot of money: after her brother's death, she inherited her parents' considerable estate. I'm guessing that until now it's been ring-fenced from Felix by a network of trusts, but if they were to get divorced, it's possible the estate would no longer be afforded the same protection. Maybe Felix has reached the point where he wants the money more than he wants her.

I take a picture of the lawyer's letter with my phone and put the folder back on the bookshelf. It's only then I notice a box file casually lying on the windowsill.

Birth certificate, passport, will, car title, house deeds. All of them right there for anyone to find. I take the deeds, and put everything else back. Another couple of minutes, and I'll be out of here.

I flip open Felix's laptop.

There's just one more thing I have to do first.

chapter 30

stacey

The picnic was Millie's idea. She suggested an afternoon at the Hurlingham Club: she and Stacey could bring Peter and Archie; Harper would come with her two little boys. No husbands: that way Felix couldn't object to being excluded.

Stacey isn't sure about Harper Conway. She's only met the girl once, at the charity gala six weeks ago, and Harper got very drunk and didn't exactly cover herself in glory. Stacey's very careful about who she admits to her inner circle: she has to be. She's been stung more than once by 'friends' selling stories about her to the tabloids. And Harper makes a living from social media: there's no such thing as bad publicity for her.

But Millie has vouched for Harper. And the truth is Stacey could use some of the younger woman's lustre rubbing off on her.

The same day she discovered Felix might lose his job, and quite possibly all their money, Stacey learned she was being bumped from the *Morning Express Show* to the breakfast slot instead. The network wanted to go in a different direction, her agent said. They didn't feel she and Brendan had the *right chemistry*.

She's being replaced by the Friday guest presenter, Zee Tobin. Zee is eleven years younger than Stacey and doesn't have a fraction of her experience. She fluffs her lines and asks interviewees *if that makes you sad* and she doesn't poll nearly as well as Stacey with their loyal *Morning Express* viewers: Zee's numbers for relatability and likeability are way below hers. But the girl's TikTok and Instagram followers are ten times bigger and the network's chasing a younger demographic these days.

Zee's also sleeping with Brendan – that must be the *chemistry* the producers were talking about.

The network presented the move as a promotion to the 'prestige' morning slot, but it's clear to everyone she's being shunted sideways. As of September, she'll be getting up at 3.30 a.m. five mornings a week while Zee sleeps in till seven and hoovers up all the lucrative sponsorships that come with hosting a mid-morning magazine show.

Stacey's career isn't over yet: there's a Zoom meeting in the works with an agent in LA to discuss a possible move to one of the US networks. But when she tried to discuss it with Felix, he instantly shut her down. *Are you insane? I'll never get another job if I leave London!*

Millie says she has to free herself from Felix. She says he's an anchor weighing her down.

'We've been lucky with the weather today,' Harper comments now, as they walk past the croquet lawn to the open-air swimming pool. 'The rain last night was insane. It took Kyle forever to get home after the Tube flooded again.'

'That's what happens when you pave over all the front gardens and dig iceberg basements so the water has nowhere to drain,' Millie says.

Peter and Archie run on ahead with Harper's two boys, Tyler and Lucas, and Millie quickens her pace to keep up with them.

'Peter's not a strong swimmer,' she says, switching a straw shopper burdened with towels and sunscreen to the other hand. 'I want to keep an eye on him. You guys can catch me up – I'll grab us some sunloungers.'

Millie's son is a good-looking boy – only to be expected with a mother who looks like Millie. His freckled face is wide and open, and his thatch of thick, honey-coloured hair flops endearingly into long-lashed tawny eyes. Stacey guesses he's going to be a heartbreaker when he's older.

Her own son is in the same school year as Peter, but he looks closer in age to Harper's boys. Pale and gangly. *Thin*. Felix says Archie looks just like he did himself at that age, and her husband has certainly grown into a handsome, if saturnine, man, his face an arresting combination of sharp planes and tight angles. But it's not just the way Archie *looks*. His whole demeanour is that of one of life's victims. He was bullied at Asher Brook Primary and now the same thing's happening at the expensive boarding school in Edinburgh that was supposed to be the making of him. She wishes he had a tenth of Peter Downton's confidence.

She and Harper join Millie by the pool. All four boys have already stripped off and are in the water, shouting and splashing, Peter in the thick of them. He seems like a strong swimmer to Stacey.

She watches Millie's boy haul himself out of the pool and dive-bomb back in, his tanned, muscular limbs in sharp contrast to Archie's feeble spaghetti arms and scrawny white legs. The two young Conway brothers follow Peter's lead, smacking into the water like bowling balls and drenching everything within a ten-foot radius. Only Archie hangs back from the ruckus, doggy-paddling at the shallow end.

'What's *he* doing here?' Millie demands suddenly.

Stacey turns towards the clubhouse. Felix is striding along-side the pool towards them, his formal grey suit – why is he wearing a suit? It's the weekend! – jarringly out of place amid the families in shorts and T-shirts and swimsuits.

Stacey puts her beach bag down on the nearest sunlounger. She deliberately didn't tell her husband where she would be. 'How did you find me?' she asks.

Felix skirts a little girl nerving herself up to jump into the pool. 'Phone,' he says shortly.

'You *tracked* her?' Millie exclaims.

Felix ignores her. 'You didn't pick up when I called,' he tells his wife.

'I'm sorry. I didn't hear my phone—'

He takes her upper arm. 'Never mind that now. I need to talk to you.'

'Get your hands off her!' Millie cries.

Stacey reaches awkwardly for her bag as her husband liter-ally pulls her away from her friends. 'It's fine, honestly. If you could just give Archie a lift home—'

'You fucking thug,' Millie hisses at Felix.

'I don't think you're helping,' Harper mutters.

Millie suddenly lunges forward and grabs Felix's left hand, the one gripping Stacey's arm. With a sharp twist, she snaps his little finger back. There's an audible crack, and Felix bellows in pain and releases his wife.

'Oh, my God!' Harper exclaims, clapping her hand to her mouth as Felix reels backwards. 'I think you broke his finger!'

'Have you *seen* the bruises on her arms?' Millie demands.

There's a sudden commotion on the other side of the pool. People are standing up, pushing back chairs, crying out in alarm. A whistle blows. For a moment, Stacey thinks it's because of the altercation with Felix.

There's a splash as someone dives fully clothed into the water.

And then she sees the small white body floating facedown in the pool.

chapter 31

millie

Harper is the first to react. Kicking off her sandals, she dives fully clothed into the water, covering the width of the pool in a couple of strokes and reaching Archie before the lifeguard has even got near. She clearly knows what she's doing: she approaches him from behind and supports his head cleanly above the surface as she brings him to the edge of the pool where I've run to help. Several other swimmers assist her in lifting the slight boy out onto the concrete.

'She's a doctor,' Harper says, as people crowd around me. 'Give her space.'

Archie isn't breathing.

I check for a pulse, and don't find one. Placing the heel of one hand on the centre of his chest at the nipple line, I start compressions, careful not to crush his ribs. When he still doesn't start breathing, I tilt his head back and lift his chin to open his airway before pinching his nose closed and covering his mouth with mine to create an airtight seal.

People are gasping and sobbing around me. Someone has dialled 999 and calls out that the emergency services are on their way. I give two one-second breaths as I watch for Archie's chest to rise, then thirty more chest compressions before repeating the cycle.

Two breaths. Thirty compressions.

Two breaths. Thirty compressions.

From the corner of my eye, I see Peter climb out of the pool and start to towel himself dry. He watches me compress Archie's chest with interest.

Two breaths. Thirty compressions.

Archie's a poor swimmer. While Peter and Harper's two little boys were larking about in the water, ducking each other and diving in from the side, Archie flailed in the shallows. I don't need to ask how he ended up facedown in the deep end of the pool. It's written all over my son's face.

The storm that's been threatening all summer.

Two breaths. Thirty—

Suddenly Archie coughs back into life, water streaming from his mouth. I roll him over onto his side in the recovery position, his top leg and arm bent to help prop him up, his head still tilted slightly back to keep his airway open. Someone proffers a thick towel, and I wrap it around his shoulders to keep him warm as he starts to go into shock.

Felix kneels beside me on the wet concrete in his expensive suit, fear sharpening his cheekbones to white blades. 'Archie, Dad's here,' he says, touching his son's shoulder. 'You're going to be OK, Archie. I'm here. Everything's going to be OK.'

He strokes his son's wet hair back from his face, his little finger jutting at an unnatural angle from his hand. It's not broken: I only dislocated it.

I glance around, looking for Stacey. She's still standing over by the sunloungers on the other side of the pool, her handbag tucked neatly beneath her arm as if she's at a cocktail party. Shock affects us all differently: I've seen as many people burst into giggles as into tears when I tell them someone they love is dead.

The paramedics arrive, and seeing them suddenly galvanises Stacey into action.

She flies to Archie's side, refusing to let go of his hand as the medics wrap him in blankets and load him onto a stretcher. Felix has to put his arm around her and gently pull her away so the paramedics can do their job.

'They're taking him to the Princess Eugenie,' I tell Stacey. 'That's my hospital. I've texted Lisa Kacer in the ED. She'll make sure whoever takes care of Archie communicates properly with you.'

'I'm afraid only one of you can come in the ambulance,' the paramedic says.

'I'll go,' Stacey tells Felix. 'You can meet me there.'

Someone throws another thick towel around Harper's shoulders as the medics wheel the stretcher back towards the clubhouse. Her wet dress flaps around her legs and she shivers uncontrollably: as much from shock as from the cold.

'Is he going to be OK?' she asks me quietly.

'He should be,' I say. 'He wasn't in the water long. You saved his life acting as quickly as you did.'

'But he wasn't breathing, Millie. Will he have – you know, *brain damage*?' she whispers.

'He's going to be fine,' I say, because it's what she needs to hear.

Tyler and Lucas cling to her, their faces white and frightened.

'Did you see what happened to Archie, boys?' Harper asks. 'Why was he even in the deep end? I didn't think he liked going out of his depth.'

The boys shake their heads, lower lips trembling as they stare at the ground.

She turns to my son. 'What about you, Peter? Did you see?'

His tawny gaze is clear and untroubled as he looks from Harper to me. 'I don't know what happened,' he says. 'I wasn't watching Archie. I was teaching Tyler and Lucas how to do cannonballs and Archie didn't want to play with us. I didn't see anything.'

Together Harper and I pack up our things. The two Conway boys are shaken and quiet, but Peter makes a play out of cheering them up with funny faces and jokes.

'What *happened*?' Harper asks me as I roll up a wet towel.

'Archie must have just got out of his depth—'

'With you and *Felix*,' she says.

I glance at Stacey's husband. He's still standing by the edge of the pool, gazing blankly towards the clubhouse as if transfixed.

'You saw what happened,' I say tightly.

I don't want to talk about it. I don't want to dwell on what just happened, because I'm more shaken by what I did than Felix himself.

Harper drops the towel from her shoulders and hitches her beach bag onto her shoulder as Felix finally breaks out of his trance and strides away.

'You're lucky you just saved his son's life,' she says. 'I know he shouldn't have grabbed Stacey like that, but he could've had you arrested for assault. I honestly thought you were going to kill him.'

'Yes,' I say, watching Felix. 'For a while there, I thought so, too.'

chapter 32

millie

I know better than to discuss what happened at the pool yesterday with Tom, beyond the basic fact of Archie's 'accident'. He's made it clear he doesn't want to hear any *psycho shit* about our son.

Peter is lying on his stomach in front of the television drawing pictures of R2-D2 – we're on a retro *Star Wars* jag – and as I watch him colour, my imagination drifts towards what should be unthinkable. I picture the hands now holding a couple of coloured pencils – hands that still haven't quite lost their baby fat – closing around the throat of a toddler. Pushing a child into the road.

Holding a boy's head beneath the water.

There's something oddly cathartic about letting myself go to the darkest places and considering what it would feel like if my worst fears came true. What I would do. What I *could* do.

I should have stopped him yesterday. I knew he was spoiling for trouble – I could see it in his eyes as we set off for the pool. It's why I ran ahead with the children to keep a watchful eye on him. But I let myself be distracted by Felix, and those few minutes were all it took.

I don't know what happened. I didn't see anything.

If I didn't know better, I'd almost believe him.

My son smiles at me over his shoulder. 'What d'you think?' he asks, holding up his drawing.

'It's very good,' I say, truthfully.

'I think I'll colour it in and give it to Archie,' he says, turning back to his picture. 'To cheer him up after his accident.'

It's as if he had nothing to do with what happened yesterday. It's a miracle Archie didn't drown: our second miracle in a month. Peter only has to be lucky once – we have to be lucky always.

My phone vibrates in my pocket. Meddie is over at a friend's house today, but I still keep my eye on my son as I slide the patio doors open and go outside to take the call, just in case he takes it into his head to microwave the cat.

Dear God, is it always going to be like this?

'Have you heard from Stacey?' Harper asks. 'How's Archie doing?'

'They kept him in overnight, just to be on the safe side, but he's going to be fine,' I say. 'They'll discharge him later this morning, after rounds.'

'Oh, thank God.'

'Thanks to *you*,' I say.

'Tyler had terrible nightmares last night. He woke me up at three in the morning screaming because he thought he was drowning.'

'Well, they've had a shock,' I say, switching my phone to the other ear. 'It's to be expected. The whole thing must have been terrifying for them.'

'He said Peter was holding his head underwater. He was trying to *drown* him.'

Is it my imagination, or is there a subtle edge to her voice?

'I don't suppose any of us slept well,' I say evenly.

'I spoke to Ty and Lucas again this morning,' she adds. 'About what *really* happened to Archie yesterday.'

This time there's nothing subtle about it.

'I don't think anyone realised Archie was so nervous in the

166

water,' I say. 'The other three can all swim like seals. I'd have kept a closer eye if I'd—'

'The boys both said Peter pulled Archie under,' Harper interrupts. 'They say he did it *on purpose.*'

A beat passes.

'They didn't say that yesterday,' I say.

'Because they were too scared to say anything with Peter standing there!'

'I think they're letting their imaginations run away with them,' I say firmly. 'The boys were all horsing around. Archie probably got caught up in the excitement and ended up out of his depth. Like I said, no one realised he couldn't swim very well. Peter might have ducked him a few times, but he'd never hurt him on purpose.'

'Like he didn't hurt his sister, you mean?'

I didn't know Tom had discussed that with her.

'Your husband told me yesterday when I called to see how Peter was coping,' she says, as if reading my mind. 'I'd never have let my boys within three feet of your son if I'd known what he was like.'

'Harper, I don't know what you're trying to imply—'

'Have you spoken to Felix yet?'

I'm taken aback by the sudden change of topic.

And then I realise it's not a change at all.

'Were you expecting me to follow him to the hospital and tackle him as he sat by Archie's bedside?' I ask coolly.

'We have to move out of our house in less than *ten days,*' Harper says.

'Even if the Porters sold me their house tomorrow, it'd still be weeks before—'

'You haven't even *tried*!' she cries, a note of hysteria creeping into her voice. 'We've had to rent a tiny flat so we can be in the right catchment area for Asher Brook before school starts, which is just money down the drain! Houses come onto the market and are sold before we even have a chance to call our agent! And you know how fast property prices are rising – even a month or two off the ladder could put houses in this area out of our reach—'

'What is it you expect me to do, Harper? Break the rest of his fingers one by one until he agrees to sell me the Glass House?'

'Tell him you'll spill the beans about the divorce if he refuses to sell you the house.'

'And if he calls my bluff?'

'Sell your house to me anyway. *You* rent a place.'

I laugh. 'You know I'm not going to do that.'

'So talk to Felix!'

I pull a couple of weeds from the raised flowerbed by the silver birch. 'Look, Harper. Honestly? It's not going to make a difference. He's not going to care. Stacey will find out about the divorce soon anyway. The only reason I haven't warned her myself is because I didn't get a chance with everything that happened yesterday.'

'So you're just going to give up?' she demands. 'What am I supposed to do? Where am I supposed to *live*?'

'You'll find somewhere else. Be patient. Houses around here are coming onto the market all the time—'

'I don't have time to be patient!'

I toss the weeds onto the small compost pile in the corner. 'Well, you don't have a choice, Harper,' I say, exasperated.

There's a long silence. For a moment, I think she's hung up on me.

'I could tell Stacey what Peter did to her son,' she says finally. 'She'd never sell you the Glass House then.'

'Oh, Harper,' I say. 'I really wouldn't threaten me if I were you.'

chapter 33

millie

Four days after Archie's accident, Stacey turns up at our house at seven in the morning with a black eye.

'Jesus Christ,' Tom says, when she walks into the kitchen behind me. 'What on earth happened to you?'

'That fucking bastard,' I hiss.

Even Tom can't ignore *this*.

He pulls out a stool at the kitchen island and motions to her to sit down. 'What can I get you?' he asks. 'Tea? Coffee? Or would you prefer something stronger?'

'It's seven a.m.,' I say.

'Coffee,' Stacey says. 'Thank you.'

'Let me take a look at your eye,' I say.

'It's worse than it looks—'

'I need to examine you properly, Stacey. He could've fractured your cheekbone.'

Gently, I palpate the area around her eye socket. A periorbital haematoma – a black eye – is caused when blunt force or trauma results in burst capillaries and subsequent haemorrhaging. The fatty tissues around the eye are soft and bruise easily when compressed against margins of bone which surround and protect the eye socket, and fluid tracks forward into the eyelid and quickly accumulates – hence the rapid swelling after an injury. As the blood decomposes and is resorbed, various pigments are released, which is what causes the lurid discolouration of a shiner.

Judging from the vivid blue and purple bruising, I'd say Stacey was hit sometime within the last twelve hours, probably late last night.

I fetch the pencil torch from my medical bag and shine it in her eyes to see if her pupils are dilating normally.

'Can you follow my finger with your eyes?' I ask.

I move my index finger from left to right, then up and down and diagonally across her field of vision. Her left eyelid is badly swollen, her eye narrowed to a tiny slit, but she manages to follow the tip of my finger.

'I don't think you have a fracture,' I say, returning my torch to my bag. 'And your vision seems normal. Once the swelling goes down in a day or two, you'll be able to cover the bruising with make-up, but you're going to have a black eye for at least a week, maybe more.'

Tom places her coffee in front of her. 'Is this Felix's handiwork?' he asks.

She looks away. We both take her silence as assent.

'You need to report him to the police, Stacey,' Tom says. 'Not just for your sake, but for Archie's.'

'He'd never hurt Archie,' Stacey says quickly.

'Until Archie fights back,' I tell her. 'You're his mother. Sooner or later, Archie's going to try to defend you, and then Felix will turn on him, too.'

I see my father's hands around my mother's throat, the vision so vivid the blood pounds in my head and my palms are suddenly damp.

With an effort, I blink the image away.

I don't want Stacey to feel pressured, but Felix has already broken the primary rule of the middle-class abuser by hitting

170

her in the face, where she can't hide the bruises. Whatever parameters they may have established in their dysfunctional marriage, they clearly no longer hold good. His attacks are escalating. Things could spiral out of control very quickly.

I should know.

'Where's Archie now?' Tom asks.

'Felix's mother, Frances, picked him up yesterday and took him back to Devon with her for a few days,' Stacey says. 'He loves staying with her. And we thought a change of scene would do him good after his accident. He's been so quiet and withdrawn since he got home. I don't know what's going on with him.'

I could hazard a guess, but now isn't the time to discuss Peter's role in what happened at the pool.

'You can't go back home while Felix is still there,' I tell her. 'It's not safe. You can stay here with us till we figure out your next move.'

'That's kind of you, Millie, but I don't want to put you out. You've done enough.'

'You're not putting us out. We *want* to help.'

'At least promise us you won't go home on your own,' Tom adds. 'If you need to get some things, I'll come with you.'

I throw a grateful look at my husband. We may not always be on the same page, but when push comes to shove we're on the same side.

I expect Stacey to argue the point, but to my surprise she acquiesces. 'I'm due some leave,' she says. 'I can't go into work looking like this anyway. But there's no need to go back home: I always keep a holdall with a few days' clothes in the car, in case I'm sent on a story. I could go and stay with a friend of mine in Exeter for a few days. She lives not too far from Felix's mother, so I'd be close to Archie, too.'

'We need to document your injuries first,' I say, getting out my phone.

'I'm not going to report it, Millie. I can't do that to Archie.'

'You need to report it *for* Archie.'

She won't. My mother never did either. Fewer than one in five incidents of domestic abuse are ever reported to the police. On average, a woman experiences more than *fifty* violent assaults at her partner's hands before getting effective help.

Every year in England and Wales there are over a million calls to the police to report domestic violence – which means there are another four million attacks going unreported. And even if Stacey were to go to the police, she'd probably change her mind later and refuse to press charges. Most abused women do. Even the rich and famous ones.

The last time my father hit my mother, he nearly killed her. If I hadn't taken care of things when I did, the next time he would have done.

My phone suddenly vibrates in my hand with a text.

'I have to go,' I say. 'Major incident on the M25. All hands on deck. I already have a blunt chest trauma en route to the hospital.'

'What about Peter?' Tom exclaims. 'I've got a meeting in Covent Garden at nine. You said you'd be home till noon today.'

I knock back my scalding coffee, burning my tongue. 'You'll have to take him with you. We can't leave him on his own.'

'I can't take a ten-year-old to a client meeting!'

'Why don't I stay here and keep an eye on him?' Stacey suggests.

'We couldn't ask you to do that,' Tom says.

'Why not? I don't have anywhere to be for the next couple of hours.' She touches her swelling eye. 'I can't go out in public looking like this. And it's the least I can do after all you've done for me.'

Archie is safely far away in Devon, and I don't imagine

172

Peter will try anything with an adult. And yet some instinct is warning me: *danger! danger!* Predators can always scent blood in the water. Stacey is vulnerable. And Peter's not a normal ten-year-old.

'Well, if you're sure,' Tom says, before I can object. 'I won't be long. The lazy sod will probably still be asleep when I get back. If he wakes up, you can just plug him into a screen.'

My phone vibrates with another text. I need to get to the hospital. Lives are in the balance.

And so I tell myself Stacey will be fine.

chapter 34

tom

I don't know what the hell is going on with Felix and Stacey Porter, but I'm fed up with their domestic drama washing up on my doorstep. My wife certainly knows which side *she's* on, but right now I'm not sure if Stacey's victim or villain.

It's hard to argue with a black eye – except Felix was sporting one himself last time we met. It makes me wonder if the Porters are one of those couples who get off on violent sex. Maybe all this is consensual. In which case Stacey Porter is deliberately misleading my wife, and I need to know why.

I'm not worried about leaving Peter with the woman either way. My son can more than take care of himself.

As soon as I've wrapped up my meeting in Covent Garden, I text Felix. To my surprise, he agrees to see me within the hour, which only makes me more bloody worried.

At his suggestion, we meet at the park in Fulham halfway between our houses. He's already there by the time I arrive, standing by the gate waiting for me. It's a miserable fucking day, gloomy and overcast: the kind of dreary August weather I remember from my childhood, before climate change was a twinkle in anyone's eye. Felix is wrapped up in a thick jacket, his shoulders hunched against the damp chill coming off the river. It makes him look like the brooding hero of a Brontë novel.

We fall into step and walk along the Embankment in silence for a few minutes. The tide is out, and there's a dank, rotten smell in the air. Felix's hands are thrust deep into the pockets of his jacket. I wish I'd thought to wear something warmer myself.

'It's not what it looks like,' Felix says finally.

'And what's that?'

'I didn't hit my wife.'

'That's not what she's told *my* wife.'

Felix stops and turns towards the river, gazing down at a tugboat churning slowly upriver through the brown water. 'I don't expect you to believe me.'

'I don't know what to believe,' I tell Felix frankly. 'Stacey turned up at my house this morning with a black eye. Why would she tell my wife you're hitting her if you're not?'

A muscle works at the side of his jaw, but he says nothing.

'You need to tell me what's really going on,' I urge. 'Millie's on the warpath, and trust me, mate, once she gets her teeth into something, she doesn't let go. If your wife's playing some kind of sick game with her, I need to know.'

'She should get as far away from Stacey as possible,' Felix says baldly.

I shiver. The damp from the river must be getting to me.

'What does that mean?' I ask.

'Stacey's like a Venus flytrap,' he says, his tone bitter. 'She likes fucking with people. She lures you in, and by the time you realise what's happening, it's too late.'

'How did she get that black eye, Felix?' I ask quietly.

He hunches his shoulders deeper into his jacket.

'It's what she *wants*,' he says abruptly. 'She likes me to choke

175

her when we . . . when we have sex. Until she almost passes out. She likes it rough. I mean really *rough*, Tom.' His voice thickens with shame. 'She creates these . . . these *fantasies* for us to act out. I have to attack her. Pretend to rape her. She makes me hit her.' He looks away again. 'It makes me sick to my stomach.'

I have no idea what to say, so I say nothing.

He turns from the river, and the two of us resume walking along the Embankment. He doesn't speak again for quite a while.

'It didn't start out like this,' he says finally. 'She was only twenty-four when I met her. She told me she was into a bit of S&M, bondage, that sort of thing, but who doesn't experiment at that age? I found it erotic at first: you know, a little bit of spanking, a pair of fluffy handcuffs. My first wife didn't like sex at all – at least, not sex with *me*. Sex with Stacey was exciting.'

I really don't need to hear this. 'Look, you don't have to tell me if you—'

'God, it's a relief to talk about it,' Felix says, his voice raw. 'I've never told anyone before.'

River water laps at the wall below us as a boat goes past, and a pair of seagulls wheel overhead. In the distance, a police siren blares. I've got no idea what to say to Felix: I barely know the bloke, but maybe that's why he feels he can talk to me.

'Things changed after we got married,' Felix says. 'It took more and more to . . . you know. *Satisfy* her. In bed. It stopped being erotic or fun for me. I started to say no. We went months where we hardly had sex at all.'

For a long moment, I think he's done talking. We walk along the pavement in silence for a while, pausing only to allow a group of teenage boys pushing and laughing and shoving at each other to go past.

'After Archie was born, things started to escalate,' he says at last. 'It didn't happen all at once, Tom. At first she'd just throw plates, or punch the wall. But one day instead of hitting the wall, she hit me instead. She cried afterwards and told me it'd never happen again, but of course it did. Things got worse after Archie went to boarding school. Once she even broke a wine bottle over my head, and I ended up in hospital with concussion.'

'*She* hits *you*?'

'I don't expect you to believe me,' he says again.

The #MeToo movement is all about believing the woman. But surely it should be about believing the *victim*.

What if Stacey's the aggressor? What if *Felix* is the one being abused?

A decade ago, I wouldn't have considered it even a possibility, but two years ago I worked on cybersecurity for a men's rights campaign group: it blew my mind when I found out a third of all victims of domestic abuse are male. According to the government's own statistics, three-quarters of a million men are attacked by their partners every year, and twelve are *killed* by them. But no man wants to admit he's been beaten up by a *girl*.

The scratches on Felix's forearms: what if they were *defensive* wounds?

I know better than to ask him why he doesn't leave her if what he says is true. He could give me a list of excuses, but at the end of the day he stays for the same reason Millie's mother stayed, for the same reason *all* abuse victims stay.

Deep down, they think they deserve what they get.

Felix stops walking and turns to face me, digging his hands even deeper into his pockets. 'I thought if I tried to give her what she wanted in bed, it'd help with her . . . frustration,' he says. 'But it's like she's passed the point of no return. The attacks are getting worse. It's as if she's been holding herself in check all this time and now she can't stop. Doesn't *want* to stop.'

'Jesus Christ, Felix. And you haven't talked about it? With *any*one?'

'We saw a marriage counsellor together a couple of times, but I was too ashamed to tell her what was really going on. The woman said we needed to visit her separately to break the *cycle of codependency*. Stacey wouldn't agree to that, and I couldn't see any point doing it on my own.' He lets out a harsh bark of laughter. 'Proves the woman's point, I suppose.'

'You can't go on like this, Felix,' I say urgently. 'You have a kid. You both need to get your shit together for his sake. Surely Stacey must realise this . . . your relationship . . . she must know it isn't normal?'

'She does, but she thinks it's part of what keeps us together.' His eyes are shadowed. 'She's got this idea we have some sort of shared sickness, and if we cure it, it'll destroy us.' He shrugs. 'Maybe she's right. I mean, it's not abuse, not really. Not if I *let* her do it.'

'Bullshit,' I say succinctly.

'Perhaps it's my fault, Tom. If I'd stood up to her when it first started—'

'Felix, this is *not* your fault.' I put my hand on his shoulder. 'You have to leave her. This isn't going to get better. Vinegar doesn't turn into wine.'

'I went to see a lawyer a few weeks ago,' Felix admits. 'But then the shit hit the fan at Copper Beech, and I've been too busy trying to salvage what I can for my investors before the company goes belly up.'

A nasty thought suddenly occurs to me. 'You said things have been like this between you and Stacey for years,' I say. 'No one's ever guessed?'

His mouth twists. 'No. We're the perfect power couple. Everyone wants to be us, hadn't you heard?'

'So what's changed?' I ask warily. 'Why is she suddenly involving my wife?'

'I don't know, Tom. But Stacey never does anything without good reason. If I were you, I'd be worried.' He looks directly at me. '*Very* worried.'

chapter 35

millie

'He's obviously *lying*,' I exclaim. 'His wife turned up at our house this morning with a black eye! What else is he going to say – she walked into a door?'

'Millie, I wish you'd just listen to what I'm trying to tell you,' Tom says with a heavy sigh. 'I'm not saying I believe Felix, although I've got to say he was pretty convincing. But we don't know what's really going on between him and Stacey behind closed doors: that's the *point*. They could both be lying, or they could both be telling the truth – some version of it, anyway. And I'm not asking you to stop being friends with Stacey. All I'm asking is that you don't take everything she says as gospel, that's all. At least accept her truth may not be *his*.'

I open the fridge and take out a head of celery, slamming it onto the cutting board. 'I can't believe you went to see him,' I say furiously. 'A woman seeks refuge at our house, and your response is to go and ask her abuser how he feels about it!'

'I didn't realise MeToo meant men are no longer entitled to a fair hearing.'

'Don't be glib.'

'I'm not being *glib*. I'm serious, Millie. Has it never occurred to you to wonder why a woman you barely know is suddenly sharing the darkest secrets of her marriage with you?'

'Right back at you, Tom,' I retort. 'You hardly know Felix, and suddenly he's spilling his soul about his—' I pause to draw ironic air-quotes, '—secret shame?'

'Yes, but he's not treating me like we're soul sisters! He only told me because he's worried about you. Come on, Millie. You viewed Stacey's house *twice*, and next thing you're off to lunch and yoga practice together and before you know it she's your BFF. That doesn't strike you as *odd*?'

'No more odd than the woman who viewed *our* house buying *you* expensive linen shirts,' I say tartly.

Tom has the grace to look uncomfortable. I have a feeling that whatever was going on with him and Harper may have withered on the vine: he's stopped mentioning her name, and the last time I checked his phone – he's restored Meddie's birthday as his password – the only suspicious texts were the ones between him and Felix.

I could be wrong, of course.

'Millie, I understand why you're upset.' He puts his hand on my forearm to still my furious chopping, and waits until I've put down the knife and he has my full – if aggrieved – attention. 'I know it can take a woman years to disclose her abuse. I'm not making light of her accusations. But I can't ignore the fact Felix just disclosed to *me*. He insists the only times he's ever hit Stacey have been in a sexual context, and at her instigation. *She*, on the other hand, has attacked him numerous times and put him in hospital with concussion.'

'According to *him*.'

He sighs again. 'Yes, according to him.'

'And you believe him?'

'I believe him, Millie, but even if I'm wrong – *especially* if I'm wrong – there's something very dark going on between him and Stacey either way. I don't want you getting sucked into it.'

I can't believe Tom's allowed himself to be taken in by Felix like this. I'm not naive: it's clear there's something dark and twisty at the heart of the Porters' marriage. Unlike my mother, Stacey has the financial wherewithal to leave her husband and stand on her own two feet, and she has a confidence in herself and her own abilities that only comes from making your own way in the world. My mother had neither. I accept Stacey's reasons for staying with her husband are complex and there's a part of her that *wants* to.

But Felix has taken the tiny kernel of truth in this ambivalence and confected it into something hideous. He's not a *victim*. He's gaslighting my husband. He's plausible and convincing and that makes him dangerous.

'Felix Porter is a controlling, abusive bully,' I snap, picking up the knife again and scraping the chopped celery into a salad bowl. 'I've *seen* how he treats his wife and the way he talks to her. When we were at the Hurlingham, he tracked her phone and then came down there and literally dragged her away from us! Don't tell me *he's* the one being victimised.'

'Millie, we don't know the backstory to that. You're Stacey's friend, so you're seeing Felix through her lens, and she's obviously not objective. Maybe there was a reason he—'

'There's no reason that excuses putting your hands on a woman, Tom!'

He acknowledges the point with another heavy sigh.

'Millie, trust me when I say this is coming from a place of love,' he says. 'But you've never had a female friend before. This isn't the way it works. Nothing about it rings true. It's all too much: inviting you into her inner circle so quickly, taking you to her fancy club, copying your clothes, even your *hair*. She's *mirroring* you. It's what people do when they're trying to connect with you and get inside your head.'

I hadn't noticed the hair, though now Tom mentions it, she

has adopted the same neat chignon I favour. As do a million other women.

I don't need my husband to tell me how inexperienced I am at friendship. And he's right: I did – I do – bask in the warmth of Stacey's attention. But it has nothing to do with flattery. It's about redemption and forgiveness. Tom should know that.

The front door suddenly slams. Moments later, Meddie appears in the kitchen and heads straight over to the fridge without even stopping to take off her backpack. 'There's never anything to eat in this house,' she complains, staring at the packed shelves. 'It's all lettuce and kale and green shit.'

'Dinner will be in less than twenty minutes,' Tom says, ignoring the *green shit*.

Meddie grabs a Babybel from its netting. 'I'm not going to be in for dinner,' she says, peeling off the red wax coating. 'I'm meeting Noah at Nando's.'

'Who's Noah?' Tom asks.

She's already heading back down the hall. 'My boyfriend,' she calls thickly through a mouthful of Edam. 'Mum says it's OK as long as I'm back by nine.'

'She has a *boy*friend?' Tom demands, as the front door slams again.

I shrug. 'He's a friend. He's a boy.'

'She has a boyfriend! She's thirteen!'

'Nearly fourteen,' I correct.

I check on the grilled chicken, and then open a bag of collard greens and start to make an apple-cider and yoghurt dressing for the salad. My chest is tight with anger. Clearly Tom and I are on opposite sides of this divide between the Porters: his willingness to automatically believe the middle-aged, middle-class man makes me almost incandescent with fury. I know, *I know*, Felix is abusing his wife. His attacks are getting more blatant: sooner or later, if someone doesn't stop him, he's going to kill her. Just by giving him airtime and sympathy Tom is enabling him.

My husband hovers at my elbow, getting in my way.

'What?' I snap finally.

'We need to talk about Peter,' he says.

I look up sharply. I can't remember the last time Tom voluntarily raised the subject of our son.

'Well, *Stacey* liked him,' I say, deliberately baiting him. 'She's offered to take him into work and let him sit in the gallery next time she's at the studio.'

'That's kind of her,' Tom says sarcastically.

'She *is* kind.'

A beat falls.

I take an apple from the fruit bowl, and cut it in half. I'm in no mood to let Tom off easily. 'If you think Stacey's so dangerous, why were you so happy to leave our son with her?'

'I didn't say she was dangerous. Don't put words in my mouth, Millie. But if I was a betting man, I'd put my money on Peter anyway.'

The words hang in the air. It's the first time Tom has come close to acknowledging the truth about our son aloud, and the relief of it rolls through me like a wave.

I've barely let Peter out of my sight since Sunday. But in less than two weeks, the school term starts again. The teachers can't watch all the kids all the time. There'll be plenty of opportunities for a boy like Peter. Bunsen burners left unattended. Children walking to school along busy main roads.

Tom refuses to meet my eye. He has an oddly hangdog air.

And then suddenly it hits me.

He *knows*.

He knows what our son is, but he's let me carry the burden

on my own because he's been too much of a coward to acknowledge the truth.

For years I've watched the darkness growing inside our son while Tom's buried his head in the sand, cutting me off at every turn: *it was an accident, Millie. He didn't mean to. He's just a kid.*

How dare he question my judgement when he's spent so long wilfully suspending *his*?

'Felix is *playing* you,' I say abruptly. 'You believe him because he looks and sounds like you. But I'm telling you, Tom, *he's* the bad guy in this scenario.' I slice the apple with quick, angry strokes. 'And I'm going to prove it.'

chapter 36

millie

The malware I introduced into Felix's laptop when I was in his office isn't particularly sophisticated, but it works. A tech expert like Tom would spot the Trojan horse in a nanosecond: there's a slight but perceptible delay when webpages load and a small icon in the corner of the screen that's a dead giveaway.

But Felix isn't looking for it. He's clearly far too preoccupied: he's spent the weekend scrolling through a variety of stock market indices and updates, opening multiple windows on his desktop and shuttling back and forth between them. Thanks to the virus I uploaded, I've been able to watch his every move on my own computer.

I close my laptop and run upstairs to find Meddie. 'I'm just going out for a run,' I say, putting my head around her bedroom door. 'You all right on your own for a couple of hours?'

She pulls one of her AirPods out. 'Where's The Freak?'

'Don't call him that. Your father's taken him to the 9/11 Memorial Exhibition in Earl's Court. They'll be back later this afternoon.'

Meddie grimaces as she plugs her AirPod back in. 'Gross. I bet he gets off on it.'

She's probably right.

It takes me less than twenty minutes to run to the Glass

House. It appears deserted – the blinds are down, and there are no signs of life. But I know Felix is in there: when I check the malware feed on my phone, I see he's still active on his computer. Stacey's staying with her friend in Exeter, so I know he's on his own.

I ring the doorbell, but Felix doesn't come to the door. I give it a few minutes, and try again.

Still nothing. I walk around the side of the house to Felix's office. The blinds are down there, too, and even when I press my face to the glass and cup my hands around my eyes, it's impossible to see inside.

I bang on the window. 'Felix! I know you're in there!'

No response.

'We need to talk,' I shout. 'I'm not going anywhere till you open the door.'

This time, I hear movement and the scrape of his chair on the expensive bamboo flooring. I return to the front of the house, and, a few moments later, the heavy glass door opens.

Felix looks like he hasn't bathed or slept in a week. He's sporting at least two days' worth of grey stubble, and he must have lost ten pounds since I saw him at the Hurlingham Club just seven days ago. The blades of his cheekbones are so sharp they could cut glass.

'Why are you here?' he asks wearily.

'Take a wild guess.'

He sighs, and then steps back with an exaggerated flourish. 'You know the way.'

I head upstairs to the kitchen. It looks exactly as you'd expect the kitchen of a man whose wife has left him to look, down to the pizza boxes littering the kitchen island and the plates and dirty coffee cups piled haphazardly in the sink.

I seat myself at one of the kitchen stools and put my bag on the counter, tamping down my anger and plastering a pleasant expression on my face. Regardless of my skin-crawling antipathy for the man, I have to focus on what I need from this encounter: Felix's agreement to sell me the Glass House. Aside from the fact that it's *my* house, it's also the only way Stacey can be free of him.

'Let's make this easy,' I say cordially. 'I want this house. You need the money. What do I have to do to make it happen?'

Felix lets out a bark of laughter. 'Jesus Christ. You don't give up, do you?'

'Any decent lawyer could ring-fence the proceeds of sale,' I persist. 'You haven't been charged with any crime. Now's the perfect—'

I break off. The expression in Felix's eyes isn't anger or even irritation. It's *pity*.

'What?' I demand.

'You've really drunk the Kool-Aid, haven't you?'

'What's that supposed to mean?'

'It's not me you need to talk to,' Felix says. 'I told your husband: *Stacey's* the one who pulled out of this deal.'

'Really,' I say flatly. 'So you were lying when you said it was *you* who didn't want to sell? Or are you lying to me now?'

'I don't expect you to believe me.'

'You're right about that.'

'She'll never sell this house,' he says. 'You think it's the first time this has happened? She never had any intention of following through. She's *fucking* with you.'

'Did she give herself the black eye, too?'

He has the grace to look away.

'You're nothing but a coward and a bully,' I say coldly. 'Men like you—'

'You know nothing about me,' Felix snaps. 'And you know nothing about our marriage.'

'I know it's sick and twisted as fuck,' I retort.

He closes the space between us, getting right up in my face. I can feel the rage radiating from him, its heat matched only by my own. 'I think you should leave now,' he says dangerously.

I push myself off the stool. 'You don't scare me, Felix.'

'I'm not the one you need to be scared *of.*'

'Let her go. Sell me the house. Take the money and get on with your—'

He seizes my shoulders, taking me by surprise, and I have a sudden, dizzying flashback to the last time a man laid his hands on me.

His arm around my neck, crushing my windpipe. His knee in my back, ready to snap my spine. His breath hot against the back of my neck.

'I've tried to help you,' Felix says. 'Don't you get it? This has nothing to do with the house. *You're* what she wants—'

I wrench myself free, my heart pounding. Felix's face blurs with that of my father and I'm suddenly sixteen again and fighting for my life.

I can't breathe.

Behind Felix, a row of Japanese steel knives glint on the magnetic bar above the stove.

I can't breathe.

I tell myself I didn't come here intending to hurt anyone.

My dark angel knows the truth.

part two

Inside the mind of a psychopath | *Original Air Date 9 July*

The transcript below has been lightly edited for length and clarity.

I have a confession to make: I haven't been *entirely* honest with you.

I know, I know. But cut me a little slack: I wanted us to get to know each other before I hit you with the whole truth. And I think we've developed a bit of a rapport, don't you? Come on, I know you're warming to me.

[Laughter]

Don't feel bad about it. I've gone out of my way to make you like me. And I'm very good at my job. If I'd ever been tried before a jury of my peers, we wouldn't be having this conversation.

First, I want to make it clear: I don't have any deaths on my conscience. Despite what you've heard, *I'm* the wronged party in all of this.

The night of the charity gala, that night when everyone met for the first time, a tragic series of events was set in motion. Until then, you just had six ordinary people linked only by a simple desire to sell their houses.

But something changed for everyone that night. Our lives got tangled together. We became part of each other's stories – with disastrous consequences.

A small quirk of fate, and it could all have turned out so differently. Sometimes all it takes is for the wrong person to cross your path at the wrong time.

I'm not to blame for what happened that autumn. It took a perfect storm of circumstances: every single person involved in the drama played their part.

What if the estate agent had got stuck in traffic the day of the viewing and someone else had got their bid in first?

What if the mortgage broker hadn't listened to her voicemail?

I can see you all sitting there smugly telling yourselves *you'd* never have taken the law into your own hands, no matter what the provocation. You're not capable of killing someone in cold blood, right?

Self-defence, maybe. Or to protect your family.

But never *murder*.

Granted, I was born without the lead boots you call conscience, so when the pressure is on, I can soar far above you.

It might have taken *you* a little longer to shake off the shackles, but you'd have got there in the end. Trust me, your red lines aren't where you *think* they are.

You've no idea what you'd do until you're put to the test. You could find out you're a very different person from the one you've always imagined you are.

Who knows: maybe you'll discover a heroism and self-sacrifice you never expected. One of the things that struck me after 9/11 was the extraordinary bravery and altruism of very ordinary people like the firefighters who kept going up the towers to what they knew was their likely deaths, or the passengers on Flight 93 who forced their doomed plane to crash in an empty Pennsylvania field to save those on the ground.

But there were the *others* too, of course. The people no one likes to talk about.

The opportunists who capitalised on the grief and chaos of the moment by inventing dead fathers and husbands and brothers to claim compensation. The liars who pretended to have crawled out of the wreckage of the towers just to get their fifteen minutes of fame. Thieves who looted Rolex watches from the dead and dying.

So don't pat yourself on the back and tell me you'd have behaved any differently in my shoes. You're as likely to be a villain as a hero.

I'm going to tell you a secret, but first I need you to promise to put aside your assumptions about *right* and *wrong*.

Can you do that?

Can you set aside your prejudices and your biases and be the jury I never had?

I told you right at the beginning I'm one of the good ones. One of the *safe* ones.

Well, that's not strictly true.

chapter 37

tom

We have five days of relative calm after Stacey's sudden appearance on our doorstep before the next crisis hits.

'Fuck me,' I exclaim, when the breaking news alert pops up on my screen.

'Fucking hell!' Millie cries, storming downstairs into my office.

I love my wife in all her moods. But there's something about her volcanic fury that brings out the best in her: she's like an avenging Valkyrie. I find myself responding to the erotic charge she brings into the small space, and my jeans are suddenly uncomfortably tight around the crotch.

'Has something happened?' I ask dryly.

'You've seen the news,' Millie snaps, pointing at my computer screen. 'Still think Felix is the victim here?'

I don't waste my breath trying to defend him. 'I saw it,' I say.

She leans over my shoulder as I scroll down the page, reading the story with me. Felix's former company, Copper Beech Financial, has officially declared bankruptcy. Thousands of low-level employees are now out of work, and they'll have neither redundancy nor pensions to fall back on: it turns out the directors have been plundering the company's pension scheme for years.

What a fucking mess. From the sound of it, Copper Beech has been taking money from new investors and using it to deliver high returns to just enough people to keep the cash rolling in: a Ponzi scheme, in other words. It doesn't matter how many safeguards financial regulators introduce: as soon as you close one loophole, the wolves of Wall Street – or the City – find another. People who invested through managed funds will be protected, but thousands of ordinary savers who invested directly with Copper Beech have probably lost everything.

Millie scoots the cat from the armchair on the other side of my desk and drops into it. 'Stacey's going to be in the centre of this storm,' she says. 'She'll be lucky to hang onto her job.'

'There's no proof yet Felix himself has done anything wrong,' I say.

'Come on,' Millie says scornfully. 'Even *you* can't give him the benefit of the doubt now. He's a director. He's just as liable as the rest of his board. And he's married to the country's most popular TV presenter. She's a *face*. This is going to be huge.'

She's right, of course. Whatever his level of involvement, Felix is going to be the biggest scalp for the media simply by virtue of the woman to whom he's married. And there's no doubt this is going to hurt Stacey badly. Her whole girl-next-door brand is built around her caring about the little guy. The people who've been ruined by Copper Beech are *her* viewers. They tune in to see her fight for them against corporate sharks like Copper Beech. How's it going to look when it turns out she's *married* to one of them?

'Have you talked to Stacey?' I ask.

'Her phone keeps going to voicemail,' Millie says. 'It must be blowing up with calls from the media. She's obviously switched it off.'

'When did you last speak to her, then?'

'What is this, twenty questions?' Millie says irritably.

I wish I knew what was eating her. She hasn't been herself all week. When I got home from the museum last Sunday with Peter, she'd taken a hot shower and gone to bed at five in the afternoon, claiming a headache. She's been unusually quiet since then: distracted and out of sorts. Until today, she hadn't referred to Felix or Stacey or the Glass House once.

I know my wife.

She hasn't just forgotten about them, or moved on. Something's brewing.

'Millie,' I say, 'what's going on?'

'What d'you mean?'

'Have you and Stacey fallen out?'

'Why would you say that?'

'Because five days ago she turned up at our house with a black eye and you were all for reporting Felix to the police, and since then you haven't even mentioned her,' I say, exasperated. 'Has something happened between you two I should know about?'

'Stacey said she was going to stay in Exeter with a friend for a few days,' Millie says evasively. 'I haven't talked to her since then.'

'I wouldn't take it personally. She's had a lot going on,' I say.

'I know,' Millie says.

'I know you don't want to hear this, but have you considered the possibility she's gone back to Felix? She might not want to tell you in case you think she's let you down.'

'She can't have—'

She stops suddenly, looking like she could bite off her tongue.

'What d'you mean?'

'Nothing.'

'Millie,' I say. 'There's no such thing as *nothing* with you.'

198

She won't look me in the eye. I know if I ask, *if I ask,* she'll tell me.

It's the closest I've come to breaking the golden rule that's kept us safe all these years: our marriage works precisely because so much of what binds us together is left unsaid.

What did you do, Millie?

If I ask, it'll change everything.

Millie, what did you do?

chapter 38

millie

A hand suddenly grabs my shoulder and I turn, expecting to find a journalist thrusting a camera in my face.

It takes me a moment to recognise the woman behind me as Harper. Her hair is caught back in a messy ponytail, and without a scrap of make-up she looks almost as young and vulnerable as Meddie.

'What are you doing here?' I ask, shaking her off.

'Where is he?'

'Felix? I've no idea,' I say.

'You must know!' Harper cries. 'You have to tell me!'

I glance across the road. At least a dozen journalists and photographers are camped on the narrow pavement outside the Glass House. Even as we watch, a Sky News van arrives and kerb-crawls down the street, looking for somewhere to park. The house has an oddly abandoned air: all the blinds are up, and the letterbox is jammed with junk mail. It's clear no one's home. It looks deserted, as if no one's lived in it for years.

I don't know what I was thinking coming here again.

A couple of snappers recognise Harper and start to take photos. We're attracting way too much attention.

I grasp the girl's arm and propel her past the journalists and down the road to my car. 'Get in,' I say.

She climbs into the Audi and pulls her knees up to her chest, wrapping her arms around them like a small child. I want to tell her to keep her thick-soled white trainers off my nappa leather, but even I can appreciate now's not the time.

'You invested money with Copper Beech?' I ask, hazarding a guess.

She nods.

'When?'

'A few days after I ran into Felix outside the divorce lawyer's office,' she admits, her chin pressed to her knees. 'When I heard he'd pulled out of the sale. I called and told him we needed the house move to go ahead or our sponsors would ditch us. He knew we had a cashflow problem. He said he could help!'

'You blackmailed him,' I say flatly.

'He said it was safe! He said everyone put their money in Copper Beech! We'd make at least ten percent in less than three months!'

Ruthless bastard. Felix already knew the company was in trouble at that point: it's why he pulled out of the house sale just a couple of days later. Which means he was also well aware Harper would almost certainly lose any money she invested with him. He probably figured she deserved it for trying to screw him over in the first place.

I sigh. 'How much did you give him?'

'Me and Kyle had a hundred and fifty thousand in our joint savings account. It was only getting one percent interest where it was. It seemed like a smart thing to do!'

'Does Kyle know?'

She shakes her head.

'You may get lucky,' I say. 'They'll probably recover some of the funds. Maybe not all of it, but—'

'We got the money through from selling our house two

201

weeks ago,' she says, her voice a whisper. 'I gave Felix that, too. All of it. I gave him everything.'

'Jesus, Harper! What were you *thinking*?'

She raises her white face to me. 'That's why I have to find him. It could take years for creditors to get paid and even then they won't get all of their money back. But if I can find him, if I can *talk* to him – he can't have spent it yet!'

I glance in my rearview mirror at the knot of reporters outside the Glass House.

The crowd is growing as news of the company's collapse spreads; it's not just photographers and journalists now, but a far sadder and more desperate demographic: ordinary people like Harper who've woken up to the realisation that every penny they've saved for their retirement, to buy their first house, to put their kids through college – it's all gone.

Harper abruptly drops her feet to the floor of the car. 'He *knew*, didn't he?' she says. 'He knew the company was going bankrupt when he took our money!'

Even though this is a mess entirely of her own making, I can't help but feel sorry for her. When the Porters broke our housing chain, I didn't tell Harper about the issues with Copper Beech at Stacey's specific request, because she was worried about the legal implications of sharing insider information with me. There was no reason for me to tell Harper why the Porters had pulled out anyway – I couldn't have known she'd try to blackmail Felix and get caught up in the Copper Beech collapse. But she's just a *kid*. I should have looked out for her.

'What about Stacey?' Harper says. 'Did she know too?'

'No,' I say firmly.

Stacey knew the company was in trouble, of course, but I'm sure she had no idea about the ransacked pension fund. She wouldn't have stood by and allowed Felix to defraud ordinary hardworking people.

'You need to talk to a lawyer,' I tell Harper. 'See if there's any way you can claw some of this money back. It's only been, what, a fortnight since you gave him the money from the sale of your house? It may just be sitting frozen in an account somewhere—'

'I'm going to kill him,' she cries suddenly.

I snap on the child locks from my side of the car. 'No, you're not,' I say.

'Unlock the door, Millie!'

'Harper, there are a dozen journalists out there,' I say calmly. 'If you storm up to his house in front of them, it'll be about five minutes before the whole world knows the financial mess you're in. Is that the smartest business decision to make right now?'

She hesitates, her hand on the door handle.

'You can spin this,' I add. 'Find a way to make it work for you. But you need to think about it with a cool head, Harper, not rush in half-cocked. Figure out a way to control the narrative.'

I'm not sure why I'm trying to save her from herself. The girl's caused me nothing but trouble: she's got the hots for my husband, tried to blackmail me over Peter, and has made a thorough nuisance of herself turning up at my office at all hours. And yet I feel oddly protective of her. If I didn't know better, I'd almost say we were friends.

Harper abruptly lets go of the door handle and slumps back in her seat. 'I want that bastard to pay,' she mutters.

'Trust me,' I say, 'you don't need to worry about that.'

harper and kyle launch the copper bottom pledge campaign!

2,028,984 views 👍 513K 👎 3.4K

This has been, like, the worst week of my life and I'm so, *so* devastated for everyone caught up in the Copper Beech scandal with us, especially all of you in our Kyper Nation, because it's just, like, *such* a betrayal, isn't it? But I think it really helps when we all come together and share our pain, and I'm really trying to hold love in my heart right now because when someone does something this, like, super-*mean*, you know it must come from a place of hurt. But when I think of the damage Felix Porter has done – I mean, there's old people out there who've saved all their lives and they've lost *everything*.

And if it wasn't for our amazing sponsors I don't know what we'd do, but we're so lucky because they've been *so* supportive and they've done just such an incredible thing and agreed to underwrite our losses so we can fight back and stand up for all of *you*.

So today me and Kyle are launching our Copper Bottom Pledge campaign! We want something good to come out of what's happened and we're calling on banks to pledge to protect ordinary, hardworking people like you. Because even when they don't do anything actually illegal, these traders are basically playing the stock market like it's some sort of casino and it's all great and wonderful until something goes wrong, because it's *your* money they're gambling with, and they need to learn there are *consequences*.

So what we think is, we think these people shouldn't be allowed to treat your pension like it's their personal ATM! We want you to *make your voices heard* and boycott banks who won't sign up to our Pledge to make these men – and it's nearly always *men,* isn't it? – accountable. There are two million of you in our Kyper Nation and we can *use that power!*

Like Kyle says, the least Felix Porter could do is stay and face us instead of running away like a total coward. He's left all of us in the lurch and just disappeared and so now we want *you* to break the internet and help us track him down!

I've put his photo on the bottom of the screen and there's a link just below the comments section where you can text him directly, and we want you to blow up his phone! And if you see him in the street take a picture and send us a message and we'll add it to our Felix Tracker!

Because we're giving you notice, Felix Porter, you and all the other men out there like you! Like that guy says in the movie — What's it called?

— Thanks, babe, I knew you'd know.

To paraphrase the guy in *Network*, we're super-angry and we're not going to take it any more!

chapter 39

millie

'You have to stop her,' Stacey says.

'I'm not sure that's possible,' I sigh. 'You've seen what Harper's like when she gets the bit between her teeth.'

Stacey scrubs at an invisible stain on her pristine marble counter: I've never seen her this rattled. 'She's going to set the media circus going again with this ridiculous vendetta of hers,' she says. 'They've only just stopped camping on my doorstep, but if she doesn't stop she'll bring them all back.'

Until now, Stacey's been lucky: less than twenty-four hours after the revelations about Copper Beech hit the headlines ten days ago, a new Royal scandal broke and knocked everything else off the front pages.

Jogging past the Glass House last week, I noticed the throng of journalists and desperate investors had dwindled to fewer than a half-a-dozen. The morning after that, it was down to a lone photographer. By the time I finished my five-mile loop even he was gone.

'Maybe you shouldn't have moved back home just yet,' I say. 'It's too easy for the media to find you.'

'*I* haven't done anything wrong,' Stacey says.

Against expectation, the *Morning Express Show*'s PR polling suggests the public see Stacey as a victim of her husband's fraud rather than a co-conspirator: the producers couldn't wait to get her back on the air. All talk about moving her to the breakfast show has apparently been shelved: as Stacey noted bitterly, any publicity is good publicity, and with the wife of Britain's answer to Bernie Madoff anchoring the programme, the *Morning Express Show*'s ratings have gone through the roof. Oscar Wilde was right: the only thing worse than being talked about is *not* being talked about.

'The press aren't going to go away,' I say. 'With Felix missing, you're the closest they have to—'

'Felix isn't *missing*,' Stacey says shortly, tossing her sponge into the sink. 'He's probably halfway to Argentina or some other country without an extradition treaty by now. But if Harper keeps up with this ridiculous manhunt of hers, the police are going to start taking his disappearance seriously. If I get sucked into an investigation, my poll numbers will take a dive and then the network will pull the plug on me without a second thought.'

'I thought the police *were* involved?'

'The fraud squad. That's totally different.'

I'm not sure I understand the distinction, but I'm not going to press the issue.

This mess is partly my fault: *I* was the one who told Harper to take control of the narrative, but a nationwide manhunt for Felix Porter wasn't what I had in mind. Stacey is right: with his absence now front and centre of the story, it's only a matter of time before the police consider foul play.

And that's not in anybody's interests, least of all mine.

'I should probably get going,' I say, pushing back my stool. 'I have a trustee meeting at work I can't miss. It was really good of you to take Peter into the studio today with everything else you've got going on. I appreciate it.'

'It was a nice distraction,' she says. 'And a promise is a promise.'

She follows me downstairs. Peter is playing computer games in Archie's bedroom: I have to call him three times before he slopes out into the hall.

'I hope you thanked Mrs Porter for taking you to the studio today,' I say.

He smiles insolently. 'What do you think?'

'Peter and I had a good day,' Stacey says. 'Didn't we?'

Peter's eyes slide away. He stares at the mirror at the end of the hall as if transfixed by his own image.

'*Peter*,' I say.

'I had a lovely time, Mrs Porter,' Peter says, treating her to his most charming smile. 'Thank you very much. I hope I can come again.'

He's saying exactly what I've told him to say, exactly what he *should* say. Only I can hear the mocking taunt in his voice.

We drive home in silence. I steal a sideways glance at my son as we wait at the lights, wondering what's going on inside his head. There's always been an opacity to him: even as a small child he was difficult to read. But there's no mistaking the new malevolence lurking beneath the surface. It feels personal, directed at *me*.

'I like Stacey,' he says unexpectedly.

'Mrs Porter,' I correct.

'She *asked* me to call her Stacey.'

'Why do you like her?' I ask. I'm genuinely curious: Peter doesn't *like* anyone.

'She's cool. She's not like other mothers. She says I can go back to her house whenever I want.'

'OK,' I say.

'She told me she wishes *I* was her son, instead of Archie,' Peter adds. I don't miss the unspoken corollary: *I wish she was my mother.*

208

'Dad got your homework from Jonah's mother,' I say as I double-park outside our house and wait for him to get out. 'Make sure you catch up on everything you missed when you were at the studio with Stacey today.'

Peter smiles secretively. 'I didn't miss anything.'

My son's smile stays with me for the rest of the afternoon.

The trustee meeting at five drags on well into the evening, and it's almost nine by the time we're done. I spend the next hour catching up on paperwork, and I'm finally about to leave my office and go home when my pager goes off.

'RTC,' my colleague says crisply, when I respond. 'Hit and run, the fuckers. CT angio confirmed an ascending AD. Looks tricky. How long would it take you to get back to the hospital?'

'I'm still here,' I say. 'Prep for surgery. I'll be down in five.'

I don't wait for the lift: speed is of the essence. An aortic dissection is a serious condition in which a tear occurs in the inner layer of the body's main artery, the aorta: blood rushes through the tear, causing the inner and middle layers of the aorta to split. If the blood goes through the outside aortic wall, aortic dissection can be fatal.

As I take the stairs two at a time, I call Tom to let him know I'm going into theatre and won't be home. My attending briefs me as I scrub for surgery: the patient is a young woman, no underlying health conditions, minor contusions and abrasions. Married, two children.

It's only when I see her on the table I realise it's Harper.

209

chapter 40

stacey

'We just need to ask you a few questions,' the police officer says.

Stacey looks at the two detectives standing on her doorstep. Not uniformed: higher up the chain than that. They introduce themselves as DCI Andrew Hollander and DS Mehdi Mehdi.

This is how it starts:

We just need to ask you a few questions.

'Please,' she says, 'come in.'

She leads the way upstairs to the kitchen. She's glad she moved Archie's school photograph to cover the hole Felix punched in the wall beside the fridge a few weeks ago: she doesn't want to give the two officers any reason to ask questions.

'I realise this must be a distressing time for you,' DCI Hollander says. 'And we are aware of your position regarding the media, so we will try to be discreet.'

'I appreciate that. May I get either of you anything to drink? Tea? Coffee?'

'Nothing for me, thank you.'

'Perhaps a glass of water?' DS Mehdi says.

He's older than his senior officer: early fifties, at a guess. Cheap suit, badly worn shoes, but his black eyes are sharp and miss nothing. Stacey knows that of the two of them, this is the one she has to fear.

She leads them into the open-plan living room. DCI Hollander perches awkwardly on the edge of one of the vintage Eames lounge chairs, but his colleague remains standing.

'May we ask when you last saw your husband?' DCI Hollander says.

She hesitates, knowing how this will sound. 'About two weeks ago.'

DCI Hollander's bland expression doesn't change. He can't be more than thirty, Stacey thinks, though she realises she's old enough now to subscribe to the cliché of thinking all policemen look young.

'Two weeks?' he repeats. 'Is that usual?'

'Not usual, no,' she says uncomfortably.

'So, you haven't seen him since *before* the news about Copper Beech became public ten days ago?' DS Mehdi asks.

She startles: she hadn't noticed him move behind her.

'No,' she says. 'I've had a lot on at work.'

'You didn't go to be with him once the story broke?'

She looks at her hands. 'We agreed it'd be better if I kept a low profile.'

DS Mehdi wanders over to the window and gazes down at the street. Stacey wishes he'd just keep still. 'So you left him to face the music on his own, Mrs Porter?'

'It was *his* music,' Stacey says, nettled.

'Did you know about the misappropriation of funds at Copper Beech ahead of the public announcement of insolvency?'

'I knew there were problems with the company,' she says carefully. 'Obviously I had no idea about anything illegal.'

'Were you and your husband getting on generally?' DCI Hollander asks.

Stacey suppresses the urge to tell the young man it's none of his business. Her husband is missing: *every*thing is his business.

'Felix and I were working through a few issues,' she admits.

'What sort of issues?'

'The usual problems you get in any long marriage,' she says impatiently. 'We were both working long hours. We were worried about money, obviously. No one else was involved, if that's what you're thinking,' she adds.

'We weren't,' DCI Hollander says mildly.

His colleague is less circumspect. 'You'd moved out,' he says bluntly. 'You were staying at a hotel near your TV studio. Were you and your husband discussing divorce?'

'No!'

DS Mehdi pulls something up on his phone, and shows it to her. 'It seems your husband may have had different ideas.'

It's a copy of a letter: *Lyon Raymond & Lyon, Specialists in Family Law*.

'You didn't know?' DS Mehdi says, watching her closely.

'No,' she says tightly. 'I didn't know.'

A beat falls.

She watches DS Mehdi move restlessly around the living room, picking things up and putting them down. He seems particularly interested in the contents of the bookshelf, turning his head sideways so he can read the books' spines.

'When did you last speak to your husband?' DCI Hollander asks.

'He phoned me the day the news about Copper Beech broke. We agreed it was better I stayed out of the way: with my public profile, it'd only make things worse if I came home.'

'Was that the last time you talked to him? Ten days ago?'

'Yes.'

'You haven't had any contact with him since then? No phone calls, no texts, no emails?'

'No,' Stacey says awkwardly.

'Nothing? Was it normal for you not to speak to your husband for long periods of time?' DCI Hollander asks.

'I told you, we were working through some issues.'

'Did he tell you he was going away?'

'No.'

'Because the thing is,' DS Mehdi adds, looking up from the bookshelf, 'no one seems to have seen him since August twenty-eighth, five days before the news about Copper Beech broke on September second.'

This is a very practised double-act, Stacey realises. Not quite good-cop bad-cop, but a skilled and slick team nonetheless.

'There were journalists camped outside our house for days,' she says. 'I'm sure Felix is just lying low for a bit, until it all blows over.'

'You think, or you *know*?'

She hesitates. 'I just assumed.'

'So you don't know where he is?'

'No.'

'According to you, you and your husband were working through a few marital issues, but the subject of divorce had never come up,' DCI Hollander says. 'You say it wasn't usual to spend significant time apart, even though you'd recently moved into a hotel. Your husband was plunged into a major crisis at work, such that you had journalists camping outside your house. And he suddenly broke off all contact with you ten days ago, and you didn't think that was odd?'

His tone is even, calm; he sounds genuinely interested in her answer.

'I told you,' Stacey says. 'I just assumed he was lying low for a bit.'

'Lying low from his *wife*?'

She drops her gaze to her lap. 'I thought . . . I thought maybe the newspapers were right,' she says, sounding ashamed. 'Maybe he did take all that money. I didn't . . . I didn't want to talk to him.'

213

'His mother, Frances, has reported him missing,' DCI Hollander says. 'She says he hasn't phoned her in over a fortnight, which is apparently very unusual for him. She says he normally checks in to see how she is at least every other day.'

DS Mehdi finally sits down opposite her and leans forward, his hands dangling between his knees. His socks don't match, she notices: one black, one grey. 'Mrs Porter, can you tell me about your husband's relationship with Millie Downton?'

She knew they'd end up here sooner or later, but the abrupt change of subject sets her nerves jangling.

'They didn't get on,' she says.

'Didn't get on? According to several witnesses, they had a very public argument at the Hurlingham Club on—' he breaks off to consult his notebook, '—on the afternoon of August twenty-first, just over three weeks ago. There was even an allegation that Mrs Porter broke your husband's finger.'

'It wasn't broken,' Stacey says.

'But the fight *did* get physical?'

'It was a misunderstanding,' she says. 'Millie thought she was *defending* me—'

'You needed defending?'

'Of course not. I told you, it was a misunderstanding.'

'This wasn't their first disagreement though, was it, Mrs Porter? Things got a bit heated between them at a charity gala Mrs Downton organised a few months ago. They were observed exchanging words.'

She must tread carefully now. Oh so very carefully.

'I don't know about that,' she says. 'Millie – Mrs Downton – she can be very . . . *intense*.'

'Mrs Downton blamed your husband for pulling out of the sale of this house to her, isn't that right?'

'She was very upset, yes.'

214

'Upset? According to one of your neighbours, Mrs Downton was seen hammering on the door and demanding to be let in on August twenty-eighth when – you say – you were staying at a hotel. The last reported sighting of your husband was when he came to the door that afternoon to let her in.'

'What are you trying to imply?'

DS Mehdi sits back. 'Your husband hasn't been seen for two weeks, Mrs Porter. He hasn't used his bank cards or his phone in that time—'

'You've checked his phone and bank records?'

'Usual procedure in this sort of case,' DCI Hollander says smoothly. 'You say you spoke to him ten days ago, but we don't see your number in his itemised phone records. In fact, he hasn't made any calls for two weeks.'

'Maybe he wasn't using his own phone when he called me.'

'Why would that be, do you think?'

She shrugs.

'You and Millie Downton are friends, aren't you?' DCI Hollander says. 'Very good friends, I understand. In fact, she was here, in this house, with you just this afternoon.'

'You seem very well informed.'

'A man is *missing*, Mrs Porter. And I'm interested in why you haven't reported it.'

'Because he's not missing!'

'Ah, yes. You just don't know where he is.'

'In case you hadn't noticed, he's not particularly popular right now,' Stacey says. 'A lot of investors are baying for his blood. He's got good reason to keep his head down.'

'Except your husband disappeared five days *before* the Copper Beech scandal broke.'

'What are you trying to say, detective?'

The man's expression doesn't flicker. 'I just wanted to ask you,

Mrs Porter,' DCI Hollander says, 'whether you think Mrs Downton may have something to do with your husband's disappearance.'

'You'll have to ask her that,' Stacey says.

He smiles. 'I thought you might say that,' he says.

chapter 41

millie

I don't have time to dwell on how Harper Conway ended up on my operating table. Her life hangs in the balance, and it's my job to save it.

Fortunately she has two things going for her: she's young and healthy, and I'm one of the best cardiothoracic surgeons in the country. But every surgery has risks, particularly when it comes to the heart. I put her chances of survival at no more than fifty-fifty.

I can't think about her two little boys at home asleep in their beds, confident that Mummy will be there to make them breakfast in the morning. My ability to put my personal feelings aside is one of the things that makes me so good at my job.

Harper isn't going to thank me for slicing her open from her chest to her abdomen, but whether or not she'll ever wear a bikini again is the least of my concerns. The visceral segment fenestration surgery I'm about to perform stresses the body in significant ways, bringing risk of major complications including stroke, heart attack, kidney failure, and damage to the colon or other organs if there's an insufficient blood supply. Harper's youth and good health reduce that risk, but if a livid scar is all she has to show for her time on my table, she'll be lucky.

Spreading her ribs, I move aside multiple organs – lungs, colon, kidney, spleen, pancreas, stomach – in order to reach the part of her aorta that needs to be fixed. I signal to my team to give her medication to thin her blood, and clamp the aorta and major branches feeding the abdominal organs and kidney before starting to repair the damaged section.

For a moment, I literally hold Harper's heart in my hand.

I've just been gifted the perfect opportunity to extinguish any threat this annoying woman might present to my son, my marriage, or my peace of mind. I don't have to do anything: I just have to perform a little less than my best. No one would ever know.

I've never performed at less than my best in my life.

It takes nearly six hours to complete the surgery, and my back aches from standing by the time I'm done. I check the flow in the branch vessels with a Doppler ultrasound, and then instruct my team to reverse the blood thinner medication.

My attending steps forward to close the incision, but I wave him away. He has all the finesse of a blind pathologist when it comes to stitching. After all she's been through, Harper deserves a little better.

'Beautiful work,' the anaesthetist says, when I'm done. 'Did you do needlepoint at school?'

I ignore him. 'Let me know when she's awake,' I say, snapping off my gloves.

I've been on my feet now for more than twenty hours, and I'm due back at the hospital for a transplant surgery in the morning. I don't want to leave until Harper is conscious, so there's no point going home; I'll snatch a few hours' sleep in one of the on-call bunks. I change out of my scrubs and text Tom as I pass through the deserted waiting area to let him know I won't be home until tomorrow evening.

A man suddenly lurches towards me and I jump, nearly

dropping my phone. It's 2 a.m. and I'm tired: it takes me a few moments to recognise the man as Harper's husband, Kyle.

It's obvious he's been crying. His eyes are red-rimmed and raw, and his hair stands up in tufts at the back of his head. He looks about twelve.

'Is she going to be OK, Mrs Downton?'

He sounds like one of Meddie's schoolfriends. I don't have the heart to point out that Downton is my married name: at work I go by Lennox.

I glance around the empty lounge, looking in vain for one of my team. I'm really not comfortable dealing with patients' families. 'How long have you been waiting, Kyle? Someone should have been through to talk to you—'

'They said it'd gone well, but I wanted to hear it from *you*.'

I guide him towards a knot of empty armchairs near us. In the small hours of the morning, we're the only people here: most patients requiring an all-night vigil are upstairs in the ICU.

'The surgery *did* go well, Kyle,' I say. 'It'll be a while before we know for sure, but the procedure went without a hitch, and I think Harper's going to make a full recovery.'

He lets out a gasp. 'Oh God!'

'I know it's easy for me to say, but try not to worry, Kyle,' I say kindly. 'You should go home and get some sleep while you can. You won't be able to see her for a while yet, and I'm going to be right here until she wakes up.'

Kyle buries his face in his hands, his huge shoulders heaving. I'm desperate to get some sleep myself so I'm fresh for tomorrow's surgery, but I can't leave the man like this on his own.

'I'm so sorry,' he hiccoughs, raising a tear-stained face. 'I know you must be busy. It's just . . . such a relief she's going to be OK. I don't know what I'd have told the boys if . . .'

219

'It's OK,' I say. 'No need to apologise.'

'I know I haven't been the perfect husband,' he says, looking down at his hands. 'I've let her down. I know I don't deserve her. But all this – it really puts things into perspective, you know?'

'Yes, of course.'

'All this bullshit with your house – sorry. No offence.'

I wave away the apology. 'No, you're right. It *is* bullshit. Never mind about the house, Kyle. All that matters right now is your boys.'

'They're OK. They're with my mum,' Kyle says.

I stand. 'I promise I'll let you know the second she wakes up.'

He gets to his feet and then suddenly flings his meaty arms around me like a giant toddler seeking reassurance from his mother. For a moment I freeze, and then awkwardly I pat his muscular back.

We both turn at the sound of voices. A porter shows two uniformed police officers into the waiting area and points to us.

'I imagine the police want to talk to you about what happened,' I say. 'I'm sure it won't take long.'

But they're not looking at Kyle.

They're heading straight towards me.

chapter 42

millie

I manage to snatch a couple of hours' sleep in the on-call room before going into a seven-hour transplant surgery. Adrenaline keeps me focused and alert while I'm operating, but by the time I get home late on Tuesday afternoon, I've had less than eight hours' rest in two days, and I'm ready to sleep the clock round.

Tom wakes me at eight the next morning with a cup of coffee.

'What's this?' I ask warily, sitting up in bed. I'm not a big proponent of lazing beneath the duvet with coffee and the papers, even at weekends: I prefer to get up and get going with my day.

'I thought you could use a bit of spoiling,' he says. He sits on the edge of the bed next to me, effectively trapping me in place. 'Have you heard any more from the police?' he asks.

'You literally *just* woke me,' I say. 'I haven't even looked at my phone.'

He reaches over to my bedside table and passes it to me. 'Could you check?'

His concern for Harper is understandable, if slightly irritating. I didn't break the news that she was my emergency patient until I got home yesterday afternoon: I take my oath of medical confidentiality very seriously, even when it concerns a woman who shares every intimate detail of her life with two million followers. It was Kyle who asked me to let Tom know what had happened: 'He'll be worried,' he said, 'and I know Harper thinks the world of him.' Sweet, dumb Kyle.

'Nothing from the police,' I say, tossing my phone onto the bedcovers.

'D'you think they could be right?' Tom asks. 'Do you think the crash was deliberate?'

'I doubt it,' I say, leaning back against the pillows and sipping my coffee. 'They said the CCTV wasn't good enough to identify the car that hit Harper's or see who was in it, but they did say there were two people in the vehicle. Felix is the only person who really has a grudge against Harper, so that'd mean he had an accomplice, which doesn't sound very likely to me.'

'You think it was just an accident?'

'It was late, it was dark and raining. I think Harper was just unlucky.'

'Why did the police want to talk to you, then?'

I shrug. 'Sometimes happens with an RTC. They want to know the extent of a victim's injuries, whether it could've been attempted suicide, if they're likely to pull through. It's just routine.'

Tom rubs his jaw. I like it when he hasn't shaved in a couple of days: it gives him a slightly disreputable air. Normally he's so clean-cut and boy-next-door. 'Where d'you think Felix Porter is, then?' he asks. 'A bit weird no one's seen him for so long.'

I'm not fooled by his casual tone. I've seen the question in his eyes, but he'll never ask it, even if it's killing him to keep silent.

'Not really,' I say. 'He's not exactly Mr Popular right now.'

'You think he's just lying low?'

'Well, they haven't found a body yet.'

'You don't seriously think he—'

I put down my coffee, and nudge Tom with my feet so that he moves and I can get out of bed. 'No, I don't *seriously think* anything, Tom,' I say. 'Felix isn't the sort of man to top himself, if that's what you mean. He's probably still working out a way to spin this so he comes out the hero.'

'Yeah, but like you said, a lot of people are out for his blood,' Tom says.

'Wanting someone dead and actually killing them are two very different things.'

I head into the bathroom. Tom follows me, clearly not finished with the subject.

'Look,' I say, picking up my toothbrush. 'The kind of people who got screwed by Copper Beech are mostly sweet old pensioners. Do you seriously think one of them went round to his house, picked up a kitchen knife, stabbed him through the heart, got rid of the body and cleaned up the crime scene without anyone being any the wiser?' I squeeze out a pea of Colgate. 'Come on. This isn't one of those kitchen island dramas, and I'm not Suranne Jones.'

'I like Suranne Jones,' Tom says.

'Excellent. She can play me when they make the TV series of our lives.'

He puts his arms around me and unfastens the belt of my dressing-gown as I lean over the basin to spit out my toothpaste. 'Well, the Glass House *is* very photogenic,' he says. 'It deserves a wider audience.'

'I have to get to work,' I say.

'This won't take long,' Tom murmurs.

He kisses the back of my neck, and I put down my toothbrush as I feel the answering beat between my thighs.

He's right: it doesn't take long.

We've always been very good at sex. After twenty years together we're both skilled at intuiting what the other wants or needs. This morning is no exception: we both feel the erotic charge in the air. Tom doesn't want me despite what he thinks I've done: he wants me *because* of it.

'I knew there had to be some benefit to working from home,' Tom smirks as we lie hot and sweaty on the bed afterwards.

'*You* work from home,' I correct. I sit up, and pull on my dressing-gown again. 'I have to get to the hospital. I need to check on my patients, including Harper,' I add, catching the suggestive wouldn't-mind-another-round glint in Tom's eye.

Shutting the bathroom door to quell any ideas he might have of following me into the shower, I turn the temperature dial all the way to cold before stepping into a blast of icy water.

I need to think.

It's only a matter of time before the police start asking questions about Felix's absence, if they haven't already: both Stacey and Tom are right about that. Harper's accident will accelerate things: first she pokes a hornet's nest by publicly declaring war on Felix Porter, and then days later she ends up fighting for her life after an anonymous hit-and-run. Despite what I said to Tom, I don't believe in coincidence. I doubt the police do, either.

I need to talk to Stacey. Whatever – whoever – the cause of Harper's accident, she and I should have a conversation. We need to get on the same page.

My skin is tingling when I step out of the shower five minutes later, refreshed and energised. Tom knocks on the bathroom door as I'm towelling myself dry. 'Millie?' he calls. 'The police are here to see you.'

Damn. I forgot to email them my statement about Harper's accident.

I wrap my wet hair in a second towel and knot it on top of my head. 'Tell them I'll be down in a minute—'

He cuts me off. 'Millie,' he says, and his voice is as serious as I've ever heard it, 'I think you'd better come now.'

chapter 43

tom

We wait in our little-used formal drawing room in silence for Millie to get dressed and come downstairs. Both detectives have refused my offer of tea or coffee, although one of them, DS Mehdi, requested a glass of water which he hasn't touched.

'She won't be long,' I say, for the third or fourth time.

'We're not in any rush,' the younger – senior – detective says. DCI Hollander. He's got one of those everyman faces that always looks somehow familiar even when you've never met them before. Dirty-blond hair, short but not too short, nondescript eyes. Nice suit, though.

'Don't mind if I look around, do you?' DS Mehdi asks.

'Be my guest.'

He wanders over to the bookcase beside the fireplace, turning his head sideways so that he can read the spines. I'm not sure what clues he expects to find in the complete works of Arthur C. Clarke and George R. R. Martin. My literary choices, obviously: Millie's not much of a reader.

'Can I ask why you want to talk to my wife?' I say.

'It's just routine,' DCI Hollander says.

I've watched *Line of Duty* and *Broadchurch*. I know what *just routine* means.

'We're talking to everyone who may be connected to Felix Porter's disappearance,' DS Mehdi adds, turning from the bookcase.

'My wife's not connected to his disappearance,' I say.

He smiles wolfishly. 'I'm sure.'

If this interview is routine I'm a Dutchman. They must know about Millie's run-ins with Felix: she nearly broke the man's bloody finger in front of at least a dozen witnesses. If she hadn't just saved his son's life Felix would probably have pressed charges, and he'd have been well within his rights.

I watch suspiciously as DS Mehdi strolls over to the low cabinet beneath the flatscreen TV, and picks up a stack of DVDs. 'Old-school,' he observes, thumbing through them. 'DVDs, I mean.'

'You can't always stream the classics,' I say.

'*Soldier Soldier*. Nice. Robson Green was great in that. Wife and I were watching him the other day in *Grantchester*—'

'Look, should I call a lawyer?' I ask suddenly.

'Why?' DS Mehdi asks nicely, putting down the DVDs. 'Do you think your wife needs one?'

Yes, I think she needs a lawyer! I think there's a good chance my wife—

That she *what*, Tom? Murdered a man in cold blood?

'Of course not,' I say. 'I'm just covering the bases, you know.'

'She's very welcome to come down to the station with legal representation,' DCI Hollander says. 'But we're not interviewing your wife under caution, Mr Downton. We only want to ask her a few questions. Shouldn't take long.'

My wife saves lives, she doesn't take them. She may not be a people person, but she's not a stone cold killer either.

It wouldn't be the first time.

No. That was different.

Something Millie said earlier, when she was talking about the desperate fraud victims, the pensioners scammed by Copper Beech, plays on a loop in my head. *Do you seriously think one of them went round to his house, picked up a kitchen knife, stabbed him through the heart, got rid of the body and cleaned up the crime scene without anyone being any the wiser?*

It was so oddly specific.

I can imagine Millie doing exactly that.

Except she's smart enough to know you can never clean up a crime scene these days, not properly. If she wanted to murder Felix, she wouldn't do it in a way that'd leave blood spatter, or DNA evidence on the murder weapon. She'd think of a way to get rid of him that'd ensure no trace of him was ever found—

Stop. Millie didn't murder Felix.

But the pieces are falling into place whether I want them to or not.

That Sunday I came back from the museum with Peter and found her asleep in bed at five in the afternoon, her hair still damp from the shower.

Her slip of the tongue a few days later when I suggested Stacey might have gone back to her husband: *'She can't have—'*

Why couldn't Stacey have gone back to Felix?

Millie, what did you do?

I know what my wife is capable of. And she's been in thrall to Stacey Porter ever since she met the woman. Felix warned me: *Stacey's like a Venus flytrap . . . She lures you in, and by the time you realise what's happening, it's too late.*

Did Stacey persuade my wife to help her get rid of her 'abusive' husband? Or did Millie buy into Stacey's carefully crafted portrayal of herself as the victim of Felix's domestic violence and simply take the law into her own hands?

It doesn't matter. I don't care what she's done. Millie will always have my unquestioning and unwavering support. No qualifiers, no *buts*.

Both detectives look up at the sound of footsteps in the hall.

'You wanted to talk to me about Felix Porter,' Millie says as she enters the room.

She doesn't apologise for keeping them waiting. She's wearing a plain sleeveless navy dress that makes her look a million dollars, her platinum hair caught up in a neat bun at the nape of her neck.

DCI Hollander stands and introduces himself and his colleague. 'It's good of you to take the time to talk to us,' he adds.

'What do you need to know?' Millie asks.

'When did you last see Felix Porter?' DCI Hollander says, matching my wife's brisk tone.

'Seventeen days ago,' Millie says precisely. She smooths her skirt neatly beneath her thighs as she sits down. 'I went round to the Glass House to talk to him. We had a row. I haven't seen or spoken to him since.'

'The Glass House?' DCI Hollander repeats.

'It's what people round here call the Porters' house,' I explain. 'It's a bit of a local landmark.'

'You had a row?' DS Mehdi says. 'What about?'

He's the one I'm worried about. My wife is a smart woman, but she's no match for modern forensics. If she's . . . *done* something, if she's made Felix disappear, they'll find out no matter how careful she thinks she's been.

'I wanted him to sell the house to me,' Millie says. 'Stacey wanted a divorce. He was being unreasonable. We argued about it.'

Millie's simply telling the truth as she sees it. She doesn't realise how cold, how clinical, she sounds.

My eyes follow DS Mehdi as he wanders out into the hall.

229

Is he looking for something specific, or is he just waiting to see if something – some *clue* – presents itself? I'm torn between following him and staying here to protect Millie.

'It wasn't the first time you'd argued, was it?' DCI Hollander asks Millie.

'I'm guessing you already know the answer to that, or you wouldn't be here,' Millie says.

DCI Hollander acknowledges the point with a slight nod. 'You didn't have a good relationship,' he confirms. 'We have it on record that you had several heated arguments with Mr Porter.'

'He was an unpleasant man,' Millie says evenly.

'How so?'

'He was physically abusing Stacey. I saw the bruises on her arms. She even came round to our house with a black eye a few weeks ago. It's why she finally left him.' She indicates me. 'Tom was here. He can tell you.'

With every word Millie is giving the detectives motive for murder. They probably think my wife and Stacey Porter are in it together.

'Mrs Downton,' DCI Hollander asks, 'when you saw Mr Porter that Sunday did he mention anything to you about going away?'

'No, though I certainly recommended it.'

'How did he seem when you left him?' DCI Hollander asks.

Millie looks amused. 'Alive, if that's what you mean.'

The detective doesn't smile back. 'How would you describe his frame of mind?' he asks.

'Angry. I told you, we'd just had a blazing row,' she says, not troubling to hide her impatience.

DS Mehdi abruptly comes back into the drawing room. He's holding Millie's running shoes in one hand. He must have fished them from the jumble of trainers and boots and plimsolls on the floor of the hallway cupboard.

'Are these yours?' he asks.

'Yes,' Millie says.

'This stain,' he says, pointing to a rust-coloured splash across the laces of both shoes. 'Whose blood is this, Mrs Downton?'

chapter 44

millie

He has no evidence it's blood, of course, but I'm not going to debate the point. I'm impatient for the two detectives to be gone. I need to get to the hospital to check on my patients, and this interview is a waste of everybody's time.

'It's Felix's blood,' I say. 'He had a nosebleed when I was at the Porters' house a few weeks ago. I helped him deal with it, and his wife will confirm it. And before you go to the trouble of getting a warrant to search the rest of my house, he got blood on my running clothes, too, and I'm happy to hand them over to you, though obviously they've been washed several times since he bled all over them.'

'My wife had nothing to do with Felix's disappearance,' Tom says. 'And she certainly didn't *murder* him! Stacey Porter's the one you should be asking questions! Felix told me a very different story from the one Stacey told my wife. He claimed *he* was the one being physically abused. It *does* happen,' he adds, as DCI Hollander looks sceptical.

'Oh, we know it does,' DS Mehdi says.

'My wife is a respected cardiologist,' Tom adds angrily. 'We have two young children! Do you seriously think she murdered Felix Porter in – what? A jealous rage? A crime of passion? Is this ridiculous investigation *really* the best use of public funds?'

I wish Tom would stop defending me. I have everything in hand. Throwing Stacey under the bus won't help.

'No one is saying Mr Porter has been murdered,' DS Mehdi says. 'Unless you have reason to think otherwise?'

'We're exploring all avenues, Mr Downton,' DCI Hollander adds. 'We're not accusing your wife of anything. We're just trying to build a fuller picture of the—'

'You don't even know Felix is actually missing,' Tom interrupts. 'He's probably sunning himself on a beach in Spain somewhere!'

'He hasn't used his phone or his credit cards since the day your wife went round to his house,' DS Mehdi says mildly.

DCI Hollander stands and pulls out a business card. He hands it to Tom, who flings it onto the coffee table with conspicuous contempt.

'Mr Porter's absence is a matter of concern, Mr Downton,' the detective says. 'We are treating this as a missing person inquiry. If you hear from him, or have anything else to add that you think might aid our investigation, we'd be grateful if you'd get in touch.'

'D'you mind if I take these?' DS Mehdi says, holding up my running shoes.

'Yes,' I say. 'I use them every day.'

'My wife's explained why Felix's blood is on them,' Tom says. 'You've no reason to suspect she's committed a crime. You don't even know a crime's been committed! And did you have a warrant to search our house?'

'You gave me permission to look around,' DS Mehdi says.

'I did no such thing!'

'It's fine, Tom,' I say. 'Take the shoes, detective. I'll find a spare pair.'

'Thank you, Mrs Downton. We'll get them back to you as

233

soon as we can. We'll be in touch if we have any more questions. And once again, we appreciate your time.'

Tom and I both accompany the two detectives to the front door and watch as they drive away. I'm quite certain they'll be back. Neither of them are fools, particularly the older one, DS Mehdi. It's almost impossible for someone to completely disappear without trace these days: even if they flee abroad, there'll be CCTV of them at a railway station or airport, and a digital money trail of some kind. Wherever you go, you need funds to survive. The chaos surrounding the collapse of Copper Beech will muddy the waters, but eventually the police will trace any bank accounts to which Felix may have had access before or after he went missing. And if all of them remain untouched, sinister conclusions will be drawn.

DS Mehdi and DCI Hollander may suspect me of having a hand in Felix's disappearance. They may suspect Stacey, or the two of us of working together. But the field of suspects is certainly considerably wider than it might have been a few weeks ago: thanks to the collapse of Copper Beech, the number of people who'd like Felix dead is probably in triple digits.

And until and unless they find a body, Tom's right: they can't even prove a crime has been committed, much less who did it.

'Where are you going?' Tom asks, as I pick up my briefcase and car keys.

'To work,' I say.

'You don't think we need to talk about what just happened?'

'Not really. I appreciate the support, Tom,' I add, 'but it wasn't necessary.'

'You know you can tell me anything,' he says. 'I've got your back, no matter what.'

'I know,' I say.

He doesn't think I murdered Felix. But *murder* is such an

234

unforgiving word. It doesn't leave room for *in the heat of the moment* or *it was an accident*. Tom may not believe I *murdered* Felix, but he thinks I might have killed him. He wonders if I lashed out in fury or in a misguided attempt to protect Stacey. But would he really have my back if he found out I'd gone over to the Glass House with malice aforethought and killed Felix in cold blood? Would I even *want* him to? Someone has to raise our children with some semblance of a moral compass, however lost our son already seems to be.

I call Stacey as I drive to the hospital, but her phone goes straight to voicemail, so I leave an urgent message for her to call me back as soon as she can.

Once I get to work, I'm too busy making my rounds to think about anything else. My transplant patient is doing well, as is Harper, who is already sitting up in bed and demanding to be allowed to upload a vlog from her hospital room.

'We don't need the security headache,' I tell her, taking her phone away. 'We've already got members of your bloody Kyper Nation trying to sneak into the hospital through the staff car park.'

'Really?' Harper says, delighted.

'Behave yourself, and I'll give your phone back to you tomorrow on condition you don't mention the hospital by name,' I say.

She doesn't remember anything about the accident: the police have already interviewed her, two uniformed beat coppers who are 'optimistic' the hit-and-run culprit will be caught. By which I take it the case has already been filed in a folder labelled *when hell freezes over*.

I tell her to stop using her vlog to agitate against Felix and Copper Beech. 'The man is officially missing,' I say. 'The police think something may have happened to him. You pursuing a vendetta against him: it's not a good look.'

'You just don't want me making waves for Stacey,' Harper says.

Once again, I'm surprised by her perceptiveness. This woman is so much smarter than she looks.

By the end of the day I've left Stacey four messages.

She doesn't return a single one of my calls.

chapter 45

millie

Peter's room is unnaturally tidy for a ten-year-old boy's. His bed is made, his few toys neatly put away in the correct storage bins: he never showed much interest in traditional playthings like Lego or cars, so eventually Tom and I stopped buying them. He's always enjoyed taking things apart – breaking them – but he's never shown the slightest inclination to put them back together. He has a fondness for collecting pieces of junk: circuit boards, mobile phones with broken screens, green knobbly pieces of tempered glass from a car break-in down the street. Everything is arranged in linear order on a shelf above his bed.

In any other child I'd wonder if his obsessive neatness was a symptom of some spectrum disorder, but Peter has weaponised his tidiness: he knows how disturbing his father and I find it.

I turn from the window overlooking our street and see Peter standing in the doorway, watching me.

'Did you find what you were looking for?' he asks.

'I wasn't looking for anything,' I say.

'Then why were you in here?'

'Just getting a feel for you,' I say evenly.

This seems to satisfy him. He sits down on his bed like a four-year-old on his first day at primary school, *criss-cross applesauce*.

He's still in his school uniform, which makes him look even younger than his years.

'Do the police think you murdered Felix?' he asks conversationally.

I'm too taken aback to correct him: *Mr Porter to you.* 'Why would you think that?' I ask, recovering quickly.

'They took away your running shoes because they had blood on them,' Peter says. 'They must think you killed him. Did you?'

'Of course not,' I say, matching his casual tone. 'How do you know about the police?'

'I heard you and Dad talking about it last night.'

It was almost midnight when Tom and I slipped out into the back garden so we could talk where neither of the kids could overhear us: sound carries in our house, and the walls are thin. Peter must have followed us and hidden in the shadows: he's light and stealthy on his feet, like a cat. We'd never have heard him.

I try to remember what else we discussed last night. We talked about Peter, I know that. Tom was angry I let him spend the day at the studio with Stacey on Monday.

So much for punishing him for trying to drown a kid! We can't keep ignoring this, Millie, and hoping it goes away.

You're the one who's had your head in the sand for ten years.

Well, I'm wide awake now.

So what is it you suggest we do?

I don't know. But we can't carry on as we are. We need to—

We need to what, Tom?

'What were you doing up so late?' I ask my son, as if that's all that matters.

He shrugs. 'I'm often up late.'

I remember his escapade a few weeks ago when our neighbour found him in his kitchen at five-thirty in the morning.

I wonder how often our son – our *ten-year-old* son – slips out in the middle of the night undetected and roams the darkened streets.

'I don't think Stacey's very sad about Felix going missing,' Peter says.

'No,' I say. 'I don't think she is, either.'

'Maybe it's a good thing he's gone.'

'Yes. Maybe it is.'

There's something about my son that's different today. It takes me a moment to realise what's missing: I've become so used to his hostility it feels odd to be in his company without it, as if I've walked into a room that's been subtly rearranged, the chairs moved or a painting changed. I know the respite is temporary, and that the barrier between us could come up as quickly as it went down: I need to take advantage of the brief detente.

I sit on the bed next to him. 'Is there something you want to talk about?' I ask, careful not to sound as if I care.

Peter doesn't reply, and for a minute I think I've overplayed my hand.

'Do you remember Mr Tipps?' he asks suddenly.

For a second I can't place the name. 'The school rabbit?' I say, as I finally make the connection.

'He bit me,' Peter says. 'I just wanted to give him a cuddle. He was so soft and warm. I could feel his heart beating under my hand. I squeezed him, and he *bit* me!'

It's the first time he's mentioned Mr Tipps in years.

My son looks at me, and his amber eyes are filled with competing emotions: hurt, outrage, confusion and frustration.

'Is that why you put Mr Tipps in the dishwasher?' I ask.

'He made me angry,' Peter says. 'I was just trying to love him and he *hurt* me. So I hurt him back.'

My gaze rests briefly on Peter's shelf of broken things.

'You pushed Meddie out of the window because she made

239

you angry, too,' I say, as the pieces fall into place. 'She teased you, and so you hurt her back. But what about Archie? What did he do?'

'He was such a baby,' Peter says scornfully. 'He made Stacey cross. He was *embarrassing* her.'

'He's her son,' I say. 'She loves him.'

'She doesn't. She told me. She likes *me* better.'

'You know you can't hurt everyone who hurts you,' I say.

'Why not?'

'Because it takes too much time,' I say.

The bridge between us is so fragile. I resist the urge to wrap my arms around him: I don't want to get bitten. 'Sometimes it's hard to love things the right way,' I say. 'They don't always want to be loved the way we want to love them.'

He scowls. 'I don't know how to do it right. I try but then it always seems to go wrong.'

My heart aches for him. I can feel him wrestling with his rage as we sit side by side on the bed in silence, his frustration a tangible presence in the room. I'm impotent either to help him or to take his burden from him.

At the hospital I've watched mothers sitting next to their children's beds, their baby's pain etched on their own faces. I've known they'd do anything to take it away: they'd cut off their own arm if they could reduce their child's suffering by even a fraction. But I had no idea what it felt like until now.

'Am I a monster?' Peter asks, his tone oddly incurious.

'What? No!'

'Meddie said I was. She said I'm a freak.'

'Meddie's your sister. It's just what sisters say.'

'You're lucky you don't have a sister,' Peter says.

Gracie running towards me, her arms outstretched. Gracie asleep in the bunk bed below mine, her thumb in her mouth, fair hair streaming like a silk flag across her pillow.

240

Gracie cold and white and still.

'You're not a monster,' I say again. 'You don't feel things the same way other people do, that's all. It's not your fault, any more than it'd be your fault if you'd been born with one leg or diabetes. You just have to learn to manage it. As if you had a prosthetic leg or an insulin pump.'

'Why?' Peter asks. 'Why do I have to be like everyone else?'

'Because otherwise the world will punish you,' I say.

Downstairs, Tom is calling me. I don't want to break this rare moment of accord with my son, but I hear Tom's tread on the stairs.

'Stacey's not your friend,' Peter says, as I get up. 'She's mine.'

I might have to have a tactful word with Stacey next time I see her: Peter's crush is getting out of hand. I don't want him to feel rejected when she gets tired of humouring him.

If she ever returns my calls, of course. It's been two days now, and I still haven't heard back from her. Although she has got a lot on her plate.

Peter catches at my hand. 'She's not your friend,' he says again.

He doesn't sound angry or possessive: it's almost like he's *warning* me.

I shiver, as if someone's walked over my grave.

chapter 46

millie

'DCI Hollander,' I say, as I come down the stairs. 'And DS Mehdi. Twice in one week. People will talk.'

The two police officers are waiting for me in the hall. Tom is halfway up the stairs, blocking their way, as if physically preventing the detectives from reaching me will somehow protect me. 'They want to interview you again,' he says. 'I've told them you're not saying anything else without a lawyer present.'

'We have a warrant to search your house, Mr Downton,' DCI Hollander announces, craning around my husband so he can watch my face.

'Based on *what*?' Tom demands.

'We have reason to believe your wife is involved in the disappearance of Felix Porter—'

'This is bloody ridiculous!' Tom explodes. 'I told you, my wife has nothing to do with it! Assuming the man's not sunning himself on the Costa del Sol, it's Stacey Porter you should be looking at! Why would *Millie* be involved?'

'Tom—'

DCI Hollander's bland expression doesn't change. 'By your wife's own admission, Mr Downton, she had a physical altercation with Mr Porter just a week before he disappeared. We'd like to take a formal statement from her at the station. At this stage, it *is* still voluntary, although your wife is welcome to seek legal representation. If she cannot afford a lawyer—'

'Jesus Christ! We've been through this! All the evidence you *think* you have is purely circumstantial! There's probably a hundred people out there with more reason to wish Felix dead. And you still don't know if anything's even happened to him!'

DS Mehdi's focus is on me even while he addresses Tom. He wants to see how I react. 'Your wife's fingerprints have been found at the home of Mr and Mrs Porter—'

'Well, of course they have! They're friends, my wife's been over there a dozen times! If that's all you've—'

'In Mr Porter's blood,' DS Mehdi finishes.

The wind is abruptly taken from Tom's sails. If I didn't love him so much, it'd almost be comical to watch.

'How do you know they're Millie's fingerprints?' Tom demands. 'She's not on the police database.'

'We compared them to a sample taken from Mrs Downton's running shoes,' DS Mehdi says placidly. 'Which she freely gave us.'

'She didn't say you could check them for fingerprints!'

'Tom,' I say. 'It's fine. Let them search.'

'Millie—'

'I told you, it's fine.'

I push past him and head into the kitchen. After a moment, Tom follows me.

'What's he talking about?' he asks, keeping his voice low. 'They found your fingerprints in Felix's *blood*?'

'He had a nosebleed when I was there, Tom,' I say, putting on the kettle. 'I imagine I had his blood on my hands when I touched something: the bannister, probably, or maybe a doorknob. Something that doesn't get cleaned regularly. It doesn't prove I killed him. Let them search our house. They're not going to find anything.'

Tom looks troubled. 'They could build a circumstantial case,' he says. 'I mean, you've argued with him, you've got his blood on your shoes, and now—'

'Stacey will confirm where the blood came from,' I say. 'And they don't have a *body*, Tom. As you pointed out, they still can't even prove a crime has been committed, much less that I'm responsible. Stop worrying. If I'd murdered him, d'you really think I'd have been this *careless*?'

Tom's face clears a little. He's willing to believe me guilty of killing Felix, but not that I'd be stupid enough to get caught. I love his warped loyalty.

I'm a cardiothoracic surgeon: nerves of steel are part of the job description. But even I am unsettled the police are back so soon, though I'm not going to tell Tom that, of course. It's not easy, but murder convictions *have* been secured without a body on nothing more than the accumulation of circumstantial evidence: suspicious bloodstains, the GPS location of a phone, a car that's been too-thoroughly cleaned. The police don't need a smoking gun. They just need enough to convince a jury that if it looks like a duck, sounds like a duck, walks like a duck . . .

I'm lucky Stacey will back me up. Even I can see bloody fingerprints require a little explanation.

'The kids are upstairs,' Tom says. 'What do we tell them?'

'Peter already knows.'

'Of course he does,' Tom says tightly.

'We tell them the truth, Tom: Felix Porter has disappeared, and the police are looking into it. I told you, they're not going to *find* anything because there's nothing to find.'

Several uniformed officers are fanning out throughout the house. DS Mehdi follows two of them upstairs, and I hear footsteps overhead as they begin their search of the bedrooms. DCI Hollander joins us in the kitchen, his not-quite-handsome, not-quite-interesting face as expressionless as ever.

I pour my tea. 'Sure I can't offer you one?' I ask.

'Is my wife being arrested?' Tom demands.

'We'd like to interview Mrs Downton at the station. As I've said, her attendance is voluntary at this stage, and she will be free to leave the police station at any time. However, should she decline to answer our questions on a voluntary basis, we may have no choice but to interview her under caution or arrest her.'

You do not have to say anything, but it may harm your defence if you do not mention, when questioned, something which you later rely on in court. Anything you do say may be given in evidence.

My faith in jury trials is limited. I'm well aware if push came to shove, I wouldn't come across well: a trial has less to do with evidence than it does with emotion. Unlike Stacey or Harper, I'm not *relatable*. It's never worried me before: people don't need to like their surgeons. But they need to like defendants.

'Are you going to prison, Mummy?' Peter asks.

Tom jolts visibly at his sudden appearance in the kitchen. Our son could creep into our bedroom and murder us in our sleep and we'd never even wake.

'Not yet,' I say dryly.

'The police want to search my room,' Peter says. 'I don't want them to take my things.'

'No one's taking your things,' Tom says impatiently.

There's a shout from upstairs. A few minutes later, DS Mehdi comes back into the kitchen holding my running hoodie.

'Blood on the cuff,' he says grimly to DCI Hollander.

'Oh, for God's sake, how many more times?' Tom says. 'My wife's told you she was with Felix when he had a nosebleed. Talk to Stacey Porter. She'll tell you.'

'We have. Mrs Porter has no recollection of it,' DS Mehdi says.

The floor falls away beneath my feet.

'What do you mean?' Tom demands.

'We asked Mrs Porter to confirm your wife's version of events,' DS Mehdi says smoothly. 'She says there was no such occurrence as Mrs Downton described. In fact, she said as far as she's aware her husband has *never* had a nosebleed.'

Tom looks at me sharply.

'That can't be right,' I say stupidly. 'She must remember. It was the same day she told me she and Felix were pulling out of the house sale. He had a bad nosebleed – she said he often had them when he was stressed.'

'There's something else,' DS Mehdi says, handing an object to the other detective. 'We found this in one of the cupboards upstairs.'

DCI Hollander examines it and then shows it to me. 'Do you recognise this phone, Mrs Downton?'

It doesn't belong to either of the children: they have very distinct phone cases. This one is plain black and glossy. 'No,' I say. 'But one of the kids' friends could have left it behind. They're in and out of the house all the time.'

He flips it around, so that I can see the back. In the centre is a dull gold logo with which we've all become familiar in the last couple of weeks: Copper Beech Financial.

Felix's phone.

chapter 47

tom

I can't accompany Millie to the police station: someone has to stay home and watch the kids. She's attending a voluntary interview, so she's able to drive herself there – no perp walk to a police car with the obligatory hand to duck her head as she gets into the back seat. It's all profoundly civilised.

And bloody terrifying.

Millie insists she doesn't need a lawyer but for once I over-rule her and contact our solicitor, Andrew, for the name of a good criminal lawyer to meet her at the police station. It's not easy to find one available at five on a Friday night: no doubt part of the calculation the cops made when they timed their visit. But we get lucky: a woman called Rebecca Miller agrees to represent Millie, though it's going to cost us an arm and a leg. But it'll be money well spent. You don't have to be guilty to require legal representation. Things can be twisted and taken out of context.

Bloody fingerprints. Felix Porter's phone at the back of our airing cupboard. A nosebleed the nation's favourite morning presenter insists didn't happen.

Millie, what did you do?

I think I know the answer to that one.

My wife is one of the smartest people I've ever met, but

247

even smart people sometimes do stupid things. I don't know exactly what happened the day Millie went to the Glass House, but I'm pretty certain she killed Felix. I realise it should bother me more than it does, but I've known who Millie is for a long time. This isn't the first occasion she's taken the law into her own hands. Her sense of natural justice may not line up with what the world considers right or wrong, but at the end of the day she's on the side of the angels. Whatever she did must have been *necessary*.

Maybe they had a row that escalated and she lashed out; perhaps he struck first and she was just defending herself. Either way, she'd have quickly realised how bad it'd look for her, given their personal history. She's a gambler, my wife: she's not afraid to take a calculated risk. She'll have weighed up her chances of successfully getting rid of the corpse against the danger of coming clean and not being believed. She has a strong stomach: I'm sure Felix's body is never going to be found. And it's very difficult – though not impossible – to convict someone of murder when you can't prove there's a victim.

But even Millie makes mistakes. When the police found her bloodstained running shoes during their cursory search two days ago, she was quick on her feet with the nosebleed story, but she must have known Stacey would blow that out of the water unless she managed to persuade her to sing from the same hymn sheet, which clearly didn't happen.

And now there's Felix's phone.

Why would Millie keep it? Surely she realised how incriminating it would be. Is there something on it she doesn't want anyone to see? Or did she bring it with her after she killed Felix, and simply hide it at the back of the airing cupboard until she had a chance to dispose of it properly?

Stop worrying, Dad, Meddie tells me, with alarming insouciance. *Even if Mum killed him, she's way too smart to get caught.*

I order the kids delivery pizza, and watch TV with them until it's time for bed. They've only just gone upstairs when Millie finally gets home around nine.

I leap to my feet as she hangs up her coat and goes into the kitchen. 'I thought I smelled pizza,' she says crossly. 'We've talked about the kids and fast food, Tom.'

'I thought we might suspend the normal rules given their mother had just been arrested for murder,' I say.

'I wasn't arrested,' she says. 'For murder or anything else.'

'So what happened?'

'Nothing *happened*. I just gave a statement, that's all.'

God, my wife can be infuriating.

'Did the lawyer meet you there?' I ask.

'She did, not that I needed her,' Millie says tartly. 'The police didn't ask me anything they haven't asked before, Tom. They don't have any new evidence. If they did, they'd have charged me. They still don't know Felix's disappearance isn't voluntary. They're just fishing.'

She reaches into the fridge for a bottle of chilled Montrachet and pours herself a large glass. She offers one to me, but I decline.

'How did Felix's phone end up in the back of our airing cupboard?' I ask.

'I have no idea,' she says.

'Millie—'

'Tom, I've just spent the last three hours answering questions,' she says irritably. 'I really don't need another inquisition from you. I've no idea how his phone ended up in our house, but I can tell you *I* didn't put it in the airing cupboard, so you'll be relieved to know the police won't find my bloody fingerprints on it.'

'Millie, I'm on your side,' I say. 'I don't care what you've done. All I care about is making sure this doesn't come back to bite you.'

She exhales. 'I know. I'm sorry. I didn't mean to snap.'

She looks tired: beneath her summer tan her face is drawn, and there are dark circles beneath her eyes. Despite her bravado, she's anxious, too.

Goddamn it, I *so* don't want to be right about Stacey Porter. The woman's the first proper friend Millie's ever made. But if my wife didn't leave Felix's phone in the airing cupboard, that leaves just one rational explanation: Stacey is the only person other than Millie who's had access to both her husband's phone *and* our house.

'It seems odd Stacey wouldn't remember Felix's nosebleed,' I say neutrally. 'You'd have thought something like that would stick in her mind.'

Millie stares into her wine glass. 'I've been trying to get hold of her for two days,' she says.

I know how much that admission just cost her. Which means Millie's blind spot when it comes to Stacey isn't quite as blind as it used to be.

'Is it possible,' I venture, 'that Stacey could have left Felix's phone here?'

'Why would she have his phone with her?' Millie says. 'And even if she did, how did it end up in our airing cupboard?'

'Because she put it there.'

Her head snaps up. 'Explain.'

'When a husband or wife disappears, the first person the police look at is the spouse,' I say. 'If I had a husband I wanted to get rid of, I'd be looking for a fall guy.'

A beat passes.

Millie is many things, but she's not a coward.

'You think she's setting me up,' she says. 'You think she manipulated me into killing her husband for her, and now she's making sure I get blamed for it.'

That's exactly what I think.

Millie puts her wine glass down and goes back into the hall. I watch as she puts her coat back on. 'Where are you going?' I ask.

'To find out,' Millie says.

chapter 48

millie

'Where are you going?' Tom asked.

I threw my school bag onto the passenger seat of my mother's clapped-out black Fiat Uno. 'To find out,' I said.

'Millie, you're sixteen! You can't drive!'

'Of course I can drive,' I said. 'You mean I can't drive *legally*.'

'At least let me come with you—'

'You've got an exam this morning, Tom. You can't miss one of your GCSEs. I don't have anything till Chem this afternoon and I'll be back way before then. He'll still be sleeping it off till lunchtime anyway. I'll be fine.'

Tom held onto the sill of the open car window, as if he could physically prevent me driving away. 'Millie, if your mother's gone back to him, you won't be able to stop her.'

'She can't,' I said fiercely. 'Not this time. I'm not going to let her.'

It had taken a spiral fracture of the radius and ulna of her left arm, a broken clavicle and the loss of both her front teeth to do it, but a month ago she'd finally walked out on my father. For good, she'd said. I hadn't believed her at first: we'd been here too many times before. I'd watched her curled up on her bed at the shelter sweating like an addict going through withdrawal as she fought her longing to call him, certain it was

252

only a matter of time before she went back. But somehow, against all my expectation, she'd resisted the urge and stuck it out. After a week at the shelter, we'd moved into a small rented flat in the anonymous sprawl of Crawley, a grey, unlovely London overspill town thirty minutes from my school. She'd talked about getting a job. She'd promised me it'd be different this time. Stupidly, I'd dared to believe her.

And then that morning I got up to make breakfast and found she'd gone.

She'd broken down and called him while I was sleeping and he'd come and stolen her away from me like a thief in the night.

She'd left me behind, because she'd known I'd have stopped her, even if I'd had to tie her to a chair. She didn't care I was in the middle of my exams, or that I was only sixteen and there was no money or food in the house. She was an *addict*. She couldn't help herself.

My father answered the door with a swagger. 'I knew you'd come crawling back,' he said.

'Where is she?'

'Where she belongs.'

He turned and walked back into the house, so confident he had the upper hand he didn't even bother to shut the door on me.

I found my mother in the kitchen, sitting at the table in her apron as if she'd never been away, stringing runner beans into a pink plastic bowl.

'You *promised*,' I said.

'You don't understand,' she said, her eyes sliding towards my father. 'He's my husband. I love him. And he's changed. It's going to be different this time.'

'You said that last time, when he broke your wrist. And the time before, when he broke your nose.'

'Your dad's stopped drinking now—'

'And the time before that, when he broke *my* nose. And the time before that, and the time before that—'

'Amelia—'

'And the time before that, when we lost Gracie,' I continued relentlessly.

She looked away.

'He's changed,' she said again.

'He hasn't *changed*! He's not capable of change! How many times does he have to break your bones for you to realise that? He's only going to stop when he kills you!'

'You heard her,' my father said. 'She's not going anywhere.'

'You were going to get a job, Mum,' I pleaded. 'We were going to get a *cat*. We have an apartment now. We can manage. We don't need him any more.'

'I can't, Millie,' she said.

She'd already receded into quiet, semi-catatonic disavowal, the state she retreated to when she didn't want to deal with the world. I'd lost. I already knew that. But I couldn't give up: not quite, not yet.

I crouched beside her chair. 'What about me, Mum?' I begged. 'I *need* you. I'm sixteen: I can't do it on my own. I need to go to school and pass my exams so I can go to uni and get us out of here. Please, Mum. If you go back to him, you know he's going to take it out on me. We have to leave.'

'Children need their fathers,' my mother said, adjusting the cushion behind her back and picking up another runner bean.

'He's not a *father*! He's a drunk and a bully who doesn't care about anyone but himself! No child deserves a father like him!'

'Is that so?' my father said, his voice dangerously quiet.

I wasn't afraid of my father, not any more. He was bigger and heavier than me, but I was quick and young. I wasn't going to back down.

'Get up,' my father said, grabbing my mother's shoulder. She winced as he hauled her to her feet: her fractured clavicle was still healing. He slung his heavy arm around her neck in a sick facsimile of affection and turned to me, smiling so widely his teeth showed.

For a moment I didn't understand. And then I saw the way my mother's hands cupped her gently swelling belly, her slightly embarrassed, proud air.

'This baby's a second chance, Millie,' she pleaded. 'For all of us. It's going to be different this time. We can be a family again.'

I wanted to be sick.

'Why?' I whispered. 'Why would you let him do this to you, Mum?'

'I tried, Millie,' she said. 'But I can't do this on my own. I'm not strong like you. This baby will be here in five months. I don't want to raise it alone.'

'You wouldn't be alone. You'd have *me*.'

'You've got your own life. Like you said, you'll be off to college in a couple of years. And your dad's not perfect, but he's a good father.'

'*Millie* doesn't think I'm a good father,' he said.

'After what you did to Gracie?' I hissed. 'You're a monster!'

'She thinks this baby would be better off without me,' my father said nicely to Mum. 'Better it's never born than it has a father like me, huh?'

I realised what he was going to do a split second before he did it, but she was blissfully unaware.

Still looking at me, still grinning that inane, hateful smile, my father drove his fist into my mother's pregnant belly.

With a scream, she collapsed to the kitchen floor. I tried to get to her, but my father easily held me back. He kicked her in the belly again and again, until I finally wrested myself free

255

of him and threw myself over my mother. She was barely conscious. A large red bloom was already spreading across the back of her skirt.

'Stop!' I screamed. 'You're killing her!'

'Good riddance,' my father said, drawing back his foot and aiming a kick at Mum's head.

I leaped to my feet, and launched myself at him.

It was what he'd been waiting for. He caught me as if I was a child running into his outstretched arms in the playground.

The next second he had me in a vicious headlock, my back to his chest. I clawed frantically at his arm as he crushed my windpipe, digging my fingernails into his skin hard enough to draw blood but unable to break his hold. Everything was already starting to turn black. His breath was hot against the back of my neck. I knew he wasn't going to stop until he killed me. And then he'd kill my mother – if she wasn't dead already.

Somehow I summoned my remaining strength and in one last, desperate move, I lurched forward, momentarily throwing him off balance as he fell with me. His hold finally loosened and I broke free and staggered to the other side of the kitchen, coughing and gasping for air.

My father didn't follow me. He was holding his head, bellowing with pain. Blood dripped through his fingers from a sickening gash on his forehead. There was more blood on the marble counter: he must have smashed his head on the edge of the stone with the full force of his bodyweight behind him.

He looked at me, his expression confused, as if he couldn't work out why I was here. And then slowly he sank to his knees.

The blow to his head almost certainly wasn't fatal. I had to call an ambulance for my mother: the paramedics would probably save him, too. And then she'd go back to him, like she always did.

No one would blame me for his injuries. Everything I'd done until now had been in self-defence.

When I picked up the cushion from my mother's kitchen chair and calmly held it over his face until he stopped breathing, *that* was murder.

Inside the mind of a psychopath | *Original Air Date 9 July*

The transcript below has been lightly edited for length and clarity.

What I did was wrong: legally and morally, at least by your lights. But it was *just*.

I've never really thought of killing my father as murder. I had to put him down for the good of the pack. Hand on heart, I can honestly say I didn't get any pleasure from doing it, beyond relief that I was up to the job. As I've said, you don't know what you're capable of till you're put to the test. You could find out you're a very different person from the one you've always imagined you are.

But I'd stepped up to the plate and got the job done. It was necessary and unpleasant, but I didn't have the kind of destabilising last-minute qualm of conscience I'd feared. In fact it was surprisingly easy in the end. If we're being honest, it didn't trouble me any more than zapping a mosquito would bother you.

My moral code, such as it is, comes down to one simple concept. *Survival*.

And the truth is, if you'd been in my shoes you'd probably have come to the same decision. The only difference between us is that you'd have agonised about it beforehand and felt guilty afterwards.

But if the outcome is the same, does that make you a better person than me? Or just a hand-wringing hypocrite?

Admittedly there was some collateral damage. That was unfortunate. But sometimes the innocent have to be sacrificed for the greater good. It's not a choice anyone makes lightly, though of course for me it's easier than for some.

And at least it was *quick*. He had a better death than some.

Honestly, it's nice to be able to get everything off my chest like this. Confession is a wonderful thing, don't you think? So *freeing*.

So you can trust me when I tell you I didn't murder Felix Porter. Because I've got no reason to lie to you.

And *his* death wasn't quick at all. It was gruesome and slow and incredibly painful. You've all read the stories, and seen the news. You know what happened to him. I may be a psychopath but I'm not a *sadist*.

It's interesting, by the way, how everyone loves to dwell on the gory details. You cover your eyes and you peep through your fingers, but you still *look*. You want to know *all* the grisly specifics. What you need, what you *crave*, is a nice bloodthirsty adrenaline rush at someone else's expense.

Well, let me give that to you. I didn't kill Felix Porter but I was *there*. And I can tell you he had a long, cruel, lingering death. He *suffered*.

It's a myth that the body protects itself by turning off our pain receptors when we're mortally injured. Nature is a sadistic bitch. Just ask any amputee who's suffered the agony of phantom pain from a limb that's no longer there.

Felix was in indescribable pain, more pain than you can imagine, and he endured every excruciating minute of it fully conscious. He wasn't even granted the blessed peace of oblivion. He couldn't talk: his vocal cords had been destroyed, and he couldn't even scream his agony. But I'll never forget the expression in his eyes: he was in hell, suffering the torment of the damned. Any one of you would have killed him in a heartbeat just to put the man out of his misery.

He knew he was doomed, and that there was nothing that could save him. Even if he'd been rushed to hospital, the only thing the doctors could've done was dose him up with morphine and speed his end.

And the worst thing was that it was *intentional*. The person who'd done this to him *meant* him to suffer before he died.

259

I told you in the beginning: I'm one of the good ones. I don't make moral choices, but pragmatic ones: I killed my father because it was necessary, not because I enjoyed it.

But not all of us are like that.

Some of us deserve our Hollywood reputations.

Trust me, I did my best to save Felix. But I didn't kill him. I didn't kill *anyone*. I was set up by a brilliant, ruthless psychopath.

And when I tell you who that was, it'll blow your mind.

chapter 49

millie

Tom puts into words what I've been thinking for the past two days: *If I had a husband I wanted to get rid of, I'd be looking for a fall guy.*

I gave Stacey the benefit of the doubt when she didn't return my phone calls after the first police visit to our house on Wednesday, despite the increasingly urgent messages I left on her phone. I told myself she had a lot on her plate: her husband had disappeared, bankrupt investors were clamouring at the door, and now she was being interrogated by two detectives investigating her missing spouse.

But everything changed the moment DS Mehdi told me Stacey had no recollection of Felix's nosebleed.

Tom's right: how plausible is it she'd forget something like that? In fact, she did more than just *forget*: she denied unequivocally that it'd happened, denied he'd *ever* had nosebleeds, even though I distinctly remember her saying he was prone to them when he was stressed.

And then there's Felix's phone.

I can't think of a single innocent explanation for how it came to be hidden at the back of our airing cupboard. Tom's right about that, too: Stacey's the only person who could have put it there. Perhaps I could accept that, in the stress

261

of the moment, she really *did* forget about the nosebleed. But actively planting evidence to incriminate me – that wasn't a mistake.

I don't need Tom to tell me how much trouble I'm in. Without Stacey's corroboration, my explanation for the blood on my clothes and shoes is weak at best. Add in the bloody fingerprints and my public altercation at the Hurlingham with Felix, and who's to say where reasonable doubt lies?

Against my better judgement, Tom dissuades me from going to the Glass House to confront her the night I get back from my interview at the police station.

'If you go tearing over there this time of night she's just going to ignore you,' he says. 'She simply won't come to the door. Go and see her at the studio on Monday. If she refuses to talk to you, you'll have your answer.'

Two days later, I take the Tube to the INN building in west London, where the *Morning Express Show*'s studio is located. Inside, the atrium is bright and airy, with acres of chrome and glass. Vast photographs of the network's stars, including Stacey, hang on invisible wires from the double-height ceiling like flags at the UN.

I give my name to the receptionist, and wait while she calls Stacey's secretary. 'I'm afraid Ms Porter is on-air at the moment,' the girl tells me a few moments later. 'Her assistant says he won't be able to tell Ms Porter you're here till they cut to the news in about twenty-five minutes. Is she expecting you?'

'Yes,' I say. 'Don't worry, I'm happy to wait.'

I take a seat on the minimalist white leather and chrome sofa. Behind the reception desk, the network's current output plays on a huge screen. The volume is off, but live subtitles roll across the bottom of the picture. Stacey is interviewing an MP and his husband: it seems the politician has been caught having an affair with his special advisor, a woman who is also married. As far as I can make out, the tabloid opprobrium that's come his way has less to do with his adultery and more to do with letting down the LGBTQ+ cause by indulging in a hetero-sexual affair.

Stacey's approach is very much softly-softly; her face is wreathed in compassion as she leans towards the MP, nodding sympathetically and exuding matronly warmth. That doesn't stop her from luring him into admitting he lied about being gay in order to win over the progressive liberal demographic in his constituency.

It's a masterclass in velvet-glove manipulation.

The interview is followed by a cooking segment, and then finally the programme cuts to the latest national headlines from INN, before going to regional broadcasters for an update on local news. Five minutes pass, then ten. Stacey doesn't come into reception to find me.

I go back to the receptionist. 'Would you mind calling her assistant to make sure Ms Porter got my message?' I ask.

She picks up her phone, and I watch her smile slip as she listens. Her expression is cool when she ends the call. 'Please wait a moment,' she tells me curtly.

She beckons to the security guard standing by the main entrance. I watch them whisper for a few moments, throwing me occasional sidelong glances, and then the security guard approaches me.

'I'm afraid I'm going to have to ask you to leave,' he says, in a tone that suggests he's bracing for trouble.

'Why?'

'Mrs Downton, I don't want to have to escalate this further. I'm sure neither of us wants the police involved, do we?'

'Don't worry, I'm happy to leave,' I say. 'I just want to be absolutely sure first that Stacey did get my message.'

The security guard glances at the receptionist, who nods. 'Yes,'

the girl says. 'Ms Porter knows you're here. Her assistant personally passed the message on to her when she came off air.'

'And Ms Porter herself asked you to tell me to leave?'

The receptionist looks uncomfortable. 'Yes.'

'And told you to call the police if I didn't?'

'Yes.'

I smile. 'Thank you so much for your help,' I say. 'Please
tell Stacey I understand perfectly.'

part three

kyperlife

harper gets to go home!

Hi there, Kyper peeps! Today's an awesome day, because I finally get to go home! Well, not exactly *home* home, because we're still stuck in our little rental flat which is a bit of a nightmare, to be honest, but you know what I mean. I've missed my boys and Kyle so, *so* much while I've been in hospital, but you guys have kept me going and I'm just so grateful for all your lovely prayers and messages. I don't know what I'd do without my Kyper Nation!

Anyway, I just hope things get sorted out soon, because it's really stressful not having our own place. I'll be honest, it's been tough on the boys having to share a room, and the flat's so small, like, you couldn't even swing a *mouse*. And there's this church next door, like right by the community centre, you know, opposite that Greek restaurant, Zorba's, and the bloody *bells*—

Oops, sorry, I keep forgetting. The police say I'm not supposed to tell you personal details but I know I can trust my Kyper Nation!

The thing is, they think maybe our Pledge campaign is the reason I ended up in hospital. Like, maybe Felix Porter was trying to shut me up, but that can't be right because I saw who was in the car that hit me and it wasn't *him*.

Isn't it weird how no one's seen him? I mean, it's been more than three weeks now, and I know you guys have been out there looking! Apparently the police think something might have *happened* to him. Like, they found *blood* at his house. It's kind of creepy, right? Mind you, wasn't there some guy who faked his own death a few years ago so he could claim the life insurance? He pretended he had an accident in his canoe or kayak or whatever, it was just found floating empty, and then he sneaked back home and lived in his wife's attic. Like for *years*. Everyone thought he was dead, even his own sons. Except his wife, of course. *She* was in on it from the beginning.

They bought a second home in Peru or Panama or somewhere, and then they went on holiday when he was supposed to be dead and someone put a photo of them on Facebook and that's how they got caught.

All I'm saying is, you never know. I mean, first Felix steals all that money and then he just *vanishes*? There's got to be more to it.

That's all I'm saying!

chapter 50

millie

'You're a good person,' Tom says, as we climb into bed.

'I think we both know that's not true,' I say. I flip back my side of the duvet and slide between the crisp sheets, newly laundered this morning. 'What else was I supposed to do?' I add crossly. 'If someone *is* trying to kill Harper, the stupid girl was practically inviting them to have another go. She more or less told two million people where she lives. If I'd let her go home with Kyle, she'd have ended up back in my hospital, only this time in the morgue.'

Tom shifts the pillows behind him. 'D'you really think the Porters had anything to do with Harper's accident?'

'I'm not sure *any*one had anything to do with Harper's accident.'

'You don't think the crash was deliberate?'

'I'm keeping an open mind,' I say.

'Harper seems pretty sure. She said in her vlog the police thought it was—'

'She made that up, Tom. She makes a lot of things up. The police aren't investigating the crash as anything other than an accident. Trust me,' I add sourly, 'they're far more interested in what's happened to Felix Porter.'

'Well, I think we both know Felix wasn't behind the wheel,' Tom says.

I let the comment lie where it falls.

'Harper didn't see who was behind the wheel of the car that hit her,' I say, reaching for a heavy glass pot of hand cream on my bedside table and smoothing it onto my hands with brisk, efficient strokes: the constant scrubbing with abrasive anti-bacterials leaves them chapped and raw. 'I just wish she'd said as much on her vlog. She made it sound like she could identify whoever crashed into her, which if it *was* deliberate gives them a bloody good reason to try again. And she knows it, too: she says she did it on purpose to flush them out.'

'That's not the stupidest idea I ever heard,' Tom says.

'Really?' I say. 'You might want to remember that if someone attacks the house with a bazooka while she's here.'

'You didn't have to invite her to stay with us,' Tom says.

'She's my *patient*,' I say tersely. 'She's only ten days out from major open heart surgery. If I'd let her go home to that miserable little flat her kids would've run her ragged and she'd have been back on my table by the weekend.'

Tom turns towards me, propping himself up on one elbow. 'Millie,' he says, 'I appreciate what you've done for Harper. I know she's not your favourite person in the world. But it's not your fault the Conways are stuck in a shitty rental flat.'

'Generous of you, but not entirely accurate,' I say.

'Still,' he says. 'You went out of your way. And you didn't have to.'

'I told you—'

'She's just a patient. Yes, I know.' He rolls away from me. 'I don't know why you find it so hard to let anyone think you care, Millie,' he says. 'I *know* you. I know you a lot better than you think. And before you start reminding me what a sociopath you are, let *me* remind *you*: good people sometimes do bad things for the right reasons. That doesn't make them bad people. Why are you always so set on convincing everyone you don't give a damn?'

'Why are you always so set on convincing me I *do*?'

He sighs. 'Millie, I get it, I really do. If you don't let anyone in, you don't get hurt. But Harper doesn't expect anything from you. She just wants to be your friend.'

'So did Stacey,' I say.

I screw the lid back onto my expensive hand cream and put it back on my bedside table, and then turn out the light.

For a long while neither of us speaks, and I think Tom has fallen asleep.

'What are you going to do?' he asks suddenly into the darkness.

He doesn't need to elaborate. I told him what happened three days ago when I went to see Stacey at the INN studio.

He was right, and I was wrong.

Stacey *played* me.

I knew it the moment the police first came to my door, though Stacey had to spell out her message with brutal clarity for me to accept it.

Deep down, I think I always knew it. I was never meant to have friends. I belong in the shadows, in dark places where it's safer to venture alone. But I let my vanity get the better of me: Stacey made me feel I was the only one who could save her. The very first time we met she read me for clues like a fairground psychic. As soon as she saw my response to the bruises on her arms, she knew exactly which buttons she had to press. I thought *I* was the one in control: congratulating myself when I persuaded her to come to the hospital gala, preening when she copied my clothes and hair.

And the truth is she was pulling my strings from the very beginning.

Tom was right when he said she didn't really want to sell the house: I remember her face when she showed us around, stroking her countertops, tweaking her blinds. I thought I was so clever wooing her into finally agreeing to part with it.

But she never had any intention of selling it to me. She simply used the Glass House as *bait*.

Tom saw the danger long before I did. He saw it, and he tried to tell me, and I wouldn't listen. I was convinced Stacey and I had a connection that went beyond the Glass House, beyond our shared experience of domestic violence.

Part of me actually admires Stacey for what she's done. I showed weakness, and she took advantage of it: that's on me, not her. She achieved something I'd never have believed possible: she made me realise how *lonely* I was. For years, Tom was enough for me, but Stacey showed me a glimpse of the mysterious and intimate world of female friendship from which I'd excluded myself for so long, and I finally understood what I'd been missing. I dared to dream I might be allowed to be part of it, to have what everyone else took for granted.

And then she showed me what a fool I was.

Stacey has reminded me who I really am. My pride is dented, but I'll regroup. It's time I stopped trying to abide by everyone else's rules. I didn't choose this path, but I absolutely will not be destroyed by it.

'Millie?' Tom says again. 'What are you going to do?'

chapter 51

millie

Harper is sitting in the kitchen sipping coffee from my favourite mug when I get back from my morning run. I have a blister on my left foot from my new trainers: the police have yet to return my running shoes. My sour mood is not improved when I see Harper propped up against my kitchen counter, leafing through one of my cookbooks, a cuckoo in my nest.

'You're out of Colombian dark roast,' she says, turning down the corner of the page to mark her place. Dog-earing books is a cardinal sin I don't even tolerate from Tom and I have to suppress the urge to snatch the book out of her hands. 'And you're getting low on milk, too.'

I open the drawer containing my coffee pods. I'm not about to defile my body with Tom's decaff, which leaves me a choice between an insipid Nantucket medium blend or – God help me – the Caramel Vanilla Cream left over from an ill-conceived foray by my husband into variety packs when we first bought the coffee machine. I slam the drawer shut again. I'll have to stop by the Lebanese hole-in-the-wall near the hospital for a decent hit of caffeine on my way into work.

I open the cupboard above the Viking range for my protein powder and am confronted instead by a neat row of condiments and spices. 'What the hell, Harper?'

'Oh, I moved that stuff to the bottom cupboard on the other side of the fridge,' she says airily, flicking the page. 'You want your spices by the cooker so they're easy to get to.'

'I want my protein powder and spices where I left them,' I say tightly.

She flips the book around and holds it up to her chest so I can see the glossy double-spread colour photograph. 'This looks amazing. What's that weird chimney thing?'

'It's a tagine.'

'Have you got one?'

'Yes. Where's Tom?'

'He said he had to get to a meeting in town after he dropped the kids at school. He'll be back around lunchtime. So, you've made this recipe? It's, like, Moroccan or something?'

'Harper, I don't have time to chat. I need to shower and get to work.'

'Oh, by the way,' she calls as I start up the stairs, 'I tidied your airing cupboard. It was super messy, so I folded everything for you. And I moved the towels to the lower shelves, so you can reach them better.'

I grit my teeth. She's been here three days, and so far she's rearranged my kitchen, my cupboards and the furniture in the sitting room: 'Oh, I like the sofa here,' Tom said, 'you can see the TV so much better, and it makes the room look bigger.'

She's bounced back to full health with irritating speed. If it wouldn't negatively affect my patient mortality numbers, I'd strangle the girl myself.

When I come back downstairs after a brief cold shower – not by choice: Harper has used all the hot water – she's in the hallway waiting for me.

'Can we talk?' she says. 'It's important.'

'I'm running late,' I say, picking up my keys. 'Maybe when I get home. Unless you're not feeling well?'

'Oh, no, I'm fine. My scar's a bit itchy, but I feel, like, basically back to normal.'

'Good. Tell Tom I'll be—'

'It was Stacey in the car,' she says.

I close the front door again. I don't need to ask her *which* car. 'Are you sure?'

'She looked right at me,' Harper says. 'She knows I saw her.'

I digest this for a moment. I'm not entirely sure I believe her, though I certainly believe Stacey *capable* of ramming her car into a young woman with two small boys at home without a second thought. But Harper has a pliable relationship with the truth, and it may suit her to position herself on #TeamMillie for now. There's no better way to do that than to find a common foe: the enemy of my enemy is my friend.

But the only way to find out if you can trust somebody is to trust them.

'Why didn't you tell the police this?' I ask.

'Because it's her word against mine. She's *Stacey Porter*. She's a national treasure. Everyone loves her. Who's going to believe me?'

'You told me you didn't know who was in that car,' I say.

'I was still figuring things out,' Harper says. 'I wasn't sure if I could trust you.'

'You realise you've just put my family at risk?' I demand. 'If she decides to come after you again. She's not some random stranger. She knows you're staying with me. She knows where I live.'

'I find it interesting,' Harper says, 'that *you* don't have any trouble believing me about Stacey.'

'I find it's always easy to believe the worst of people,' I say dryly.

'It wasn't Felix in the car with her,' Harper says.

'Then who was it?'

275

'I don't know,' she says honestly. 'It all happened in a split second. I was sitting at the lights when I saw the car coming right at me, and I just saw a glimpse of Stacey behind the wheel, and someone next to her – I don't even know if was a man or a woman, but I know it wasn't Felix. Too short, wrong profile. Next thing I know I'm waking up in hospital feeling like I've got a baby elephant sitting on my chest.'

She follows me as I go back into the kitchen and put a pod of the despised Nantucket blend into the coffee machine. 'I want to help,' she says.

'Help with what?'

'Whatever you're planning. You've got a plan, right?'

Of course I have a plan.

'She tried to kill me,' Harper says. 'And Tom says she's lying to the police about Felix's nosebleed to screw you over. Whatever you think of me, Millie, we're on the same side. Let me help.'

'I'm thinking,' I say tersely.

What threat could Harper pose that would induce Stacey to take such a monumental risk? She couldn't be sure she wouldn't be picked up on CCTV, however careful she was. She'd have had to get a car from somewhere – a rental, maybe – because she could hardly use her own. Harper's ridiculous crusade to get her vlog followers to boycott banks that won't sign up to her 'copper bottom' pledge has nothing to do with Stacey – it's a meaningless gesture. And Stacey must know Felix isn't likely to be found by Harper's 'Kyper Nation' or anyone else. So why the need to silence her?

And the question *du jour*: who the hell was with Stacey in that car?

chapter 52

stacey

No one knows where Felix is. He's been missing for more than four weeks now, and the police have no more idea of his whereabouts than they did at the beginning.

The media think he's done a runner with the funds he embezzled from Copper Beech. The consensus seems to be Argentina, though Rio and Spain's costa del crime are popular alternatives. But public interest in the story is already waning, and with it the media's appetite to pursue it. A middle-aged, middle-class white man having a midlife crisis and going AWOL – well, it's not very sexy. Stacey's a journalist. She wouldn't bother with it either.

She reaches into the shower and turns it on, perching on the side of the bath as she waits for the water to run warm. Everyone on the *Morning Express Show* has been tiptoeing around her for weeks now, pulling their mouths into sad little moues of sympathy whenever they catch her eye. She saw the same expression on their faces when she interviewed a woman whose husband caught Covid and ended up in a life-changing coma: part pity, part there-but-for-the-grace-of-God relief. When she watched the playback of the interview afterwards, she saw the same expression on her own face. No one knows how to respond to a woman who's not widowed, but bereaved all the same.

They all rallied round though when Millie Downton tried to ambush her at the studio last week. As she told the security staff, Millie had already been to her house on numerous occasions, banging on the windows and harassing her. Stacey explained she didn't want to report the woman to the police: she felt sorry for her because she was clearly in need of some sort of help. So security just had a quiet word, and she's not heard from Millie since.

Steam billows into the bathroom as Stacey opens the shower door. Felix always prefers cold showers, he finds them bracing, but she likes the water hot enough to almost scald. Hot enough to scour away the conversation she just had.

The police have told her to prepare herself for the worst. Officially, they're still investigating Felix's disappearance as a missing persons case, but the fact he hasn't used any of his credit cards or his phone in a month is ominous, DCI Hollander told her gravely, no doubt about it. They've got forensic accountants going through digital records at Copper Beech, but so far they haven't found any suspicious external transfers connected to her husband. In fact, the only transactions they can find show money coming *in*, not going *out*, the most recent of which was a large deposit from Harper Conway, which is still sitting untouched in a frozen account at Copper Beech. If Felix *did* salt money away to fund his disappearance, he's covered his tracks exceptionally well.

The police aren't treating Stacey as a suspect any more: they're focusing on Millie Downton. They seem to accept Stacey isn't involved.

Stacey has freely admitted she and Felix were having marital problems – no point lying about it – but as she told the two detectives, they were both still hoping they could work it out. They have a child together, after all. She'd never want any harm to come to Felix, of course, but she's sounded off about him now and then to her girlfriends, of course she has, *I'd be better off without him*, that sort of thing, it's what women say when they've had a row, isn't it, it doesn't mean she didn't love him. But now she's dreadfully afraid Millie might have misconstrued what she said and taken matters into her own hands and done something terrible. *Will no one rid me of this turbulent priest?* Stacey said. (Then she had to explain to DCI Hollander and DS Mehdi it was a quote attributed to King Henry II in 1170 when he sounded off about his aggravating Archbishop of Canterbury, Thomas Becket, which prompted four knights to travel to Canterbury where they killed Becket in his own cathedral, thinking they were doing the King a favour.) *Maybe I said something that made Millie think I wanted something bad to happen to Felix*, she told the detectives. *I know she had a bit of a crush on me, but I never thought it'd go this far.*

The thing is, Stacey said, Millie has a history of domestic abuse, and she can't help wondering now if she triggered the other woman. Stacey flushed scarlet as she explained she and Felix enjoyed an enthusiastic and vigorous sex life; a bit too vigorous, sometimes. There were . . . well, there were *bruises*. Sometimes. A black eye when she fell off the bed and couldn't stop her fall, because her hands were . . . God, this was so embarrassing . . . well, *tied together*. DCI Hollander got a bit pink around the ears himself at that point.

She turns her face up into the hot spray and closes her eyes as the water sluices over her breasts and shoulders. She doesn't know what was going on in Millie's head, what deluded narrative she's been telling herself, but as she told the two detectives earlier, she feels responsible for not picking up on it before. She was the one who invited Millie to her tennis club, to her *home*. If something she said or did has led Millie to hurt Felix—

The police officers rushed to assure her it wasn't her fault, but, as she told them, if anything's happened to Felix, she'll never forgive herself.

She's not sure why they haven't arrested Millie, to be honest, given the wealth of evidence they've amassed against her. She's told them Felix has never had a nosebleed, and certainly not when Millie Downton was with them: the woman had Felix's blood on her shoes and clothes, and she left fingerprints in his blood on the underside of the stair bannister. How can that *not* be sinister? It's incredibly unfortunate Stacey had the house professionally cleaned the same week Felix disappeared, as she does twice a year (the cleaners are on an automatic contract: the police checked into that). The forensic team's UV lights didn't pick up any traces of blood in the kitchen or anywhere else in the house, nothing to indicate foul play other than those incriminating fingerprints; but then they wouldn't after the cleaners had been through with their bleach.

She rinses the shampoo from her hair, and gently massages conditioner into her scalp. The worst thing is, she can see how Millie ended up thinking this way. She should never have confided in her – a woman she scarcely knew! – about the problems she and Felix were having. But there's no denying things had escalated in the bedroom to a point where she wasn't comfortable, and she needed to tell *some*one.

The level of violence between them: it might be consensual, but even she could see it wasn't healthy.

Felix clearly felt the same way: he'd gone behind her back and engaged a divorce lawyer. Who knows what he'd told Tom about the state of their marriage, but it probably wasn't very complimentary. There are two sides to every story, after all. She doubted he'd painted her in the most flattering light. And if Tom had passed details of their marital troubles on to his wife – well, it would've just fed into Millie's misguided conviction that Stacey needed rescuing.

And then there's Harper Conway. Stacey hasn't trusted the young woman since the first day she met her, she thinks, soaping her legs. Harper is publicity-hungry and a lot savvier than she lets on. And she's got more reason than most to carry a grudge against Felix, given he stole all her money. Who knows what poison she's been dripping into Millie's ear? As she told the two detectives, she knows it sounds completely crazy, but what if Harper took advantage of Millie's obsession with Stacey and somehow manipulated her into . . . well, into hurting Felix?

They didn't take her seriously – she's aware how paranoid she sounds – but she didn't really expect them to. It's like she's trapped in a complex, elaborate maze of smoke and mirrors designed to make the innocent look guilty and the guilty seem innocent: nothing is as it seems. No one is to be trusted.

Stacey rinses the conditioner from her hair. The police may believe her for now, but she doesn't kid herself she's out of the woods yet. Millie Downton is a dangerous woman, and she's not just going to leave things as they are. Stacey's glad Archie is safely away at school, out of Millie's reach.

The hot water is starting to turn tepid, so she finally turns off the shower and gropes for a towel. She needs to be proactive now. She's losing control of events, and she has to turn that around. She's got to work out Millie's next move, and be one step ahead. She can't rely on the police to do it for her.

She knots the towel around her, and pads into her bedroom.

The next thing she knows, someone has grabbed her from behind and is flinging her facedown onto the bed.

chapter 53

millie

'There's no point screaming,' I tell Stacey as I twist her right arm behind her and press my knee into the centre of her back. 'No one will hear.'

She doesn't struggle. She turns her head sideways on the duvet so she can speak. And breathe. 'Are you here to kill me or talk to me?' she says.

'I'm still deciding.'

'Well, while you do that, can you let me up?'

'Are you going to try anything stupid?'

'I think you can see I don't have a weapon,' she says dryly.

I release her and climb off the bed, keeping a sharp eye out in case she lunges for one of the heavy lamps on the bedside tables.

Stacey rolls cautiously onto her back and then pushes herself into a sitting position, holding the white fluffy bath towel around her chest to protect her modesty. 'How did you get into my house?'

'The same way I did when you asked me to break into your husband's study,' I say. 'You might want to actually use that expensive alarm system of yours now and again.'

Stacey smooths her wet hair back from her face with the palm of one hand. I can see her weighing up her options: she can't outrun me, and one glance at the nearest bedside table tells her I have her phone. She must know I'd beat her in a fight. I work out every day, and years of broadcasting from a sofa have made her soft and weak.

'Are you going to tell me why you're here?' she asks.

'Really? We have to play that game?'

'What game?'

I fold my arms, and lean against the mahogany and wicker chest of drawers behind me. John Hutton for Donghia, if I'm not mistaken. She won't have got much change from twenty thousand pounds.

'I pretend I have no idea what happened to Felix,' I tell her, 'you pretend you didn't set me up to take the fall for his murder, I threaten you, you tell me you don't know what I'm talking about, blah, blah, blah. I'd expect those kind of games from someone like Harper Conway, but I thought you were smarter than that.'

'What is it you want?'

'Ahh. Better.'

'You must want something, or you wouldn't be here.'

I smile wolfishly. 'Psychopaths don't need a reason to be psychopaths. I assume you know the fable about the scorpion and the frog?'

'Remind me.'

'A scorpion wants to cross a river but he can't swim, so he asks a frog to carry him across.' My tone is relaxed, but I don't take my eyes off Stacey's hands for a second. 'The frog hesitates, afraid that the scorpion might sting it, but the scorpion promises he won't, because they'd both drown if he stung the frog in the middle of the river. So the frog agrees to carry the scorpion, and he climbs onto its back. And then halfway across the river the scorpion stings the frog anyway, dooming them both. The dying frog asks the scorpion why he stung him, knowing they'd both die, to which the scorpion replies, "It's in my nature".'

'Are you the scorpion or the frog in this fable?' Stacey asks.

'You tell me,' I say.

'I liked you,' Stacey says. 'I really *liked* you.'

'I liked you too,' I say. 'Why did you set me up?'

She rolls her shoulders and stretches her long white neck from side to side. 'Hypothetically speaking? Well, if I wanted to get rid of my husband, I'd be the first person the police would suspect. So I'd need a someone to distract them, wouldn't I? Someone to provide reasonable doubt.' Her lips curve. 'Someone who had a motive to want Felix dead. And you *really* didn't like my husband, did you?'

'I assume that was your intention.'

'You saw what you wanted to see.'

'And Harper? Where does she fit in? Why did you try to kill her?'

'Why *would* I try to kill her? What are you talking about?'

'She saw you behind the wheel of the car that hit her.'

'She's lying,' Stacey says.

'Of course she is,' I say. 'But not necessarily about this.'

'I think about you all the time,' Stacey says unexpectedly. 'I think about your hair, and the clothes you wear, and how you look when you're sleeping. I wonder if you masturbate, and who you think about when you do.' She leans forward, her breasts swelling against the edge of the bath towel. 'I wonder what it must be like to slice into someone and watch their blood flow over your fingers and to hold their life in your hands. Literally *in your hands.*'

'I think about you, too,' I say. 'I wonder what happened in your family to make you the way you are. I wonder why you chose to have a child. I think about why you picked me for your little game. I think about what it's like to go into a studio every day and expose yourself to the scrutiny of ten million people.'

'Not quite ten million, but thank you. I appreciate the compliment.'

'You're welcome. I took the scissors out of your bedside table, by the way,' I add. 'Just in case you were tempted.'

Her hand stops inching across the duvet. 'What are you going to do, Millie?'

'Ah. Well, that *is* the question, isn't it?'

'You could just walk away.'

'I think we both know that's not going to happen,' I say. 'You took that option off the table when you told the police Felix had never had a nosebleed.'

'Did you really expect me to take your side against my husband's?'

'I expected a little *loyalty*,' I say, 'after all I've done for you.'

'Are you going to kill me, too?'

'Nice try,' I say.

'I thought we weren't playing games,' Stacey says, standing up.

'Oh, Stacey. We've only just started.'

The air between us hums. *This* is what has been missing from our relationship: the dangerous, deadly rivalry that adds fire and blood to the charm of conquest. Our friendship was a fraud, but this, *this* is real: the merciless struggle for survival, red in tooth and claw, honest and authentic. Strip away the lunches and the yoga and the confessional intimacy of any female friendship and this is what you'll find: savage, brutal, ruthless competition. It's the dark truth hidden away like a portrait in the attic, withered, wrinkled and loathsome of visage.

We circle each other like gladiators.

'You broke into my house,' Stacey says. 'You must know I'll call the police the minute you leave.'

'You have no proof,' I say. 'Your security system is disabled, including the CCTV. I checked.'

285

'*This* time,' Stacey says.

It takes me a moment to realise what she means: she's talking about the time I broke into the Glass House to steal the house deeds for her. I didn't worry about the CCTV then because Stacey herself had disabled the security system for me. It never occurred to me she'd leave the cameras running.

'Ah,' I say. 'Well, that was rude.'

'You've repeatedly broken into my house. I've got witnesses to confirm you've harassed me at work. People have seen you hammering on my door.'

'I can see how it might look,' I say dryly.

'I've tried to be kind,' Stacey says. 'To let you down gently. I told the police: this is as much my fault as yours. I led you to expect too much. I let it go too far. I never thought you'd take it out on Felix.'

'Video can be incriminating,' I say. 'A picture's worth a thousand words. It's easy to see how someone might get the wrong idea even when there's an innocent explanation. If there was a video of a woman punching and hitting her husband for example,' I add. 'A husband who'd then gone missing in suspicious circumstances. Well, it'd be easy to see how the police might jump to conclusions.'

It's Stacey's turn to pause. 'Hidden cameras,' she says.

'I didn't need to hide a camera,' I say. 'Just download a virus to Felix's computer, which gave me access to the camera. Though when I checked it last night, the content turned out to be a bit unexpected, I must admit.'

'It's not what it looks like,' she says.

'But what it looks like is all that matters,' I say.

The silence stretches between us. 'So,' she says.

'So,' I say.

Stacey drops her hands, letting her towel fall to the carpet. Her breasts are white and full, her belly soft. She puts her hands on my shoulders, and lifts her mouth to mine. For a long moment we drink each other's breath.

Adrenaline and desire flood my system, a high like nothing I've ever experienced: not running the roofs of train carriages in the dark, or free-climbing a cliff in Yellowstone National Park, or making love to my husband, or holding a human heart in my hand. It's the danger she poses. The *risk*. Every nerve in my body is on fire. I don't think I've ever felt this alive.

But I don't forget what Stacey Porter is capable of, not for one second.

These violent delights have violent ends, and in their triumph die, like fire and powder, which as they kiss consume.

Shakespeare knew a thing or two about love.

She sees my answer in my eyes. Her hands drop to her sides.

'It's not too late to row back from this,' I say. 'You could tell the police Felix had a nosebleed. All the evidence they have against me is circumstantial. I'll make sure you're safe. We can both still walk away.'

For a moment, I actually think she's going to agree. Honour satisfied on both sides. A hard-fought draw against a worthy opponent: perhaps we'll even stay friends. She has my respect, which is a commodity I parse out even more carefully than friendship. We could be quite the team.

'Ahh,' she says, tilting her head to one side with a regretful smile. 'If only my memory was just a little more reliable.'

'Then it's war,' I say.

'Then it's war,' she says.

chapter 54

millie

'You wouldn't even know the woman existed if I hadn't tracked her down,' Harper says. 'If you're going to see her, I'm coming with you.'

'You're supposed to be convalescing, Harper. You should be in bed, resting. Or better yet, go home to your family. I'm sure your husband and children are missing you.'

'You said it wasn't safe to go home.'

'Well, after a week living with you, it's a chance I'm willing to take.'

'You'd send me back to that *tiny* flat just days after *open heart surgery* with two little boys and a husband I haven't shared a bed with in nearly a month, a husband with *needs*—'

Harper is like a psychotic savant: she knows exactly which buttons to press. 'Fine,' I sigh.

She grabs her white leather bomber jacket and follows me out to the car. 'It's not that I don't love Kyle,' she says. 'But we've been together since I was fifteen. That's, like, almost half my *life*. I mean, you can have eggs for breakfast every day, you can really *love* eggs, eggs can be totally your *thing*, but sometimes you just don't want to see another egg in your life, you know?'

'Please stop.'

'I'm not ready to go back home,' she says.

'That much is obvious,' I observe. 'But you can't stay with me forever, Harper.'

'I know.'

She struggles with her seatbelt, and I lean across to help her with it. 'Your incision is still healing,' I say. 'You really should be resting.'

She puts her hand on mine as I click the belt home. 'It's not really about Kyle,' she says.

The intensity of her tone gives me pause. 'Then what *is* it about?'

'I'd give my life for my boys,' she says fiercely. 'I love them to death, they're my world, but sometimes I just feel like I can't *breathe*. They need me so much. Not just to do stuff for them, the cooking and things, I can live with all that, but I don't just have to keep *them* safe, do I?' She releases my hand suddenly. 'I have to keep *me* safe too, and the responsibility of that – ever since the accident it's like there's been this tight band round my chest and I can't seem to get any air. I feel like I'm drowning. Loving them is . . . it's *killing* me.'

There's a sudden silence in the car. Something passes between us: a moment of shared recognition that knits us together like bone. Motherhood means living simultaneously in joy and desperation. When I got pregnant with Meddie, my biggest fear was that I wouldn't be able to love her. It never occurred to me that loving her too much would be what nearly crushed me.

'They'd survive,' I say gently, 'if anything happened to you. Children are resilient. You and I are living proof of that.'

'I want my boys to do more than just *survive*.'

'I'm not going to let anything happen to you, Harper.'

'You can't make promises like that. Stacey tried to *kill* me.'

'Did she?' I say quietly. 'Or did you just need a reason not to go home?'

The lights change and I turn onto the Fulham Road, over-taking a black cab stopping for a fare and slotting neatly behind a bus. The taxi driver gives me the finger.

'You don't believe me,' Harper says flatly.

I feel a brief, unexpected flicker of regret as the moment of understanding between us breaks and we retreat to our own sides of the divide.

'You lied to me before,' I say. 'You said you didn't know who was in the car that hit you. You only told me it was Stacey when I said it was time for you to go home.'

'It *was* Stacey,' she says.

'Then I believe you. Stop talking and put the address in the sat-nav,' I say. 'We don't have much time.'

Stacey isn't going to sit on her hands and wait to see how things play out. She knows that without a body the police don't have enough to charge me, or they'd have done it already. She has to box me into a corner from which there's no coming back.

Gambling is in my nature. And it's in Stacey's, too. Neither of us is in the habit of playing it safe. We both have incriminating video of each other: in theory, our mutually assured destruction should keep us both safe. But I guarantee she'll roll the dice anyway and give the police the CCTV footage of me breaking into her house and her husband's office, calculating I'll be arrested before I have a chance to mount an attack. It's what I'd do.

She never needed the house deeds, of course. It was a set-up to give her video that'd make me look guilty, and it was a brilliant move. I was so invested in her domestic abuse narra-tive I never stopped to question why she needed the deeds so urgently. I didn't question anything. Even when I hacked into Felix's desktop camera I was trying to find something that'd *help* her.

I've probably got a few hours at most before the police arrest me. The video I have of Stacey attacking her husband is suggestive, but it's nowhere near enough to get me off the hook. I need more ammunition if I'm to persuade the police to take Stacey seriously as a suspect. And Harper's ridiculous Kyper Nation may just have secured it for me.

The girl has more than two million followers. That's two million pairs of eyes looking for Felix Porter; Stacey Porter's name on two million lips. Stacey's kept her secrets hidden for nearly twenty years, but even she couldn't bury them deep enough to survive that kind of scrutiny.

It takes Harper and me more than an hour just to drive out of London. We don't reach the sleepy West Sussex village Harper entered into the sat-nav until mid-morning. We follow the directions until we turn onto a quiet road and find ourselves outside a small bungalow opposite the weathered lychgate of a beautiful medieval church.

'Number 59,' Harper says, pointing as I pull into the kerb a few houses down from the church. 'It's that one, there, with the blue door.'

'A car's in the drive,' I say. 'Fingers crossed that means she's in.'

We get out of the car: I'd rather Harper stayed behind but I know better than to ask. The door of Number 59 is surrounded by a trellis of ivy reddening in the weak autumn sunshine, and the small handkerchief of lawn is lush and just the right side of overgrown. Dense bushes of heather spill from the flowerbed and over the low brick wall fronting the road. Snatches of Radio Three and the smell of bacon waft through the open kitchen window as we walk up the short drive.

Susan Temple was Stacey's foster mother for four years after her parents died in a car crash when she was fifteen. The accident is a matter of public record, but Stacey's never

291

mentioned the woman who took her in afterwards: her version of events has her brother as her legal guardian until his own death from an overdose four years later. Susan Temple's been struck from the record.

I want to know why.

chapter 55

tom

The footage my wife leaked online this morning has gone viral. The nation's morning sofa sweetheart caught on video slapping and punching and kicking her husband, her *missing* husband: it's a tabloid wet dream.

Less than three hours after *MailOnline* picked up the story, INN rushed out a craven ass-covering statement: *Stacey Porter has been suspended from the* Morning Express Show *pending further evaluation of information that has recently come to light. We take all allegations of domestic violence extremely seriously regardless of gender, race or sexual orientation, and are deeply saddened by recent events. We can say unequivocally, that, prior to Friday morning, current INN management was never made aware of any complaints about Stacey Porter's conduct, but these allegations represent an egregious violation of our company's standards and we have no choice but to take them extremely seriously.*

'I'm not sure that was the wisest move,' I tell Millie when she returns from wherever she's been with Harper mid-afternoon. 'You've just poked the bear – Stacey's going to be out for blood. More importantly, you've just put Felix's disappearance back on the front page.'

'I realise this is going to come as a shock to you,' Millie says, 'but *I* didn't kill Felix Porter, Tom.'

'You don't have to—'

'Tom,' Millie says, enunciating each word clearly and concisely. 'I. Did. Not. Kill. Felix. Porter.'

'Are you sure?'

'I think I would've noticed.'

My wife isn't a cold-blooded murderer: that's a *good* thing. That doesn't mean she isn't capable of killing if the need arises. She took care of her father, after all. She just isn't responsible *this* time.

'So if you didn't kill him, where is he?' I ask.

'I have no idea,' Millie says, exasperated. 'Assuming he isn't sunning himself by the pool in Argentina or Panama, I'd say Stacey killed him. And she's *already* out for my blood, Tom. This won't make any difference. She set me up to take the fall for Felix. I've been two steps behind her all along. I need to get out ahead of her if I'm to have a hope in hell of coming through this. Frankly, I'm surprised the police aren't already here to arrest me.'

'About that,' I say.

'What? Have you spoken to them?'

'No need,' I say. 'There's not much point being married to a computer geek if he can't hack a simple CCTV system. Stacey downloaded the footage of you breaking into her house onto Felix's computer instead of her own laptop. Rookie mistake. I used the trapdoor from your original virus to wipe the download *and* the original CCTV file. She didn't send it to the police – I checked her digital history. She's got nothing on you now.'

'Have I told you how much I love you?' Millie says.

'All in a day's work. Though next time you want to hack into someone's computer,' I add, 'talk to me first. It took me hours to make sure that virus you uploaded couldn't be traced back to you.'

'I didn't want to involve you,' Millie says.

'I *am* involved,' I say. 'If something involves you, it involves me. You should have told me when Stacey asked you to break into Felix's office in the first place. You know the rules.'

'It wasn't about *us*. And sometimes I think you enjoy that sort of thing a little too much, Tom.'

'Well, you're safe now,' I say, choosing to ignore the implications of that last remark. 'Stacey's on the back foot. She'll be too busy saving her own skin to take any more pot shots at you.'

'She's cornered,' Millie corrects. 'That makes her more dangerous than ever.'

'But now the police have that video of her—'

'Don't be naive, Tom,' she says, putting a pod of coffee in the machine. 'It's bought me a bit of time, that's all. By tomorrow morning, Stacey will have given a tearful press statement on her front steps admitting to being a long-term survivor of domestic abuse, and claiming the video has been taken out of context and she was just defending herself. She'll say she's traumatised and seeking counselling, and she'll be back on the *Morning Express Show* next week launching a campaign to support women who fight back against their abusers. Everyone loves a redemption story. Just ask Martha Stewart.'

'What about Felix?'

'What *about* him?'

'Well, he's still missing. She can't explain *that* away.'

'Without a body the police can't even prove a crime has been committed,' Millie says, tossing the used coffee pod into the bin. 'And all the available evidence points to *me*, not her.'

'So where were you and Harper this morning?' I ask.

'Are you sure you want to know?'

'We're in this together, remember?'

'One of Harper's fans got in touch with her,' Millie says, pulling out a kitchen stool. 'Apparently the girl's mother is best friends with the daughter of a woman who fostered Stacey when she was a teenager. We went to see her this morning. It turns out Stacey was in and out of the foster care system four or five times *before* her parents died.' She takes a sip of coffee. 'The first time her parents put her into care was when she strangled the family cat with barbed wire when she was seven.'

'Jesus!'

'According to Susan Temple, the foster mother, Stacey showed all the early traits of a psychopathic child: lack of empathy, extreme tantrums, chronic lying, failure to show guilt or remorse. There were numerous incidents over the years. About six months before the car crash that killed her parents, she attacked another child at school with a rounders bat. She smashed him in the face and blinded him in one eye.'

My jaw drops. 'And they didn't lock her up?'

'Oh, they did. But she was a model patient, took her meds, and eventually her parents took her back. Two weeks later, they were dead.'

'An accident?'

Millie shrugs. 'No one could prove it wasn't. Her father had been drinking – he was under the limit, but the police didn't dig any further. Susan Temple isn't in any doubt: it was a straight stretch of road, and Stacey's father swerved into a tree for no apparent reason.'

'I can't believe none of this has ever come out,' I say. 'Stacey's in the public eye. How's she kept this under wraps so long?'

'She was a juvenile. The records were sealed. And she's never put a foot wrong since. Whatever she might have got up to in private, she's managed to stay under the radar. Susan Temple tried to raise the alarm a couple of times after the crash, but no one wanted to know. She says she's been waiting twenty years for someone to come and ask questions, but no one ever did.'

'Have you got proof of any of this?' I demand. 'Can you use it?'

'I'm still trying to figure that out,' Millie says.

'Well, I hope for both your sake and this woman's that Stacey doesn't find out you've been to see her,' I say. 'I can't imagine she's going to be happy.'

'Where are the kids?'

'Meddie's gone out for pizza again with this *Noah*,' I say, making his name sound like a dirty word. 'Peter's upstairs in his room.'

'We need to keep better track of them,' Millie says.

'You think Stacey might go after them?' I exclaim.

'I don't know, Tom. It's not a chance I want to take. Frankly, I don't want Peter anywhere near her. I worry he—'

A noise behind me makes me jump. Millie and I both turn. 'How long have you been standing there?' I demand.

Peter's flat eyes tell me nothing.

chapter 56

millie

'Where are you going?' Tom says.

'You can't ask me that,' I tell him.

Tom follows me into the bathroom and watches as I twist my heavy hair into its neat chignon and pin it in place. 'What time will you be back?'

'You know the rules, Tom,' I say.

He trails me as I return to the bedroom and pull a pale cream tweed jacket from the wardrobe. '*You* know the rules,' he says. 'Back before nightfall.'

'The children aren't babies any more.'

'That's not the point.'

'Why? Are you worried I'm setting Peter a bad example?' I say, glancing in the wardrobe mirror and straightening my shirt collar so that my silk lapels are even. 'I think that ship has sailed, Tom.'

He moves behind me, snaking his arms around my waist. I turn into him. When he kisses me, his mouth is hungry, urgent. His tongue forces its way between my lips, and I can feel his erection against my thigh.

This is how it is between us.

This is how it's always been.

I saw his disappointment yesterday when I told him I wasn't

the one who killed Felix Porter. I am his dance with the dark. He needs me to be who I am so that he can be who he is.

I know what he wants from me. Tom's always been aroused by my shadowed side. It's what kept him from Harper's bed, what keeps him from the bed of any other woman but me. He tells me I'm a good person, but he doesn't really believe it. It would break his heart to know the truth about me.

I killed my father, but I'm not the person Tom thinks I am. I break into homes, but instead of stealing, I leave flowers. I slice through flesh and dip my hands in blood, but I save lives: I don't take them.

So this is my gift to him today: a consolation prize for the truth about Felix. He doesn't know where I'm going or what I'm doing, but he *imagines*. His fantasies are what makes him hard. He thinks I don't tell him because I'm afraid he would be shocked. And he would: but not the way he thinks.

Because I love him I've kept my secret for nearly twenty-five years: not for my sake, but for *his*.

It's Saturday: once I get out of Fulham, the traffic west to Abingdon is surprisingly light. It's a journey I've made many times before; I know where the speed traps are, which traffic cameras work and which are dummies. I stop for petrol at the garage I always use, eschewing the bitter reheated coffee on offer when I go inside to pay, and instead crossing the forecourt to the greasy spoon on the corner of the block. The owner, Harry, greets me with a smile when I hand him my travel mug, and returns it filled with the best coffee I've had outside Brazil, along with a piece of homemade shortbread – still warm – on the house.

'Haven't seen you in a few weeks,' he comments as I pay. 'Everything all right?'

'Fine, thanks, Harry. It's just been a bit chaotic at home.'

'Send your girl my love,' Harry says, as he always does.

He proffers my change, and I wave it away, as I always do. 'Thank you for the shortbread,' I say, raising it in tribute.

Harry's smile broadens. 'Hope she enjoys it.'

I get back on the road, sipping my coffee as the grey built-up streets give way to country roads and vivid autumn foliage. Eventually I reach the outskirts of Abingdon, securing the lid of my travel mug just before the hump-backed bridge that would have spilled it. Shortly afterwards I turn right between a pair of stone pillars onto a long, sweeping gravel drive. It's another half-mile before the warm yellow stone of Alexander Manor comes into view.

The receptionist is new to me. I hand her my ID, and she pecks away at her computer with neatly trimmed nails: all the better to show off the small princess-cut diamond on the fourth finger of her left hand.

'Have you been here before?' she asks, handing me a sticky 'V' label.

'Yes. I know where I'm going,' I say.

I ascend the broad curve of stairs to the second floor. Built in the eighteenth century, Alexander Manor was once the seat of an old Sussex family that endured for seven generations before being abruptly extinguished by the First World War. Requisitioned as a military hospital in 1916, it was finally returned to civilian use in the mid-Sixties and for the last four decades has been used as a private care home. Unlike most such institutions, it smells not of pee and bleach but beeswax and history.

Coloured motes of light from the stained-glass windows dance across the oak panelling, and long-dead ancestors look down sternly from the walls.

I head down the corridor to a bright, sunny room at the end. I imagine this was once the private sitting room of the mistress of the house: I can picture her gazing from the window down the graceful curve of her drive.

Watching a boy on a bicycle bringing her a telegram telling her the last of her four sons was dead.

'Hello, my darling girl,' I say, as I enter the room. I hold up the paper bag containing the shortbread. 'Look what I've brought for you.'

Gracie doesn't move. I crouch beside her wheelchair, positioned near the tall window so that she can see the view, and touch her cheek so she knows I'm here. After a moment, she turns her head towards me, and I tell myself I see recognition in her eyes.

'Here,' I smile, breaking off a piece of shortbread and handing it to her. 'It's your favourite.'

Under my guiding fingers Gracie slowly brings it to her mouth. She doesn't close her lips as she sucks on the shortbread, and drool spills down her chin. I reach for a tissue from the box on the table near us and gently wipe it away.

The night Tom and I ran from my father, the night when I was nine and my mother told us to *Run!* and we sped barefoot over broken glass to the sanctuary of the Spar shop on the corner, I didn't think about my four-year-old sister cowering upstairs beneath the bedclothes. I didn't think about anything but getting as far from my father as possible before he killed me, before he killed Tom.

I didn't think about Gracie.

It was my job to look after her, and I left her behind.

My father insisted my baby sister had fallen down the stairs. She couldn't contradict him, because she couldn't talk. Or walk, or brush her hair, or smile at a familiar face, or grow up and go to school or fall in love or do anything else by herself ever again.

My mother was so ashamed of herself for going back to him she told everyone Gracie was dead. She didn't even tell me my sister was alive – no, not alive, *existing*, abandoned in a

301

mental institution – until the morning of my father's funeral seven years later. She thought it *excused* him: the fact that Gracie wasn't dead after all. *I don't want you to think the worst of him,* she said. *Your dad's not as black as he's painted.*

I didn't tell Tom then, because I didn't want him to have to share the burden of guilt I felt for leaving Gracie behind. I visited her whenever I could, and later, once I was out of medical school and could afford it, I moved her to Alexander Manor, where I was sometimes allowed to stay with her overnight.

My 'prison breaks'.

I let Tom imagine I'm doing dark deeds in dark places when I'm visiting my sweet, broken sister because I love him just a tiny bit more than I hate myself. He's drawn to the darkness in me: I'm not going to be the one to disillusion him.

It's almost dark when I say goodbye to Gracie, the chill of autumn hanging in the air. I get into my car and turn the heating up, my headlights picking up a swirl of ground mist as I turn onto the gravelled drive. I should be home by eight-thirty if the traffic isn't too heavy.

I glance in my rearview mirror as Alexander Manor recedes into the darkness behind me and almost swerve onto the grass.

'Jesus fuck!' I exclaim.

'You went digging around in my past,' Stacey says, meeting my eyes in the mirror. 'Did you really think I wouldn't start digging around in yours?'

chapter 57

millie

I'm a cardiothoracic surgeon: keeping cool under pressure is what I do best. 'How did you get into my car?' I ask calmly.

'You left it unlocked when you went back into your house for your handbag,' Stacey says. 'You really should be more careful, Millie. London can be a dangerous place. There are all sorts of dodgy people around, and this is an expensive vehicle. In the time it took you to get your bag your car could've been stolen.'

'Careless of me,' I say. 'I'll have to remember to lock it next time.'

'If there is a next time,' Stacey says.

I shift in my seat to get a better angle in the mirror, trying to see if she has a weapon. I can only make out her head and shoulders in the dark: she could have a knife or even a gun in her lap.

'Keep driving,' she says, as I slow for the intersection with the main road.

'And if I don't?'

'Well, that would be a little awkward for both of us, wouldn't it?'

I pause at the junction, my hand on the indicator. 'Where are we going?'

'Home,' she says.

'Yours or mine?'

She laughs. 'It doesn't much matter, does it? We live less than a dozen streets apart, so either way we're heading in the same direction.'

We could be car-pooling on the school run. I turn left onto the unlit lane at the end of the drive, my headlights picking out the cats' eyes down the centre of the road. Stacey has never been more dangerous than she is now, cornered and on the back foot.

'It wasn't very nice of you to leak that video,' she says chidingly. 'Do you know how much extra work you made for my agent? She was up all night drafting a press release for me.'

'She might as well earn her commission,' I say. 'What angle did she come up with?'

'The obvious one: self-defence after a decade of abuse. You didn't see my statement to the press? It was all over the news this afternoon.'

'Forgive me. I've been a little distracted.'

Stacey glances out of the window. It's started to drizzle: my windscreen wipers scrape against the glass. 'I think you might've done me a favour,' she says. 'I've already had a couple of domestic abuse shelters contact me asking me to be their patron. The Centre for Women's Justice — or was it Justice for Women? — want me to join their campaign for penal reform for women who hit back against their abusers. Did you know nearly forty percent of female murder victims were killed by a current or former partner, against just four percent of male victims?'

'I think we both know Felix wasn't the abuser here, Stacey.'

'Do we, though?' she asks. 'It's all a question of perspective, isn't it? That video, for instance. It looks bad for me on first viewing, but once you see the photos of my bruises and black eye, well. That changes things.'

The grey shadow of a fox darts across the road, and I brake to avoid it. 'I told you those photos would come in useful.'

'And you were right, Millie. I'm the first to admit it. As soon as Justine – that's my agent, the bloodsucking leech – as soon as she made the photos available to the press, everything changed. Hashtag *believe the women*: you've got to love it. I've already had three grovelling voicemails from my producer, but I think I'm going to make him sweat a bit more before I return them.'

It doesn't matter what I do: Stacey will come up smelling of roses. The police are never going to believe me over her. I'm not *likeable*. I'm not *relatable*.

'So why are you here, Stacey?' I ask. 'If everything's worked out so beautifully for you? What do you need from me?'

'I didn't kill my husband, Millie.'

'Nor did I,' I say tersely. 'Though you've done a very good job at making it look as if I did.'

'No one's ever going to convict you,' Stacey says with a dismissive wave of her hand. 'It's all circumstantial. Smoke and mirrors. It'll blow over. You'll be fine.'

'So what was the point? Why drag me into it at all?'

She doesn't reply. When I glance in the rearview mirror, she's staring out into the darkness. I could stop the car and refuse to play this game any longer. Maybe she has a weapon, maybe she doesn't: I find it hard to believe she's going to do me any harm. The last thing she needs is another corpse on her hands.

She turns her head. 'Why are you such good friends with Harper?' she asks abruptly.

I meet her eyes in the mirror. 'We're not friends.'

'She's living in your house,' Stacey says.

'Because you drove a bloody car into hers and tried to kill her,' I say.

'You only have her word for that.'

She's right, of course.

'She says she saw you at the wheel,' I say.

'Did she tell you your son was with me when I did it?'

It takes a considerable effort of will to keep the car on the road. 'You're lying,' I say.

'You know I'm not.'

My knuckles tighten on the steering wheel. 'Stay away from him,' I snap.

'What's that worth to you?'

'He's my *son*.'

'You tried to destroy my career with your little online stunt yesterday,' Stacey says. 'You've been digging around in my past trying to find more dirt to use against me. Your son told me that, by the way. Gave me all the details. He's very loyal. Just not to you.' She opens the window a couple of centimetres, letting in a sharp blast of cold air. 'Please pass my best on to your husband, too, won't you? He did a nice job wiping my computer.'

We're getting closer to London now: the trees have given way to streetlamps and unlovely buildings, and I'm forced to slow as the traffic snarls.

'Look,' I say, keeping my temper on a tight leash. 'I told you before: we can both still walk away from this. Whatever's going on with you and Felix, I want no part of it. I just want to be back in my OR where my only concern is keeping my patient alive. What I *don't* want,' I add sourly, 'is to be hijacked in my own car. What I *don't* want is to be looking over my shoulder every five minutes, or wondering if my son is going to slide a knife between my ribs on your behalf while I sleep.'

'OK,' Stacey says.

'OK?'

'A truce. That's what you want, right? You go your way, I'll go mine?'

'Yes,' I say warily. 'I'd be happy if I never saw you or your damn house again.'

'Fine,' she says. 'A truce. But it comes with strings attached, Millie.'

'Yes,' I say. 'I thought it might.'

chapter 58

millie

Sunday is a difficult day. I spend most of it watching my son as he guzzles Cheerios, milk dripping down his chin, or lies on his stomach playing with his Lego, wondering what my tousle-haired, clear-eyed, freckle-faced boy is really thinking. The question isn't *whether* he crept out of the house after he'd been sent to bed and walked half a mile in the dark to Stacey's: I already know he's capable of that. His invasion of our neigh-bour's house a few weeks ago wasn't an isolated incident: he was far too slick and confident for it to be a first time offence. He sneaks around in the dark, listening in corners and watching from the shadows. Disappearing in the night to the Glass House would have been – literally – child's play.

The real question is *why*.

Did he know what Stacey was planning to do when he slipped silently out of the house that night? Was she waiting for him outside in her stolen car? I find it hard to imagine she'd want a ten-year-old boy along for the ride, but the two of them have been drawn to each other from the day they met. It sounds ridiculous: a child and a grown woman, a successful woman, a mother herself. But there's a darkness between them, a kinship, that makes me fearful. Harper says the intense bond between them *creeps me out* and I can't say I disagree with her. Together, they're far more dangerous than either of them would be alone.

I think of murderous pairings like Myra Hindley and Ian Brady. They brought out the psychopathic worst in each other, committing vicious, sadistic crimes together that were almost inconceivable in their brutality. Would they have tortured and murdered children had they been acting alone? They recognised something of themselves in each other, something misshapen and ugly and deformed, and drew strength from that black affinity.

Age isn't a barrier to this sort of evil partnership: the killers of toddler James Bulger, abducted from a shopping centre before being tortured to death and abandoned on a railway line near Liverpool, were just ten years old themselves at the time.

Exactly the same age my son is now.

I cast my mind back to the morning five weeks ago when Stacey came to our house with a black eye, the same day Tom asked her to babysit Peter. It was only a few days after my son had tried to drown hers in the swimming pool at the Hurlingham Club. I remember every instinct warning me of *danger!* but my fear was for Stacey, not Peter. It never occurred to me for a split second that the threat was not *to* either of them, but *from both* of them.

Two days later, Felix Porter disappeared.

If my son was partly responsible, if he's kept this dreadful secret for five weeks – and I know better than most people the secrets children are capable of keeping from their parents: they know all of ours, but we know none of theirs – then I have to help him, because sooner or later Stacey will tire of her game of cat and mouse, and then his life won't be worth spit. Because despite her denials, I'm quite certain Stacey *has* killed Felix. And now I'm equally sure Peter helped her.

Tom knows this too, but he won't admit it to himself, much

less to me. He insists Stacey's lying: that it can't have been Peter in the car with her. Which means he doesn't have to choose between saving our son or saving the world from him: he abdicates that bitter responsibility to me.

I don't wrestle with the decision. I've always lived in the shades of grey that lie somewhere between right and wrong. Peter is my son. It doesn't matter to me if he is *good* or *bad*. As long as he is safe.

Tom doesn't trust Stacey or her truce, but she knows what I will do to protect Peter, and so she knows my protection extends to her now, too. I can't threaten her without endangering him. And from her point of view I've served my purpose: the evidence swirling around me has disturbed enough sediment to muddy the waters for the police. We've achieved an unlikely stasis.

On Sunday afternoon, I tell Harper it's time to go home. She protests because she thinks that morally my house is hers, *you can't send me back to that tiny flat*, but I'm done with this now. I'm done with the Glass House. I'm done with it all.

Monday is a much better day. On Monday I'm back in theatre, back where I belong: I'm on my feet for more than nine hours without food or a break performing three complex surgeries back-to-back, but Monday is not a difficult day. When I finish I feel energised and revitalised, and after I've checked on my last patient I change into my running clothes, deciding to leave my Audi in the car park overnight and run home.

I'm lacing up my new trainers – they're still uncomfortably stiff – when my phone beeps with an incoming text from Tom.

Peter wasn't at pickup. Does he have practice?

It's forty minutes since school ended. Peter doesn't have any after-school activities on a Monday: he should have been waiting for Tom to collect him as usual. The first wings of anxiety beat in my chest.

Maybe he got the tube with M? I text back.

She's home. He isn't with her.

I call Peter, but it goes straight to voicemail without even ringing. I tell myself his battery is probably dead from watching too many TikTok videos beneath his desk during class.

The Find My Phone feature is enabled on both the kids' mobiles. Even if Peter's phone is switched off, it will give me his last location by pinging off other users' phones. A minute later I have my answer: the school, which tells me nothing I didn't already know.

My phone vibrates again.

It's from Stacey this time: a photograph of my son sitting at her kitchen counter eating ice-cream.

The bird of anxiety takes flight.

We had a deal, I text.

Keep your hair on. He just turned up at my door. Come and get him.

Tom offers to collect Peter himself when I update him with the news, but I tell him I'll go. I need to make sure Stacey understood I meant what I said yesterday.

I'm halfway down the stairs when I'm paged to attend an emergency cardiac tamponade. I text Stacey to let her know I'll be there as soon as I can and head down to the Emergency Department. It's only ninety minutes later, when the crisis is under control, that I realise I forgot to press *send*.

I erase the redundant message and text a new one.

Held up at work. On my way.

Three grey dots appear, and then disappear. I wait a few moments but Stacey doesn't reply.

I'm reversing my car out of its space when my mobile pings again with an incoming text.

Too late now.

chapter 59

stacey

Stacey meant every word of her promise to Millie Downton. She managed to spin the video Millie leaked online to her advantage, but the damage has been done: she's back under the media spotlight just when she most needs it to move on. She has no wish to go toe-to-toe with Millie again. She's enjoyed the hero-worship from Millie's son – if only her boy, Archie, was as charismatic and enterprising – and taken no small degree of pleasure from Millie's obvious irritation, but he's not worth incurring her mama-bear wrath. The woman is a psychotic tigress when it comes to her children.

Most mothers are. It's not something Stacey's ever really understood.

So when she comes up from the cellar and finds Peter peering in through the heavy glass front door on Monday afternoon, she's not pleased. The boy can keep secrets – he's certainly proven that – but she doesn't want to give Millie any excuse to resume hostilities.

On the other hand, she doesn't want him telling his mother what he knows either.

So she lets him in, and feeds him Coke and ice-cream before texting Millie to come and collect him.

'I told you this had to stop,' she tells Peter, putting the tub of Ben & Jerry's back in the freezer. 'No more coming over here unannounced. Your mother doesn't want you to see me. She thinks I'm a bad influence.'

Peter grins. 'That's funny.'

Stacey doesn't smile back. It isn't funny. It isn't funny at all. But she certainly appreciates the irony: a freckle-faced ten-year-old boy and a thirty-eight-year-old grown-ass professional woman – of course people will assume *she's* the bad influence.

Her coffee has gone cold, and she pours it down the sink. Instead of draining, the coffee pools in the bottom, lifting small fragments of onions and peas on a tide of black caffeine. Stacey reaches beneath the sink for the plunger to clear it.

'Harper's going back home tomorrow,' Peter says as she pumps the plunger.

'I'm sure your mother must be relieved,' Stacey says.

He spoons another mouthful of ice-cream into his mouth. She wishes this boy had been born hers. They could have done so much together. He really *is* an exceptionally good-looking child, with those amber eyes and sweep of tawny hair. At ten years old he's already learned to weaponise his looks: she can only imagine how dangerous, how *effective*, he'll be in a few years' time.

'They know,' he tells her, slyly. 'Harper saw you in the car.'

The cold coffee starts to drain, and she puts the plunger back beneath the sink and straightens up. 'Knowing and proving are very different things, Peter,' she says.

'You don't have to worry about Millie,' he says. '*She* won't say anything.'

It's odd hearing him use his mother's first name.

'I'm not worried,' she says.

'You should be,' Peter says. 'You should be worried about *Harper*. She talks too much. I hear her at night recording her vlogs. She talks about *you*.'

Stacey pictures him creeping through the house in the dark, listening at doors, hiding in shadows. She hopes for her sake Harper locks her bedroom door.

Peter gulps his Coke, and then lets out a small burp and grins. Sometimes it's easy to forget he's still a child. 'What are we going to do?' he asks.

'*We* aren't going to do anything.'

'You've let it drag on too long,' Peter says. 'You know what you have to do. You just need to *do* it.'

Sometimes it's easy to forget he's not like other children. 'It's not that simple,' she says.

'Yes, it is. Stop pretending you haven't decided. You know you're going to do it anyway, so just get on with it.'

'Your mother will be here soon,' Stacey says.

'*I* could do something,' he says, as if she hasn't spoken. 'Before Harper goes home. We have to stop her or she'll ruin everything. You said I was a big help last time,' he adds. 'You said you couldn't have done it without me.'

Stacey glances down the street. She doesn't know what's keeping Millie: she should be here by now. 'I shouldn't have involved you,' she tells Peter.

She's not thinking of him when she says that. She's aware she took an insane risk, an unforgivable risk, by involving a ten-year-old. She still isn't quite sure why she did it. Perhaps she was just tired of being alone.

Stacey has never had friends. But she learned the hard way survival depended on fitting in. She didn't ever want to go back to the place they sent her after she smashed the face of the boy who tried to kiss her with a rounders bat. So she figured out how to censor what she really thinks. She learned to mimic the appropriate reactions and behave the way the world expected her to behave, to hide in plain sight, to blend in: she's done it so well she's built a career based on her ability

314

to empathise and *feel your pain*. But the constant effort required to pretend to be normal is *exhausting*.

And it's *lonely*.

It's like being immersed in a foreign language: sometimes she just wants to speak plainly and be understood.

Peter understands.

Stacey saw what Peter did that day at the Hurlingham Club. She saw him pull Archie beneath the water while everyone was distracted by the antics of the two Conway boys, and for a moment, as she watched and *did nothing*, she allowed herself to imagine Archie gone and Peter her son instead.

Peter saw her watching him, and something passed between them: an understanding, a recognition that transcended *ten-year-old boy, thirty-eight-year-old woman*. She *saw* him. He was a child like she had been: a child who lied all the time, who broke things, who bruised his classmates, who hurt people. He couldn't help it. He was biologically wired not to feel shame or fear or guilt. He'd been born without the ability to empathise, to *put yourself in my shoes*, just as some people are born without limbs. It wasn't his fault – any more than it had been hers.

She wanted to teach Peter everything she knew, to mentor him, to protect him, to see him flourish and become who he was born to be. For the first time in her life she understood what it was to feel like a mother.

So she told him about Felix.

Her phone rings suddenly, and she glances at the number: DS Mehdi again. She wants to ignore it, but he's already called twice this afternoon, and the last thing she needs is for him to turn up at the house.

'Stay here,' she tells Peter, as she shuts herself in her bedroom. 'Wait for your mother. She won't be long.'

DS Mehdi is just checking in, he tells her, but Stacey knows the avalanche of publicity around the video is making the detective look at her seriously again. He's always been the one she feared. She's on the phone longer than she'd like, and when she finally ends the call and goes back into the kitchen, Peter isn't there.

She knows where he is.

She goes downstairs. The door to the cellar is open. She can hear a strange gurgling, a *scratching*, like a rat caught in a drain. She's not someone who experiences fear, but something speeds her down the cellar stairs so fast she can't feel her own feet.

Peter is waiting for her at the bottom. He smiles up at her, those beautiful tawny eyes clear and untroubled.

'I was just tidying up for you,' he says.

chapter 60

millie

Stacey's front door is not only unlocked, but *open*. I go into the house, fear gnawing an acid path through my insides. *Too late now*. What did she mean by that? If she's done anything to Peter, if she's harmed a single hair on his head—

I head up to the kitchen, taking the stairs two at a time. An empty bowl smeared with chocolate and vanilla ice-cream is on the counter. A dirty coffee cup bearing the imprint of Stacey's signature pink lipstick sits beside the sink. The kitchen has the deserted air of a hastily abandoned shipwreck.

My anxiety builds as I go back downstairs and check the bedrooms. There's no sign of Peter or Stacey.

It occurs to me she might have tired of waiting for me and driven Peter home instead, but a quick text soon establishes that's not the case: Tom hasn't heard from either of them, and I can't see Stacey leaving her front door wide open anyway.

Something bad has happened, I can *feel* it.

I check every inch of the house again. Stacey still hasn't responded to my texts, and when I call her, her phone rings out on the kitchen counter. She'd never have left her phone behind if she'd gone out. Something's *wrong*.

I stand in the hall by the front door, debating what to do next.

And then I see the cellar.

The door is just a fraction ajar, which is the only reason I notice it. It's been ingeniously designed to blend seamlessly into the wall at the foot of the stairs: I've walked past it a dozen times and never noticed it was there. I know this house almost as well as the architect who designed it, and I'm quite certain there isn't a cellar on the plans. There was a small workman's cottage on this site before the Second World War, if I remember correctly: the basement must be part of that.

'Stacey?' I call, opening the cellar door wider. 'Peter? Are you down there?'

No answer.

The stairwell is unlit. Using the torch on my phone, I grope my way carefully down the dangerously steep flight of concrete steps, one hand on the rough stone wall for balance. When I reach the bottom, I find the cellar floor is beaten earth, the ceiling so low I have to dip my head to avoid hitting it on the old beams. It must be an ancient root cellar. I can't imagine it's been used in years.

'Peter?' I call again. 'Stacey?'

I cast my torch around me. The cellar is about ten feet square, and there's nothing in it but a few broken tools. Everything is covered with a thick layer of dust and cobwebs. It looks like no one's been here in decades.

I almost miss it at first, concealed as it is by a partial collapse of the ceiling, but then I see it: another door directly opposite the stairs. Two heavy bolts at top and bottom have been pulled back from their locks. Drag marks scored in the earthen floor show it's been opened, and very recently.

My heart pounds as I grab the doorknob and pull. It's black as pitch in here: without the daylight spilling down the stairs from the house above, this room is even darker than the root cellar. My field of vision is restricted to the narrow circle illuminated by my phone torch. But I can feel cold air on my face: there must be a vent or duct to the outside somewhere.

I yelp as my shin makes contact with cold metal, and swing my phone down.

'Oh, dear Christ,' I whisper.

Felix is still alive, stretched out on a bare, stained mattress atop a narrow metal bed frame. He shrinks back from the sudden glare of light, turning his head away with a gargled yelp.

I drop to the floor beside him. 'It's going to be OK,' I tell him. 'I'm here now. I'm going to look after you. I'll get you out of here.'

The bottom half of his face is oddly black, and it takes me a moment to realise it's not dirt but dried blood. The stench coming off him tells me he's been lying here in his own filth for weeks: I can smell not just urine and excrement, but the sickly-sweet decay of sores and infected wounds.

His pulse is weak and thready, but it's there. He tries to speak, but the most he can manage is a thick, choking sound. His eyes bulge frantically. I hook my finger in his mouth, trying to clear his airway. When I remove it, several of his teeth spill into my hand.

'Dear God,' I mutter, appalled.

The only time I've ever seen injuries like this was years ago when a plumber came to the Emergency Department after drinking a glass of drain cleaner which he'd mistaken for his glass of beer. I have no idea what's happened to Felix, but if I don't get him help soon, he's not going to survive.

I swing my phone torch wildly around the room. It's bigger than the last, and looks as if it was finished more recently: the floor is concrete rather than earth, and it obviously has electricity as a bare bulb hangs from the ceiling. There's a large chest freezer in the corner of the cellar, and, to judge from the hum, it has power, too. I can't imagine how anyone ever got it down here. I don't even want to think about what Stacey might be keeping inside it.

I prop my phone on the floor against the wall so that my hands are free to help Felix. His left arm is bent at an unnatural angle over his head, and I realise he's handcuffed to a thick metal pipe running along the basement wall. His muscles must have atrophied in that position: he stiffens in agony when I try to move him. He's just skin and bone: he must have lost at least thirty pounds. What I can't understand is why Stacey's bothered to keep him alive. If she wanted him dead, why not simply kill him? Why prolong the agony like this? It's unspeakably cruel.

I need to get help, but I don't want to leave Felix. I pick up my phone to see if by some miracle I have signal down here, but before I can use it, something heavy hits me from behind and everything goes black.

chapter 61

millie

Pain.

A pain so overpowering I can't think.

Pain.

It feels as if my eyelids are weighted shut. Just the movement of air in and out of my lungs when I breathe is enough to make my head explode. I gasp and see flashes of blinding light behind my eyes, and then oblivion returns.

The next time I wake, the pain has diminished to a throbbing ache at the back of my skull, leaving just enough space for me to feel the soreness in my neck and shoulders, the numbness in my left arm. Something sharp digs into my back: I'm propped against a stone wall. Concrete beneath my legs and buttocks. Darkness around me, and the reek of urine, sweat, blood and faeces.

And fear.

Vomit suddenly rises in my throat and fills my mouth, and I turn my head, spewing it onto the ground. I feel weak and dizzy from the concussion. I can't move my left arm. My thoughts are disjointed and confused, floating past me like soap bubbles on the breeze. Every time I try to catch one it bursts in my hand.

I must pass out again, because I'm jolted back to consciousness by a sudden burst of bright white light: the harsh glare of an overhead bulb. It takes several minutes for my eyes to adjust, but finally my mind is coming back into focus. I remember what happened: looking for Peter and Stacey, finding Felix, the sudden blow to the back of my head. I have no idea how much time has passed: a few minutes, an hour, a day.

I glance at Felix on the metal bed next to me. He's not moving. I can't see the rise and fall of his chest. I don't know if he's still alive.

I try to move towards him, and my left arm screams in protest: I'm handcuffed to the same metal pipe as Felix. One tug tells me it's not coming free.

'Ah. You're back with us,' Stacey says.

She's standing in the doorway to the small root cellar, safely well out of my reach. I try to speak, but only manage a harsh cough. She points to a bottle of water next to me. Pain shoots through my tethered arm from my wrist to my shoulder as I jam the plastic bottle against my chest so I can open it with my free hand. The water is tepid, but it clears my throat.

'Where's Peter?' I rasp.

'He's here,' she says vaguely. 'Sorry about the headache,' she adds. 'I'm afraid this was the only way.'

'Where is he?'

'I told you, he's here,' she says impatiently. 'You'll see him soon enough.'

Adrenaline is an extraordinary hormone. It's an amazing thing to have coursing through your system when facing danger – people have been known to lift a car off a child with its help. It increases the flow of blood to muscles, releasing sugar into your bloodstream, along with a cascade of other effects that make your body alert and more able to fight off an attacker or outrun a flood.

My mind is suddenly crystal clear. Stacey deliberately left the door to the cellar open. She knew I was coming to the house to collect Peter: she *wanted* me to find it.

She wanted me down here, in a cellar no one knows exists.

I scan the room, assessing my options. Stacey is blocking the only doorway. No windows or skylights. There's a large cage of machinery in the far corner next to the chest freezer: a mechanical pump of some kind. At a guess I'd say it's for the swimming pool. The small external access hatch above it is probably the source of the fresh air I can feel. Even if I could get free and reach it, it's far too small for me to climb through.

My only hope is to talk my way free.

'Felix has been down here all along,' I say. 'You've kept him locked in here for five weeks.'

'Literally right under everybody's feet,' Stacey says. 'All those people looking for him, DCI Hollander and DS Mehdi telling me they'd leave no stone unturned to find him, and he's been right here all along. You've got to admit it's funny.'

'No one even knew the cellar was here?'

'Exactly. Not even Felix, until I showed it to him. It's not on any architectural plans. I only found it by accident a couple of years ago, when I was considering putting in an outdoor shower and discovered the internal dimensions of the corridor upstairs didn't match the external measurements. I located the stairs to the cellar by a process of elimination. Felix said it's like one of those secret dungeons in a medieval castle – what's the name for them?'

'An oubliette,' I say.

She comes a little closer to me, but she's still out of my reach. I deliberately let the bottle of water slip from my hand so it rolls towards her, and she takes another step in my direction to catch it. She's not foolish enough to hand it to me, though: instead she simply tightens the lid and rolls it back.

323

'Why keep him alive?' I ask conversationally. 'Why not save yourself the trouble of looking after him?'

'I didn't want to kill him,' she says, sounding almost indignant. 'That was never the plan.'

'Then why is he here?'

'It was *his* idea,' Stacey says.

I'm stunned. 'Felix wanted you to *chain him in the cellar*?'

'Not exactly,' Stacey says. She perches on the chest freezer, gently swinging her legs. 'It's a long story.'

'I'm not going anywhere.'

She laughs. 'Fair enough. Would you be surprised if I told you it was all about money?'

I think as rapidly as my aching head will allow. 'Copper Beech,' I say, after a moment. 'Felix was siphoning off funds. And you knew about it? Of course you did: Felix never did anything without you. Except you wouldn't be able to access the money,' I add slowly, working it through. 'Not if they thought Felix had absconded with it. They'd be watching you too closely. But if he was dead, that'd be a different matter. If he was dead, and someone else was arrested for his murder, no one would be looking at either of you. You'd just have to wait for the fuss to die down, and you could disappear and start again. By the time anyone figured it out, you'd be long gone.'

'This is why I like you,' Stacey says admiringly. 'You get it. Going after the pension funds was Felix's idea. His plan was to leave the country and have me follow him later, but it's not that easy to slip abroad these days, not with all the facial recognition software out there. Do you know how hard it is to avoid cameras these days? We needed the police to think he was dead, and one single image on CCTV at an airport or train station would have sunk that idea, so Felix came up with the plan to hide down here until things blew over.'

The police aren't stupid: they'd have been watching Stacey either way. But she and Felix created a false narrative of marital problems that threw all of us off the scent, and I played my part for her perfectly. Who'd suspect them of collaborating in a scam together when they were living apart and consulting divorce lawyers? The physical abuse on both sides: perhaps that was all part of it, too.

Although, I think, casting a glance at Felix's motionless form on the bed beside me, perhaps not.

'So what happened?' I ask, indicating Felix. 'He can't have planned for *this*.'

'He was never supposed to be down here this long,' she says. 'We only meant for him to be here a week or two at most, and then, once everyone stopped looking for him, he was going to slip quietly out of the country. I'd join him later. There's no future for me here. They want to move me to *morning television*.' Her expression darkens. 'But then Harper stirred everything up with that ridiculous campaign of hers to find him. There was too much attention: from the press, from the police, from that ridiculous Kyper Nation of hers. Felix got impatient. He wanted to call the whole thing off. We . . . disagreed.'

I can't hear him breathing. He hasn't moved once in the entire time Stacey's been talking.

'He's dead,' she says, matter-of-factly. 'He died a few hours ago, while you were still unconscious.' She sighs. 'I suppose it's for the best, really. He was in a lot of pain.'

She sounds almost regretful.

'What happened?' I ask, keep my voice level.

'Drain cleaner,' she says carelessly. 'Terrible way to die.'

She could be talking about the weather.

'I really am sorry I had to involve you, Millie,' Stacey adds honestly. 'This was never part of the plan. I told you, I *like* you. You were just supposed to be a distraction – the police would never have had enough evidence to convict you, not without a body. I told you on Saturday we had a deal, and I meant it. But then when Peter came over this afternoon—'

'He found Felix,' I say flatly.

'Oh, he knew Felix was here,' Stacey says. 'He's known since the very beginning.'

chapter 62

millie

I should be more surprised. My ten-year-old son has known Stacey had her husband handcuffed to a pipe in the cellar and he's kept it secret for five weeks. But I understand better than most the secrets children are capable of keeping.

'Was he . . . was he part of it?' I say. 'Did he help you bring Felix here?'

'No, I told you. That was Felix's idea. I told Peter about Felix because he deserved to see what he could do, what he could *be*, given the chance.' A note of admiration colours her voice. 'You really should be proud of your son, Millie. He was an extraordinary kid. The way his mind worked—'

She isn't making any sense. It's clear to me, even if it isn't to her, that she intended to kill Felix all along. That's why she involved Peter: as her acolyte, her disciple. Maybe she needed him to help her finish what she'd started. An unholy, homicidal alliance.

Twenty years ago, a forty-one-year-old man killed seventeen people in a series of sniper attacks across America with his young accomplice, who was just seventeen at the time. An unequal partnership, but a partnership nonetheless: psychopaths brought together by a sinister kinship that transcends age and defies definition.

Just like my son and Stacey Porter.

'Why did you have to drag him into it?' I say. 'He's *ten*.'

'A ten-year-old who tried to drown my son. Hardly an innocent, Millie.'

'So this was, what? Revenge?'

She laughs. 'Oh, Millie. No. This was *reward*.'

I have no idea what she means: I can't think straight. My head is throbbing again, and my arm aches unbearably from the pressure and restriction of being raised and cuffed to the water pipe. I shift in an attempt to ease it, and a blinding shaft of pain leaves me breathless and light-headed.

'I told you,' Stacey says. 'You should be proud of Peter. He saw weakness in my son and took advantage of it. He did what he had evolutionarily adapted to do. He was an apex predator – a *winner*. Natural selection favours winners: it's what survival of the fittest means. *He* was the one who made me see I couldn't let Felix leave the cellar just because things were taking longer than we'd planned.' She shakes her head in admiration. 'I wish my son was more like him.'

'He's not a *winner*,' I say. 'He's—'

I break off as her words finally sink in.

'What do you mean, he *was* a winner?' I say slowly. 'Why do you keep saying *was*?' Dread seeps like ice through my limbs. 'Where is he, Stacey?'

'He's here,' she says irritably.

'*Where*?'

'He shouldn't have interfered,' she says. 'I had a plan. But Peter thought he was smarter than me. He thought he could do what he liked and it'd be too late for me to be able to do anything about it. He had no right. This was *my* plan. Felix was *my* husband.'

Fear coalesces in the pit of my stomach.

'What have you done?' I shout, lunging towards her. 'Where is he, Stacey?'

328

The handcuff pulls me up short, almost dislocating my shoulder, but I yank against it anyway like a chained dog until the metal cuts deep into my flesh and blood flows warm and sticky over my wrist. 'Where is he, Stacey? *What have you done with my son?*'

'Oh, for God's sake,' Stacey says, exasperated, smacking her palm against the freezer. 'Enough already. I told you, he's *right here*.'

'What d'you mean he's—'

And then I get it.

'Oh, dear Jesus. He's *inside*.'

She laughs. 'I did *tell* you he was here.'

A howling gale of grief and fury sweeps through me: I want to strangle the woman with my bare hands, I want to gouge out her eyes with my nails and force them down her throat.

It takes every ounce of self-control to hold my rage in check. There's no point begging or pleading or threatening her: she's a psychopath, incapable of fear or empathy. My only hope is to appeal to her self-interest: to her *ego*.

If there's any hope left in a world without my son.

'Is he dead?' I ask calmly.

'I'm not sure,' she says, glancing down at the freezer and sounding genuinely curious. 'He was alive when I put him in, but that was an hour ago.'

When I was a young resident at a hospital in London, a five-year-old boy was brought into the Emergency Department. His brother had shut him in the chest freezer in their garage after a quarrel. The boy had been in there for four hours before he was found by his distraught father. Hypothermia had slowed his metabolism and reduced his oxygen usage, which was the only reason he hadn't suffocated. He had severe frostbite on his fingers and facial extremities – nose, ears – but he survived.

Brain-damaged. Unable to see or hear or walk or talk.

'Explain it to me, Stacey,' I say reasonably. 'Why does it benefit you to do this to him? To us?'

'I didn't have a choice,' she says, sounding almost apologetic. 'Sooner or later, Peter would have talked about Felix. I could have just left your son down here, and you'd never have known what happened to him, but I thought you deserved better than that. I thought you'd want to be with him.'

'He's ten, Stacey. Who'd have believed him?'

'You,' she says.

I try not to look at the freezer, try very hard not to think of my son, my child, curled up inside. 'I have very little credibility with the police where you're concerned,' I say. 'We had a deal before. You could leave the country as you planned. I won't say anything because that'd just incriminate Peter.'

'What about Felix?'

'What *about* him? You could leave him here. No one knows this cellar exists. Or I could help you move his body. I'd be implicated, then, too. We'd be partners in crime. I couldn't say anything even if I wanted to.' I force a laugh. 'You could sell me the Glass House after all and it could be our secret.'

She's tempted. I can see it in her eyes.

'It's the perfect crime,' I say. 'You actually got the victim to collaborate in his own murder. It's brilliant. Because you intended to kill him all along, didn't you?' I smile conspiratorially. 'I think we both know he was never going to walk out of here. It's why you told Peter, isn't it? You wanted someone to appreciate the beauty of it all. Everyone wants their work respected.'

'Felix wasn't a *victim*,' Stacey says, 'whatever he told your husband. He was with me because he wanted to be. He *needed* me. And defrauding Copper Beech was *his* idea. Except he didn't think it through, as usual. *I* was the one who had to step in and sort out his mess.'

'I'm not the enemy, Stacey,' I say.

330

'It's too late,' she says impatiently. 'I don't have time for this.'

'At least let Peter—'

'Don't be boring, Millie. You've always been so much better than that.'

'I need a knife,' I say, holding my voice steady. 'You owe me that. Don't leave me down here in the dark to die of thirst. I'm not Houdini,' I add, shaking the handcuff against the pipe. 'I can't pick the lock or cut through metal this thick. But if you give me a knife, I can make sure the end is quick.'

She cocks her head to one side. 'I don't want you to waste time shouting for help,' she says. 'No one will hear you. I'm going to take your car and phone back to the woods near Alexander Manor. Tom won't ever know exactly what happened to you, but he'll assume you decided to take care of Peter and then yourself. We all know the path your son was on, so he won't be that surprised. In fact,' she adds, suddenly darting forward and holding a screen in front of my face, 'let's unlock your phone and have you text him yourself.'

She's out of reach again before I have a chance to react. Her thumbs speed across the screen as she texts my final message to my husband.

She turns to go, and then abruptly stops, bends down, and skitters something across the floor towards me. 'It's a Stanley knife,' she says. 'It's not particularly sharp, but it'll be enough for what you need.'

She shuts the door to the root cellar behind her. I listen to her footsteps as she walks up the stairs. Even though I'm expecting it, a bolt of terror shivers through me when I hear the hall door overhead shut behind her. No one knows we're down here. No one even knows this cellar exists. I could shout for a week and no one would ever hear me.

But Stacey has left the light on.

And she's left me a knife.

chapter 63

millie

Stacey has left me with a stark choice: wait in vain for rescue, and die from dehydration within a few days – if I'm lucky.

Or I can use the knife.

The human body is about sixty percent water, and, under normal conditions, an average person loses about a litre of water each day by sweating and breathing, and another one to two litres by urinating. If it's not replaced, cells throughout the body will shrink as water moves out of them and into the bloodstream, part of the body's efforts to keep the organs perfused in fluid. All the cells will shrink, but the ones that count are the brain cells. As the brain becomes smaller, it takes up less room in the skull and blood vessels connecting it to the inside of the cranium can pull away and rupture.

But my kidneys will probably shut down first. Lack of water will cause my blood volume to decline and all my organs will start to fail. My mouth will dry out and become caked, my lips parched and cracked. My eyes will recede into their sockets. The lining of my nose will start to bleed. Mucus will thicken in my lungs, causing respiratory failure. My temperature will rise. I'll have convulsions.

Death will be a relief.

I look at my left wrist, shackled to the pipe. I know exactly where to slice it open: given my expert anatomical knowledge, I can target the arteries precisely and the pain will be minimal. I will bleed out within fifteen minutes.

Tom isn't going to save me. When my car and phone are discovered near Alexander Manor in a day or two from now, and the police start investigating, he'll finally learn the truth about Gracie. He'll wonder what else I've hidden from him. Perhaps he'll believe I might have decided to 'take care' of Peter and then myself, as Stacey intends. Even if he doesn't, even if he comes here, to the Glass House, he'll never find me, not in time. I know every inch of this house and I had no idea this cellar was here.

I don't know if Stacey was telling the truth, and my son is truly trapped inside the freezer, or if it's another of her sick mind games. But if he is inside it, and if he's still alive, it won't be for long.

Stacey's given me a simple binary choice between a long, protracted death or a savage, swift one. But I have a third option.

An unthinkable one.

It might not work. Even if it does, there's no guarantee I'll make it out of this cellar alive. I don't think Stacey's bolted the door to the root cellar door, but if she has, I won't have a hope. And if by some miracle I *do* survive and get out of here, the life I knew will be gone forever. The person I am now will be gone. My life will be destroyed. I'll survive, but I won't be *living*.

It's not hyperbole to say I'd be better off dead.

But it's not just my life at stake.

I pick up the knife.

chapter 64

millie

In April 2003, an American mountaineer and mechanical engineer called Aron Lee Ralston dislodged a boulder as he made a solo descent of Bluejohn Canyon in south-eastern Utah. The rock trapped his arm and pinned his right wrist to the side of the canyon wall. After five days without food or water, dehydrated and hallucinating, he had to break his forearm and amputate it with a dull pocketknife to break free. He then made his way through the rest of the canyon, rappelled down a twenty-metre drop, and hiked eleven miles to safety.

As a surgeon, I read his autobiography and watched James Franco play him in the film *127 Hours*, and wondered how desperate you'd have to be to find the strength to do such a thing.

Now I know.

I'm cool and collected as I pick up the rusty Stanley knife. Resilience isn't just about exercising your strengths: it's about finding the strength in your weaknesses. The inability to tune in to my emotions has sometimes made it hard for me to move through the world, but now it's my saving grace. I'm a rational person: an analytical, problem-solving scientist. Self-pity isn't an option. I can't use brute force to break the handcuff: I've tried. My son doesn't have time to wait for an unlikely rescue.

I've known since the moment Stacey told me my son was trapped here with me I only ever had one choice – which means it wasn't a choice at all.

I tug off one of my running shoes, and unthread the shoelace, tying it as tightly as I can around my wrist, using my teeth to pull the knot firm. I need a tourniquet, or I'll bleed to death.

I have one advantage over Aron Ralston: my anatomical knowledge.

As any surgeon – or butcher – will tell you, severing a limb at the joint is the most efficient method: the bones are held together by sinew and tendon and muscle and cartilage, all far easier to part than bone. I know exactly where to cut to remove the last two fingers and knuckles of my left hand.

I'll never operate again, of course. My surgical skills may be about to save my life but using them now will ensure I never set foot in an operating room again.

For most people, losing two fingers would be upsetting, distressing, shocking even: but in the end it wouldn't impact their lives to any significant degree. You can still do up your buttons with six fingers and two thumbs. You can still ski downhill and send a text and roll pastry and bathe your child. But for a pianist, or a gymnast, or a world-class heart surgeon, it's life-changing.

I'm a surgeon, but I'm a mother first.

It takes me less than three minutes to hack through the flesh and tendons of my left hand and sever my little and ring fingers and two knuckles. The pain is indescribable, as if I'm vaporising my hand with a white-hot laser, but I'm driven by the momentum of a strange euphoria: *I am not going to let my son die in this place.* I don't black out, or lose consciousness, or shed a tear. It's almost like childbirth: my pain means my son gets a chance to live.

As soon as it's done, I wrench myself free from the handcuff and tug off my running hoodie, wrapping it around my mutilated hand to staunch the bleeding. I can't let myself pass out, or I'll bleed to death before I ever regain consciousness and this will all have been for nothing.

I wrench open the chest freezer with my good hand. Stacey didn't lie: Peter is curled up on the bottom. He isn't moving, and when I lean inside and put my index and middle fingers to his carotid artery, I can't find a pulse. His skin is white, his lips blue, his hair frosted with ice. I don't know if he's alive. I don't know how I'm going to get him out on my own.

I climb into the freezer with him. Blood from my mangled hand spatters across the sides of the freezer as I fumble my baby into my arms. I'm shivering uncontrollably in the cramped space, though I don't know if it's from shock or the cold or a combination of both.

Somehow I haul him onto my lap. He's dead weight, slumped lifelessly against my chest. I still can't tell if he's breathing: the cold will have slowed his respiration so much it'll be hard to detect even if he is alive. The adrenaline that has got me this far is suddenly ebbing, and I don't think I have the strength to get myself out of the freezer, never mind my son.

And then I feel it: his heartbeat.

Slow, but steady.

I am not going to let my son die in this place.

With a sudden renewed burst of energy, I heave Peter up to the lip of the freezer, bracing myself beneath him as I take his weight. It costs every ounce of strength I have left to lower him onto the concrete floor without dropping him. I clamber out and collapse beside him, enveloping his body with mine to warm him.

'Sweetheart, come on,' I plead, chafing his arms with mine. 'Wake up, Peter. You need to *wake up.*'

336

He doesn't respond. The strain of moving him has loosened the tourniquet around my hand and I'm starting to feel light-headed again from the blood loss. I use my teeth to tighten it, and then cradle my boy against me, rocking us back and forth as I gaze up at the cobwebbed ceiling. I was so focused on rescuing Peter I didn't think beyond this moment, but if I can't figure out a way to get us out of here, then I will have saved my son from a quiet, peaceful, quick death from hypothermia only for him to endure an agonisingly protracted one from dehydration. I might as well put him back in the freezer now.

And then suddenly the light goes out.

Stacey must have realised it was still on and switched it off from upstairs. For a moment I panic: the cellar is as black as pitch, and I can't even see my child in my arms.

But he's breathing. I feel him stir, and the soft puff of his breath on my face.

I'm a scientist. I'm blessed with a rational, analytic brain. I'm going to think us out of this cellar.

'It's OK,' I tell Peter, hugging him close. 'It's going to be OK, sweetheart. I'm going to get us out of here.'

I am not going to let my son die in this place.

kyperlife

harper to the rescue!

👍 LIKE 👎 DISLIKE

Welcome back, my lovely Kyper peeps! I know you haven't heard from me for a couple of days and I'm super sorry about that, but it's been a crazy week. The good news is, this time tomorrow I'll be back with my boys and Kyle at our teeny little rented mouse-house, though we're not going to be there for long. I can't tell you how I know that, but just trust me, OK?

Look, I wasn't going to say anything, and maybe I shouldn't, but I've just got this bad *feeling*, you know? I'm sure everything's going to be fine, but just in case – God, I'm sure I'm being super ridiculous and superstitious, but you know when you just get that *sense*?

Anyway, I can always delete this afterwards. Like, I'm *sure* I'll just delete this later. Because it's all going to turn out fine—

[Pause]

Fuck it. I've had enough of playing this game. I'm going to delete this as soon as I get back anyway, so I might as well drop the act and just spit it out.

So. Stacey Porter, our big-hearted, award-winning, 'People's Choice' national treasure, is the one who crashed her car into me. She tried to kill me to shut me up about her pension-stealing husband, but that's not the big reveal.

Millie Downton's ten-year-old son, Peter, was in the car with her. Bit of a twist, huh?

Actually, not so much, not if you've met him. This kid's a total freak show. He tried to drown Stacey Porter's son in a swimming

338

pool a few weeks ago, though no one will admit it. You'd think Stacey might be a bit upset, but instead she practically adopted Peter Downton and then took him on a homicidal joyride to take me out.

I haven't told Millie he was in the car. I can't quite bring myself to burst her bubble, not after everything she's done for me. And I didn't put two and two together myself and realise it was him till yesterday morning, when I saw him in profile drinking a glass of milk and the penny dropped. But when I tell you I think the kid's involved in Felix Porter's mysterious disappearance, I'm not messing around.

Doesn't matter he's only ten. He's super creepy and kids like him, they *hurt* people.

And the thing is, Millie's missing. She and Peter have been gone all night, and we don't know where they are. Millie's husband says he's not worried because she sometimes stays out all night, and she did text him yesterday to say she was taking Peter on a road trip or something. But she didn't turn up to work today, the hospital's already called three times, and I don't care what Tom says, something's *wrong*. I know this family has its own way of doing things, but I don't know why he's not more worried about her. She sent Tom a really weird text last night about taking Peter for a walk in the woods or something, it didn't make any sense. I made him ping her phone this morning and it shows her located somewhere in Abingdon, of all places. But Peter's not with her. *His* phone is still at Stacey's house. According to Tom, he walked all the way there from school by himself yesterday, which is fucking weird to begin with. Millie told Tom she was going to the Glass House to pick him up. And now she's totally fallen off the grid.

So, anyway. I'm going to go to the Glass House now to see what's happening for myself. Tom says we should just wait for them to come back, but I told you, I've got this *feeling*.

[Pause]

If I don't – if anything happens to me – then this will automatically upload to my vlog in twenty-four hours. I'm sure it's all going to be fine, and I'll delete this and go back to playing KyperLife, God help me.

But if it's not. If I don't come back.

You know where to look now.

chapter 65

millie

It's pitch black in here: absolute darkness, crow black, blacker than night. It's impossible to know how long we've been down here, or whether it's day or night outside in the real world, which already seems as hazy as a distant dream, a vacation taken long ago.

The protective effect of the adrenaline has worn off and the pain in my butchered hand is agonising. I can't seem to quite stop the bleeding, either, though the tourniquet has slowed it. The cold from the concrete basement floor is seeping into my bones. I just want to sleep, but if I do that, there's a real risk I might not wake up, and if I die, my son dies with me. So I drag us both across the floor to the cellar wall and force myself to sit upright, cradling Peter in my arms, reciting the periodic table and the bones of the human body and the steps of a coronary bypass aloud in an attempt to keep myself awake.

'Mummy?'

His voice in the darkness jolts me. 'Peter! You're awake!'

'I'm cold,' he says.

'I know you are, sweetheart,' I say, unable to keep the relief from my voice as I tighten my embrace and try to infuse what bodily warmth I have left into his limbs. *If he's cold, he's awake.*

If he's cold, he's going to live. 'I'm right here, Peter. Try to move your legs if you can.'

He doesn't respond. He doesn't ask any questions. I don't know if his torpor is physical or psychological, but I need to get him moving. I need him to *fight*.

'Come on,' I say. 'Up we get. Come on, Peter,' I urge, as he slumps, inert, in my arms. 'We have to get up. We have to move and stay warm.'

Fireworks explode behind my eyes as I force the two of us to our feet, the pain in my hand so intense I have to steady myself against the wall. Peter whimpers as the blood starts to circulate in his legs, piercing him with pins and needles, but I refuse to let him rest. We stumble across the cellar in the dark, and when we reach the opposite wall, I turn him around and propel the two of us back. I'm grateful for the darkness so he doesn't have to see Felix's bloody corpse on the bed.

I don't know what he knew about Felix and when, but he's not responsible for the man's death. That's on Stacey. Whatever she tells herself now, she never intended her husband to walk out of this cellar alive. Dragging my son into it was just a sideshow to the main event. A bonus. She saw the darkness in him and she took pleasure in drawing it out and setting it free.

But he's *ten*. The fight for his soul isn't lost yet.

I turn us around again, and once more we lurch across the cellar. My son deserves the chance to live. The better angels of his nature deserve the chance to win. I'm not going to let what happened here in this cellar with Stacey be the sum of who he is.

'I'm hungry,' Peter says.

'Try not to think about food,' I say.

He sags against me. 'But I can smell McDonald's, Mummy.'

It's not McDonald's he can smell: it's woodsmoke. Someone

342

must be burning autumn leaves in one of the gardens nearby. Air is getting into the cellar from somewhere. And if air can get in—

I tell Peter to keep moving, and clamber onto the top of the chest freezer. The air is cooler near the ceiling, and I hold up my good hand in the dark, trying to feel where the faint breeze is coming from. If it's the hatch I saw above the pool pump, there's a chance Peter could scramble through it: he's slight and agile.

Inching carefully along the slippery lid of the freezer, I lean out above the pump cage. This is definitely where the air is coming in: I can just about reach the edge of the maintenance hatch above the pool pump with my fingertips. But it's so *small*. It's not designed for someone to access the cellar, merely for a mechanic to be able to reach in and fix the pump if required. It can't be more than thirty centimetres in diameter at most. Even if I'm able to prise it open from the inside, I don't know if Peter can wriggle through it. I'm not even sure I can lift him up high enough to try.

I climb back down and feel my way across the cellar in the dark. I need something to stand on so that I can reach the hatch properly and try to open it.

'Stay where you are a moment, Peter,' I call. 'I have to move a few things.'

There's an ugly thump when I roll Felix's body onto the floor, like the sound of a bag of flour splitting when it hits the ground. I flinch, but I don't have time to dwell on it. I drag the metal bed frame across the cellar in the dark, praying the sound of the legs screeching across the concrete floor doesn't carry.

'What are you doing?' Peter asks.

'Trying to get us out of here,' I pant.

Standing on the bed, I grope for the hatch above my head,

343

and then insert the blade of the Stanley knife and run it around the rim, trying to clear it from dirt and debris. My shoulder is already aching. Dust clogs my throat, and sweat trickles into my eyes as I work at the seam of the cover with the rusty blade. I can't find any screws holding it in place, and unless it's locked from the outside, it should pry loose, but despite my best efforts, it doesn't budge.

'Do you want me to try?' Peter says, his voice small in the darkness.

I doubt he'll succeed where I've failed, but I need to keep him occupied. And he has two hands to my one.

'Can you climb up here next to me?' I ask. 'Careful now. That's it. OK. There's a sort of manhole cover above our heads, Peter, and I want you to see if you can push it open with both hands. It's really stiff. I'll need to lift you up for you to reach it.'

'But I can't see!'

'Feel your way. Come on, Peter. You can do this.'

The throbbing in my left hand intensifies as I lift him up. My palm feels hot and inflamed: the beginning of an infection. If I don't get antibiotics soon, sepsis will spread through my body and kill me, but I'm not worried: there are plenty of other ways for me to die down here first.

'It's stuck,' Peter pants. 'I can't move it.'

'Try again.'

Peter bangs on the hatch with his fists, dislodging dirt onto the two of us. 'Help!' he shouts. 'Help! Can anyone hear us?'

I cough. I feel dizzy and light-headed from a combination of concussion and blood loss, but I can't afford weakness now. 'Save your breath, Peter. Hitting it won't help. See if you can loosen the cover at the edges.'

'It's jammed, I told you,' he says, banging the cover again. 'Help! Someone help us! We're stuck down here!'

344

'There's no point shouting,' I say. 'No one can—'

And then we hear it.

A familiar voice, faint but clear, calling my name.

'Harper!' I shout. 'Peter, jump down. Harper!'

'Millie!' she yells. 'Millie, where the hell are you?'

'We're in a cellar!' I shout, thumping against the pool hatch. 'Stacey locked us down here!'

'How do I get to you?'

'There's a door at the end of the hallway upstairs,' I shout. 'It's hard to find—'

I break off as the cellar is suddenly flooded with daylight: Harper must have been able to open the hatch from her side. She's talking to me, but I'm still trying to adjust to the searing brightness blinding me after so long in the dark. I feel nauseous, and fight back the urge to vomit. I think I'm about to pass out.

'Mummy,' Peter says, tugging at me. 'Mummy, help me up! I can climb out! I can show Harper how to open the cellar door!'

The light is briefly blocked by Harper as she peers in. 'Can you fit through, Peter?'

'I think so.'

Through sheer willpower, I hoist my son up towards the hatch again. It's a tight squeeze, and for a moment I think he's not going to make it.

But then, suddenly, miraculously, he's free.

'Call the police, Harper!' I shout. 'Don't go into the house alone!'

'I'm coming!' she calls. 'Just hold on, Millie! I'm going to get you out of—'

And then abruptly she's gone.

SETtalks | psychologies series

Science ♦ *Entertainment* ♦ *Technology*

Inside the mind of a psychopath | *Original Air Date 9 July*

The transcript below has been lightly edited for length and clarity.

You all know the story of what happened at the Glass House: the horror of what took place in that cellar. You've watched the news and read the papers and seen the documentaries.

In the annals of crime, it's not the *worst*. It wouldn't even make it into the top ten. But there's something about the Glass House Murders that keeps the story on the front pages anyway. You just can't get enough of it, can you?

Maybe it's because it all started over the purchase of a *house*.

Ridiculous, isn't it? I mean, we all know about property feeding frenzies, but this takes gazumping to new heights.

I think it's because it has such a great cast of characters. It's got made-for-TV written all over it, doesn't it? A famous television presenter who claimed she locked her abusive husband in the cellar for five weeks at *his* instigation as part of a complicated Ponzi fraud. A brilliant heart surgeon who *cut off her own hand* to save her son from being frozen alive in a chest freezer. A popular vlogger who stirred up a hornet's nest and then jumped right into the middle of it.

And at the centre of it all, there's the Glass House. It's a character in its own right, like Downton Abbey or Manderley. The kind of dream home we'd all kill to own.

It's no wonder you're obsessed with the story. I don't hold it against you. You should know by now I'll never judge you. You can show me your darkest selves and I won't look away.

Frankly, it's a miracle anyone got out of there alive. Felix Porter was the first to die, of course. He was locked in that cold cellar in the dark for thirty-five days while the police came and went with no idea he was right there, beneath their feet. As he starved to death, his body began to eat itself, cannibalising the protein in his muscles as a fuel source to keep him alive. His body atrophied. He developed bed sores, his bones almost poking through his withered skin. He was slowly decomposing alive.

But starvation isn't what killed him.

No, it was worse than that, worse than you can imagine. Felix died because he was desperate for a sip of something, *anything*, to drink, and when his loving wife gave him a mug of cold coffee, he drank it. Except it wasn't coffee, of course.

She gave him *drain cleaner*.

She'd been using it to unblock her sink that day. The corrosive chemicals blistered his lips, burned his tongue, peeled the flesh from around his mouth. His oesophagus was so damaged he couldn't breathe and bled into his chest cavity. His teeth fell out. His vocal cords actually *dissolved*. It took him hours to die: long, torturous, agonising hours that must have felt like an eternity. Killing him would have been an act of mercy.

Surely the death of the person who inflicted such pain was a *good* thing?

I wish I could say I'd had the courage to wield the axe, as it were, but someone else beat me to it. Not that I expect you to believe me. After everything that's gone on since then, I can't blame you for thinking the worst of me.

The truth is, all I've ever wanted is to fit in. To have friends: to be loved and cared for, just like you. But I was left to sink or swim on my own. No one gave me an instruction manual. No one taught me how to speak your language. I had to figure that out alone. So I did my best to mimic you without ever understanding what *normal* meant. Is it any wonder I made a few mistakes along the way?

But I learned from them.

I'm immune to guilt and I'm immune to fear, but I have a very good instinct for self-preservation.

I've lifted the veil and shown you my soul. I've told you who and what I am. I've admitted my crime: I killed my father, and I accept now that by your lights, what I did was wrong. It might surprise you to learn I actually *miss* him. I may not be able to feel fear or remorse, but that doesn't mean I'm incapable of love.

But the Glass House Murders – that wasn't me.

I didn't kill any of those people. I'd tell you if I had. I've done the work on myself. I've owned my past behaviour – it's the reason I'm here now.

I've told you the truth. I'm one of the *safe* ones.

You can trust me now.

chapter 66

tom

This damn house.

I look up at the spectacular glass facade through the wind-screen of my car. There's no denying it's an extraordinary property, but it doesn't exert the same magnetic pull on me as it does on my wife. All this craziness only started when Millie went to view the Glass House four months ago. I suppose it's fitting if it ends here, too.

I reread the text Millie sent me yesterday. It makes no more sense now than it did last night. I was tired then, so I didn't question the idea that Millie had taken Peter off on an impromptu road trip to see if she could get him to open up to her about what's going on in his head, but in the cold light of day I realise she'd never take him out of school without damn good reason. And I have *no* idea why her phone is located in Abingdon. Maybe Stacey took Peter there for some reason and she went after them, but that makes even *less* sense.

I slide my phone back into my jeans and climb out of my car. I put on a good front for Harper when she was at panic stations earlier and wanted to call the cops, but I'm rattled. Millie's never taken Peter on one of her prison breaks before. And now Harper's gone running off to find them, and if I don't follow her I'm going to look like a total shit.

My alarm grows as I walk up the road. The door to the Glass House is not just unlocked, but wide open. *No one* leaves their front door open in London unless they're literally walking through it – not if they don't want to be robbed or murdered in their beds. But there's no sign of Stacey or anyone else going in or out of the house, no signs of life at all: no shopping bags in the hall, no lights on, no TV or radio playing. I've got a really bad feeling about this. It just seems *off*.

I glance back down the street. Stacey's yellow Mini convertible is parked a couple of houses away, which presumably means she's here. Maybe she's upstairs, or out by the pool, and didn't realise she'd left the door open.

I finally screw up the courage to go inside, bracing myself for some sort of jump scare, like I'm in a teen slasher movie.

What I find is my son, sitting cross-legged on the floor at the end of the hallway in his school uniform, looking for all the world like he's waiting for assembly to start.

'What the hell is going on?' I demand, relief making my tone sharper than I intend. 'Are you all right? Where's your mother?'

'Stacey and Harper had a fight,' he says.

'What sort of fight? Where are they now?' I glance up the stairs to the kitchen, and then back out into the street. 'And where on earth is your mother?'

'Stacey locked us in the cellar,' he says. 'She put me in the freezer. Mummy got me out, and Harper came to rescue us, but then Stacey caught us and she and Harper started fighting.' He delivers all this in a strange monotone, as if he's rehearsing lines from a play. 'Harper told me to call you. But I couldn't find my phone and then there was an accident and I didn't know what to do.'

The only thing I can get my head around in this insane catalogue of horror movie clichés is that there has been an accident and *I still don't know where my wife is.*

'Where are they?' I shout. 'Peter, *where are they*?'

He points dumbly towards the other end of the hall. A half-hidden flight of stairs leads down into the dark.

I run towards the stairwell, shouting Millie's name. A faint sound comes from the cellar: a thump, then a low groan. A wash of panic floods through me as I pull out my phone for light and take the stairs as fast as I dare, terrified of what I might find at the bottom. If that woman has hurt Millie, if anything has happened to my wife, I will kill her, I swear to God.

I almost trip at the foot of the stairs. My foot connects with something warm, soft: some*one*.

'Oh, Jesus, no,' I breathe.

But it's not Millie crumpled at the bottom of the concrete steps.

I crouch down beside Harper. She has a deep gash on her forehead, and it looks like her leg is broken: I'm sure her knee isn't supposed to hinge like that. I feel queasy: I'm not good with blood. I think – oh, Christ – I think I can see bone poking through her skin.

'Don't try to move,' I say, swallowing hard. 'It's going to be OK, Harper. I'm going to get help.'

'Millie,' she whispers.

I catch a glimpse of tangled limbs in the shadows just beyond Harper, and swing my phone upwards in a panicked arc.

Stacey must have broken Harper's fall. She's sprawled on the cellar floor, her neck twisted at an unnatural angle, her eyes wide and sightless. I'm not a doctor, but even I can see at a glance she's dead.

Harper grips my hand. 'Millie's . . . down here,' she gasps. 'Stacey . . . tried to . . . stop me—'

'Don't try to talk,' I say fiercely. 'I'll find Millie. You don't need to worry about Stacey any more. We're going to get you out of here.'

351

'Peter,' she pants.

'He's OK. He's upstairs. He's fine.'

'Peter—'

'I'll be right back,' I say, gently freeing myself from her grasp.

I step over Stacey's body, the gorge rising in my throat. There's another door beyond her, bolted shut. 'Millie!' I shout, yanking the bolts free.

My wife is propped up against the wall, her left hand cradled oddly in her lap. She looks pale and filthy, her face drawn and hollow-eyed. She's aged ten years since yesterday.

'What kept you?' she says.

chapter 67

millie

I can see at a glance there's nothing I can do for Stacey. Her neck is broken: she must have died instantly in the fall down the cellar steps. It was a quicker and kinder death than she gave her husband.

I crouch next to Harper, sprawled at the bottom of the stairs like a broken marionette, and triage her injuries as Tom runs upstairs to call the emergency services. I daren't risk moving her. Her pulse is weak and thready, and I don't like the sound of her lungs. She has an open fracture of the left tib and fib, and I suspect a pneumothorax on the left side, probably caused by one or more broken ribs. I'm worried about the gash on her forehead, too. And that's before we get to any hidden internal injuries.

'The ambulance is on its way,' Tom says, returning with a thick blanket he must have dragged from one of the beds upstairs. 'What can I do to help?'

'Stay with her,' I say, tucking the blanket around Harper. 'I need to sort out my hand again, Tom, and see if I can stop the bleeding. There's a strong chance I might faint. I don't want you to panic. If I pass out, you need to make sure the tourniquet is tight. And try not to throw up over me,' I add, as he goes green.

He looks away as I tighten the shoelace around my macerated hand. 'What the *hell* happened here?' he says. 'Peter said Stacey put him in the *freezer*! What the actual *fuck*?'

'Felix is dead,' I say grimly, gritting my teeth through the pain as my vision swims. 'Stacey's kept him locked down here ever since he disappeared. He's in the other part of the cellar. Don't look,' I add. 'You don't want to see it.'

'Jesus,' Tom breathes.

I swallow down nausea and then go back to Harper and check her pulse. Her eyes are closed, and her skin is pale and clammy. Her injuries are severe, but they'd probably be survivable in normal circumstances. But she's still recovering from major heart surgery: given what her body has already been through in the past few weeks, I'm not sure she's going to survive this. I pray to God I'm wrong. If it wasn't for her bravery, neither Peter nor I would have survived in this cellar more than a couple of days at most. We owe her our lives.

'Peter knew Felix was here,' I tell Tom, keeping my voice low.

Tom's jaw drops. Even in the dim light spilling from the hallway upstairs, I can see horror and shock in his eyes.

But not disbelief.

'He *knew*?' Tom echoes.

'Since the beginning.'

Tom rubs his hand across his face. 'Christ Almighty.'

'Stacey was the adult here,' I say. 'Whatever Peter may or may not have known, he's only ten. She probably terrified him half to death. What happened here is on her.'

Tom looks at me over Harper's head. He doesn't need to say anything. We both know what our son is. Stacey and Peter had a meeting of minds, a partnership of equals, regardless of the age difference between them. *He was the one who made me see I couldn't let Felix leave the cellar.* Without her acolyte to egg her on, would she still have doomed her husband to his

354

excruciating death? Who was the real master here, and who the disciple?

'This is on Stacey,' I insist. 'She tried to kill our son. She put him in the *freezer*.'

'She put him in the freezer,' Tom echoes.

I wonder if the words sound as hollow in my mouth as they do in his.

This isn't just on Stacey, and we both know it. For all her monstrous behaviour, Stacey wasn't entirely irredeemable. She felt some compunction about what she did; maybe even regret. Her relationship with Felix was far more complicated than we'll ever know: I think she loved and hated him in equal measure. And she wanted me to be with my son when he died: however warped her thinking, she was trying to do right by me. She gave me the Stanley knife, either to give me an easy way out or a fighting chance: I honestly think she meant it when she said she liked me. And she certainly admired my son. Was actually *fond* of him, in her own way.

I don't think Peter is fond of anyone.

I think my son is incapable of empathy. I think he could kill a man as easily as swatting an ant, without doubt or hesitation.

There must have been a reason Stacey turned on Peter. A reason she tried to kill him. Something he'd done that she found unforgivable.

He thought he could do what he liked and it'd be too late for me to be able to do anything about it.

There's a story in Native American culture that describes the battle between two wolves that live inside us all: one wolf is evil – it is anger, violence, resentment, darkness, despair. The other wolf is good – it's love, hope, light. Which wolf wins?

The one you feed.

It's not too late for Peter. I can still save him, if Tom will let me.

'How could he?' Tom whispers. 'How could he be part of this . . . this *horror* show?'

'He's our son,' I say. 'He's *ours*.'

Tom puts his hand over his mouth, as if physically holding back words.

'He's our son,' I insist. 'He's *my* son.'

'This isn't you,' Tom says harshly. 'Don't you dare put this on yourself. He didn't get this from you. You're nothing like this. You're not a monster. You save lives, Millie, you don't take them. You *save* lives,' he says again.

He's right. The dark wolf in me is strong, but I've worked hard all my life to starve him into submission. My childhood forced me to armour myself against the world, to detach myself emotionally for my own self-preservation. But I'm not a psychopath: if I were, I wouldn't distinguish between the good wolf and the bad. I wouldn't even know they were different.

I'd be like Peter.

My son's forced me to confront what *true* psychopathy looks like. But he can't help the way he's wired any more than I could help the family I was born into. I have to save him if I can.

'We can't tell anyone he knew,' I plead. 'We've got to protect him.'

'Who'll protect everyone *from* him?'

'Tom,' I beg. 'Please. We don't know. We don't know he did anything wrong. We don't *know*.'

Harper moans softly on the cellar floor beside us. In the distance, the sound of sirens grows louder. The ambulance is nearly here. 'Hold on,' I tell her urgently. 'Think of Kyle and the boys. You can do this, Harper. Hold on for them.'

Her breathing is getting shallow. I'm a doctor: I know the signs.

She's twenty-seven years old. She has two little boys called Tyler and Lucas.

She saved my son's life.

I stroke her hair back from her forehead. 'It's going to be OK,' I lie. 'You're going to be fine. You just have to hold on a little bit longer.'

'Peter,' she whispers.

'He's OK. You got him out. You saved his life, Harper.'

'Peter,' she says again.

I lean in close.

'Peter . . . pushed . . . us.'

chapter 68

millie

'You heard what Harper said,' Tom says, appalled. 'We can't just ignore it.'

'Peter says it was an accident,' I say. 'They were fighting together at the top of the steps. He was trying to *help*. I heard Harper tell you Stacey tried to stop her rescuing me,' I add firmly. '*That's* what I heard.'

Tom insists we have to speak up, to tell the police everything that happened, leave nothing out. Even if Peter was just a bystander, even if he's incapable of understanding what he did was wrong, Tom says, *we* aren't.

But Harper is dying, and no one is left who knows the whole truth but us.

And Tom loves me. He loves me unconditionally, and so when I ask him to protect Peter in these last few moments before the police get here, when I *beg* him, he agrees.

So we show the police the cellar where Stacey kept her husband chained in the dark for five weeks. They see the chest freezer where she left our son to die. They find my severed fingers on the floor. We tell them what happened, and all of it is true. Every word of it true.

But it isn't the whole truth. Even Tom doesn't know that.

I look at my son now as he sits between us in the back of

the police car taking us home from the hospital, where one of my colleagues patched up my ruined hand as best she could. I have more surgeries ahead of me, many more surgeries, and physical therapy, and even then I may never regain full use of my hand. I will certainly never operate again. So I look at my son, the child for whom I've sacrificed my career and a large part of who I am. And I wonder if I made the right decision.

Because in the chaos and confusion of the police and paramedics' arrival, as Tom explained to them what'd happened and I waved off medical attention and insisted they tried to save Harper first, somehow we lost sight of Peter.

I found him in the kitchen. He didn't notice me come up the stairs, and I stood there for a moment, watching him pour the contents of a Coke can into Stacey's empty coffee mug beside the sink, before crushing the can flat and shoving it in his pocket.

And I knew in that instant there was only one reason he'd do that.

My son is the one who put drain cleaner in a Coke can and gave it to Felix. And then he put what was left into a coffee mug Stacey had used, a coffee mug with her lipstick on the rim and her fingerprints on the side.

My son killed Felix in cold blood. He pushed Harper and Stacey down the cellar stairs so no one would find out the truth.

And if I want to save my son, I can't ever tell anyone.

part four

chapter 69

millie

I can't believe how tall Peter is. It's a renewed shock every time I see him these days, as if unconsciously I carry around an image of him at ten years old in my head. I remember my own irritation at my grandparents' and my parents' friends' refrain every time they saw me – *Haven't you grown!* – and bite back the words.

He was a beautiful boy, and now at nineteen he's grown into an exceptionally handsome young man. His honey-coloured hair still flops beguilingly across those clear, untroubled tawny eyes. His mouth is soft and full, his smile when he sees me wide and joyous. But there's a squareness to his jaw now, a firmness, an integrity: he has an old-fashioned, rugged masculinity that puts me in mind of bygone movie stars like Burt Lancaster or, more recently, Daniel Craig. There's nothing metrosexual or ambiguous about Peter.

'I wasn't sure you'd make it,' he says, putting down his book. 'We were about to give up on you.'

'I was in theatre,' I say. 'There were a few complications.'

'How did it go?'

'It went well,' I say, dropping my coat over the back of a chair, and sitting on the sofa opposite him. The window near me is open, and I can smell the scent of roses and mown grass.

'I have a new resident. Apollo. He's very gifted. He has an instinct you can't teach.'

Peter's mouth quirks. 'Apollo?'

'I should introduce him to your sister,' I say.

'Medusa and Apollo. Now there's a match the gods would like. How is she, by the way?'

'She's fine,' I say. 'Better than fine, actually. Harvard Medical School just accepted her for their graduate programme. She only found out yesterday. She's planning to fly up to Boston next month and start looking for a place to live.'

'Chip off the old block,' Peter says.

I never thought I'd be the kind of parent to live vicariously through my child, but watching Meddie follow in my footsteps has brought me intense pride and pleasure.

She was valedictorian of her undergraduate class at Johns Hopkins, and getting into Harvard now will put her on the radar of all the big teaching hospitals in America. I wish she wasn't so far away, but I can understand her need to put four thousand miles behind her and the past. Tom's death four years ago hit her hard.

It hit us all hard.

'D'you think she'll end up going into cardio, like you?' Peter asks.

'Neurology,' I say. 'She says it's more cutting edge. There's still so much left that we don't know about the brain.'

'You must miss it,' Peter says. 'Being at the forefront, I mean.'

For someone born without the ability to empathise, sometimes Peter can be surprisingly intuitive. Reflexively I touch my left hand. The scar has long since healed, though from time to time I still feel phantom pains in fingers I left on a cellar floor nine years ago, nature's sly little joke at my expense. Years of physical therapy have given me back more of my dexterity and skill than I'd dared hope, but I'll never be a world-class surgeon again. I'm a jobbing butcher now: heart bypasses, shunts, valve replacements. I still save lives, but no one comes to me for their Hail Mary pass: the inoperable surgery no one else would have the ego or ability to perform. I'm nothing special now.

And yet, oddly, I'm OK with it. I wasn't at first, of course. It took me years to come to terms with my loss. But I've learned there's something deeply satisfying about grooming the next generation of raw talent. I feel the pride of a parent when one of my students beats me at my own game.

'It's four years today,' Peter says suddenly.

As if I could forget.

'Yes,' I say.

'Do you still miss him?'

Grief isn't something that abates. You simply learn to live with it, in the spaces around it. A scar forms: to the outside world, it looks as if you've healed. But the pain never goes away.

And yet, somehow, you adapt. You manage with eight fingers instead of ten. You survive. Grief shapes you in unexpected ways: you are never the person you once were, but you figure out a way to move through the world.

Tom loved me unconditionally. He saw me for who I was, and it's only now he's gone that I'm able to understand what that really meant and see myself through his eyes. I am flawed, so very flawed, but I'm not the sociopath I once believed myself to be. I didn't think myself capable of great love, but the over-whelming, all-encompassing nature of my grief after Tom died showed me that loving him was my greatest achievement. He always knew that however damaged I was, no matter how many mistakes I made, I was also fundamentally a good person. Even the very worst thing I ever did, killing my father, I did to save a life. I gave up the thing that mattered most to me besides my family – my career – for my son. I *tried*. Can any of us ever do more than that?

'I'm sorry,' Peter says. 'I'm sorry that he's gone.'

Intellectually, I think he means it. It's not his fault he's unable to *feel* it.

'Did you see my talk?' he asks.

'Your SET talk?' I say. 'Yes. I watched it online.'

He leans forward, his hands clasped loosely between his knees, eyes alight. 'Did you like it?'

'It was very good,' I say. 'Very articulate. You presented yourself well. It was all bullshit, of course, but I'm sure it went down a storm.'

'They want me to do a series for one of the streamers,' he says, leaning back. 'I'm the poster child for rehabilitation, apparently. I've been asked to take part in research studies at Cambridge and Yale. Everyone wants to know what makes me tick.'

'Inside the mind of a psychopath,' I say.

He laughs. 'You've got to admit, it's a catchy title. Everyone loves a psycho. You're all just fascinated by us, aren't you?'

'I'm sure the parole board will be impressed.'

'My lawyer says I've got a good chance at the hearing next month,' Peter says. 'Will you be there? He says it makes a big difference if the victim's relatives support the application.'

Nine years ago, I protected my son and let Stacey Porter take the blame for Felix and Harper's deaths. I kept silent about what I'd seen, what I knew. I persuaded Tom to delete an eerily prescient vlog Harper had made that incriminated Peter. And for five years he rewarded me by being the perfect child. He played for his school's football team. He volunteered for charity fun runs. He worked out at the gym. He had a girlfriend. Even

Tom believed Peter had turned a corner. We fed the good wolf, and the good wolf was winning.

And then one day, a day just like any other, our fifteen-year-old son came home from school and slit his father's throat.

'Do you ever wish you'd chosen differently?' Peter asks suddenly. 'Do you ever wish you'd saved your hand that day in the cellar, instead of me?'

It's a question I've asked myself a thousand times over the last four years. If I'd let Peter die in that freezer, Tom would still be alive. Afterwards, if I'd done as Tom asked and told the truth, the whole truth, I would still have my husband.

Instead, I watched Peter get taller and broader and fitter and stronger, until he was strong enough to kill the man I loved.

There was no reason, because psychopaths don't need a reason. He did it because he *could*. He saw it as perfectly reasonable: the young lion ousting the old for the good of the pack. His expensive legal team blamed it on the pills he'd been taking from someone he'd met at the gym, some version of 'roid rage'. They pleaded the charges against him down to manslaughter, and he was sentenced to just eight years at a low-security facility, a prison with rose gardens and rowing machines and flatscreen TVs. But he and I both know what Peter did had nothing to do with pills.

I don't blame Meddie for fleeing abroad, but Peter's my son. He is the sum of my mistakes. And so I will always be here for him. I will always love him. It's too late now to tell anyone what really happened at the Glass House, because any proof was destroyed years ago when the house was torn down to prevent it becoming a ghoulish shrine. But I will be at his parole board application, and I will tell them they should never release my son, although I'm fairly certain they won't listen.

I'll remind them of the fable of the scorpion and the frog.

I'll tell them my son shouldn't be blamed for what he did to Tom because he can't help who he is, or the way he was wired; but that he's not sorry, is incapable of being sorry, and if they release him, he will sting again.

I will tell them it's just in his nature.

ACKNOWLEDGEMENTS

My lovely sister, Philly, my beautiful broken butterfly, died very suddenly just as I was finishing this novel. Losing her at 53, after the death of my baby brother Charles at just 40 seven years ago, has broken my heart. My last novel, *Stolen*, was dedicated to Philly: she was tickled pink. I know they're both cheering me on from somewhere, and I hold them in my heart with every word I write. Thank you, sweet sister, for showing me what love truly means.

I am so very lucky to have such a brilliant and committed team behind me at Avon and HarperCollins which has worked tirelessly to get my books into the hands – and ears! – of readers in what has been another very challenging year for all of us. I could not hope for better publishers, and I thank all those who've laboured behind the scenes to make this novel a success.

Special thanks to my wonderful new editor, Cara Chimirri, who has been such a fabulous cheerleader for my books, and has made this novel so much better in every way. It's a joy to work with you.

Thanks also to my brilliant agent, Rebecca Ritchie, for her passionate support and endless patience in the face of my self-doubt. Your friendship means the world to me.

And thanks to my marvellous copy editor, Rhian McKay,

369

for her meticulous eye for detail. Your deft catches have saved me so much embarrassment!

Ellie Pilcher and Ella Young in Marketing, Sammy Luton in Sales, my lovely PR Becci Mansell, Claire Ward, Elisha Lundin, Charlotte Brown (those Audio sales are amazing!), Robyn Watts, Melissa Okusanya, Dean Russell, and in the US Jean Marie Kelly and Emily Gerbner – you are all so fabulous at what you do, and your energy and enthusiasm are what makes Avon such a wonderful home for my novels. Thank you all.

Thanks to my dearest stepmother, Barbi, for reading the manuscript when it was only half-written, and giving me exactly the kind of clear-eyed advice I needed to get it back on track. Without you, I'm not sure I'd ever have finished the book at all.

And thank you to my lovely friend, Dr Lucy Pollock (author of *The Book About Getting Older*, such an important book!) for casting an eye over the manuscript and checking for medical howlers. Any mistakes are absolutely my own!

Thanks, too, to all the sociopaths and psychopaths on social media who inspired me with their dark and brutally honest confessions. You truly are the most fascinating human beings . . . though I'm not sure I'd ever want to meet you.

Thanks always to the NetGalley readers and bloggers and book lovers who take the time to review my novels – it really does make a difference and is so much appreciated! I love hearing from you, my readers, so please feel free to contact me via my website, www.tessstimson.com.

Most of all, thanks to my husband, Erik, my sons, Henry and Matt, and my daughter Lily, who provide me with inspiration on a daily basis. That may not always be a good thing, but when your mother is a writer, no disaster is ever wasted.

April 2022

Don't miss Tess Stimson's other addictive
psychological suspense novels . . .

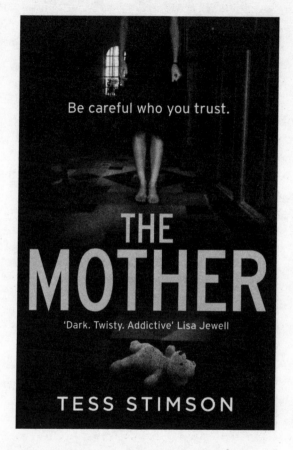

Be careful who you trust.

THE
MOTHER

'Dark. Twisty. Addictive' Lisa Jewell

TESS STIMSON

'More chilling than *Gone Girl* and twistier than
The Girl on the Train' Jane Green

Out now

Both of them loved him . . .
One of them killed him.

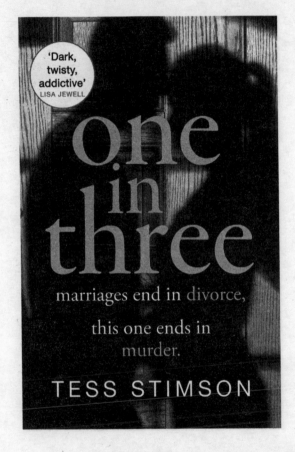

'Dark, twisty, addictive'
LISA JEWELL

one
in
three

marriages end in divorce,

this one ends in
murder.

TESS STIMSON

'Tense, twisty, and that ending – wow!' Jackie Kabler

Out now

You thought she was safe.
You were wrong . . .

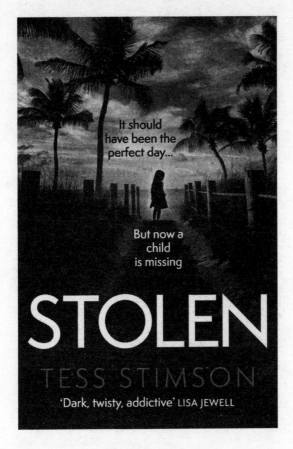

It should
have been the
perfect day...

But now a
child
is missing

STOLEN

TESS STIMSON

'Dark, twisty, addictive' LISA JEWELL

Out now